Mrs Reed scrutinised the shed floc
fluid and closed the door. Two b
despairingly on the grimy shed wind
followed Audrey traipsing up the c
sunshine.

'I have to hurry Ann.'

Audrey lugged a swollen bag of freshly dug potatoes, cabbages, cups and flask in one hand and her husband's new hoe in the other. Her boys raced to the five bar gate and sat on it kicking their legs.

Mrs Reed lagged behind melodramatically, holding the contaminated bag away from her, barely gripping the knotted handles with gloved thumb and forefinger as she might a china teacup.

'Don't you boys open that gate,' Audrey shouted, 'It's a busy road, so wait for Mummy.'

Mrs Reed mumbled something about the heat and Audrey barely responded.

'You know, I've just had another thought who did this, Audrey. I'm not casting aspersions, but Harry Tait and I have never hit it off.'

Audrey turned, eyeing Mrs Reed dubiously. They had just passed Harry Tait's flourishing plot.

Harry's allotment was the penultimate garden on the right by the tap and trough, just before the uphill bend to the entrance. It was a prize garden, a truncated fan shape filled with myriad vegetables and flowers. Today it was gaudy with plate-sized dahlias of the brightest yellow, ripening chrysanthemums and the neatest wigwam rows of French beans. Bright green lettuces in neat cloches and huge brassicas covered with fine mesh cages formed the ribs of the fanned display.

A tidy red gravel path led to the garden apex where a smart white summerhouse complete with varnished decking and scalloped wooden canopy provided a shady vista for Harry to oversee his endeavours. It was pretty with honeysuckle and edged with blue lobelia and orange marigolds. Knee-high white picket fencing marked the entire plot border and Mrs Reed eyed the neat rows of caned dahlias and beans jealously, as she continued to expound her new theory half way up the bank.

'I think Harry's been acting a bit shifty recently, she panted, 'and he's here until goodness-knows-what-hour these light evenings. He thinks he owns the place.'

'Oh, come on, really Ann. Harry Tait? That's ridiculous; he's a widower and he's a genuinely lovely man.' Audrey looked at Ann askance. 'Are you telling me that after gardening here for thirty odd years he's suddenly decided to use your shed as a toilet? Knowing Harry, his shed's probably got one plumbed in or he'll certainly have a nice shiny bucket,' she quipped.

'Hmmph,' Mrs Reed responded.

They reached the gate and stopped to catch their breath. The heat was energy sapping and Audrey swapped her bag and hoe-hand over while supervising her boys.

'Down you get and keep in. Don't run ahead,' she ordered, lifting the stiff gate open with difficulty, letting Mrs Reed through first before heaving it back into its catch.

Mrs Reed swiftly padded the ten yards to the station entrance, consciously silencing her booted footfall before guiltily dropping the knotted bag into the station bin and cutting and running hastily to Audrey's side.

'Yes, I think it must have been Harry Tait and I've good reason,' she persisted.

'Rubbish! Audrey vented irritably, 'It will be someone from the last train or someone caught short on the way home from the pub.'

'Why my shed then, Audrey? Why didn't they do it in Harry's shed? It's closer.'

'You mean his summerhouse Ann?' Audrey corrected.

'Well, it's more of a double doored shed I would say, but that's beside the point. Why didn't they use his … summerhouse then?' she said grudgingly.

'For a start, it's too easy to see from the main road and secondly Harry will have a good mortice lock on the French doors,' Audrey speculated.

'So you say you've good reason to suspect him?' Audrey probed cynically.

'Yes, I'll tell you, but you mustn't let this go further.' Mrs Reed waited for a response, but Audrey feigned indifference, so she continued regardless.

'When Albert was alive he'd invited Harry to join the Lodge and Alby bent over backwards to propose him. After giving all the right signals for a long time, Harry for some reason told Albert it wasn't for him. He said something about it not gelling with his beliefs. What do you think that meant Audrey? We thought he might be a Catholic, but his surname didn't match, but anyway, I took it as a bit of an insult when he didn't join and Alby felt a little betrayed as he'd put a lot of legwork into introducing him to folk and even got him a decent sized bit of carpentry work at the council. Him suddenly pulling out of the deal was a bit off, don't you think?'

Audrey remained silent and waited for Ann to continue.

'Well, they had a few words and because the next job went Dougal Smith's way he accused Alby of being in the "Mafia of the Mediocre" as he termed it, or something ridiculous like that. That new bit of council business was the luck of the draw, Alby said, but it was the final straw between him and Harry; we washed our hands of him.'

'I wouldn't know, Ann. Vic was also asked to join the masons by Derek Driscoll and he wasn't interested either, so I can't comment on Harry's reasons, but Vic had his too, not least because he thinks the Masonry thing gives people unfair advantage.'

'Well Vic is very much mistaken Audrey. Alby and I are dedicated churchgoers, so that unfair advantage nonsense is groundless.'

Audrey didn't think it polite to correct Ann's mid-rant present-tense reference to her late husband.

'Well, all I can say is there's good men in that Lodge and friendship is all about caring and sharing connections isn't it? Alby always gave work out on merit.'

'I don't doubt it, Ann,' Audrey responded sceptically, 'but each to their own. Vic has far too many responsibilities already and no time to be going to a men's club in the evening. He plays piano at The Kittiwake on Tuesdays and Thursdays as soon as he finishes dinner, and we've got the boys and the allotment now, not to mention all the jobs at home.'

'Oh, it's nothing I would fall out about Audrey; Alby never had a bad word to say about Vic. Anyway, I got side-tracked—and this was the thing I was leading up to—I wasn't going mention it at first, but Harry said something a bit perverse to me last month you know, Audrey.'

'Perverse? Harry?' Audrey queried. 'What did he say?'

Mrs Reed hesitated, the tip of her tongue briefly touching her top lip. 'He said I had a lovely back.'

'A lovely back?' Audrey laughed. 'That's hardly perverse Ann,' her attention momentarily returning to her children, 'Slow down you boys!' she commanded. The boys halted and stood on tiptoe to peer over the railway bridge as the pair caught up. Another lorry rumbled past mingling diesel fumes with the mousey stink of the Badman's Oatmeal flowers wafting from the steep verge.

Mrs Reed raised her voice to counter the traffic noise, her stiff hair shaking indignantly, 'Well, I had a low-cut back on my blouse and I could feel his eyes boring into me every time I bent over, sitting on the deck with that pipe of his, pretending to read his paper. Honestly, I felt very uncomfortable and it was only a year since Alby passed. I think his flirting entirely inappropriate, don't you Audrey? Well, I made short shrift of his advances as you can imagine. And doing something like that in a shed is just the kind of thing a pervert might do if they got the cold shoulder.'

'Oh, come on Ann, really? Harry's always been an old flirt, but he's a friendly chap and he's not the sort of person to take vengeance on a woman who knocked him back. You can tell he was a ladies' man and quite the looker twenty years ago. You should be flattered. He's always chatty with me, and even if he's an old tom cat he's quite funny, and generous with sweets for the boys.'

'Are you talking about Mr Tait, Mummy?' John asked.

'Yes boys, he gives you sweeties doesn't he when he's talking to Mummy.'

Mrs Reed smiled a fake smile at the triplets who were now trailing their hands along the metal railings by the bridge embankment, 'Well isn't that kind of Mr Tait, boys?'

She promptly turned back to Audrey, speaking guardedly.

'Well it was the way he said it. That look in his eyes.'

'Ann, I know you're upset about the shed, but you're blowing the whole thing out of proportion and to consider Harry some kind of pervert, you're completely mistaken. You have to be very careful about accusing people. It really could be anyone; most likely a complete stranger.'

'Well, I hope it doesn't happen again, that's all I'm saying. I'm going to get a padlock for the door to make sure it doesn't. Twenty odd years without needing a lock. What a state of affairs.'

Mrs Reed turned into her privet hedged drive while Audrey continued towards the cul-de-sac, past Thora Hedley's house by the narrow cut, her boys stamping their feet to make a pleasing twanging echo between the houses.

John, the middle triplet blurted, 'Mummy, the balloon we found around the back of Mrs Reed's shed had stuff in it and we put it on the fire and it starting bubbling.'

Aghast, Audrey bent down, levelling with her children on one knee in fretful entreaty: 'You must never, EVER touch anything you find like that on the allotment or anywhere else. Do you hear? I've told you before about the poisons in the sheds and you should have told Mummy straight away. I'm very cross with you! You didn't put it anywhere near your mouth or touched your lips with your fingers did you?'

'No, Mummy, it was just a balloon Mummy!' Mark's chin began quivering.

Audrey pulled a floral embroidered handkerchief from her dress pocket and vigorously wiped each boy's fingers in turn, starting with Mark, her agitation clearly upsetting her young sons.

'Let's get you home quickly and wash your hands. Hurry up.'

'Did Mrs Reed think Mr Tait did the poo in her shed, Mummy?' Alan asked as the pace home urgently quickened.

'Of course not Alan. Don't let me catch you saying such silly things. That's not what Mrs Reed said. She said she thought Mr Tait might have seen what had been in her shed because a big dog or fox has been around the allotments and she thought it might be that. And Alan, you mustn't repeat things you hear adults talking about in private, do you hear me?'

'Yes, Mummy, like the time when Uncle Paul said Helen was a right tart at your Silver Wedding?'

'Yes, like that time. Remember, you must never ever repeat that to anyone, do you hear me?'

'But we heard you say to Mrs Reed that the poo wasn't an animal's.'

'No, I was thinking aloud and I meant to say it didn't look like a small animal's, but I had forgotten about that big fox. Do you remember the Cry Wolf story I told you about? The big fox at the allotments is nearly the size of that wolf and hopefully Mr Tait will catch it in one of his cages and put it in the woods where it belongs because it's obviously lost.'

'Does Mr Tait have cages, Mummy?'

'Yes, to trap rabbits and foxes - and naughty boys.'

'No he doesn't Mummy!' Alan grinned doubtfully.

*   *   *

Mrs Reed wasted no time in recounting the befouling episode to all her neighbours. The 'deposited lot' was re-clarified as a 'bowel movement' as some of her more naive acquaintances thought her euphemism related to a mistaken delivery of compost or horticultural sand.

Wisely, she suppressed the temptation to vilify Mr Tait directly for any part in the incident, reassessing her suspect as just 'someone from the allotment, or perhaps a gypsy from the travellers' fair at Whitley Bay' in case the suggestion of an allotment perpetrator was too slanderously specific.

Meanwhile in Wellbank Infant School the autumn term had started along with a new teacher, Miss Corrigan who tasked the class to write down what they did in the holidays. To the amusement of twenty year old Janet Marwell, Mrs Corrigan's assistant support, the short illustrated story by Mark, the eldest triplet was a highly amusing distraction from the staffroom hubbub during morning playtime.

Mark's 'Lotment shed' tale featured a big brown amorphous scribble inside a wonky shed outline with the word POO adjacent. The *Chubbi-Stump* crayon sketch roughly defined a Mrs Reed stickwoman, identifiable from her red face and big black boots splayed outwards, while "Mummy" wore a blue flower dress and held a square board.

Repressed sniggers rattled the young ladies' thick-rimmed Education Authority cups and saucers as Mark's story was shared covertly in the smoky staff room:

> *"Mrs Reed blamed Mr Tate for doing a poo in her shed even tho it was a giant fox and Mummy had to clean it with carbord. Mummy cleaned the shed and Mr Tate cort the fox in a cage to stop Mrs Reed being cross".*

That evening Janet brought this, her first marking assignment home, and passed the exercise book to her family after dinner. Although Janet's brother found the story very amusing, her parents, Sheila and Henry did not.

'From the mouths of babes!' Sheila's deep voice reverberated across the dinner table, as her tacit husband, Henry reddened and became very serious.

'You know who that woman is, don't you Janet? That's Ann Reed from Hillsden Avenue,' her mother rapped the table mat with a stout forefinger, 'and if that boy's story is true – and you can trust most things you hear from bairns - then that young lad has overheard her accusing Mr Tait of doing something not very nice at all.'

She paused to clear the plates and continued, 'It's absolutely disgraceful and not the first time that snooty woman has got people into trouble. She was behind Edna getting fired from the Co-op when she told the manager she'd seen her keeping toilet rolls back for her friends—you remember don't you, Henry? Edna from the Co-op? During the power cuts?'

Henry grunted and rose from the table, grabbing his pipe and jacket from the hallstand before striding stony-faced the half-mile to The Beacon pub...

*   *   *

When Mrs Reed returned to her plot on Saturday, Harry Tait raised himself up from his haunches by the potato bed, leant on his fork purposefully and grinned.

'I hope *The Caped Crapper* hasn't been at it again Ann, but if I see him flying about I'll tip you the wink.'

Mrs Reed froze, flushed, mouth agape in mute silence, saving a barely audible *harrumph*.

'These long summer evenings I sit in my shed and enjoy watching the world go round you know, Ann,' Harry gloated. 'Lots of 'birds and bees' as well as villains about, but funny, no foxes at all,' he smirked.

'And that reminds me. You may want to ask your lass, Abigail, what she was doing here with the chap from behind the bar in The Red Lion last week. I thought she was engaged to the Harper lad from St. Andrew's? Be sure your sins will find you out, eh? Does his dad, the vicar know?'

Mrs Reed stumbled dumbstruck towards her plot, shaking her head disdainfully, while Mr Tait's shock disclosure echoed almost rhythmically inside her head to the crunch of her gumboots on the clinker path.

She traipsed the long fifty yards to her shed as casually as she could, perceiving Mr Tait's triumphant stare needling her. Dizzy, she unbolted the door and fumbled with the rusty latch, quickly entering and pulling it nearly closed behind her. She slumped trembling on the school seat, panting for breath in the stifling corner, the harsh tang of disinfectant burning her sinuses as the dry grey residue of Jeyes fluid continued to outgas.

Harry meanwhile had gone inside his summerhouse, locking the door behind him with a shiny key. This was his sanctuary and he knew no one would see through his nets as he fumbled to find his gardeners' bible from the top shelf: 'The Culture of Vegetables & Flowers' by Suttons. Furtively he flicked through the pages, opening the marrow section as he pulled out the neatly folded full colour page torn from a magazine, his hands trembling and breath faltering in anticipation.

Ann Reed sat, perspiring; pondering; wishing her Alby was there. He would have a word or two to say to that Harry Tait, but first she was going to have a word with Alby about hanging some newspaper squares on the shed door on a string rather than expecting people to tear up magazines themselves, it simply wasn't acceptable to expect people to tear their own, especially in the dark during a blackout. *Can't let a night time visit to the netty guide Hitler's bombers to our towns and cities,* she remembered her mother's warning.

She noted the slightly ajar shed door. She would have an urgent word with Alby about fixing it; *toilet door hinges don't mend themselves* she thought, but she'd do that after her hospital appointment that Abigail had arranged for her to 'get an accurate and timely diagnosis'; when was it again? And what was it she was being accused of? *Early Onset Dementia* or some other nonsense. *Hmmph. It's disgraceful to accuse people of things like that.* Where had she put the appointment card? Had Abigail moved it? She had hidden things in her doll's house before. Alby might know.

Mrs Reed squatted uncomfortably; holding the shed walls with outstretched arms to balance herself. She would have to remember to tell the police that someone had stolen the toilet. Alby had many friends in the Constabulary. They would find the culprit.

Ann hitched up her skirt and stood up, confused. Someone had deposited their lot in the shed again.

It was quite unacceptable. Criminal even.

She wondered if her friend Audrey would help her clean it up before the coffee morning.

A summer gust rattled the door wide open and a string of dry shallots swayed from the shed ceiling. A bluebottle buzzed in enthusiastically.

///woods.fancy.frog

"INANE"

Disappointingly, the cottage rental in Suffolk was more of a terraced house and was in the centre of busy street in the historic village.

'It's 2259 for the key locker Pete,' Tina said, reading the printed email instructions for entry.

'You sure? 2259? Ah, got it. It was a bit stiff.'

Pete jiggled the key in the mortice on the ancient black and white studded front door and pulled the handle towards him. The difficult lock finally yielded and the old door creaked open as he, Tina, Stu and Mary, four fifty-something friends stumbled indoors relieved, as loud traffic trundled by.

The foursome had just finished a tiring fourteen mile hike cross-country from Borley, sharing a single garlic sausage filled French stick between them for an on-the-go lunch, and a litre of bottled water per couple. Now they were hot and thirsty for tea or coffee and they jostled for space in the cramped porch, their rucksacks colliding irritatingly.

A narrow and steep flight of stairs lay immediately ahead of them and Stu and Pete moved up a few steps to give the girls room to un-boot and remove the cagoules tied around their waists. They heaved off their hiking boots relieved to feel cool tiled floor through their socks, and piled their rucksacks into the corner, bundling through the living room door immediately to the left of the porch coat hangers, re-establishing their personal space.

'They must have photographed this place at five in the morning with a wide angle lens for the "Cottage to Let" advert. It's so tiny and on a very busy street,' Tina complained.

'It's double glazed thankfully. Once you're in you can't hear much and besides, it's 5pm and all the offices are clearing out, so it'll be much quieter later,' Stu reassured.

'We hope,' said Tina sceptically.

'It looks cosy enough though Tina,' Mary encouraged, scanning around the small oak beamed living room with its floral country cottage fabric curtains and matching twee two seater sofa and armchairs. 'Designed for titchy Tudors.'

'And pretty clean. As long as the kettle works we're good,' Tina added.

'And Wi-Fi,' Pete chipped in.

'Yes, and working Wi-Fi, defo,' Mary agreed, smiling.

A side unit with small television and digi-box stood to the left of a fireplace adorned on each side with horse brasses with a roughhewn oak mantelpiece holding a tiny china clock and two Coalport posy bowls.

'Granny-city,' Stu commented, stroking a petal.

They shuffled through a connecting archway into a stone-flagged kitchen diner. A modern oven and washing machine were separated by low floral pleated drapes on wires that screened off pan and crockery shelves.

'A bit basic, but some decent white goods, I suppose,' Tina said, filling the kettle up over the Belfast sink.

'Coffee and tea and sugar cupboard here with ketchup and salt and pepper,' Pete noted, 'and milk and eggs in the fridge.'

'We'll get dinner stuff at the supermarket after coffee, do you think?' said Tina.

'You don't just fancy fish and chips or something?' Stu looked at the others for comment. 'I just don't think I've got the will to cook tonight or do dishes, I'm so knackered.'

'Yeah, I must say, I'm pretty jiggered too and Pete and Stu will probably leave all the hard work to us,' Mary teased, nipping Stu's bum.

'Sure, whatever, I don't mind at all,' Tina nodded, 'Shall we look at the bedrooms while the kettle boils?'

The two couples picked up their rucksacks and chased up the narrow stairs, wrestling to see who could bag the best bedroom.

Two double rooms, one with single beds; a bathroom with shower and separate toilet greeted them.

'Guess we should toss as usual for the rooms, unless you have a preference?' Tina winked at Mary, knowing she would prefer the single beds over the double room tonight given the farting discussion they'd had while 'the boys' marched ahead on the hike.

'Stu and I will take the singles if that's okay, I was so hot last night in Borley I couldn't sleep, and it's going to be hot again tonight.' Mary opened the pretty leaded windows and closed the curtains to block the late afternoon sun.

'That's fine by Pete and me, if you're sure,' Tina approved.

'That's the trouble with England; it's never hot long enough to invest in air-conditioning, but when it's hot, it's unbearable. Can you imagine how foreigners feel when they stay in your average UK hotel in the summer and have to sweat it out? Even some four star hotels in London you still have to open the windows and the concierge brings you a fan.'

'The fan is to help you roast evenly,' Stu proposed. 'In some hotels the windows don't open more than a couple of inches.'

'Or at all. I'd rather do an Airbnb any day, about half the price too,' said Tina.

After coffee and a change of socks, the four headed into the town centre to a quiet cobbled market square. The ubiquitous British War Memorial was hub to three pubs, two tea rooms, a wine bar bistro and two charity shops. An Indian takeaway trumped the fish and chip option and *Tikka Masala, Dhansak, Rogan Josh* and a *Biryani* were carried back eagerly to the cottage.

'Careful not to drip any of that on the lounge carpet,' Mary advised Stu and Pete as turmeric-stained ghee pooled in the bottom of the two brown carriers, 'or we'll lose our £500 deposit.'

'Good call, we'll eat in the back garden on the picnic bench,' Pete replied.

The garden grass was short and parched from the late summer heatwave. A green parakeet screeched from a sycamore, and curry spices mingled with a pleasant charcoal smoulder from a nearby garden.

'Close your eyes and smell the air,' Pete encouraged. With the traffic noise it smells and sounds just like Bangladesh, especially with that parakeet.'

'Even more like Bangladesh if Stu does one of his classic farts,' Tina prompted.

'No Stu; not while we're eating,' Mary warned.

Stu sniggered like a schoolboy.

'Talking of Bangladesh, did I ever tell you about my Bengali friend Amon's grandma when I lived in Bracknell?'

'No, what did she do?' Tina asked.

'Grandma-ry things.' He paused for laughter, but only received groans.

'No, but seriously, on the school holidays when we were about twelve he showed me an alabaster jar on her dressing table. Any idea what was in it?' Stu paused.

'Go on, tell us,' Mary pressed, not wanting to do the guessing game.

'It was something quite gross, I warn you. It had a layered substance in it which was dark brown in the bottom and light tan in the middle and white and crispy on top. I remember Amon took the lid off, got a Bic pen and pushed it into the jar.'

'What the heck was it?' Mary demanded.

'I'll tell you when you've finished your poppadums.'

'Oh, just tell us Stu, we can handle it,' Pete urged.

'Okay. It was fingernails.'

'Fingernails?' Mary puzzled, wincing.

'Yep, and toenails too.'

'Urgh that *is* gross. Why were they layered?' Tina asked.

'I have no idea, but it looked like they were in some kind of ointment or thick waxy oil, with the freshest cuttings on top.'

'You cannot use the adjective *freshest* with toenails, Stu. That is just so, well, wrong.' Tina's face showed disgust.

'Yeah it was very wrong,' Stu sniggered. 'His grandma had been collecting them for decades and putting them in this jar and Amon - the little twat - shoved the pen in my bloody mouth when I was gawping into the jar and he thought it was hilarious. I almost chucked up.'

'My brother Dan and I got him back the next day with Dan's sucky-button.'

'Sucky-button? That sounds gross too,' Mary commented.

'It was, Dan would smear chewed food into his shirt buttons when my mum wasn't looking during dinner, about the second and third button down, then it would dry. Later he would pin you down on the floor with his knees on your arms and he would force the button into your mouth. He used to put on a mocking psycho voice saying *Dan has a lovely, delicious surprise for you. I know you've been waiting to savour it, so open up like a good boy and get your special treat.*'

'You boys are so disgusting,' Mary remarked, as all of them fell about laughing at the grossness of Stu's older brother and the horribleness of the teenage torturers.

'I still don't understand why Amon's granny would do that?' Mary puzzled.

'Never found out. Amon didn't know either, or he didn't want to tell me. I found out they have lots of demi-gods out there in Bangladesh that they pay homage to including a god of faeces, so perhaps there was a toenail and fingernail clipping demon she had to placate.'

'That is ridiculous! And even more crazy and perverse that she had dedicated her time to such an inane obsession, she must have been mental,' Tina remarked shaking her head.

'Yeah I know, but each to their own as they say. We've all had a crazy collection or obsession at some point. I had an obsession with *Sea Monkeys* when I was twelve; you must remember the shrimp

33

things they advertised on the back of kids' comics that you hatched in a fishbowl?'

Stu drained a full bottle of chilled Pinot into four large glasses and looked around the table at the blank faces.

'You don't remember *Sea Monkeys?*' Stu was incredulous, 'The adverts showed pink prawn and human hybrid creatures living in an underwater castle, wearing crowns on their heads and playing games.'

Pete typed in "Sea Monkeys" on his phone and scrolled through the images.

'Oh, yeah, I do remember those things. You put a bag of powder into salt water and they hatched, but they were tiny. My sister had some. What a con trick, we thought they'd really look humanlike just like the advert.'

'So did I. The leaflet you got inside the pack was even more of a con, it showed them hurtling around on go-karts and motorbikes I seem to remember. I spent weeks of savings buying a fishbowl, fake plastic weeds, a piece of coral and a Sea Monkey vacuum cleaner which was just a crappy eye-dropper. They did hatch, the tiny salt shrimp eggs, but as you say, they were so small you had to magnify them. I actually killed mine by focusing the sun from a big magnifying glass onto the coral to heat up the water, which they did not appreciate.'

'Sea Monkey murderer!' Tina barked, laughing.

'Funnily enough, Stu, you talking about comics reminded me how obsessed I was with Bazooka Joe when I was about ten,' Pete volunteered.

'The American bubble gum?' Mary quizzed.

'Yeah, the one your mum hated you spending your pocket money on, but it was the ultimate prized sweet.'

'Why did mums hate you getting bubble gum or chewing gum? My mum did too,' Tina remarked.

'Because they thought you would choke on it, or that it would stick to your heart or some nonsense like that, but you were much more likely to die from a gobstopper. They were renowned for kids choking,' Pete said, unemotionally.

'Seriously Pete, were they really *renowned*? Did you honestly ever know any kid in your school suffering death by gobstopper or any other type of choking? It must have been incredibly rare, like an urban myth from the *The News of the World* that freaked mothers out.'

'Yeah, probably was, but I thought gobstoppers were boring anyway. My friend Giles told me that the little gritty bit in the very centre of a gobstopper was highly explosive like *Semtex* and that you could blow a tooth up on it if you bit down too hard. I believed him.'

'Wasn't that golf balls? My dad said the inner core of golf balls was explosive,' Stu added.

'Yeah, I remember that golf ball story too, they're different design now anyway, they used to have a giant rubber band inside, I opened one once and stretched it for miles and there was a small, hard rubber ball at the very core which didn't explode.'

'You're going off subject Pete. Tell us about the Bazooka Joe collection,' Mary interrupted.

'So, Bazooka Joe was the most prized sweet when you were nine or ten years old. Hated by mums probably because you sometimes got the gum stuck on your clothes, your face, or worse, in your hair.'

'I would stick gum on the tip of paper aeroplanes and aim for someone's head in class,' Stu reminisced.

'You boys are pure evil,' Tina shook her head.

'That first bubble you blew was something quite memorable, wasn't it?' Mary said.

'Yes. It took a few weeks of practice to crack it. Early on you would try stretching the chewed gum out in your fingers and holding it externally on your lips and blowing. Eventually you would just kind of get the knack, like riding a bike. Suddenly your brain and tongue and lips would coordinate in perfect unison for that first bubble and what a triumph! You wanted all your friends to know you had done it.'

'You would need about three pieces in your gob to do a monster bubble, though - one of the big ones that would pop and waft into your eyelashes and the bridge of your nose,' Mary added.

'Yeah, and after a while, if you over-chewed the gum, it would only make small bubbles that made a crack,' Stu recalled, nostalgically.

'If you remember too, as well as the bubble gum,' Pete added, 'inside the wrapper was a mini comic strip starring Bazooka Joe the character. You could save Bazooka Joe comics to send away for a prize or you could just collect a few, but you'd have to send some money along with it, about forty pence if you couldn't collect the 500 comics for a plastic telescope or camera. They even did Swiss Army knives and axes, can you believe it?'

'Knives and axes, stop exaggerating,' Tina mocked.

'I'm quite serious, in the 1970s boys carried knives for whittling and throwing at trees. All of us did, didn't we Stu? No one got stabbed back then, but anyway, I got a Bazooka Joe gold plated bracelet with my initial on it. It was pretty good, not plastic either.'

'Was there a character called Monty or something? I remember the comics being like Roy Liechtenstein style, in primary colours,' Stu recalled.

'Well, there was Bazooka Joe with his eye patch and some kid in a cowboy hat,' Pete replied.

'Do you think Roy Liechtenstein was the Bazooka Joe artist then?' Mary quizzed, quite serious.

The table burst into uproarious laughter while Mary flushed.

'You're making fun, but Salvador Dali designed the *Chupa Chups* lollipop logo, so it's not that stupid a question,' Mary countered.

'True. I heard that too, it was on the Dali documentary on TV, so apologies Mary.'

Tina had googled 'Bazooka Joe artist' on her phone and pulled up an image of Bazooka Joe and His Gang.

'Isn't it amazing that you can get an answer to almost any question you want instantly on Google? Look, the Bazooka gang are *Mort, Herman, Tex, Pesty, Jane, Joe, Pat and Tuffy*.'

Tina held her phone out.

'Mort and Pesty, they were the two I remember and I vaguely remember the pigtail girl, Jane.' Stu said.

'Yep, she's quite tasty that Jane bird,' Pete laughed wheezing at his own ridiculous comment.

'So was it Roy Liechtenstein then?' Mary persisted.

'No Mary,' Stu shook his head contemptuously, 'Bazooka's marketing department would probably just have paid some person in an ad agency to do the comics for them, probably some precious pony-tailed prat.'

'I did work experience in an agency in 1990,' Mary affirmed grumpily, 'and there was a bloke who did illustrations for the agency who was lovely actually. He smoked a pipe and was the most talented and unpretentious person you could meet. He had worked in a massive London ad agency in the 1960s, like the kind in *Ad Men* on Netflix. He said that people just saw it as a job and didn't get paid much and it wasn't that glamourous, but he did meet Andy Warhol, and Peter Blake, the Sergeant Pepper album designer once, so it's not that massive a leap of logic to think they sometimes might have contracted artists for big advertising work,' she sneered.

'Interesting, you never told me that Mary, about the work experience,' Stu responded huffily.

'Didn't really last that long, just a few weeks,' she shrugged haughtily, remembering 'Roberto'.

They paused, finished their curry and cleared the plates. Pete lit the candle inside the hurricane lamp on the picnic table as the sun set.

'Okay, your turn again Stu, you must've had another inane quest or obsession other than Sea Monkeys?'

'Hmm, fossils. I liked collecting fossils. I once spent all day looking for a fossil my mum had chucked into the dustbin. She thought it was just a piece of gravel, but there was a fish fin on it. I had to go through all the dustbin with all the cigarette ash and bean juice to find it.'

'That's not really an inane quest Stu, that's just finding something that got lost,' Mary taunted.

'I've got one,' Pete interrupted.

'I had an inane quest trying to make a perpetual-motion slide.'

'A-what slide, Pete?' Mary quizzed.

'A perpetual-motion slide. Actually a ramp or gradient would be a better description. I wanted to make a ball roll forever using gravity.'

'You didn't succeed then given that we never saw you in the Sunday Times' Rich List,' Stu teased.

'Er no, but for a day or two I was frenzied. I think I was still a bit delirious with a fever as I was off school poorly, and I'd read a book with optical illusions in it. Do you remember the eternal stairs illusion that looked like they were going up for ever?'

'I'll Google it,' Stu said, typing 'endless stairs' into his phone. He rapidly brought up a selection of images and flashed it around the table.

'That's the bugger. So I figured I could pile up books on the bedroom floor in steps like the picture, but could never get the last one to overlap correctly. I thought if I could see it on the illusion, I could build it.'

'That's not really a quest Pete, more of an experiment gone wrong,' Tina objected.

'Abba then, I was obsessed with the blonde bird, Agnetha.'

'So were about a billion other blokes,' Stu affirmed.

'Not to my level of obsession. I was about fourteen and had the Abba Arrival album, the one with the helicopter on the front, and I was so obsessed about meeting her I tried to figure out where the photo of the helicopter had been taken by analysing the background scenery. It must have been in Sweden somewhere I thought, and by analysing the types of grass in the picture foreground and the relief of the scenery I could make a stab at the Swedish location, then just hop on a boat to Norway, ride a bus to Sweden and get a job in a local garage, or a corner shop nearby; maybe even a job gardening in her mansion, then I would gradually be able to woo her with my spotty teenage charm,' Pete chuckled self-deprecatingly.

'You are a bloody stalker, Pete, a furtive pocket-billiard-playing prowler,' Stu laughed loudly.

'I'm beginning to think you guys mean *insane quest* not inane quest,' Tina shook her head, chuckling.

'I know, it's pretty sad,' Pete agreed, 'A ridiculous schoolboy fantasy, you know, like: *There I was in the back garden when Beyoncé's helicopter made a crash landing and everyone aboard was dead apart from Beyoncé who only had a couple of minor cuts. I am the only person who can drive her to the concert in time, but on the way there is a nuclear war and we are the only survivors and end up having to breed to save mankind.*'

Everyone rolled in laughter.

'Okay Tina, what about you? You must have had an inane obsession, you can share it with us,' Stu demanded.

'Well I liked Bay City Rollers when I was about ten and had all their posters up, but actually I had this really stupid thing that keeps coming back to haunt me to this day, but you'll think I'm mental.'

'No we won't, Tina, not after Pete's Abba confession; spill the beans,' Mary urged.

'Alright then, as long as you don't mock.'

Tina paused and pursed her lips as though she was about to change her mind.

'Come on Tina, let it out,' Mary persevered.

'Alright. You'll think me so stupid, but for forty years I have been obsessing about a TV programme I saw when I was about ten years old one Saturday morning. I knew it was a Saturday because I was in a great mood; it was sunny and my dad kept telling me to hurry up as we were going out for the day in his new car, but I just wanted to see the end of the show.

'I can remember it was a bit science-fictiony and one of the men in the show was on this planet where evil amphibians lived and he was imprisoned in a cage in the middle of a lake and was gradually being turned into a frog creature because they were putting a frog potion in his food and drink. The only way he could escape was to drink the potion until he was sufficiently froglike enough to slip through the narrow bars of his cage, and only then would he be able to drink an antidote, I presume back on his ship.'

'So what was it called, the programme?' Pete asked.

'I have no idea. I spoke to lots of people over the years trying to remember the show, but zilch, *nada*; so I ended up wasting hours and hours of time racking my brains. I even looked at scanned copies of old TV Times on microfiche in the library to see if I could find the show.'

'How long ago was that, Tina? Microfiche went out with The Ark,' Mary asked.

'About twenty five years ago I started looking, and trust me, it was an obsession.'

'Sounds it. So I presume you understand the benefits of the modern search engine,' Stu joked.

'Yes, surely by now you've *Googled* the plot and solved the mystery?' Mary tilted her head quizzically.

'No. I did start my quest again once *Alta Vista* and *Google* came out when I was about thirty in 1995, but the search engines weren't well populated back then, so I had to go back to the local library to request back issues of the Radio Times - this time, from 1974 and 1975 - to flick through their programme listings on Saturday mornings from April to September. I found *Lost in Space* and thought that this must be the right show and I read through every single episode plot, but there was nothing near to the frog thing that I could discover.'

'Hey Tina, you are an enigma, wrapped inside a mystery, and shrouded in a paradox,' Pete scrutinised her, amazed at discovering this hidden side of his wife's personality. 'So when you're doing 'urgent research' on your computer and I have to cook the dinner and do the chores, this is what you're really doing?' Pete eyed her sceptically.

'No Pete, genuinely; I knew you'd say that, but my investigations are very sporadic and usually when you're out,' she blushed, guiltily.

'Anyway, I thought I was going crazy; that I had imagined the whole thing and I had to get it clarified. I had to know.'

'Then around 2005 I had another revisit. Googled it multiple times, using different searches. All I knew was, it was an American show, but the quest never came to anything. I was frustrated and still am as I have never found anything in the listings. I even tried doing a Sunday morning TV programme search in case I had mistaken my happy Saturday vibe for a Sunday because it was school holidays or a bank holiday the next day, so Sunday might have *felt* like a Saturday, so I went through the whole tedious search process again using Sunday morning UK TV nostalgia 1974 and 1975.'

'Could it not have been a year earlier or a year later?' Pete suggested.

'No, because my dad died in 1975 and his new car was bought in 1973 and he replaced it again with a new dormobile in 1974, so it must have been one of those years.'

'I can't believe you haven't mentioned this before as it seems such a thing for you,' Pete quizzed sympathetically.

'I did ask you about the show a few years back, but you were drunk and you have obviously forgotten. Anyway it's not important to anyone but me and I'll forget about it for ages, but then I get that crazy urge to try one more time.'

'I remember *Puf'n Stuf* and *Lidsville* with Timmy and his magic flute,' Stu pitched in.

'How can you guys remember such trivial crap so many years ago?' Mary shook her head in disbelief.

'Hey, TV was the most important thing in my house growing up; on a par with food. I remember in the summer holidays when all the kids came running into their houses to watch *The Banana Splits*. That show was like the Pied Piper of Hamelin, when the theme tune

41

rang out every kid in the cul-de-sac ditched their bikes and footballs and ran inside for American technicolour fun.'

'If you had a colour TV that is,' Pete interjected. 'We were the last people in our street to get one and we used to watch *Wacky Races* at a friend's house. I always remember how gaudy the colours were on the early sets, like really garish.'

'Well, the frog show was definitely in colour too, but I've kind of accepted I'll never know what it was now.'

'Ah, poor Tina, an unfulfilled desire; that missing jigsaw piece, never to be found,' Stu teased.

'You make fun Stu, but I have actually questioned my sanity because of it,' Tina stated, earnestly.

'This conversation is ridiculously crazy, but fascinating,' Pete laughed, patting his wife's hand a little condescendingly. 'Any more crazed confessions?'

'I think I've had my fill of wine and stories tonight Pete,' Mary said, 'I still have to plan tomorrow's route so we can get a Ploughman's Lunch half way and get back here before the supermarket shuts. We don't want to be heating up garage pasties and microwave chips for dinner.'

*   *   *

The couples began their day hike at 9am as hot August sunshine quickly broke through the early cloud and warmed the historic streets, gift shops, and tea rooms serving breakfasts. They had a circuit of ten miles today on the flat, through cornfields; woodland walks, river footpaths and a couple of minor villages with two village pub lunch options.

By 11am they were in quiet country lanes linking villages and had just walked by a historic medieval church with gargoyles.

Mary and Tina lagged behind again, chatting.

'I wonder what your average medieval obsession was.' Tina spoke suddenly, revivifying the previous night's topic. 'Sharpening the tip of your joust? Stitching your kirtle?'

'Probably finding sufficient menstruation cloths,' Mary suggested drily.

'I think they used moss bags for that,' Tina advised. 'Can you imagine the daily anxieties you must have had that would terrify us cosseted westerners? I guess daily survival was the obsession for most, especially if you had kids.'

'Keeping the pottage topped up with leaves and herbs. No Bazooka Joes for the children back in those days, just a stick of sour rhubarb and autumn berries,' she laughed wryly. 'Though I guess toothache was a big deal for adults, given that agonised looking gargoyle with the cloth holding its jaw,' Mary replied, pointing up at the church gables.

'Yes, toothache must have been a thing. My dentist said that abscesses were a really common cause of death before antibiotics. Aside from health worries, I guess people would have had similar thinking processes to us today.'

'Hmm, I don't know,' Mary pondered, 'Foraging food; preparing for winter; finding sufficient wool to weave into cloth for clothes; collecting firewood, and moss; agonising childbirth; burying your own dead; rinse and repeat; it was very different from today.'

'And confessing their sins to the local priest— if they even had time to sin in between all the scavenging and burying and menstruating,' Tina added, chuckling.

'You're so right; most people's main concerns today are incredibly shallow; like how much their house is worth, and how much pension is in their pot, not dandelion and herb leaves.'

Mary thought silently for a minute or two until she unexpectedly blurted out, 'Actually Tina, I have a bit of a confession to make myself.'

'Pray, tell, thou sinner,' Tina's ears pricked up in anticipation of a juicy morsel of gossip.

'It's nothing too sinister, but you'll think me weird.'

'No I won't, Mary, The Sisterhood doth never judge,' Tina reassured satirically.

'Well, talking of inane quests, I am in the middle of one at the moment.'

'I'm listening.'

'About two years ago I dreamt about someone from university from thirty years ago. It was someone I'd had a very short fling with and I dumped him after about a week. I just never gave him any thought at all, then all of a sudden, I dream about him. Can you believe that? Out of the blue, for no reason I had a dream about him and we were madly in love.'

'Okay, so you dreamed you were in love, but you woke up and realised you weren't because you're in love with Stu.'

'Well, that's the weird thing. I suddenly felt that this person was my true love and that I had to pursue him again, find out where he was living and what he was doing, I felt that the dream was somehow guiding me into his arms again. I felt so much passion.'

'That's crazy, Mary, nothing good comes from reacting to a horny dream. What was his name?'

'Mitch. I knew him as just Mitch, but couldn't remember his surname at all.'

'So how were you going to track this Mitch down if you only knew his first name? Presumably you looked up the old university alumni to clarify?'

'Yes, I thought it would be easy, that he would be listed in my year at uni, but he was like a ghost, no one at all called Mitch in any of the listings in the year above or below. I couldn't even remember what course he was on, so figured Mitch must have been short for something like Mich for Michael, or a middle name like Mitchell, so I went through all the old alumni lists looking for people with first name Michael or a middle initial M. I even contacted a couple of girlfriends who were at uni with me and they just sent me off on another wild goose chase looking for people called Michael Scott and a Michel de Santis and some other Michaels they could remember, but they weren't the Mitch I was looking for. Then, all of a sudden I remembered a conversation with him when I'd asked him his full name and he said Mitch *blah blah* and my response was

'Does he now?' and he said, 'Oh, I get that a lot'. His surname was a verb, a past tense verb.'

'So his surname was 'a doing word'?' Tina chuckled at her primary school synonym.

'Yep.'

'And?'

'I went through the alumni lists again and I found nothing. I drew a complete blank, because none of the surnames were past tense verbs.'

'Needle in a haystack, Mary.'

'Yes, but I had the same obsession to find out the name as you did for your daft frog show. I thought I was going crazy too, like I had imagined this person, the fling and all, but he'd visited my digs with a video once and a couple of albums.'

'Which were? *All The President's Men* was the film, but can't remember the albums, some Irish rebel songs stuff which I wasn't into.'

'Irish then, a member of the IRA?'

'Ha ha, no, he wasn't wearing a black balaclava, but he might as well have been for the difficulty in tracking him down.'

'Go, on, tell me more.'

Stu and Pete were a hundred metres or more ahead of the girls now, walking a footpath adjacent to a beech wood and pretty wildflower scrubland.

'I remembered one other thing he said to me, that he was brought up in a place called Greatstone in Kent. I remembered that because we stayed there once when I was ten and rode on a miniature railway there, which we discussed.

'Anyway, I figured that if I could just remember his surname that I would be able to find his Facebook profile and just see what he looked like today so I tracked down an old telephone directory from the 1970s for South East Kent. Took me ages to find it. Had to look on eBay to find one and it cost me fifty quid.'

'Can't believe you paid that much money for a crappy old directory. To think how many of those we binned back in the day.'

'I know, wish I'd kept a few, but I digress. I started the laborious task of scanning through each of the surnames from A to Z to see if any jumped out at me, or A to Y as I knew he wasn't a Z.'

'What the…'

'I know, crazy stalker behaviour. I obviously skipped the Xs and the Qs as impossibles, but I started with the As. It was no easy feat, hiding my obsessive paper-thumbing from Stu in the evenings, hiding an old directory under the bed to see if a name would trigger my memory.'

'It must have taken you days just to thumb through the A's,' Tina mused, amazed.

'Yes, I know, but obsession causes you to do these things, like you going to libraries to look at microfiches, but funnily enough the phone book quest lets you dispense with huge tranches of pages in one swoop, for example Adams isn't a verb and there was about ten pages of Adams and Adamsons, so that kind of boosted me to keep on going, and Smiths and Jones and Robinsons too, a joy to reach those ones.'

'Just when you felt like giving up, you got a boost from seeing the remaining page count dwindle,' Tina said.

'Well, you might think that, but the further I progressed through the directory, the more I started to give up hope, especially when I finished S. I realised that T and W were more likely candidates for his name than V and U, but then I started thinking I'd got this far and still hadn't found his name, so what if I had just simply missed it. I also discovered I had to be careful because some names sounded like past tense verbs but weren't spelt the same, such as *answered* could be spelled Anserd or *clawed* spelled Claude.'

'Homophones?' Tina interrupted.

'Is that what they're called? Well yes, *homophones* made me realise that I could have easily missed the obvious by misreading the phonetics of his name.'

'Mary, you must've been like a crazy homophonic-phobic nightmare to live with during this quest especially when you were pre-menstrual,' Tina shook her head with amused incredulity.

'Yep. Stu doubtless put up with a lot.'

'So what happened next?'

'I reached the end of the directory after about six months, with nothing clarified. I worked out I must have wasted about two hundred hours searching that bloody book.'

'Oh, Mary, that is just as frustrating as my *Radio Times'* quest.'

'It was strangely cathartic actually. I came to the conclusion that life is too short to waste following some ethereal whim. I reached the point where I didn't feel any passion or love for Mitch anymore, just obsessive focus on finding the answer to the quest.'

'So you never found out then?'

'Yes, I did,' Mary hesitated.

'Go on, I'm desperate to know.'

'Okay. Well there's a reason why I persuaded all of us to go to Suffolk for a walking holiday.'

'What are you saying, Mary?' Tina looked at her askance.

'I found out he's landlord of the Shepherd's Purse where we're going for Ploughman's Lunch today.'

'You are kidding me, Mary, surely not.'

'No Tina, I confess I was a bit more persuasive than usual about the benefits of visiting Suffolk, nice as it is.'

'Come to think of it, you did seem to override the objections of Stu and Pete who wanted Scotland again. So how did you find this out? What happened?'

'I simply re-read all the alumni surnames as homophones and I noticed it straight away, then I googled his name and it turned up he was living here in Suffolk, but he has no Facebook profile or anything. I just found a press cutting of him and his wife Barbara with all the villagers, something about the pub as a wildlife haven in the local Suffolk rag, but it was so small and there were so many people in the photo I couldn't make him out at all.'

*   *   *

The small hamlet of Abbswell had a War Memorial, a timber yard and a pub. Mary and Tina sat down at one of the picnic tables with Heineken umbrellas in the garden while Stu and Pete wandered in to the bar to buy the drinks and order food.

'Look at the sign, Tina,' Mary whispered, motioning with her eyes and a subtle nod, 'above the entrance.'

Over the front porch, hung a sign, Proprietor: Mr Robert M. Dougmee. Licensed to sell all intoxicating liquor on or off these premises.

'Rob M. Dougmee? Is that his name?'

'Yes, Robert Mitchum Dougmee. He, er, really 'dug me' back in 1989.'

'Dougmee, of course, I get it now, and Mitchum after the actor, Robert Mitchum. No wonder he disguised it with 'Mitch' and now just the initial.'

'Have you seen him yet?' Tina asked.

'Nope, no idea, this is so nerve-wracking for me.'

'The boys are coming back with the drinks, shush.'

Pete and Stu returned with a tray of drinks and peanuts.

'Got some good news for you Tina,' Stu affirmed, smiling broadly.

'Just been checking something on the pub Wi-Fi.'

'Does *Land of the Lost* bring back any Saturday morning memories for you?'

Tina looked quizzically at Stu who was tilting his iPhone screen towards her.

'Look at the lizardy reptile creatures on the screen, called 'Sleestaks', could these be the evil frog creatures that will lead you to the lilypad of closure?'

'*Land of the Lost*; I already checked that series, but well done boys and thanks for trying. Yes, it was a Saturday morning show in 1975, and American too, but none of the plots match,' Tina sighed.

'Oh, man we were both sure we'd found it,' Pete slumped down on his seat, clearly disappointed.

'Not to worry, boys, Ploughman's coming,' Tina observed as an overweight, beer-bellied bald man shuffled wheezing out of the front door, balancing Ploughman's Platters on his arms.

'Four Ploughmans. Here you go, enjoy,' Mitch Dougmee puffed. A look of recognition flashed slightly across his face as he did a double take of Mary and he appeared about to say something when a grizzled farmer dismounted from his station wagon, 'Usual for me Mitch when you're ready.'

Mitch swung on his heels and wobbled back indoors.

Tina convulsed with laughter, tears running down her cheeks as the boys looked at her perplexed. Mary went bright red and thumped Tina on her thigh.

'What are you girls laughing at? Something hilarious obviously,' Stu smiled, mystified.

'Just a girl's joke,' Mary responded, her pursed lips cracking into a broad grin.'

'We were just laughing about the local talent on offer in Abbswell,' Tina volunteered.

The two men shook their heads, smiling and the girls continued giggling as the couples opened their little foil butter pats simultaneously and spread it on the French sticks.

'Glad the butter is soft,' Pete said keen to change the subject. 'The landlord says the pub is a wildlife haven; little blue butterflies and toads. There is a Toad Crossing road sign around the next bend,' Pete remarked.

'The chap who brought our lunches out? I thought he looked a bit like Toad of Toad Hall,' Tina commented still laughing. I think Mary fancies her chances.'

Mary gave Tina another thigh slap and brought her napkin up to hide her flushed face.

'Stop it Tina, you're making me hysterical.'

Stu and Pete shook their heads, irritated by the girly closed-ranks and ploughed into their platters, realising they would never get to the bottom of the joke.

As the four left the pub, they took a few photos at the Toads Crossing sign before checking the map and circling back towards the Airbnb.

'I've just realised something Mary,' Tina said as the two men walked briskly ahead, 'All these years I've been searching for my half-man, half-frog while you were searching for your dream toad.'

The girls laughed and upped their pace to catch up with the boys for the hike back.

'You know, I've had a thought. I never did put 'toad' in the search bar,' Tina said, her face bright with fresh inspiration. 'I always searched for *frog*, but it could have been a toad. That tiny tweak might reveal the show.'

'Give it up Tina. GIVE IT UP,' Mary exclaimed, grabbing her forearm and looking her sternly in the eyes. Nothing worthwhile has ever come from searching for hybrid amphibians from the past.'

'I don't know. It led to a pretty good Ploughman's,' Tina replied, her fingers twitching to make that one final search…

///bunk.bulb.took
"IVOR D."

Shona and Andy dropped their cases onto the baggage trolley and trundled it from the rumbling carousel into the cool air-conditioned corridor of Adelaide airport, enjoying the calm hiatus before the paparazzi pandemonium of Arrivals.

'Sleeve Andy! Button up, we'll let them get a close up after the Brekkie Show, but not before. Keep it under your shirt, literally,' she instructed her celebrity charge.

'Sorry, Shona. Thanks for the reminder. It's just so bloody hot. Oz in January is like New York in July. It must be mid-80s and it's just gone eight. My English armpits are struggling. Have you any deodorant; and is that our limo driver ahead?'

Shona squinted into the near distance at the placard holding taxi drivers, waiting chauffeur-cum-security detail and the throng of reporters and fans beyond.

'Yes to both questions, but spray not roll-on. The chauffeur's a big guy and he'll bundle you straight over to The Pullman. We've just got to punch through that pod of paparazzi first. If need be I'll fob the jackals off and get a cab. Phone you when I hit hotel Reception; the manager's briefed for your secret back door entry.'

'You sure Shona? I don't want a repeat of Germany. I've still got that love bite from the Leipzig lurrrve monster.'

'Your own fault for being such a handsome and talented pop idol daaarling.'

'Who's doing the Breakfast interview? Not that cokehead again?'

'You slimed it in one - Scott Valant, the smarmy face of Oz breakfast TV, now powdering his nose with the finest Colombian just for you.'

'Great,' Andy grimaced.

'I know, but you've got *Rockslot's* sexy vixen, Janine Johnson at 1pm to make up for it - naughty boy. You ready?'

'It's now or never; we've been spotted.'

'Head down and smile, you know the drill,' Shona reminded as they reached Eruera, the hefty six-foot-five Maori chauffeur holding his 'Mr A Shaw and Party' electric placard.

'Ma'am, Mr Shaw, follow me closely and briskly,' he instructed lifting the two suitcases in his stubby grip as though trivial burdens, veering them out to the side and front in a V formation like a locomotive cattle guard to repel the uproar of reporters surging towards them:

'Who is Ivor, Andy? What are you hiding from your fans?'

'Give us a peek, Mr Shaw.'

'Got secrets you want to share, Andy?'

Shona sacrificed herself, dropping titbits to the Press hyenas while Andy ducked into the waiting limo; relieved to find privacy behind tinted windows and the caress of air-con as the succession of camera shutters faded. A *schadenfreude* smirk betrayed his amusement seeing Shona engulfed by a rowdy ball of hacks with their impudent microphones, but he knew she relished the argy-bargy of the business as well as being handsomely paid to be his counsel.

It was January 17th and high summer; an overhead gantry thermometer on the airport freeway read 85 degrees. The short ride from the airport to the hotel reminded Andy of Tampa. He didn't feel out of place here like he did in Indonesia and the Arab nations and being a Brit, the left hand drive was a homely change. All too soon, the journey ended as Eruera pulled around the back of the hotel.

He stepped out of the cool limo into the blasting sunshine on York Street, beads of sweat instantly appearing on his forehead as he fumbled in his jeans for a tip.

'Sorry, I'm out of tips, Eruera, my assistant carries it, but I'll make up for it on the return leg.'

'No problem at all, sir, but my daughter will be mad with me if I don't get a selfie.'

'Sure man, let's get inside and take a few.'

After greeting the manager who led them through the trade entrance to hotel reception with the cases, Andy was pleased to oblige, snapping poses with his stock thumbs-up and wink alongside the big grinning Maori.

'Have a great gig tonight, Sir and thank you,' Eruera shook hands and nodded courteously.

Reception staff at The Pullman were used to celebs popping in, as many of the South Australian TV networks arranged whistle-stop interviews to promote tours and albums at the airport hotels. This week Andy Shaw's performance at Thebarton Theatre, was a big deal for Adelaide and The Pullman was a good location for his pre-gig interviews.

Shona knew the rota. Breakfast TV was the big puller and they were going to pre-record an interview at 11am with Scott Valant for Friday's morning show. Andy's gig was 8pm to 10pm and the one-hour slot with *Scott's Brekkie Krew* preceded an afternoon *Rockslot* interview, so he only had a little time to unwind. The rest of the band were staying at a large Airbnb at the beachfront in Glenelg while the roadies set up.

As founding member and handsome lead singer of Britband, *Moonlight Teapartie*, Andy, from Hertfordshire was the lynchpin of all the Australian PR activity and would join the rest of the band an hour before the concert.

As Andy waited for Shona in reception, some thirty vertical feet away, Scott Valant's team were setting up an improv-studio in The Lincoln Suite. Scott, a thirty something narcissist powered by cocaine, was an excellent talk show host as long as he had his entourage of suppliers, though if the snow was in short supply he would improvise with a quarter bottle of Grey Goose.

'Let's hurry it up. Fix that second tripod head on the slider, Brian. Come on you guys, get it together, Andy Shaw's PR has arranged 10.40 for mike and makeup. This is our last chance for the network to extend our contract so get with it.'

'Done, Mr Valant.'

'It's lucky they're running late so they don't realise how bloody inept we are. Make sure you get that camera up to my eye line this time, Bri. I've got one hour max to nail him on what he's hiding up that sleeve.

'Is that okay for you, Mr Valant?'

Scott's team, whom he referred to as *Diane le Powder, Jake the Bulb and Brian the Lens*, already understood the time constraints and fussed efficiently and professionally in spite of Scott's imperious order giving.

'No, I want an over the shoulder in on my shadow side and I want more headroom in front of my face than behind it. Sheesh Brian! Hurry up man; Diane, dust my forehead again and I want you straight to make-up on Andy.

'You got the b-cam ready, Jake? I'm liking the framing, but not sure if we...That's the lift door, here they come.'

Scott's beleaguered team breathed collective relief when Andy and Shona arrived at 10.55am.

'Lincoln Suite, found you a little late,' Shona breezed in, her arms outstretched to hug Scott as Andy stealthily sprayed his armpits in the corridor.

'Hey! Shona! But where's my boy?'

'Andy is coming,' Shona reassured as he wafted in seconds later smelling of Impulse body spray.

'Andy, dude! Great to see you guys again; mwah! Mwah!'

'Hi Scott, mwah aussi, mon ami!' Andy offered his cheek to Scott, loathing his own penchant for plausible sincerity.

'Both looking and smelling *gor-gee-oh-so!* Grab yourselves a brew while we make our tweaks. We're pre-recording for tomorrow's 8.30 slot, but Andy should sit straightaway for mike and makeup.

You may not remember these bods - Diane, Jake and Bri?'

'Sure we do - hi everyone,' Shona waggled her fingers towards the crew while Andy thumbsed-up.

Diane moved swiftly with lids unscrewing and brushes tinkling, 'Andy, you relax in my chair here and I'll freshen you up after your flight.'

54

'Great, I feel a bit greasy with the humidity.'

'Sure you do, we've all got Adelaide Armpit this morning; so I'll just put a little of this cleanser on, like so, and dab a little matt serum on you to stop you shining.'

'He's a rock star Diane, he's meant to shine a little,' Scott sniffed.

'Wow that cleanser smells divine, thanks Diane.'

'Where'd you stay last night Andy?'

'I stayed over in the Carlton in Perth. A good five star option and as they say, 'celeb-safe'. No spy-cams or bugs guaranteed, we hope, though I don't do much to be ashamed of these days now I'm hitched.'

'You really gotta worry 'bout surveillance,' Scott was suddenly serious as this was a subject close to his heart. 'You can't ever let your guard down when you're in the public eye. Always some paparazzo trying to dig dirt.'

'I've grown out of all that extramarital stuff anyway,' Andy pursed his lips. 'Too much guilt and fear to deal with the next day. I've got kids now, so I want to set an example to them.'

'Hey, that's a good line, mate, save that for the interview, you cool about talking about your kids, dude?'

Shona interrupted, 'Yes, Scott, generically, not specifics; the usual stuff about what Dad likes to do when he's not on tour, but appreciate it if you stay on topic and focus on the gigs.'

'It's pre-recorded honey-pie. Uncle Brian cues it up afterwards with the intro music and we clip to fit with the sponsors' ads. So don't worry, I got the list of 'no-goes' including Kate Zoopz and the Brisbane cancellation.'

'Good because Kate Zoopz and Brisbane are walk-aways and remember we've got *Rockslot* at 3pm so we're needing to cut things fine.'

'Worry not, my sweet. I got the schedule and Network wants me to be a good boy so they can tempt you guys back.'

Diane dropped her makeup brush into the jar with a tinkle.

'You're done Andy; de-greased and delicious. Have a quick preen in the mirror and we'll get you and Scott comfy in the giant cornflakes.'

'Oh yeah, I remember those monster orange beanbags; you feel so secure, like you're getting cuddled.'

'To lull you into a false sense of security, Andy, so Scott can charm out your deepest secrets,' Shona cautioned, playfully.

'Ooh, you're such a cynic, girl,' Scott camped it up, 'I just like my guests to snuggle and chill out.'

Andy slumped into the beanbag's caress as Scott made final checks.

'Bri, come a bit further out and get that camera to Andy's eye line man. Hope you're using the 120d aperture with that light-dome?' Scott knew that most of what was said in rock and pop interviews was garbage, but at least the lighting should be right.

'Diane, check Andy's mike, it's slipped and Brian, move that backlight to bring out Andy's head and shoulders.'

'Sorry, Diane,' Shona interrupted, 'can you just cut that freak hair off Andy's ear? It really stands out in the backlight.

'Oh sure, I just spotted that too.' Diane snipped while Scott sniffed impatiently before lowering himself in position in the facing beanbag, tapping his mike and adjusting his fringe.

'Oh..kayy; Shona? Andy? Team? We all good now? Let's roll.'

Brian looked into the viewfinder, 'Standby…Two, three, four, five...Speed.'

Nine thousand five hundred miles away a gentle rattle of cups announced the arrival of Nurse Barbara wheeling the elevenses tea trolley into the day room of the Minnesota care home.

'Mr O'Brien? Shaun? Shaun? Wake up,' she whispered, prodding his shoulder gently.

'What time?' Shaun queried groggily.

'My, you're a sleepy head today; you were snoring, disturbing the Sudoku ladies in the corner. Here's your hot tea for elevenses, that'll fix you.'

Shaun took his glasses off and rubbed his eyes.

'Ah, you are a heavy-eyed Harry today. Would you prefer me to wheel you back to your bedroom until lunch?

'No woman. I'm sick of bloody bed. It's those pills you keep giving me as soon as I wake up. And why can't you Yanks learn to make proper tea. Not only do you make me drink it from a lidded cup like a baby, but it's always lukewarm and tastes like piss. I keep telling you, use tea leaves and a strainer; one spoon for me and one for the pot, but scald the pot first.'

'Now Shaun, I've told you before, we can't get your Irish tea leaves in Minnesota, just Lipton's bags; and you need those pills for your Parkinsons' to stop the trembling. We're trying to keep you healthy you know.'

'Keep me healthy for what?' Shaun banged the beaker of tea down on the tray table in front of him, 'For more jigsaws and the stink of meat pies and colostomies? It's not Parkinson's that makes me shake, it's being stuck in this stinky boring dump.'

'Now don't be silly Shaun. There's folk who'd love to live here. It's one of Minnesota's finest residentials, with a long waiting list,' Nurse Barbara insisted.

'Well I'll speed things up for them,' he said, straining toward the trolley, 'Just let me take that full bottle of pills.'

'Now don't be silly, Mr O'Brien. You mustn't talk like that.'

'Brought up in a bloody home and now I'm going to die in one,' Shaun slammed his palms on the tray table.'

'Now you stop that tantrum nonsense in front of me, Mr O'Brien. I don't know what's got into you this morning. Here, have a cookie. Scottish shortbread and look, chocolate gingers, you like them.'

'Humph. My son put me in this prison to get me out of his hair. His wife hates me, you know. She's turning the grandkids against me. So tell me, what do I really have to live for?'

'Oh, now don't be silly, spring will be here soon,' she paused, 'Ooh, and there's a Tammy Wynette impersonator coming this afternoon.'

'Tammy bloody Wynette? I never liked the first one never mind a phony. Has she got big tits? Ah, no,' he laughed coarsely, 'that's Dolly Parton. I'll hang around if the Wynette woman has big tits.' He grabbed the tea beaker and started to unscrew the lid, 'Well, has she?'

'Stop that, Mr O'Brien, you know you mustn't talk disrespectful in front of staff and residents. Where are your manners today? And don't take that lid off, you'll spill hot tea on your shirt.'

'Oh, just wheel me outside in the snow to die, woman.'

'Now come on, I'll trundle you to the corner to watch the TV with your headphones and you can fill out this week's meal choices while you're watching. I'll collect it in a few minutes. Look, it's a National Geographic about dams.'

Shaun's eyes glinted, 'I designed turbines for hydroelectric power in the eighties. Did I tell you about my innovation for the rotor mechanism?'

'I think you might've done, Mr O'Brien; but you can tell me again when I've done my trolley round.'

Shaun, distracted by images of generators and complex gravitational vortexes, absent-mindedly enjoyed his lukewarm tea as electrical schematics flashed through his brain before he fell back to sleep during the advert break.

On Friday morning at 8.30am in Adelaide The Brekky Krew theme tune played with canned applause, signalling the start of the show.

It's Friday and it's KERRRrunchtime with Scott and his Brekky Krew, the booming Rastafarian voice-over exclaimed as Scott broke from chatting with Andy to grin directly at B-cam.

'Good morning Krunch fans! Stop yer brewin' and halt yer chewin' because joining me, Scott Valant on the comfy cornflakes this morning, in a very sweaty Adelaide, we have *the Emoji of Englishness*; *the Tsar of Twitter trending*; the *blond British bad-boy* himself – *Moonlight Teapartie's, Andy Shaw*.

'Welcome to South Oz mate and thanks for taking time out of your schedule to join your *Krunchtime* fans.'

'Hiya Scott, hi Krunchtime fans,' Andy responded with a little wave into camera as the applause died down.

'You're wriggling Andy. Isn't our cornflake cool enough for your hot superstar bum? January in Oz a bit too sweaty for your British backside?'

'No, I'm fine, Scott; just adjusting,' Andy was impressed with Scott's ability to switch on instant camera charm.

'Take your time and de-wedgie yourself, mate. You Brits are normally digging double-deckers out of snow drifts this time of year while we Aussie's bake on the beach, isn't that right?' Scott sniffed silently.

'Too true Scott, but that's what roadies are for, shovelling and digging and...'

'Or sleeping six abreast in the back of a Ford Transit with the drum kit?' Scott cut in, 'Remember those days, Andy?'

'Oh man, don't remind me.'

'You've come a long way, literally and metaphorically since your early Sheffield gigs in the UK. Tell us about that, or more to the point, how does it feel to be playing in Adelaide's Thebby tonight?'

'Thebby? Oh, yeah, The Barton Theatre, right. Amazing venue.'

Scott replied in a snobbish British accent, '*The Barton Theatre? One sounds so posh, mate...*But yeah, our Thebby's really fantastic; and it's another sell-out for you guys?'

'Yeah, selling out is a bit of a habit for us these days.'

'International rock stars don't do empty seats, mate,' Scott briefly brought his hand to his septum to mask another sniff; 'So the Oz tour started in Perth on Wednesday?'

'Yeah, we kicked off completely jetlagged. Fantastic audience kept us on our toes though. Love all you 'Sandgropers'!'

'Hey, impressed you know the lingo, Andy, but you won't fall asleep on us will you?'

'Don't worry, just poke me.'

'Ooh er!' Scott puckered a campy pout to camera.

'Oh, man. I gave you that one, Scott.'

'You certainly did, mate.'

The over-dubbed whistles and claps subsided. It really was difficult to tell the show wasn't live.

'But let me check, Andy - all your Oz gigs are supported by one of our own - The Skinseeds, is that right? A huge Oz band in their own right, wouldn't you say?'

'Yeah, The Skinseeds - great support act with really dreamy melodies, kind of a mix of Arthur Lee and Love with a techno backdrop.'

'The perfect line up for Oz summer evenings.'

'One hundred percent, Scott.'

'Talking of 'skin' seeds, Andy, can you roll up your sleeve so the viewers can clock your very mysterious skin illustration?'

'I knew you'd be slipping that one in somewhere, Scott, but so soon?'

'Yeah, mate,' Scott laughed, 'You were fifteen minutes late for the interview so I'm pulling my cheeky punches faster than usual. Isn't that right guys?' Scott shouted.

'You were fashionably late, Andy,' Diane affirmed off camera.

'So come on Andy, show us what's hiding up your sleeve-y weave-y. We know it's the only tat you've got, so naturally it must be very special. Is it special Andy? We all saw the blurry picture in the tabloids last week; it looked like a name – 'Ivor D.' something? Is that right? Ivor? Some gay thing? You can tell Scotty, Andy.'

'No Scott, you know me, I'm a ladies' man through and through.'

'Let me guess then. Hmmm. Ivor D... Ivor...Ivor...*Ivor Declaration* to make? Or perhaps, *Ivor Denial* to hide behind? Are you coming out in Oz, Andy?'

'Nope. Defo not a gay thing.'

'Careful mate, protesting too much and all that, but I'm still thinking… *Ivor D. something*. Is it a secret clone name then? Ivor Double? You know all about the 'Andy is a clone' rumour?'

'Yeah, yeah, but you're trying too hard Scott; though it might be handy to have a clone of myself to do your interview.'

'Cheeky boy! Don't think we won't show you the door, mate. I've more megastars queuing up outside than you've got hot groupies.'

Scott yelled off camera again: 'Tell Beyoncé to cancel the Superbowl; a *Krunchtime* slot's just opened.'

'You're a card, Scott. Why don't you ask me about the new album instead?'

'I'm going to, mate, but let's have a peek up that sleeve-y first...This *Ivor D* character must be really important. Huge stars like you don't get a new tat without inviting curiosity. Come on man, your Australian fan is desperate to know - and so am I,' Scott teased.

'It's hard not to hate you, Scott,'

'I'm your number one fan, Andy'

'That's a really bad Kathy Bates' impression.'

'You reckon? Come on mate, spill the beans before I hobble you with me mallet.'

'Careful Scott, your Aussie charm might just penetrate my inner sanctum.'

'Ooh er, penetrating inner sanctums?'

'Oh man, I did it again,' Andy shook his head self-deprecatingly, reaching for his sleeve.

'Well my Oz charm obviously worked because it looks like you're unbuttoning. Pan in on Andy's forearm, Brian so the audience can see at home.'

'Do I get a drumroll?'

'No budget for that, Andy.'

'Wow Andy, it looks very ornate close up. What does it say? Let me read to the audience: *Ivor D. In memoriam* - very minimalist, but stylish. So Andy, pray tell us more about - *the late Ivor D.* - Obviously someone you were close to?'

'Okay, you win Scott; persistence over charm, mind you. I was saving it for Janine Johnson on *Rockslot*, so you're privileged. My PR girl's tutting.

'Hey Janine and I are buddies. We share, man,' Scott beamed, delighted at his scoop as whistles and applause overlaid the recording.

'I'm plugging your album and tour, remember,' he grinned.

'Okay Scott, but you're wrong about Ivor and me being close. I never met him.'

'More intriguing by the second, carry on mate,' Scott leaned forward with keen interest.

'Well; Ivor relates to my grandfather and the love I had for him. He died last year...'

'Ivor D was related to your grandfather?'

'No, no Scott. Patience, patience. My granddad died last year and it prompted me to get inked.'

'We're all intrigued, carry on.'

'When I was about ten, my granddad met me at the school gates. He smoked a pipe and I remember the lollipop lady and parents eyeing him shadily because no one smoked and he was setting a bad example.'

'Smoking a pipe?' Scott camped up the outrage. 'Was Granddad like a 'terrorist'? Did a black helicopter overshadow him in whisper-mode?'

'Ha, yeah, I know what you mean, but no one said anything because he was smartly dressed; like really old fashioned smart, with a trilby hat and polished shoes and black trousers with a crease. He'd sometimes carry an umbrella and use it like a cane.'

'Sounds like Neville bloody Chamberlain.'

'Yeah, actually that's a good comparison, Scott; Chamberlain, though without the piece of paper. I was really proud of him; he looked a smart gent with impeccable manners and because of that it defused any criticism.'

'They must have thought he was a time traveller.'

'For sure...' Andy nodded, smiling.

'A real anachronism and clearly another ladies' man and rule breaker like his grandson, eh? But where does Ivor D fit in all this?'

'I'm coming to that, Scott, hold your horses.'

'Sorry, Andy, they're champing at the bit, but I'll zip it; hope to die.'

Andy paused, 'Anyway, I had a bit of a cold that day and I remember wiping my runny nose with my school blazer sleeve.'

'Urgh, gross man! You're on *Krunchtime*, the brekkie show remember; no one wants to talk snot when they're eating soggy Sugar Puffs.'

'You're right Scott. I'll keep it clean. Anyway, Granddad said, 'You want to use a hanky, not your sleeve, or you'll end up like Ivor Delaney'. So I said, 'Ivor who?' And he explained Ivor Delaney was a little boy who lived in the Dublin Barnardo's home with him back in the 1950s. He was a friendly wee laddie, but always had a jewelled sleeve.'

'A jewelled sleeve, mate?' Scott guffawed, 'Sounds more like a Disney Princess.'

'Yeah Scott, well it starts off with a 'shiny' sleeve when you first wipe your nose and later it turns to crystals – so I hear. Granddad said little Ivor's sleeve was... well... shiny and jewelled owing to his continual snotty schnozzle.'

'Brekkie show, Andy, brekkie show! Anyone eating 'Lucky Charms' cereal out there? Hope not.'

'I know, Scott, but seriously, poor little Ivor didn't have a mum to wipe it for him and so he was remembered for perpetual dewdrops running from his nostrils which always ended up on his sleeve.'

'Dewdrops — a much more pleasant euphemism, mate. He didn't use tissues or a hanky then?'

'Don't know, it was a long time ago the 1950s. Clean hankies probably weren't that easy to come by and tissues were probably not a thing. I think they had to use newspaper or that shiny bog-roll back then,' Andy shrugged.

'You're right, oucha! I got acquainted with that in a youth-hostel dunny on a school trip in the Nineties.'

'Sure you did, Scott you're much older than me. Anyway, back to Ivor.'

'Sorry Andy, I'll do my Trappist monk impression; vow of silence and all that.'

'So as I was saying... My granddad – Alfred, or Alfie to his friends - shared a dorm with Ivor and other boys in the home - and every Saturday morning they were allowed out to the pictures to buy sweets and watch Flash Gordon's adventures in space. It was the week's highpoint...'

*   *   *

'We are doomed, Professor Gordon. That planet is rushing madly toward the Earth and no human power can stop it'. Professor Hensley's words merged with the rustle of sweet wrappers; the sucking of black bullets and crunching of barley sugars in Camden Picture House, Lower Camden Street, Dublin.

Eight-year-old Ivor sat in the front row, gummily ruminating the liquorice shoelace that blackened his teeth, his eyes wide with foreboding as *Ming the Merciless* sent *Flash Gordon* to fight in the arena. Black dribble ran down his chin. He wiped it with a swipe of his ragged grey pullover sleeve.

'He fights well, the Earthman. He shall not escape the pit!' Ming the Merciless mocked.

'*No, Father, not that!'* Princess Aura pleaded.

The Planet Mongo terrified and the beautiful women tantalised, as spaceships whizzed and monsters gnashed like locusts through Ivor's imagination. He was awestruck; until Shaun O'Brien disturbed his reverie.

'Ivor. Psst! Me and Alfie have seen this one before. Ming the Merciless makes Flash fight the ape men in the arena.'

'Shut up Shaun, be quiet,' Ivor protested.

'Shut your faces you eejits, I can't hear and this is the best part,' Alfie cut in.

'Shut your face Alfie, you've seen it too,' argued Shaun, punching him in the leg.

'Well, I haven't seen it, Shaun, so don't spoil it for me,' Ivor grumbled.

'Shurrup, Delaney, I willin'me hole.'

'Get my daughter out of there', Emperor Ming commanded, *'The pit!'*

'No. No!' Princess Aura screamed, *'He's earned the right to live'.*

'It's nearly finished anyway. Race you and Alfie to the Bayno,' Shaun sprang from his seat, 'Hurry up eejits or you'll be last out.'

The credits rolled to the scratchy orchestral score while a domino effect of thumping sprung cinema seats merged with a frenzy of footsteps as hordes of children raced to the exits. A mass of chattering heads shoved and stampeded past the doorman through the bottleneck alley and onto the street. The bright sunshine tore into them like a flare from Mongo's sun.

'Hoy, stop your roughhousing you lot, slow down or you'll get a clip from me,' the old doorman warned.

'But we're running to The Bayno for sticky buns and cocoa before it shuts,' Alfie explained.

'Bayno? You mean The Iveagh Play Centre on Bull Alley Street? Well, mind your manners laddie, you'll knock the shoppers over.'

'It better still be open,' Shaun panted, 'Bloody hurry up Ivor.'

'I'm coming, Shaun. Slow down,' he wheezed.

Shaun and Alfie ran on ahead waving their arms in music-conductor mockery, singing a clipped version of The Bayno anthem to the tune of *Tip-toe Through the Tulips*, their rhythmic exaggerated skipping scuffing the soles of their shabby shoes:

Tip-toe to the Bayno,
where the kids go,
to get their buns and cocoa,
Come tip-toe to the Bayno with me

The boys skidded to a stop at The Bayno entrance on Bull Alley Street.

'Bugger! We're not jammy today. You eejit, Ivor, you were too bloody slow; It's one o' clock and now everyone's leaving and we've missed the free buns.'

'It's not my fault, Shaun. You were only ten seconds in front.'

'Aye, Shaun, we were. You can't blame Ivor. Anyway, the play park's still open. Race you to the teapot lid. Come on!'

Every Saturday was like Sports Day in The Bayno's rectangular yard. Boys played football and battled; girls skipped with ropes or span in rings and rhymed, while adults loosely supervised from teak park benches next to the raised play area; reprimanding queue jumping and bad behaviour with a stern glance from over a newspaper.

A ten foot high brick wall backed the park where children could peer over into the amenities yards if they mounted the high top of the 'chimney pot' on the climbing frame. A sandpit area, and roundabout dubbed The Teapot Lid, was on the left, and to the right, the popular Witch's Hat.

'Climbing frame for me,' Ivor shouted.

'Teapot Lid for me and Shaun!'

'You're on your own Delaney,' Shaun heckled.

'I don't care, I'm climbing to the top of the chimney pot.'

The park was gradually emptying as Ivor climbed, daydreaming.

'Higher and higher Rocket Pilot Delaney climbs. Whoosh! Whoosh! Up into space he goes, to the Planet of Peril to fight the ape men and win the hand of the evil princess.'

Ivor craned his neck back and gazed bravely up at the azure vastness of cloudless sky. A wind-whistle piped wistfully through a small hole in the tubular frame and he felt a strange disconnection from the hubbub and screams below, remembering a sad tune his mother would sing to him when he was very small.

'In Scarlet Town where I was born,
There was a fair maid dwelling…'

He couldn't remember the rest, just that one line.

The wistful fluting blew sadder as the summer breeze gusted fitfully. His thoughts drifted far away into a lovely memory of a pale morning in a flower garden, his beautiful mother bathing him in a metal bath and singing; the final remembrance of her sweet voice and gentle caress. He wished he could have heard her sing it one more time before she was taken to Heaven and he was sent to St Benedict's.

'He's at the top of the world spinning around Saturn's rings like a needle on a record. He can hear the loneliness of space like a sad song—*Mammy, I can nearly reach the clouds from here—the sky is bright blue like your picnic dress.*

'I'm so sad without you, but I hear you singing your song in heaven when the wind blows: 'In Scarlet Town where I was born, hmm, hmm, hmm...fair maid dwelling'...

'..I am going to be a famous space pilot and fly to the stars. I will swordfight Emperor Ming the Murzilust and make you proud.'

A sudden fear of falling upwards into blue infinity jolted Ivor and he wobbled, looking quickly down to steady himself, tensing his fingers and locking his knees against the aluminium frame as a noisy clanging of a bell brought him back down to earth and the shrill business of the playground.

'Oy, Ivor, Shaun – Witch's Hat, now! The park's closing.'

Ivor launched downward, descending like a willowy macaque through the grid of the frame, joining Alfie and Shaun to bag the prized spaces.

'The bell gave me a fright, Alfie. I nearly fell....'

'Hurry before those girls get on,' Alfie was focused.

Six children simultaneously disembarked the hat and it clanged to a bumpy stop while three sullen looking girls in blue pinafores and white blouses quickly took their seats.

'Ah no, Ivor you were too bloody slow.'

'It's okay, Alfie we'll whirl it fast to scare them off.'

'You girls separate out. Sit there, and there, and there,' Shaun bossed, 'and me and the boys will zoom it up.'

'Who are ye to tell us where to sit? It's our turn, we were here first,' the oldest girl protested.

'No stupid, it bangs on its hub if you don't balance it,' Alfie said.

'We want our turn by ourselves and swing on it, not spin.'

'It's not a swing. It's a witch's hat,' Shaun disputed.

'No it's not; it's called The Ocean Wave and we swing on it.'

'You are very pretty, but you should share,' Ivor stared longingly at the oldest girl's chestnut tresses and green eyes, just like Princess Aura's.

'What's that to you if I'm pretty you snotty nosed freak?'

'My name's Ivor Delaney and I'm not a snotty nosed freak.'

'Well it's a bastard's name and… ' She paused, '… I know yous three; yous are the shabby bastards from St. Benedict's. We can tell, cos y'all stink o' piss.'

'Houl yer whisht! The bleedin' state of ye, you Narkey Holes,' Shaun snarled.

'You don't swear at us like that,' the youngest chipped in.

'Aye we will, and I'm no bastard; my daddy and mammy died. Bloody let us on,' Ivor said firmly.

'Go 'way outta that!' Princess Aura scowled, 'We don't want to catch lice from you jackeens. Stay away.'

'I willin'me hole!' Shaun jeered, 'Ivor, jump on next to Alfie; rockets lit... Spin! Spin! Into space... Hold on tight!'

Shaun ran holding the frame before releasing it in a powerful surge. An intermittent squeak sounded faster and faster as he continued to spin it while the girls screamed and Ivor and Alfie laughed raucously.

'What class of eejits are you? Stay away from us and stop spinning now! You'll wreck the gaff and you're scaring my friends. My brother will kill yous if you don't stop.'

'We're not scared of your brother and there's no time left to wait our turn. The park's closing.'

'Shurrup Shaun, her brother will banjax us, he's fifteen,' Alfie shouted.

'It's fine, three against one,' Shaun countered.

'Flash Gordon is leaving Earth and hurtling to the Planet of Peril,' Ivor narrated.

'We are whirring like a gyro, Dr Zarkov! Now passing through Saturn's rings! Whoosh!'

The screams from the girls turned into a whimpering, desperate protest. The youngest started crying.

'Stop, please, let us off! Stop! You jackeen eejits...Please stop! I'm going to fall off. Help!'

'The rockets are lit, it is too late to stop. Whoosh!'

Abruptly Shaun felt a sharp slap on his head. The older brother was shouting.

'What state da ya? Ya thick langers; *Gidditz*!'

'Ow! That knackers!' Shaun held his head in both hands.

'Slow it down now and leave my sister an' my mot alone or I'll murder yous. You two Benedict's bastards gerroff too.'

The older brother hit the rotating bars with his stocky hand to slow the rotation, finally grabbing the frame and skidding on the concrete as the mechanism whined and clanged on its axis to a shuddering stop. The girls whimpered.

'Aw, stop blubbering, we didn't hurt yous!'

Shaun received another slap on his head and face and a kick in his back.

'Ow! Leave me alone.'

'You're some thick bollocks. I'll bloody banjax ya.'

'Gerroff! Ow! Argh! Ya bloody bogger,' Shaun spluttered, red-faced.

'Look at de state o' de head on dat sham,' the older boy mocked, 'I told yous gowls to *gidditz* and ya still here? Do yous all want some? Ay?'

'Leg it!' Ivor yelled.

Alfie, Shaun and Ivor sprinted out of the park along the street to the Iveagh building entrance as a defiant Shaun paused to taunt the older boy still standing at The Witch's Hat, 'Gerr-up-ow-ra-da! Your ma's a floozie!' he goaded before the three dodged into the main building to hide inside a large hall where ladies were packing up needlework class and chairs and trestle tables were being stacked and folded away.

'Walk, don't run,' a severe looking lady reprimanded, 'Disport yourselves in the correct manner you boys, or you will not be allowed back. It is time to leave anyway, so please move to the front doors and be civil.'

They obediently slowed to a walk, heads bowed as they scampered back to the entrance.

'You shouldn't have shouted Shaun,' Ivor stated scanning around nervously, 'He'll banjax us next time and we won't get to play here without looking over our shoulders every second.'

'Check the street to see if he's coming before we go back out,' Alfie panted, 'He can't hurt us with grown-ups around.'

Now Bull Alley Street pavement bustled with children lining up to walk side by side in twos carrying needlework samplers or still-wet paintings and crayon drawings.

'The coast is clear me hearties!' Shaun sniggered. 'Race you back through St Paul's. Mind the bus.'

A bus horn blared loudly as the three pelted across the road, laughing.

'Did you hear when Spotty told us to *gidditz*! That night-watchman on the building site shouted *gidditz* when he chased us, remember?'

'Aye, he's probably Spotty's da,' Shaun roared with laughter.

'Gidditz! Gidditz! Gidditz!' Alfie chanted, whacking stinging nettles with a stick as they ran until they slowed to catch their breath.

'I'm starving,' Shaun complained.

'I'm not, I've got liquorice and black bullets.'

'Well give us some, Ivor, you greedy langer.'

'No, Shaun. I saved mine for now. You and Alfie ate yours in the pictures. Anyway, Matron said we might have jam tonight.'

'But I'm hungry now and it's just rhubarb jam and it's for Sunday tea, not tonight. I saw her and Father Laidlaw eating it on scones with cream yesterday,' Alfie revealed.

'Gutsy bastards,' Shaun griped, 'The old bag better leave some for us instead of stuffing her face.'

'And cream too,' Ivor added.

'That fat cow? No chance will she. Give us a bullet, Ivor.'

'Just one then, Shaun; here. Miss Bly said it's liver and potato and semolina and rosehip syrup pudding tonight.'

'Grand. Better than bone broth and bastard marrowfats.'

'Or pickled herring salad - the most disgustingest thing ever,' Alfie clutched his gut and mimicked vomiting.

'It's ages yet 'til dinner. Let's go to the games room. Are you eejits coming or what?' Shaun bolted around the corner while Alfie and Ivor raced to catch up, hurtling up the steps to push open the heavy front door of the terraced Barnardo's town house.

A red tiled entrance hall contained a Victorian hall stand with mirror and a disproportionately small *Sacred Heart of Jesus* picture in a cheap frame, mottled with foxing and barely visible in the dim light of the single fanlight window above the front door.

The home was quiet apart from Miss Bly, Matron's twenty-five-year-old assistant housekeeper, clattering and coughing from the distant scullery. At the top right of the hall, adjacent to the stairwell was a dark brown painted door leading to the high-ceilinged games room with its recessed brick fireplace which remained unlit from Easter to All Saints Day. By the hearth was a hooky rug with two decaying leather armchairs to the left and right stuffed with horsehair, their holey arms waxy with newsprint and their cracked cushions so deeply slumped, they were comfortable.

Bookshelves to the right of the fireplace contained piles of magazines, newspapers and hymnbooks with the lowest shelf housing a wooden draughts and chess set with missing pieces and a crushed Chinese Chequers box bound with a rubber band. To the left of the door stood a shabby upright piano with a number of dead keys and a small granite bust of Liszt.

It was a Spartan sight compared to the shiny cinema screen that morning, though Dublin's faint traffic noise was welcoming for Ivor; signalling activity and excitement in the world beyond the drab confines of the home. He thought of America with skyscrapers like silver rocket ships gleaming in the warm Hollywood sunshine and he ached for palm trees and neon and sylph ladies wearing expensive furs with gorgeous hair, red lips and white teeth; a million miles from the washboards, mangles and genuflecting of Dublin's brawny Dettol fishwives.

'I hate this bloody games and reading room. What eejit would want to read matron's boring old church pamphlets? And there's nothing to play except solitaire,' Alfie complained rustling through the leaflets and rattling the box of wooden chess and draughts pieces.

'There's draughts or 'Mousey Mousey', Shaun.'

'I'm bored of draughts and the mice have had their tails chewed off.'

'Hey Alfie, I know!' Ivor's eyes sparkled, 'We should lie down on the proggy mat and stare up at the ceiling and pretend we're flying into space. Turn the light on Shaun.'

'I'm not your slave, Delaney.'

'No, Shaun, but if you lie down and squint at the bulb and ceiling rose, it looks like a galaxy and that moth is a giant bat creature attacking.'

The three boys stared at the moth tapping against the bulb.

'What? A bat creature attacking? Like this?'

Shaun whipped Ivor's shirt up and slapped his stomach hard.

'Ouch, ya ruddy bastard! That kills.'

'You should keep your shirt tucked in, Snotty... And another bat creature swoops down on Alfie...'

'Ouch, Fatty Arbuckle, ye! Gerroff!' Alfie fumed.

'Aha, you dare to insult Flash Gordon, you puny ape men,' Shaun raised his fists and swayed like a boxer.

Alfie hurled himself fast and low to grab Shaun's waist: 'Flash Gordon wrestling match!' he announced, forcing Shaun onto the rug.

'Matron will kill us if we're noisy,' Ivor said, stealthily easing the door closed.

'Not if we do silent wrestling,' Shaun puffed, writhing out of Alfie's grip, 'I'll be Flash and you two can be the fanged ape-men in Ming's Arena. I will defeat you both and earn the right to live.'

Shaun began to circle his prey, quickly grabbing Ivor in a headlock and forcing him wheezing with laughter onto the floor.

'You will fall into the pit and die,' Shaun heckled, victorious.

'Aargh! Aargh! Ow,' Ivor exclaimed as Shaun grappled him on top of Alfie.

'Sword fight!' Shaun took the brass fire poker from the hearth-tidy.

'Grab your weapon ape-man. Get the broom next to the piano, Ivor.'

Circling around the room, the two contenders clashed, metal banging against wood.

'Ow! You eejit, you whacked my knuckle,' Ivor protested, dropping the shank.

'Shush. Keep your gob shut, Snotty.'

'You've made it bleed.'

'Don't be soft, Delaney.'

'Here Shaun, fight me instead with the window pole, not the poker,' Alfie raised his broom to battle, 'Wood against wood. If I win I'm Flash Gordon.'

'Flash Moron you mean,' Shaun mocked.

'No, Alfie, you're Ming the Murzalusk,' Ivor corrected.

'Ming the Merciless, you eejit,' Shaun panted.

'Merzilust then. How do you know, Shaun?'

'Cos I've ears and a brain, Delaney. Take that monkey guts,' Shaun poked the blunt window pole into Alfie's stomach.

'Ow, that hurt you eejit,' Alfie clutched his belly, angrily thwacking Shaun's window pole with his broom handle.

'A gut wound for a slow and painful death,' Shaun cackled.

'But Flash the brave hero fought on in spite of the blood,' Alfie hissed.

'You're an ape-man, moron. I'm Flash,' Shaun insisted as Alfie poked the broom shank into his ribs.

'The hero kills the impostor with a stab to the heart!'

'You missed,' Shaun winced, 'it was nowhere near my heart.'

'Yes it was Shaun, Alfie beat you. I saw.'

Shaun was defiant: 'No! The ape man could not hurt Flash, because of invisible armour under his shirt.'

Shaun lunged towards Alfie who deflected the pole with a whack of his broom shank, smashing it into the leaded window. Tinkling glass marked a sudden tense silence.

'Shaun, what have you done? Matron's going to banjax you,' Ivor whispered.

'It was Alfie, he hit my pole. I was just standing.'

'Fudge off Shaun! You did it, I …'

'Shush, someone's coming,' Ivor tensed as stomping footsteps heralded an abrupt turn of the door knob. The games room door swung open.

'Miss Bly!' Ivor exclaimed.

'Gerr-up-ow-ra-da and stop your thumpin', there's no horseplay in here. I can't hear myself think. It's like a boxing match from the kitchen. What are you doin' O'Brien with that window pole? Put it back at... Oh! Mother Mary, what is that? Glass? Who's put the pane out? You've made a complete haymes in here.'

'It was just an accident, Miss. Alfie and me were trying to kill a moth before it ate the curtain. It's just the small pane, Miss.'

'Don't you give me your lies, O'Brien. It's a holy show you've made and just a small pane is it? It's no cheap thing to get a window fixed - and on a weekend.'

'Well, you're going to have Matron to deal with, but you're getting all that glass swept up and it's straight to bed after dinner, no pudding.'

'But Miss, it...'

'No buts from you Delaney; you're just as involved as those two. Get the dustpan now and sweep it all up. I dread to think what Father Laidlaw will have to say about this. You'll be lucky to get bread and water before Mass tomorrow.'

After dinner, Shaun, Alfie and Ivor marched up the loud wooden stairs with Miss Bly looking up behind them.

'You'll all get into your pyjamas and brush your teeth - without wetting the powder, O'Brien, then I'll be up to inspect. After prayers, I don't want to hear a peep from any of you.'

After five minutes Miss Bly stomped into the room and secured the blackout curtain as the three boys knelt and said The Lord's Prayer.

'Now into bed and get to sleep at once with no more shenanigans and you'd better hope Matron is in a reasonable mood when I tell her the tale.'

The two-bunk dorm had one bed empty this week as Michael Fitzwilliam was holidaying with an aunt in Liverpool. Ivor, on the lower bunk, played with a small carved wooden car from under his pillow, making a subdued rocket noise.

'Whoosh, whoosh, whoosh. I'm going to be a spaceman,' he whispered, 'I will conquer evil Emperor Ming.'

'Shut up Shaun, Miss Bly will ruddy-well hear. We don't want early bed tomorrow too,' Alfie warned.

'I don't care, Alfie, I'm going to escape from here and live in America in a silver skyscraper and then I'm going to be a spaceman.'

'How will you ever get to be a spaceman, Delaney?'

'Easy. First I will learn to be a jet pilot, then I will get a job flying rockets and then I will go to space.'

'You won't get further than Ha'penny Bridge in a bogey-cart, Snotty.'

'Aye, Ivor,' Alfie cut in, 'How do you think you can even get to America in the first place?'

'Simple, I'll stowaway at the docks. And what do you eejits know, anyway? I ruddy well will be a spaceman and be famous and all the world will see me up in the stars. Whoosh! Whoosh! Whoosh!'

'You need to know about engines to be a pilot, Delaney.'

'That's rubbish. As long as you aren't scared of heights you can be a pilot and then if you're brave enough you can be a spaceman.'

'Well, you're not brave, Delaney, that's why you ran from that spotty eejit.'

'You ran too.'

'Aye so? I was just sick of him hitting me around the head, protecting yous.'

'Anyway, I'm going to build engines and be rich while you're still making up baby stories about being a spaceman.'

'You won't say that when you see me fly in a rocket one day O'Brien, you big gobshite. I'll have the whole world looking at me through telescopes in outer space. Just you wait. Whoosh!'

'Shut your ruddy mouths! I'm not getting wrong because of you eejits. Shush, I think I can hear matron.'

*   *   *

Back in the Lincoln Suite, Andy Shaw's iPhone vibrated in his pocket as the *whoo-whooo-whoo* of his ring tone interrupted the *Brekky Krew* interview.

'Oops, sorry Scott, my bad,' Andy sniggered, 'Sci-fi Theremin ring tone!'

'Very apt Flash Gordon. So what happened to Ivor? And why the Ivor tattoo?'

'Ah, the tattoo, yes,' Andy paused pensively.

'My granddad said Ivor had been poorly a few days and he took really bad one night all feverish…'

*   *   *

Shaun O'Brien and Michael Fitzwilliam lay undisturbed in their bunks, but Alfie woke from a fitful sleep recognising Miss Bly in the dim doorway and Matron leaning down at the low bunk opposite in the lantern glow.

'Matron, the ambulance men are here.'

'Show them up, Brianna. Quickly now.'

Alfie listened drowsily to heavy boots on the wooden stairs as cool Dublin air, tainted by the odour of cigarettes and ether wafted from the ambulance men's tunics.

Ivor wheezed, startled at the touch of a cold stethoscope on his chest as matron's warm hand tenderly pressed his forehead. A haunting lilt of a young woman arose from somewhere far away, serenading Ivor's spirit.

'In Scarlet Town, where I was born
There was a fair maid dwelling
In Scarlet Town where I was born,
Her name was Barbara Allen...'

'Is that you, Mummy? Are we going to Scarlet Town?' Ivor slurred.

'Shush now, Ivor; it's Matron. You're a little delirious.'

'Mammy,' he stuttered, 'It's so sunny today. Your blue dress... I see flowers all around.'

'What's wrong, Matron? Is Ivor alright? Who are the men?' Alfie quizzed.

'Quiet now, Alfie, go back to sleep; Ivor's not well.'

Ivor's voice became momentarily strident, 'Are we going for a picnic?'

Shaun mumbled and fidgeted on the upper bunk.

'Don't worry now, Ivor, the man's got you.'

'I'm so cold, Mammy...'

'Keep that blanket over him now,' Matron instructed, following the men out of the room.

Alfie drifted back to sleep as the dreamlike lantern shadows dimmed and the ruffle of overcoats and subdued footsteps echoed into abstraction.

Minutes later, a stretcher was solemnly secured into a quiet ambulance, the dank air sealed outside as the door banged shut. A coarse grey blanket was pulled tenderly over Ivor's cold, damp head; the urgency over.

*   *   *

'My granddad said Ivor died the same day as John Cobb in 1951 or '52, I forget the year.'

'John Cobb?' Scott queried.

'Yeah, the jet powered speedboat man. They remembered seeing the newspapers with the pictures of the crash scene the next day. Ivor's demise completely offset by John Cobb's death.'

'Yeah, but two rocket fans on the same day.'

'True, Scott. True. I never thought of it like that.'

'What a story, Andy. You've transformed what began as a snotty stomach-turner for Krunchtime viewers into a genuine heart-tugger. But the tattoo? Why the tattoo? Why Ivor?

'I dunno,' Andy mused, 'Perhaps because Ivor's life and my granddad's memory were intertwined; I see the Ivor tattoo as a symbolic tribute to my granddad and his childhood. My right wrist is a place I look to every time I'm tempted to complain.'

Scott rebuffed the urge to make a smutty remark.

'If I'm tempted to feel entitled, I think of little Ivor with his runny nose and his short and insignificant life. He lacked opportunities and never realised his ambitions. I feel so sad about that.'

'Wow,' Scott exhaled, 'so do we.' There was real sincerity in Scott's inflexion.

Andy rolled his silk sleeve back over the tattoo and secured the cuff, imagining Ivor's ragged pullover sleeve.

'That's some tale Andy. How do we follow that one Krew? It's a big lump to swallow for breakfast. Not much room left to digest your next album now, mate,' Scott looked at his watch purposefully.

'No worries, Scott. It was my fault for reminiscing...'

'You're forgiven, and it's a timely reminder how important it is to appreciate family and friends and keep 'em close... That said', Scott quickly reverted to character, 'I hope you'll be keeping us guys close and tuned in to all your Moonlight Teapartie antics this week. We'll certainly be following you guys for the rest of the tour; shiny sleeves an' all.

'Big hand for Andy everybody - and whoa! – I forgot – a very big hand—and shiny sleeve—for the late Ivor D. too. Be sure to check in with the crazy Krunchtime Krew next time you're in Oz, Andy.'

'Sure guys; thanks.'

'Fantastic... *Moonlight Teapartie's* Andy Shaw everyone.' The show applause faded out as the credits rolled.

*   *   *

An hour later in Dingle Road, Dublin, an old style telephone bell rang jarringly in a chintzy hallway. The repetitive *brr-brr* seemed interminable to the long distance caller who was about to hang up when the line connected with a crackle.

A frail voice spoke guardedly: 'Hello? Yes, I'm Miss Bly; Miss Brianna Bly. Who's calling? The Sydney Morning Herald? What on Earth? You found me in where? National Children's Home... Dublin Local Authority Archives? Why? Yes, I did work in St Benedict's. Uh huh, until 1963. Andy who? Andy Shaw? Yes, I have heard of *Moonlight Teapartie*; I may be ninety three, but I watch TV you know. His grandfather? Alfred Shaw? Oh my. Yes, I remember Alfie, yes; and Ivor Delaney too.

'Young wee chisellers they were; Ivor died very young, double pneumonia I recall. Yes. Yes. Shaun O'Brien. Oh yes, I still get a card from Shaun at Christmas. He's in America now. Retired. Very successful engineer you know. Uh huh. In fact I have an old photo of the three of them at The Bayno Christmas Party in my bureau drawer. I'll send you a copy. No, I have a scanner. I may be old, but I have some mod cons. Oh, how lovely. Yes, you have permission and I'll give you my email. Uh huh, very pleased to be of help.'

*   *   *

Two days later, *Moonlight Teapartie's* New York charter flight landed in freezing fog at LaGuardia Airport. Andy was wearing a grey hoodie, hopelessly seeking anonymity from the press, but in spite of being wedged between Shona and the roadies a CNN mike wielded by a gorgeous and sassy reporter was thrust into his face.

'Andy, did you think your tattoo reveal would be so internationally, er, disruptive?' she asked him flirtatiously.

Andy, drawn by her beauty halted mid step as his entourage stumbled and collided to a stop behind him.

'No man, but I guess when you're an influential band like *Moonlight Teapartie* you have this power to affect culture,' he responded, completely charmed.

'Indeed, a cultural legacy comparable to The Beatles, and now linked to another phenomenon – that of Ivor D., the boy from your grandfather's childhood. Have you heard?'

'Heard? What? Has his snotty nose come back to haunt me?' Andy joked.

'Paradoxically, yes; you could say your story has raised Ivor from the dead.'

'How so?' Andy was curious.

'They found his photo. Thanks to *Teapartie* fans his image has already become the most shared meme in history.'

'No way man, that's crazy.'

'Crazy but true, look at the screens behind you.'

Andy turned to see a digital billboard with alternating adverts; the first an environmental campaign for the rainforest - *#Savetrees use your sleeve;* the second an image of Ivor photoshopped on dumbbells below a purple *Monstah Motivatah* logo with the headline, 'Stop whining, start shining.'

'Monstah Motivatah?'

'Er, New York's workout guy?'

'Oh.'

'Even the Irish Taoiseach mentioned him today when he visited The Whitehouse.'

'No way!'

'What do you think Ivor would say now he's achieved such recognition seventy years after his death?'

'Oh man, I don't know; he'd defo banjax my Granddad for mentioning his shiny sleeve,' he laughed.

Shona's unyielding arm eased Andy away from the interview as the pretty reporter pressed home a final question:

'Could Ivor's cultural footprint end up - forgive the pun – 'outshining' *Moonlight Teapartie*'s?' she teased.

'Now that would be ironic,' Andy winked as Shona guided him to the waiting coach.

'Viral' hardly did justice to the phenomenon of Ivor D. Around the world, bouncing from ground station to satellite and back down to earth, an unknown boy from Dublin became the most shared and edited image in history as antennas, buildings, and electronics transmitted, received, copied and repeated the familiar pixel arrangement of Ivor's party hat, runny nose and toothless grin billions of times with the words: *B'lieve in D'Sleeve*. It was a universally understood meme and *Moonlight Teapartie's* international fan base embraced it.

Ivor's face popped up everywhere, from grainy Andy Warhol style silkscreen prints, to bus back adverts, giant banners and even in a digitised corn circle in Wiltshire.

A cruise ship *LE Ivor Delaney, Pride of Dublin* set to sea with the headline: *The Face that Launched a Thousand Ships*; Dublin's New Year light show recreated Andy's tattoo using drones; the St Patrick's parade in New York had a float for Delaney-surname sharers wearing ostentatious jewelled sleeves; a tissue advert extolled the strapline: *Don't Grieve your Sleeve, Pack a Wype*; a

Moonlight Teapartie tribute band called themselves *Delaney's Dewdrops*; Time Magazine explained *How the Ivor Meme Defined Ireland's Lost Generation;* The New York Post ran an article: *Delaney's Dublin: Barnardos and Bayno;* Delaney's Polishes boasted: *Sleeve it to us to bring outshining results; a*nd a snotty nosed *Ivor the Frog* meme asked: *Will it be Shiny or Slimy, Sir?*

Meanwhile, oblivious to the world beyond the pine-scented disinfected corridors of the Minnesota care home, Shaun O'Brien pretended to be asleep and ignored the muted knock on his bedroom door amid the rattle of cups.

'Mr O'Brien. Shaun. Shaun? Rise and shine. It's a lovely morning and your hot tea is ready. You don't want it getting cold. Shall I turn on your television to wake you?'

The TV pinged on to Fox News.

'There you go, Shaun, nice cup of tea. Be sure to take your pills, I'm watching now - I've put them on the corner of your tray.'

'Where's my glasses? Must you open those bloody blinds?'

'Come now Shaun, don't be such a bellyache. It's a lovely sunny morning...'

'Not hot enough.'

'Oh, it's a while until spring of course, but lovely blue sky.'

'Not the weather; the tea. Bloody lukewarm again. I've told you the rhyme: *Unless the kettle boiling B filling the teapot spoils the T.*'

'I'll take it back downstairs and heat it for you, but let me watch you take those pills first and I'll be back with your breakfast tray. Shall I turn the news up?'

'No.' Shaun gulped the pills and stuck his tongue out. 'There, swallowed.'

'Well done, Mr O'Brien. I'll go and reheat your tea.'

Shaun looked with renewed interest at the breakfast news. A large rocket steamed on a launch pad.

'Turn the TV up woman, I can't hear a bloody thing.'

'I just asked you and you said no, Grumpy,' she tutted, adjusting the volume, 'Anyways, I'm back in five with your breakfast.'

The TV anchor narrated excitedly over the crackly NASA countdown:

'And finally, in just a few seconds, NASA is launching the highly vaunted successor to Voyager I and II from Kennedy Space Center.

'The 'Pleiades Probe' carries an updated Golden Record - a message from humanity to the cosmos...'

'Wait, what the heck – who is that?' Shaun bellowed, sweeping his tray table aside as an image from seventy years ago gut-punched him.

'Come back, woman. Quickly, hurry!' Shaun flailed in the duvet creases for the remote control.

'What is it Shaun? Are you okay?' the nurse rushed in.

'Look, I know those boys. Look, the photo! It's me as a young lad with Alfie and Ivor from the home. Why's it on telly? Oh turn it up woman quickly, find me the bloody control.'

'The countdown has begun. TWENTY...NINETEEN...The updated record, no longer a golden floppy disc, but a contemporary platinum USB drive...'

'It's the 1950 Bayno Christmas party!'

'.. will rocket humanity's message toward the constellation of Pleiades along with thousands of pictures of Earth and its culture; from images of pyramids and silver skyscrapers to presidents and popstars; FOURTEEN...alongside icons of sport, science and the arts...TWELVE...Martin Luther King, the Pope and King Charles all feature, but most topically of all, that timeless image of childhood the world is now so familiar with; EIGHT...the joyful grinning photo of Ivor Delaney and his pals at a happy Christmas party long ago in old Ireland'.

'Me and my pals at the bloody Bayno Christmas party!'

'The Pleiades Probe will slingshot past the Moon...ONE...zooming onwards through the Solar System and far, far into deep

space...LIFT OFF...Go Ivor, go with our best wishes and shine for humanity!'

'Now don't get too excited now, Shaun…'

'Oh, shut up woman. Look at us – Alfie, Ivor and me - we're all going up into space just like Flash bloody Gordon.

'Well, well, well, Ivor! You've got me as red faced as old house-matron,' Shaun wheezed, clutching his chest.

'You said we'd see you up in the stars one day, Delaney and there you are! You did it; you really did it, you sweet, snotty-nosed, shiny-sleeved jackeen!'

///throw.spider.dizzy
"FAIRY LIQUID"

Georgina watched Alec snore on the sofa with a mix of fear and disgust. It was Friday evening and he'd been out drinking since noon. He would be in a foul mood when he woke up, she realised, shouting for cigarettes and looking for more booze. He was horrible most nights, but Friday nights were the worst. Her mummy, Helen would probably be sore and crying again tomorrow. Last weekend Mummy had her hair pulled all the way up the stairs and was forced to do something she didn't want to do in the bedroom, saying 'No, no, no,' and crying lots.

Georgina hoped it wasn't going to be the same again tonight.

Alec had been living there about two years now. When he first came he seemed friendly and used to be nice to her and her mum, buying her toys and sweets and Mummy seemed really happy. Then he got another job and he was in the house a lot more during the day and would go out in the afternoon and come home very late, shouting about stuff and banging things about a lot. Then one night Mummy fell down in the kitchen after they'd had a fight and she had terrible black eyes.

Her mum told her to keep a big secret which was that booze-drink turned Alec into a monster, but that he was nice the rest of the time. The trouble was, Alec seemed to drink booze-drink all the time these days.

Grandma didn't like Alec. Mummy had stayed away from Grandma's for ages after falling in the kitchen, as she didn't want Grandma to think Alec had done anything bad to her.

That evening, Mummy crept quietly into Georgina's bedroom and did a shush sign as she sat on the bed and pulled out a storybook from inside her big brown floppy bag.

'Mummy will read a story, but we have to be very quiet so we don't wake Alec up.'

'Okay, Mummy, is Alec still asleep in the lounge?'

'Yes. He's been to the pub today and he's tired, so we must be super quiet, okay?'

85

Georgina turned to her dolly and did a *shush* sign too, putting her finger on her lips.

'When is he going to work again, Mummy?' she whispered.

'Monday is his next shift, so it's a lie-in day tomorrow but you can watch TV in the lounge with the volume right down. When I get up you can play in the garden because it's going to be sunny again. I've bought you more bubbles, or you could take them to Grandma's after.'

Georgina loved it when Alec went to work because the house would be lovely and peaceful until he came home again, but if he was home it was best to go around to Grandma's or at least be in the garden away from all the stink of cigarette smoke and noise. Alec would always be watching boring TV like football and horseracing and racing cars, or watching really loud programmes with people clapping and laughing and it would give her a headache. When Alec came in the lounge, she would always have to stop watching her programmes and go upstairs to her room.

'Okay, Mummy, that's a good idea. Henry and Tinks played at Grandma's with me last time. We were very noisy and I don't want Alec getting mad as it's difficult being quiet here.'

'That's a good idea. You can be as loud as you like in Grandma's garden.'

Henry and Tinks were Georgina's best friends. They were brothers; Tinks was the more boisterous - like Georgina - in contrast to Henry who was quiet and dreamy owing to his condition, but they were both fun company and cheered her up. Although they went to a different school they would often go out into the street and play together after school and at weekends, especially during the warm days and light nights of the summer. Tinks was the naughtiest and would always be encouraging her and Henry to get dirty or go somewhere they weren't supposed to, like the Red Hospital - a derelict tuberculosis sanatorium built in the 1930s and just yards beyond the fence at the bottom of Grandma's garden. It was now a burnt-out, roofless shell with charred timbers securing various sections of corrugated iron walls that rattled in the wind.

Georgina was pleased she had something fun to do tomorrow. She sat up in bed enthusiastically, plumping up her pillow as her mum sat down beside her and cuddled her. Six year old Georgina mirrored her mum, putting her arm around her dolly, shuffling into a comfortable position for the story and leaning into her mum's shoulder as the paperback was opened. 'Read the story now, Mummy. What's it about?'

'It's a new one I got from the library; another Roald Dahl one because you liked *Charlie and the Chocolate Factory* so much, didn't you?'

'Of course I did,' Georgina looked at her mum in disbelief, 'It was the best story ever, Mummy,' she affirmed.

'I thought so. This one is just as exciting and it's called, *George's Marvellous Medicine*. I think you'll really like it because it was one of my favourites when I was little.'

Helen looked suddenly serious; focusing on a noise downstairs. She stared towards the door, biting her bottom lip.

'Is Alec waking up?' Georgina asked concerned.

'No. I think he was just coughing in his sleep.'

Silent seconds passed as Georgina and Helen relaxed again, turning back to the book. Georgina loved Storytime; it was rare now for her to get attention from her mum while Alec was in the house. He would always ask for stuff or interrupt whenever Mummy was talking to her or playing a game with her. He never played games with her himself anymore, or if he did it was only to pretend he was being nice in front of Mummy. When Mummy wasn't looking he would sometimes pull mean faces at her that looked really scary and then pretend he wasn't doing anything or was 'only joking' if anything was said.

'What's the story about, Mummy?'

'Oh, it's about a boy who makes a medicine to make his grumpy grandma nicer.'

Helen read the first chapter describing the wicked Grandma and Georgina was hooked. She got to the bit where George had to look after his Grandma when his mum and dad were out. It was a scary bit where she threatened him with evil magic spells to turn his fingernails into teeth. Georgina couldn't wait for the next chapter tomorrow and she fell asleep with lots of scary and exciting images running through her mind.

In the early morning Georgina tiptoed downstairs and saw the bottles, empty glasses and full ashtray on the coffee table in the lounge. She could smell the stale smoke and the glass top was sticky with drink rings. There was a mess of loose tobacco and pieces of Rizla packets torn up. Alec had been drinking cocktails and smoking again. Thankfully she hadn't heard any argument last night because she was fast asleep. That wasn't to say there wasn't one, but usually she would wake up with all the noise.

There were lots of pretty rainbow coloured liquids in the bottles. The orange one and blue one looked gorgeous in the light through the porch windows and the red and green bottles were lovely too, especially the red one which looked like rubies. The green one was quite dark with a pretty Green Fairy on the label. The lid smelled of liquorice. Georgina couldn't wait until she was old enough to drink cocktails as they always looked so pretty, but her mum said she was too young and should stick to drinking squash or lemonade or coke as they tasted nicer anyway. She didn't really believe that because sometimes she would sip the leftovers in her mum's glass and they mostly tasted nice.

Georgina wondered which one of the drinks turned Alec into a monster. She remembered a funny *Tom and Jerry* cartoon where Tom turned into a monster cat when he drank a special multi coloured mixture, then when Jerry put something in the mixture he turned giant while Tom shrunk to mouse size and got chased by Jerry.

The thought prompted her to watch cartoons on the TV - on a really low volume like Mummy told her. She tiptoed into the kitchen to get some Rich Tea biscuits and some orange squash.

Alec and Mummy were still in bed at ten o'clock even though it was a really hot morning with bright sunlight streaming through the vertical blinds making it difficult to see the TV screen. Georgina felt lonely watching TV alone, but at least she got to watch what she wanted and not some boring sport show.

There was a cartoon on - for babies, so instead she watched something about sharks and creatures of the deep, though the volume was so low that the sound of her own crunching made it difficult to hear the words. Besides, a phrase from last night's story kept looping inside her head distracting her:

The whole point of medicine was to make a person better. If it didn't do that, then it was quite useless.

Georgina finished her biscuits and lined up all the colourful bottles on the coffee table in rainbow order and thought about medicine ingredients. She had a great idea to make some of her own *Marvellous Medicine* and resolved excitedly to do it at Grandma's house with Henry and Tinks.

After a lonely wait she recognised the sound of stealthy creaking from the small landing. It was her mum getting up quietly to go to the toilet - Alec stamped around and did loud coughing and hockling when he got up. Georgina was pleased to see her mum's pink slippers appear through the top bannister bars followed by her short pink dressing gown as she rustled softly down the stairs into the lounge. She sat gently down on the sofa next to Georgina.

'I'm sorry I overslept sweetheart, but I'll get us both ready and you can go and spend the day at Grandma's,' she whispered. 'She's going to make your tea tonight and you can have a bath at hers. I'll come and pick you up at seven o'clock, okay?'

Helen accidentally sat on the TV control, changing the channel to some kids' quiz show with lots of shouting, sirens and applause. The din reverberated throughout the small house as Georgina and her mum flailed around trying to locate the control that had lodged between the sofa arm and cushion. In a fumbled panic Helen pulled it out, dropping it clumsily onto the glass coffee table where the batteries came rattling out.

Suddenly a thumping came from the room upstairs. Alec was stamping his foot on the floor above, one leg out of the bed. The light fitting rattled as Helen yanked the TV plug from the wall socket and the screen went blank.

'Keep the fackin' noise down or I'll put my foot through it,' he hollered in his Cockney accent.

Mother and daughter looked at each other anxiously, barely breathing, just listening intently for more movement from the bedroom above. None came. The colour had drained from Helen's face. They stared at each other, straining to hear and Georgina started tittering nervously. The titter became infectious and both mother and daughter quaked with repressed laughter as relief tempered with fear triggered a bout of hysterical giggles. Georgina stood up and did a mimed impression of Alec stomping on the floor, wagging her finger at her mum, mouthing, 'Keep the fackin' noise down,' as she made a fake karate kick toward the TV screen.

It was good to see Mummy laughing. She hadn't seen that for a long time.

'I'd better go and make him a cup of tea,' Helen whispered.

'We haven't got milk mummy,' Georgina warned.

'Oh, no, I remember, Alec had all the milk with cereal late last night. I'll have to pop to the garage to get some.'

Helen crept back upstairs to pull on tracksuit bottoms and a T-shirt. She returned to slip on some sloppy trainers from a pile of shoes in the small porch which opened on to the front street.

As the front door closed, Georgina thought it best to tiptoe to her room and get dressed for Grandma's, but as she put her foot on the bottom stair she sensed a dark apparition looming over her.

'What's all the fackin' noise? Doors slamming and TV. Bloody get up here.'

Georgina walked fearfully up the stairs hoping her mum would come back quickly from the garage shop.

Alec grabbed the back of her hair as she reached the landing, knelt down and put his scary unshaven face close to hers.

'You'd better watch your cheeky mouth you little cow or I'll make sure you get what's coming to you sooner.'

Georgina winced at his disgusting breath. She thought it smelled like the old dog bones and pigs ears in the boxes at the pet shop.

He pushed her backwards and she hit her head on the bedroom door. It didn't hurt, but she could feel the hate and worse, saw something in his eyes that was different to what she had ever seen before and it terrified her.

She ran into her room and closed the door, repressing tears and sniffling into her pillow. Seconds later the door opened, dragging over the carpet pile.

'Dry your eyes you little cow before your mum gets back and don't you dare complain to her, or else next time she's out I'll throw a massive spider in your room and lock you in with it.'

Georgina was terrified of spiders and Alec knew it. She wanted to tell her mum, but realised he meant what he was saying. She was relieved to hear the front door key in the lock and her mum kicking off her shoes in the porch.

'She's been cheeky again,' Alec said lying on the bed in his underpants, beckoning impatiently with arm outstretched for his cup of tea, 'I've had to tell her off.'

'Why, what's she said?'

'She was barging in front of me to get to her room on the top of the landing and I told her to have some manners and she gave me some lip.'

'What sort of lip? That's not like her at all,' Helen eyed Alec suspiciously.

'She needs to buck her ideas up and have some respect.'

'Don't be hard on her Alec, she's only six remember. I'll go and have a word with her.'

'Nearly seven. And don't bother, we've sorted it, just letting you know she needs to zip that cheeky mouth of hers.'

'She's not cheeky, are you sure she…'

'Do you want an argument about it or what?' he interrupted crossly.

'No, I'm just saying, go easy…'

'I'm just saying too - so drop it!' Alec's eyes momentarily flashed hot with aggression. Helen flinched inside and changed the subject.

'I'm taking her to her grandma's in twenty minutes, so she'll be out of your hair. Do you want a bacon sandwich before I go?'

91

'Yeah.' Alec flicked onto Sky Sports on the bedroom TV, distracted by football.

Helen got Georgina ready in a pretty orange summer dress with white daisies on it and a pair of white crocs. Alec stayed in the bedroom, shouting angrily at the football.

'Grab any toys you want to take and put them in Mummy's bag and you can wheel a board game in dolly's pushchair. Georgina took some teddies and *Buckaroo*.'

Two short alleyways linked the cul-de-sacs on the short walk to Grandma's house. Flowering shrubs and climbing roses cascaded over the high tops of fences and warm summer air gave a pleasant twanging resonance to Georgina's footsteps as she stomped between the red brick walls of adjacent semi-detached houses.

Georgina thought Grandma's house was old fashioned with bay windows and stained glass fan shapes above them, but it was much bigger inside than her mum's, with high fancy ceilings and a really big, long back-garden to play in.

She was getting hot and impatient in the sunshine as Mummy and Grandma were taking ages chatting about grown up stuff by the front door. Grandma stood with her arms folded, a headscarf over her curlers and a serious look on her face, talking quietly and shaking her head. Mummy said, 'I know, Mum, I know,' because Grandma was telling her off about something. Thankfully Tinks and Henry came out to play while she waited for Mummy to finish talking.

Georgina made a finger-monster from a snapdragon flower in the front garden rockery and chased Tinks with it. Henry was in his special wheelchair propped by a mossy rock to stop it rolling; placidly staring up at the summer sky, waiting patiently for Georgina and Tinks to include him in their fun and games.

Eventually Mummy said a curt goodbye to Grandma and gave Georgina a kiss on her cheek before strutting briskly out of the driveway. Grandma seemed annoyed with Mummy, shaking her head to herself as she unbolted the high side gate into the back garden.

'Come on poppet, we'll get you in the back where I can keep an eye on you. I see your friends are here too,' Grandma nodded towards the boys.

'Yes Grandma. Me, Henry and Tinks are going to make *Marvellous Medicine* today. Please can we have a bowl and some spoons and scissors so we can make a mixture?' she asked excitedly.

'That sounds nice, is the medicine for me? Will it make me young again?'

'No Grandma, because it's not meant for you. I'm going to make it for a monster to drink.'

'Oh well, at least you don't consider me a monster, so that's something.'

She patted Georgina on her head affectionately with an old cool hand that smelled of potato peelings.

'So if it's for monsters, then you and your friends will be having some, will you?' Grandma joked, poking Henry and Tinks gently on their tummies.

'No of course not, Grandma! We're not monsters either,' she responded, giggling as Henry and Tinks stared at Grandma gormlessly.

'I know you're not real monsters, sweetheart, but don't be getting any mess in the house or on that lovely dress and don't be going into Grandma's shed. There's lots of sharp rusty things in it and poisons for the weeds. I'll get you a nice big mixing bowl and spoon from the kitchen and you can use your play scissors, not Grandma's sharp ones, and remember what I said about walking with scissors, always hold the pointy end away from you and never run with them.'

In spite of the shed containing lots of paints and things that would be perfect for a medicine mix, Georgina had no plan to enter the shed. It was the last place she would go because there were cobwebs the size of hammocks draped from the shed window to the top of the rusty propane cylinder.

'I would never go in your shed Grandma because of the spiders.'

'Don't be daft, love, spiders won't harm you, not the English ones anyway.'

'I don't care Grandma, I hate them; there was a thunderstorm when I was little and a giant one was on the bath towel and Mummy didn't see it and I screamed when she was going to dry me.'

'I remember that. I don't much like the big ones either, but as long as they keep you out of my shed, that's fine. Anyway your mum has left you these bubbles so there's no need to be getting into mischief, just play nicely.'

'Okay Grandma, I'll do the bubbles later, but I have to do the medicine first.'

*   *   *

Grandma's back garden lawn was pretty with dandelions, daisies and red clover. Washing flapped lightly on her clothesline that cut horizontally east to west, obscuring the view to the woods beyond. A steep flagstone garden path led down from the back door alongside a roughhewn flower bed that sloped the entire hundred and twenty metre length. It was gaudy with mature roses, foxgloves and tall blue delphiniums. A high creosoted fence separated the neighbouring houses, assuring privacy and ended in a low hedge by a shallow stream at the bottom. The stream was flanked by a decrepit chain-link fence with gaps you could push through for paddling or for crossing over to the woods beyond. Today the stream was fringed by tall summer weeds that buzzed with insects and pretty damselflies.

Georgina thought she always had the best adventures on sunny days in Grandma's garden as she snaked in and out of the clothesline giggling with Tinks. She weaved Henry's wheelchair through the flapping duvet covers and pillowcases so he didn't feel left out until she was breathless.

Parking Henry's chair sideways on the path, she took hold of Tinks by his arms, spinning around until they were both really dizzy and falling on the ground looking up at the sky, the world teetering like a drunk. Georgina loved the rocking sensation and how everything settled back to normal in dizzying see-saw pulses. Henry looked on silently, a little jealously, as she brushed dry straw from Tinks's back from the last grass cut. Georgina was very maternal with her friends and they liked it.

There was a sudden thump and loud creak as Grandma heaved open the stiff utility room door with her shoulder; decades of gloss paint strata wedging it tight into the old door frame during the warmer months.

She clattered some items on the crazy-paving patio.

'Bowl, spoon and scissors and some pop and sweets too,' she shouted. Georgina ran over excitedly and picked up the bag of sherbet chews, old metal spoons and craft scissors as well as a bottle of icy cold Fanta.

She held up the bright yellow Tupperware bowl and exclaimed to her friends, 'Today we are going to make *Marvellous Medicine.*'

Georgina sounded deliberately upbeat, more so to enthuse Henry who was looking a bit sad. Even though Henry's best friend, Tinks would play with him a lot when she wasn't around, neither of them had the same enthusiasm unless Georgina was there to spur the play along. She was a catalyst for fun and the boys would show off in front of her with Tinks's silly antics and daft games usually getting them all into some muddy trouble.

Because they had grown up together, neither Georgina nor Tinks minded that Henry was disabled, but it was still hard for him, having lost his legs when he was little he wasn't able to do all the things that she and Tinks could, though thankfully his wheelchair was very modern and Henry was light enough for six year olds to push around.

She told them about Alec and what he had said about the spider. She knew not to tell Grandma because she would say something to Mummy who would say something to Alec who would just laugh it off as a joke, but then punish her for being a grass.

'Tinks and me will help make your marvellous medicine and then you and your mummy will not be scared of the monster anymore,' Henry wheezed, while Tinks nodded enthusiastically.

Georgina gave the bright yellow plastic bowl containing the metal spoons and scissors to Henry to hold. Tinks helped Georgina wheel him half way down the sloping garden path.

'I think the mistake George made in the story was he didn't put any pretty things in the medicine like flowers. We should do that,' Georgina instructed Tinks who, with her help, plucked rose and poppy petals from Grandma's borders. Georgina grabbed a cool handful of pink and peachy roses that reminded her of Fruit Salad chews. They smelled gorgeous.

'If we pick lots of pretty flowers it will make a person pretty inside,' Georgina said, nipping some tiny violets up from the undergrowth. 'This little purple flower will give purple-coloured happiness,' Georgina held up the flower to Henry's nose to sniff the petals.

'It doesn't smell of anything,' Henry observed.

'That doesn't matter Henry, it's the colour that counts.'

'There's little blue and white and orange ones too so you can put some of those in and I will stir it up,' Henry advised, pointing out the lobelia and marigolds as Georgina dropped another handful of petals into the bowl.

'Oi, don't be wrecking my garden you vandal!' Georgina spun around and looked up sheepishly at her grandma now bellowing from the top bedroom window. 'There's plenty of nice dandelions and daisies on the lawn, not the flowers from my borders.' Grandma pulled a face, feigning outrage.

'Can we pick some of the roses, Grandma?'

'No, you can only pick up rose petals that have fallen.'

'Alright Grandma,' Georgina responded, disappointed, as the bedroom window banged shut.

'Dandelions and daisies are nice, but they're a bit boring,' Georgina declared to her two friends.

The bedroom window swung open again. 'And don't be picking laburnum pods. You know what they are because Grandma has shown you and not foxgloves either, they're both poisonous.'

'We're not silly Grandma, you've told us lots of times about the poisonous ones and you haven't got any laburnum in your garden anyway,' Georgina added smugly.

'Well, Grandma knows that, but the wind might have blown them over or a bird might have dropped some. You never know,' Grandma knew her logic was questionable, but she wasn't going to be outsmarted by a six year old.

The three friends paused, momentarily disconsolate until Henry pointed.

'There's plants with little pompoms you can reach over the fence by the stream.' He squinted towards the bottom of the garden, spying the misty looking drifts of tall white flowers just over the fence.

'Yes, that's a good idea Henry, we'll get some of those,' Georgina and Tinks regained their gusto, trundling Henry and the bowl down the final forty feet of path to the stream, out of sight of Grandma.

Georgina and Tinks leaned over the fence and grabbed handfuls of the mini pompoms, dropping them into the bowl and mashing everything down with the spoons, cutting bigger bits up with the play scissors.

'Tinks and I will quickly pop over the stream into the wood to see if there's any more flowers there.'

'No Georgina, we're not allowed in the woods because that's where the Red Hospital is and there are lots of funny men in there,' Henry warned.

'It's okay Henry,' Tinks piped, 'because I'm with Georgina and you can be the lookout and shout if anyone comes near. There are lots of pink flowers in there.'

Georgina looked at Henry reassuringly as she grabbed Tinks's arm, 'We'll be very quick won't we Tinks?'

Georgina lost sight of Henry as they brushed through the tall plants and into the gently trickling stream. They jumped, startled, as a duck flapped loudly into the air in a flurry of quacking.

'Phew, what a shock Tinks, I almost dropped the petal pot.'

Henry sat tense and motionless in his chair watching his two friends disappear across the stream into the trees beyond.

In the near distance, the rusted hulk of the old hospital emerged faintly through the low curtains of beech branches. Georgina gripped Tinks's arm tightly in excited trepidation. Two small dark windows with charred wooden frames appeared like eyes staring at them as they drew closer, though the bonny willow herb swaying in the breeze adjacent tempered their unease.

'These are nice Tinks, we'll pick lots of these.'

They skipped excitedly around the perimeter plucking pink blossoms in handfuls, being careful not to get stung by nettles and brambles. Georgina collected elder, dog rose and more violets.

'Which ones shall I pick Georgina?' Tinks enquired.

'Anything pretty. You can get the low ones and I will get the high ones.'

Tinks found a scarlet pimpernel flower and a ragged robin.

'Is this alright Georgina?'

'Let me see if it is pretty. Hmmm, yes it's pretty so that goes in the mix.'

'What about this one?'

Tinks grabbed a handful of low dark green shrubs carpeting the woodland floor.

'No Tinks, not those. They are quite dull and ugly, so we don't want them in.'

'But we'll make that plant sad, if it's not allowed into the mixture,' Tinks said.

Georgina remembered *The Ugly Duckling* story her mummy had read to her and thought about Henry sitting by himself not having any friends except her and Tinks and she felt sad.'

'Okay, you're right. I've changed my mind, we can put some of those in, after all, we've got lots of white and pink and red and we need some green in there too.'

'I can't just pick one leaf in case that leaf gets lonely, or the mummy leaf might miss the daddy leaf and baby leaf,' Tinks added, plucking up more dark green leaves. 'There, the whole family is together now, so they're all happy,' Tinks affirmed, piling them on top of the bowl.

'Perfect!' Georgina approved, sweating now as the rusty corrugate of the old building radiated stifling pockets of heat in the noon sun.

The Red Hospital was no longer red, Georgina noted, but dark brown with rust, though some of the ancient crimson paint was still visible in flaky remnants by the hinge areas in a double doorway recess and under timber sills.

She peered apprehensively through the doorway into the open hospital structure, spying broken white tiled floors and corridors strewn with collapsed roof and tree branches. Grass grew between the cracks and, near where she stood, scorch marks on the tiles marked evidence of bonfires lit by naughty boys.

It was strange to see the pillars and framework of old rooms stretching into the distance. She thought how spooky it would be here at night, but this morning as dappled green shadows from the beech trees danced to summer breezes blowing softly all around, the site had a serene loveliness, save the dark far end of the building where an old intact flat roof overshadowed a line of vandalised toilet basins and wall mounted sinks. Adjacent, in the sunshine, was a line of derelict tiled compartments housing bath tubs that sprouted ferns and tiny saplings.

A raucous crow cawed, shocking the tranquillity and two pigeons clattered from the far side of the building into the woods beyond.

Georgina noiselessly turned to make a shush sign to Tinks who was sitting by the petal bowl taking a rest.

'Someone must be coming,' she whispered, looking at Tinks fearfully.

A distant twig cracked, emanating from the space behind the toilet block. Long seconds of silence followed, then another crack confirmed someone was approaching, furtively. Georgina stared at Tinks mutely.

Cautiously she picked up the neon yellow bowl and placed the scissors and spoons on top of the petals, stashing the bowl in long grass to conceal its flamboyance. She peeped silently around the open doorway but saw no one. The building was appallingly quiet. She figured the noise was probably just a big curious bunny or deer, but then a clang from the shadows like a metal rod bouncing on a tiled floor made her tense in fright.

Barely breathing, she grabbed Tinks by the arm and hunkered down beside him in the grassy undergrowth directly below the windows.

Georgina waited, straining to distinguish the sounds of the beech wood from the unnatural. Tinks just stared, terrified.

'I...' she began to whisper when another twig abruptly cracked, nearer now, followed by slow footsteps that stopped for some seconds and resumed, moving inexorably closer—too close for them to make a run for it.

Georgina found a small rivet-hole in the metal to peep through, a little below the charred window frame. Kneeling in the long grass she saw the sinister outline of a hooded man by the line of broken toilets. The dark figure moved slowly towards them, head bowed, stepping cagily towards the centre of the derelict structure out of the shadows, but now obscured by two brick pillars. He cleared his throat and spat.

Georgina ducked, staring directly at Tinks and panted guardedly, alert to the smallest sound. She spied through the peephole again. To her relief he was heading back toward the toilets; however, as though aware he was being scrutinised, he stopped and unexpectedly glared over his shoulder in her direction.

Georgina gulped in fear. It was Alec. She could see him clearly now as a shaft of sunlight illumined his smelly grey track suit bottoms, baggy trainers and dark blue hoodie. Although she was concealed, he appeared to be staring directly at her, eyeball to eyeball from fifty yards away. She froze, neither daring to blink nor look away. Could he see her through the tiny hole? Was her orange dress visible? To her relief he turned; distracted; snorted and spat again.

Ducking down, she heard his slow footsteps, the crunch of beech husks underfoot betraying his position. He kept stopping, then walking again. What was he doing? Now he was moving closer - terrifyingly close. She dared not move to look through the peephole and simply gripped Tinks who was wide-eyed with fear. Alec had stopped on the other side of the wall just inches away, separated by an ancient sheet of rusty corrugate and decayed timber struts. She could hear him breathing; sniffing; the sound of his track suit legs chafing together as he shifted around. He was whisper-talking to himself, or as her mummy called it, chuntering. It sounded like he was having an internal dialogue with someone, responding to his own whispers in a strange wiry little voice, almost like a cartoon character. He flipped the lid of his petrol lighter—a sound and smell Georgina had learned to hate ever since he moved in—and clinked it shut, as blue cigarette fumes drifted out of the window just inches away.

Alec sniffed, laughed at something and walked away. Georgina released her pent up breath and gulped in lungful's of fresh air. She raised herself to the peephole as his footsteps receded, watching him walk towards the central pillars more stridently than before, confident he was alone.

'What's he doing?' she whispered to Tinks, 'He seems to be heading to the bathtubs...Yes, he's bending down to look underneath one.'

Alec stood up again and looked around, double checking no one was observing him. He swiftly squatted down and reached under one of the baths, straining and fumbling around behind the taps, eventually standing up holding a black bin bag. He unknotted the top and rustled around inside, taking out what looked like one of her mum's small blue Tupperware boxes. Checking around again, he shoved the bag back.

'What's he doing with that box?' she whispered, poor Tinks's arm pressured by her unrelenting grip.

'He might be collecting spiders in it, Georgina,' Tinks responded anxiously, 'to put in your room, because that's where you find them mostly, in baths.'

Tinks, in spite of his rufty-tufty boldness in most situations, did not like spiders either, but he didn't mind any other type of creepy crawly, or slimy worm, or frog.

'I don't think he is Tinks, because you can get spiders most places other than here, including sheds and garages,' she responded, failing to reassure herself.

Her face was pale as she looked back urgently towards the stream, attempting to gauge the distance; wanting to make a fast dash for it, though she couldn't leave without picking up Grandma's bowl and spoons because she didn't want her to know she'd been to the Red Hospital.

Georgina squinted once more through the rivet hole. Alec had gone. She didn't know whether to be relieved or more frightened, half expecting him to loom around the corner from the right or left. She heard a clang and a distant twig crack indicating he was leaving the same way he came.

Very quietly she gathered up the petal bowl, hiding it in front of her chest and swapped hands to hold Tinks by his left arm. Sidestepping crunchy twigs they stealthily moved through the undergrowth beyond the willowherb, feeling horribly exposed in the open section of trees, but quickly reaching the stream and splashing across in a hurry, stumbling on small boulders that clacked together and losing some of her prized petals in the water.

Lurching through the tall weeds by Grandma's garden, still gripping the bowl and Tinks's arm, the two squeezed through the chain link fence and back into the garden out of breath. Henry was sitting up in his chair expectantly as Georgina plopped the full bowl of leaves and petals into his lap heroically.

'You've been ages,' Henry said, 'I was expecting Grandma to shout and I didn't know what to say, but it's okay now.'

'Tinks and I saw Alec collecting a box in the Red Hospital,' Georgina said.

'We think a box for spiders,' Tinks added, 'So we have to make sure Alec gets his medicine before the monster decides to frighten Georgina with them.'

'How are you going to do that?' Henry looked confused, 'How will you give him his medicine without the monster finding out?'

'I am going to borrow Mummy's nutri-juicer and put the juice in a bottle.'

'Will she let you use the juicer?' Henry asked, sceptically.

'As long as I rinse it out and put it back tidily she won't mind or even know I've used it,' Georgina affirmed smugly. Her mum had been letting her do lots of grown up things by herself recently as Alec had been grabbing more and more of her mum's time and attention, while her mum ran around fussing, trying to find things to please him to stop him shouting and turning into the monster. One day, while her mum had driven Alec to the football, Georgina had even made her own soup for lunch, putting boiling water in the pan herself from the kettle and stirring the soup powder into it. There were still hard lumps in the pan, but her mum was pleased with her and it tasted nice once it had cooled.

'Come and get your beans, Georgina,' Grandma shouted from the utility room door.

Sweating, Georgina pushed Henry up to the top of the garden, took the bowl and ran inside to the cool of the kitchen while her friends waited.

'That looks just like a big mess of dead flower heads and stalks,' Grandma commented wryly, inspecting the bowl. It's got lots of tiny little black bugs in it too. Do you want me to put it in the compost?'

'No Grandma!' Georgina protested, almost spitting her beans out, 'It's the mix for the medicine and it's taken ages to collect. I'm going to mix it up properly when I get home.'

'Well, that's good because I've just tidied and I certainly don't want any buggy stuff inside my clean kitchen. I don't think your mum will be happy if you take it back home either; there's enough mess for her to deal with, with that boyfriend of hers,' she shook her head critically.

'No, but you don't understand Grandma, I really have to make it and I won't make a mess at Mummy's, I promise.'

'Well, that's fine, but I need my bowl and spoons back before they disappear into the back of your mum's cupboard.'

Georgina gulped down her beans on toast as her Grandma took the spoons and scissors out of the bowl and scooped the leaves and petals into a carrier bag with a no-nonsense hand.

'There, your mum can deal with your messy mixture.'

'Thank you, Grandma,' Georgina said, slurping a beaker of tepid orange squash thirstily, 'I've finished, so can I get down from the table please?' she asked, pushing her plate aside eagerly.

'Yes, but don't be making yourself sick rushing around after bolting your lunch.'

On the contrary, apart from rolling down the bank a few times, the remainder of Georgina's afternoon was restful and reflective, lying on the lawn staring at clouds and making daisy chains for Henry and Tinks. Grandma apologised she couldn't play the *Buckaroo* game because she had too much to sort out, but Georgina played it with Henry and Tinks who lost every time because they were both too clumsy. At bath time Georgina's fingers were stained with chlorophyll, her cheeks and nose red with the sun and her arms and legs tingled in the hot water with bramble scratches.

Her mum arrived to pick her up at 7pm as she was finishing her tea of cheese sandwiches and midget gems. Grandma was packing away *Buckaroo*.

'Don't forget your bucking bronco, and that bag of mess,' Grandma joked as a damp haired Georgina followed her mum onto Grandma's front street.

Henry and Tinks accompanied them back to the cul-de-sac; her mum helping push Henry up the kerbs as they sauntered lazily back in the warm evening sunshine, the petal mixture bag swinging rhythmically from the handle of Henry's chair. She left her friends abruptly when she reached her front drive and surreptitiously rolled the petal bag into a tight sausage while her mum rummaged in her bag for the front door keys. Even from outside Georgina could hear the TV blaring with gameshow sounds.

'Go straight up and play in your room while Mummy hangs up washing and I'll read the next chapter,' she said, opening the door. Alec was stretched out on the sofa smoking a cigarette and drinking a can of lager. He was still wearing the blue hoodie and tracksuit bottoms from earlier, but he'd kicked off his trainers and his sweaty bare feet were resting on the sofa arm.

Georgina said a sheepish goodnight and ran up the stairs with her bag to get away from the noise. Alec grunted in acknowledgement.

When Georgina got into her room she opened the bag of medicine mixture. Some of the petals were turning brown. It smelled of warm fields and cut grass. She didn't know when she would get a chance to use her mum's nutri-juicer so she hoped it would still be okay tomorrow. She could always put it in the fridge vegetable drawer to keep it cool, but Alec would probably ask her what was in the bag if she went back downstairs.

She popped the bag under her bed and began worrying about what was in the Tupperware box that Alec had taken, but then her mum came in with a bag of crisps and a pack of Rolos. 'Here's a few nibbles for us. You must brush your teeth after the story though.'

'Okay and thanks Mummy, how did you know I was still hungry?'

'Girls your age are always hungry. Be quick though and I'll read the next chapter. Alec is going to the pub to meet friends from work and he wants me to drop him off.'

'When?'

'After the story, sweetheart, Mummy won't be long, half an hour at the most.'

'But Mummy, last time you went out to the pub you were hours and I got frightened.'

'I know, and I'm sorry, it's just that Alec bumped into friends of his and we just got chatting and the time just flew and the taxi was late, but tonight I'm just dropping off.'

'Are you sure, Mummy?'

'Half an hour, I promise.'

'Okay,' Georgina responded, 'You can read the story now before you go.'

Tonight's chapter was all about how George got the shampoo and toothpastes and nail varnishes and mixed them all up in a saucepan with washing powder, curry and chilli powder and peppercorns.

Georgina was gripped and eager for the next chapter when a shout came from downstairs.

'Are we going out or what? Hurry up, I told Stevie I'd be in The Chequers by now.'

Georgina's mum jumped to attention, 'Coming!'

'Goodnight sweetheart, we'll do two chapters tomorrow night, I promise, and I promise I won't be late.'

Georgina heard the front door close, the car doors slam and pull off the drive. She looked out of her bedroom window. The sun had set behind the houses opposite, and a blackbird sang a beautiful song from the chimneypot. It sounded like it was singing especially for her. She stayed staring at it for a minute and then she looked to the right up the street. She figured she would give her mum and Alec a minute or two in case they had forgotten something. It was all clear.

She snatched the carrier bag from under the bed and ran downstairs to the kitchen. The nutri-juicer was next to the bread bin. Unscrewing the lid was a struggle and it stank rotten inside, so she rinsed it before reaching into the carrier bag, pulling out a handful of petals, green leaves and flower heads and cramming them in with a wooden spoon, turning the lid as tight as she could with her small hands.

The nutri-juicer whizzed, but kept missing the wedge of petals at the base of the container. She unscrewed the lid and put some water in and tried again. This time it worked. Lots of green sludge. She was disappointed that the peachy rose petals and the yellow buttercup petals hadn't given their hue to the mixture. Tinks's leaves had turned everything dark green like spinach which she hated. No one would want to drink medicine this ugly she decided. Dipping her finger in she put a tiny blob on her tongue tip. It tasted bitter and carroty, but it didn't smell bad, just warm and froggy, a bit like the school amphibian tank, so that was a good thing.

With renewed enthusiasm she slopped the thick sludge into one of the little foil trays her mum made brownies in and stirred; adding some yellow food colouring and a teaspoon of sugar to make the pulp a bit brighter and sweeter. She dipped her finger in again and it tasted okay, before spitting into the bin.

The revving of a car in the street reminded her that Mummy would be back soon. She had to clean up quick and put the medicine in a bottle.

She shook out the nutri-juicer remnants into the bin, rinsed it and put it back by the bread bin. What bottle would she use for the medicine? She didn't have much time, so she scurried into the lounge and opened the sideboard. She needed something green to disguise her green medicine. One called Midori was unopened, but the other was the bottle with the fairy on, called Absinthe. There was half a bottle left and Georgina figured it was the perfect colour to get Alec to take the medicine without the monster finding out.

She scampered back into the kitchen thinking it funny that Fairy Liquid cleaned dishes and the Green Fairy medicine would clean away a monster. She squeezed one of the corners of the foil tray to make a little spout holding back the spinach bits in the tray to carefully pour the liquid into the crusty bottleneck until only slow drips were left in the tray. Screwing the sticky lid in place she gasped in horror. The top inch of the Absinthe had turned cloudy. She jiggled the bottle and all of the drink inside turned into green milk. Alec would *never* drink green milky medicine and she knew how mad he would be to see one of his precious booze drinks spoiled.

Headlights from the front street shone into the living room. Mummy was back in the driveway.

Grabbing the bottle, she slid it behind another inside the sideboard and darted upstairs into bed. She would decide what to do with it tomorrow.

Georgina heard her mum close the porch door and drop the keys on the coffee table. Alec wasn't with her because there was no talking, but what would happen if he came back and wanted some Absinthe?

Helen ran upstairs and peeped around the bedroom door.

Georgina turned to face her pretending she'd been asleep.

'Are you alright sweetheart?'

'Yes Mummy,' she said with fake drowsiness. 'Is Alec home too or is it just you?'

'It's just me, poppet, Alec is bringing a curry home when he's finished at the pub.'

'Can we have some more of the story then before he gets home?'

'Oh go on then, we'll have a little snuggle up and I'll read a few more pages.'

They reached the bit where George was just about to put the giant saucepan of his medicine mixture onto the stove to boil it up, complete with horse, cow and pig pills. Georgina wondered if she should have boiled hers as she knew how to cook soup, but it was too late now, then she remembered she had left the foil tray full of green pulp on the bench. She was trying to think of an excuse when a noisy car revved down the road with music thudding and brakes squealing. It stopped outside the house. Her mum sat up attentively, leaned over and pulled the curtain back to look out.

'It's Alec with the curry. I'd better warm plates. Sorry poppet, we'll read more tomorrow night. Get some sleep, you've had a busy day.'

Her mum kissed her on the forehead and jumped up before Georgina had a chance to own up to the mess.

'Mummy, I made a bit of a…' but the car door opened spewing men's voices and laughter cutting her short. Alec's voice resounded above the music as he thanked his pal for the lift.

'Cheers Stevie, enjoy the gear. Catch up next week.' Anyone hearing him in the street would think he was a nice, friendly person, Georgina thought, but he was horrible in the house.

She had two problems: The biggest was the cloudy bottle. Alec would guess it was her and he would never drink the medicine to get rid of the monster, so today's adventure was a complete waste of time. Even worse, he would get that Tupperware box and terrify her with a big spider for sure.

She heard Alec bang the inner porch door as he stomped inside and strained to hear if some ruckus would soon be starting. She could tell he had been drinking.

'Curry,' he said emphatically, 'You serve it 'cause I queued for it,' he ordered as he slumped onto the sofa.

'I don't want much,' Helen responded, 'Just a tiny bit of tikka masala and a poppadum. I'll pop it in the oven and warm it up with the plates while I get in my dressing gown.'

Georgina could hear her mum in the kitchen, unbagging the curry and making a noise with baking trays as she spread out the foil containers of pilau rice, chicken tikka masala, lamb dhansak and vegetable sides to warm up.

In the lounge, the TV pinged on loudly, there was a car chase going on and guns firing. She could hear Alec coughing and doing his sniffing thing.

Her mum came upstairs to the toilet. She heard her flushing and then getting ready for bed, opening her wardrobe door and jangling wire hangers.

Alec was clattering around in the kitchen, chuntering again. He slammed the cutlery drawer and then the oven door opened and slammed. He swore.

Georgina was worried. He slammed things before he got really angry. She prayed he wouldn't go into the sideboard tonight for cocktails. She sat up in bed in dread, hearing him heaving around in the lounge with sideboard sounds and the rap of a heavy bottomed tumbler on the glass coffee table.

He watched TV for about five minutes then she heard him back in the kitchen. The oven door opened and she heard him clattering around for cutlery. He had dished his curry out and was back in the lounge because she could hear his knife and fork scraping on the plates and he burped really loudly. To her relief, there was nothing to indicate he had discovered the green fairy bottle yet.

Her mum swished downstairs in her dressing gown and Georgina listened.

'You didn't put any out for me, did you?'

'Nah, I didn't know what you wanted and I couldn't wait. There's a bit of tikka masala left though. And you forgot to put the saag in.'

'Oh, sorry. Is it cold? The saag?'

'I put it in myself and I've mixed it with the hot stuff, but yeah, it was cold,' he complained, slurring. 'Pass my voddy, will you?'

Georgina heard the clatter of a plate on the glass table and another loud burp. Alec's lighter clinked open and shut as he lit a cigarette. She had a tummy ache and the TV was loud with gruff American voices and an American woman speaking:

'It must be torturous running after a man who doesn't even care about you. Who's in love with someone else. Who hates you!'

Long minutes later Georgina was drifting off to sleep, confident her misdemeanour was undiscovered, when shockingly she heard Alec erupt.

'What the fackin' 'ell? That little bitch has been in the sideboard. Look!'

'What do you mean? What's wrong with it?' her mum answered nervously. You've obviously put some water in it accidentally. It's what happens with Oozo. You can't blame her.'

'It's not fackin' Oozo, it's fackin' Absinthe. There's a difference.'

'No, I know, but don't blame Georgina. It's more than likely that...'

Her mum repressed a squeal as Alec's broad hand slapped her on the back of her head.

'Go and get that little bitch down here now,' Alec panted, breathlessly.

'No, please Alec, no. We'll deal with it in the morning. She's fast asleep, please be quiet.'

'I'm not fackin' around, if you don't get that little cow from her bed now, I'm bloody going to do it myself.'

'No you will not, you'll wait until tomorrow morning and we'll both deal with it.'

'We'll see about that!'

Alec blustered upstairs as Georgina's mum followed, grabbing his ankle. He kicked back and she slipped downstairs to the bottom on her front scuffing her breasts and screaming as he stormed onto the landing, barging open Georgina's door Hulk-like with a bottle in his left hand and cigarette in his right.

Clinging to her duvet terrified, Georgina saw the seething monster swaying in the doorway.

'What are you playing at with my booze, you little cow?' He gulped a mouthful of the cloudy absinthe and shivered. 'What have you put in it? Have you tasted it?' He sniffed the bottle and thrust it toward her as she cowered under her duvet, saying nothing. The glowing end of his cigarette crackled like some evil coal dimly highlighting his dark eyes as he took a long and contemplative draw and smiled evilly.

'If you don't tell me, I'm going to get the biggest spider and put it in your room tonight,' he snickered.

Before she could protest her mum appeared behind him on the landing. 'Leave her alone. I'll buy another bottle tomorrow, just leave it!'

'Ah fack it, you stupid cow, get out of the way,' Alec shoved passed Helen, flicked his burning cigarette into the toilet bowl directly opposite Georgina's bedroom before he banged back downstairs laughing.

'Incy Wincy's coming to get you to crawl up yer spout!' he cackled.

Georgina's mum dashed into her room and cuddled her daughter tightly, stroking her forehead. 'I'm sorry,' she whispered, 'We're not putting up with this much longer.'

'You won't let him get a spider, Mummy, will you? I think he's gone to get one from a Tupperware box.'

'Shush, shush, no, of course not, he's only pretending. He hasn't got any spiders and I won't let him near you,' she reassured.

'Please don't let him in, Mummy, please close the door tight,' she whimpered tearfully.

Her mum hurried downstairs and sat on the sofa to intercept any further moves by Alec to the bedroom, though thankfully he had calmed down after emptying the bottle of cloudy Absinthe into the sink and dumping the empty into the kitchen swing bin.

'Sodding waste of expensive booze. She can bloody well replace that from the money in her savings jar. Pass me another fag, and pass the voddy.'

Georgina's mum shoved the packet of Marlboro over to Alec urgently, knowing cigarettes calmed him down; nor would she be getting smacked around the head if he had a precious ciggie in one hand and a drink in the other. The lighter clinked and Alec poured a double vodka into his glass. He took a swig and a long draw of the cigarette before rising from his seat to grab his hoodie hanging on the bannister post. He pulled out a Tupperware box from the bib pocket.

'I'm having a line, right? Any complaints?' he challenged.

'No, but you promised me about all of that,' Georgina's mum meekly protested, measuring her criticism against the need to preserve the peace.

'Yeah well, it's none of your bloody business. I deserve a bit of comfort for all the grief I have to put up with, with you and your daughter. And how do you think I pay for your booze and curry? Anyway, I've got heartburn starting and I don't want to hear your lip,' he rubbed his abdomen.

Alec popped open the plastic lid and removed a cling film ball sealed with a tiny rubber band at the top. He gazed at it reverently, opening it like a magician captivated by a precious elixir; lovingly spooning a small heap of powder onto the coffee table with his long pinkie nail, tapping it loose on the glass. He licked his nail ceremonially and rubbed his gums with his finger before taking out a credit card and working the powder like a savant; keeling and chopping and keeling again for minutes until satisfied it was as silken as French chalk. He pulled a small metal tube from the tub, flared at one end, and sniffed back the six inch line in one long fulfilling snort, slumping his head on the sofa back, grinning. He sat staring into the distance for a minute, nodding pleasantly.

'Look, I'm sorry for slappin' yer love, I just lost me rag. I've had a lot on me plate, literally!' Alec joked about the torn naan and

112

leftover curry remnants on the dishes in front of him. He turned amiably towards Helen. 'My heartburn has gone instantly. Just what the doctor ordered.'

Alec poured himself another double vodka and pulled his bare feet up to rest them on the glass table, sighing contentedly.

Georgina fell into a fitful sleep dreaming of Tinks and Henry and monsters as the jarring TV sounds faded into a peaceful short summer night. She woke quietly and rested, hearing early birds chirping. They sounded so happy to be alive, she thought, but her quiet dawn meditation was ousted by a sudden loud groaning and being-sick sounds from her mum's room.

'What's wrong Alec? Are you okay?' Mummy's voice was quaky. Georgina strained to hear as the groaning and vomiting continued followed by a low growling like a wild animal and thudding across the short landing. Alec was banging against the walls and knocking pictures down like a big bear. Her door banged open, the carpet pile stopping it halfway, revealing a low shape lunging into her room. Alec was on his knees, naked; rabid. Georgina reeled as the monster trained its eyes on her with dragon intensity. Alec clinched his gut with his left hand and pulled himself up, gripping the bedside table with his vomit covered right hand. He rose in a leering, unstable crouch.

Georgina shoved back defensively, balling herself into the wall corner of the bed, wrapping her duvet around her legs and pulling it over her nose and mouth. That evil little voice she'd heard yesterday coming from Alec's mouth in the Red Hospital quavered again like some sneering ventriloquist, 'You…You're going to Hell…'

Alec's sweat-beaded face was pale green in the dawn glow as he swayed ever closer, drooling and clawing the air just inches from her face as he continued to grip his abdomen, his groin pain intensifying. Georgina recoiled, disgusted by his clammy nakedness and gripped her duvet screaming, 'Mummy!'

Unexpectedly, Alec jerked upright to attention and raised a trembling finger, facing the bedroom wall to his right. He looked confused and squinted as though recognising someone vaguely familiar.

'Oh, it's…It's you, is it?' Alec's usual voice returned and he pawed the air in front of his face, is if brushing away some ethereal cobweb. The wiry little voice responded as though a Rumpelstiltskin imp had again hijacked his vocal cords, tweedling back absurd gibberish to incant its terminal conundrum: '*It's time…Gulthor squeenah mubbleeant!*'

Sensing impending horror Alec flailed his arms wildly towards the vision, fending off an invisible assailant as he stumbled backwards terrified, falling with a crash and smashing his right temple into the corner of Georgina's glass-topped chest of drawers. Georgina closed her eyes tight shut as a disembodied squeal vented from his throat and a stench of rotten eggs and vomit filled the room.

Her mum stumbled in, pushing the door against Alec's twitching bulk as she squeezed forward; arms outstretched to Georgina who jumped up with duvet around her as her mum cradled her head into her shoulder to shield her from the vile nakedness on the carpet.

'Oh, there's blood. I have to call the ambulance. Please don't look, Georgina, just run downstairs and put the TV on,' she pleaded.

'Alec? Alec? Answer me. Can you hear me? Please get up.' Alec's face was ashen, his eyes staring.

Georgina listened to her mum hurry across the landing, putting her phone on speaker to Emergency Services.

'Ambulance please. It's an accident. 10 Lonsdale Bank. SP21 2ZU. It's my partner. He's fallen and banged his head, but he was being sick and dizzy. It looks like he's fainted. No, no. I can't tell. What? Is he breathing? I don't know. Yes, faintly. Tilt his head? He's on his side and been sick, but he's too heavy. No. No. How do I do that? His wrist? No, I can feel a faint pulse. I don't know how to do that. Please, please just send someone. Please hurry up.'

Georgina had turned on the television. There was some cartoon on Freeview called *Escape from Dinosaur Valley*. The Stone Dwellers were collecting 'Better Berries' in the scary Allosaurus-infested creek which reminded her of yesterday's adventure. She would tell Tinks and Henry about it.

It took two commercial breaks for the ambulance to turn up. Her mum kept running up and down the stairs a lot, putting on a jumper, jeans and trainers. She paced up and down and kept looking anxiously through the lounge window.

The man and lady from the ambulance ran upstairs with a machine that made a high pitched whine and a thump. They kept saying, 'Clear!' before each thump. Then one of them rushed back down to the ambulance and pulled a metal chair thing upstairs. They carried it down again about one minute later. Alec was strapped to it and his head was lolloping to one side. He made a gurgling sound. Georgina glimpsed his face. His skin was really white and his eyes were bulging. Mummy was sobbing when suddenly Grandma appeared in the lounge looking serious. She gave Mummy a hug and rubbed her back, saying, 'You should go.'

The ambulance people made the seat thing go flat like a bed on wheels and they clattered out through the porch and slid Alec into the ambulance on his side. Her mum got into the back with the ambulance lady and the doors were shut. It sped up the street, lights flashing.

Grandma put the kettle on and sat down next to Georgina, telling her not to be worried; that Alec wasn't well and that Mummy would be home soon.

*   *   *

The coroner's report was unequivocal, determining the mechanism of death as *'Fentanyl and cocaine overdose exacerbated by concussion and alcohol intake causing seizure and myocardial infarction'.*

The stomach remnants of curry were noted and a bacterial faecal culture ruled out food poisoning, affirming the exemplary record of the restaurant and corroborating the fact no other recorded food poisoning outbreaks had occurred locally that Saturday night. Also, according to her notes, some of the same meal had been shared by a partner, with no ill effects.

The coroner confirmed the dangers of taking cocaine and fentanyl together are *'indefinite and depend on the mixture and the susceptibilities of the individual'* and that *'in England widespread*

115

polysubstance use with synthetic opioids in the mix is rare, so the medical consequences are unchartered at this point'.

Like Georgina's saddle-stacking game, *Buckaroo*, there is always a tipping point; a last straw or plastic shovel or even perhaps a foil tray of Tinks's green petal mixture looking like *saag aloo* that is just too much for a mule, or monster to handle.

Given the deceased had a criminal record of drug dealing and medical history of a heart murmur as well as a previously recorded cocaine overdose, this was hardly a 'truly unknown' case though if the coroner hadn't been so pressed for time she might have made more of the stomach contents and have requested further toxicology. Specialist chromatograph tests would have revealed the presence of toxic *Oenanthe Crocata* or water hemlock, and highly poisonous *Mercurialis perennis* or Dog Mercury without her even flagging up a search for their presence, but the circumstances of this case seemed to be cut and dried and besides, she also had two other autopsy reports to finalise before Friday; two PhD dissertations to mark; and the family vacation to Italy on Saturday to pack for.

Grandma and Georgina had a nice morning out at the precinct by the playpark and Henry came along too, though this time Henry was carried under Georgina's arm, leaving his wheelchair in the porch because today it was Ragdolly's turn to use it as a Cinderella carriage. Tinks stayed at home because he had to go to Mrs Hedgehog's naughty-boy class in Primrose Wood Teddy School after running across the road without looking both ways causing Mr Squirrel the lorry driver to slam on his brakes and spill his hazelnuts all over the woodland road.

That evening, Mummy came back to Grandma's house with a bag of pyjamas and teddies. She was quiet and sad, but not as sad as Georgina thought she would be. Grandma cooked spaghetti in tomato sauce with cheese and mini sausages. It was gorgeous and Mummy even laughed a few times. Mummy was going to stay the night with her in Grandma's spare room, just like being on holiday.

Georgina pulled Tinks out of the bag by his stubby arm. Tinks's brown felt patches on his ears and paws had a salty looking watermark because he and Henry had been left in heavy dew

116

overnight in the toy pushchair at the bottom of the drive. Tinks needed the brown felt in his ears and paw pads patching anyway and Grandma was going to do that at the same time as stitching Henry's legs back on, but tonight, Georgina, Henry and Tinks were going to enjoy more bedtime story.

Georgina held Henry's paw as he bounced excitedly on his sausage-shaped body into bed beside her. She stuffed Tinks next to him, giving his sweet little face a kiss. He didn't have a mouth, just a little black embroidered nose and two brown felt eyes.

'Mummy,' she revealed pensively, remembering Alec taking a swig of the absinthe, 'Tinks and me made *Marvellous Medicine* and it killed the monster.'

'That's nice poppet,' Helen said distracted, rubbing her forehead and staring at the wallpaper pattern, pondering.

'Mummy, did you hear me?'

'What? Oh, sorry. Yes,' she said, snapping out of her trance, 'Well done Tinks,' she turned, patting him on his rough little head and jiggling him. She picked up the book and inhaled a big shuddering draught of air, holding it for long seconds, eventually exhaling a protracted sigh as her tense body relaxed.

'Now which page did I get to?' Mummy asked.

Georgina—her confession acknowledged—shuffled down in the bed comfortably, resting her head on Mummy's arm, Henry and Tinks sitting obediently motionless beside her as she grinned joyfully at the funny scratchy pictures in the story.

Mummy turned to Georgina, smiling softly and gave her a squeeze. Georgina smiled back and reciprocated by giving Tinks and Henry a squeeze and a loving head pat.

The bedroom was gorgeous with pink sunset-fire illuminating the floral paper through the net curtains as the blackbird sang his reliably beautiful evensong from the chimney opposite. Mummy riffled the book pages to a new chapter.

"DELICIOUS"

The distant church bells pealed nine o'clock and three children aged four, ten and eleven stood eagerly scanning the field above the low wicker fence.

'Will he be coming soon Mama?' They squinted at the horizon where the dawn blurred into a drizzle burdened sky now lightening with the hope of early sunshine on this, the shortest day of the year. The youngest, Margery piggybacked sleepily on the shoulders of her older brother, Gilbert.

Joan, the twenty five year old mother responded happily, 'He should be here presently, children,' Girls, brush out your kirtles, and rag your face Gilbert, wipe those cinder streaks off your cheeks – it's not Ash Wednesday and no way to look for Thomasing with the merry widows.'

The dole-giver, Eustace was on his way to the last cottage on his list at Low Law. The Christmas tradition of dole-giving on St Thomas's Day was one of the most anticipated events of the year for the labourers in his father's, Sir Anthony's, tenure. He checked the one remaining hessian sack was still hooked to his saddle as he cantered away from the excited farmsteaders at High Law whom he had left with a dry gingered wheaten loaf; an apple, plum and peafowl pie; a small hen, a pouch of dried fruit, four apples and six pears. He trotted relieved to this, the final farmstead in his father's pay with the remaining dole. The children had been up since first light doing chores and impatiently awaiting his arrival.

'Have you girls had a dry wash?' Mama asked inspecting Agnes's forehead and wiping it with her cold hand. 'Margery, grab your porringer with a little water and bring me your rag. We want to be looking like a young maiden not like a driggle-draggle who sleeps in the hogbog.'

Margery skipped obediently to fetch her face cloth and bowl from inside. The low thatched eave dripped plops of water from the subsiding drizzle. She held her porringer up to dampen the rag as though supplicating Heaven.

'Here Mama, you can wipe my face now.'

Mama rubbed her daughter's wan face roughly.

'Stop fidgeting. A good scrub will put a red rose in each of your cheeks. Don't you want to look pretty for Master Eustace? As quick as he has been with the dole, we can eat and go to the fayre. Your father will meet us after his labours. And remember to sing for Master Eustace.'

'Yes Mama,' the three chorused.

Lean harvests of the previous three years had tightened flesh on bones and taken many children home to the Lord, especially toddlers who barely suckled because their mothers had to prioritise the babies. In the previous year, 1552, many young men in High and Low Law villages had died of The Sweating Sickness including the landlord's eldest son Eugene. Eustace sixteen, was the new dole-giver.

'I can hear a horse coming,' Agnes said, ears sharp as a hare in a frosty field. Her younger siblings strained to hear the snorting steed's distant canter as it slowed to a promising trot which shifted to steady crunches as the stallion moved from soft earth to cinder path. Eustace appeared over the horizon with hessian sack swinging from his saddle as reliably as his older brother had done in previous years.

Mama's mouth watered at the anticipation of this year's sack contents. The harvest had been reasonable in 1552 after three disastrous harvests in a row and it was likely they would receive a little more than previous years; the late Master Eugene was known for a charitable spirit and his brother, it was hoped, shared his disposition.

The children lined up obediently and readied to carol in harmony as the horse hoofed and sidestepped restlessly.

'Whoa, whoa,' Eustace ordered, punching the feisty horse in the head with his chubby fist.

'Good Master Eustace, we share our rhyme to thank you for your gifts:

'St. Thomas Day,
St. Thomas gray,
The longest night
and shortest day
Bless our food both warm and dry
Herbs for sauce and meat for pie
But throw in fruit for moist and cold
To balance humours young and old.

Thank you Master Eustace.'

'Thank your landlord, my father and Mary, your new queen,' Eustace yanked on his reins impatiently to steady the restless steed now irritably circling and thumping its front hooves.

'I am your master it is true, but I am merely their servant. You jack, take this sack and give it to your mother and hold my horse while I pizzle.'

Eustace dismounted heavily, he was portly for his years and stood in contrast to the leanness of his tenants. The family stood attentively until he had finished his business behind the tall elm; Mama's polite smile softening her lean cheekbones and disguising her keenness to open the sack, restraining the girls' fidgeting with a sinewy grip on their bony young shoulders. Eustace finally completed his long and fitful urination with a shiver and a fumbling of breeches.

'Return the sack to the kitchens when you have emptied it. Do not forget,' he ordered gruffly.

'We will Master Eustace, and thank you,' Mama replied, blushing.

Eustace pulled himself up onto the saddle and waved his hat with a flourish towards the pretty face of Agnes, a fine looking farm girl he thought as he flamboyantly heeled his steed to an abrupt canter on the track joining farm to village. As soon as he was out of sight the children and their mother hurried inside gleefully.

Gilbert and Agnes bustled by Mama's hips and Margery shoved between them on tiptoes to see the sack opened on the trestle board.

'Master Eustace wants this sack returned, though it is in need of a good stitch or two at the seam.'

Mama glowered at her brood and paused before carefully pulling out the contents onto the board.

'Please give me room to move children.'

'Mama there is a hen and a meat pie and a ginger loaf and apples and pears and a pouch of raisins,' Agnes piped joyfully pointing each item out with a grubby finger.

'Don't prod the food with your muddy hands. I have eyes to see and ears to hear, Agnes,' Mama responded genially.

'And I've a big gob to receive,' Gilbert hooted pointing at his wide mouth as Margery squealed with delight at her brother's jest.

'I've a big gob too, look!' Margery copied Gilbert's expression and wiggled her tongue, giggling wildly.

Mama chided, 'That's enough playing the dalcop, young Margery, save your mouth for chewing and praying; and set an example to your sister, young man.' She tapped Gilbert on the head lightly with the hollow rap of a wooden spoon causing infectious laughter that even coaxed a broad smile from Mama's face; after all it was a day of celebration and the darkest day of winter could not assuage the anticipation of the day's merriment, nor the welcome extra surprise of a wrap of raisins buried in the sack corner.

'Now please settle children, sit on the bench quietly and you'll get some dole after dinner. We'll have a tittynope of ginger loaf after soup and when we return from the fair your father will decide what we do with the rest.

'And who is going to thank the Lord for his provision this St Thomas Day?

'Agnes, it is traditional for the man of the house, but since your father is not here and your brother is being a ninny I think you should say it.'

'Bless us, O Lord, and these, Thy gifts, which we are about to receive from Thy bounty. Through Christ, our Lord. Amen.'

'Amen,' the others responded while Mama ladled hot barley and turnip broth from the hanging cauldron above the fire into four wooden porringers on the board, placing Margery's aside to cool.

'Praise well spoken, Agnes.'

Agnes flushed with pride and Gilbert tapped his foot against the trestle leg resentfully.

'Sit still and lift elbows from the board, Gilbert. If you tip it your father will knacker you and I've a mind to do the same if you spill your soup.'

Gilbert insolently lifted his shoulders in a half shrug and placed his hands between his legs. Mama glowered at him crossly.

'Sorry Mama, I am excitable because of the fair,' he mumbled.

'Indeed we are all excited, but your sisters are keeping their manners. Now eat your soup without slurping.'

'Do you think the Egypts will be there this year Gilbert?' Agnes asked, sorry for her brother's chiding and feeling for his humiliation.

Mama responded before Gilbert could answer.

'Egypts are again at the fair Agnes. Fairs are always good trade for vagabonds and rogues; but they're lifters and they foxship men with dice games Stay away from them and their hounds,' she warned, remembering last year's trouble when one of their dogs mauled the leg of a prize calf.

'They surely breed their curs with bears,' she scowled.

Gilbert and Agnes bolted their soup and waited for Margery to finish hers, eyeing the delectable ginger loaf warming on the mantel corner.

'Hurry little Margery, pretend you are a trout gulping tiddlers, see how quickly you can eat it,' Agnes coaxed.

With renewed vigour Margery spooned her barley pottage enthusiastically into her mouth, spilling some on the board.

'Ah, ah, ah! Don't encourage sloppy eating, Agnes; the loaf will still be there when Margery has finished. Margery, eat properly and slowly or you won't go to the fair.'

'But I've finished, Mama, look.'

'Hmm,' Mama responded sceptically, checking the bowl was empty.

'It's fortunate I'm minded to be lenient because of the day.'

She spooned out five raisins from the pouch for each of them, neatly placing them in a small pile on the board in front of each child.

'Wait,' she instructed, sawing through the dark base of the ginger loaf to make a roundel which she cut ritualistically into precise sixths. Gilbert sat like a hungry dog careful to see who would get the biggest share. Mama passed one piece to Agnes; one and half pieces to Gilbert and Margery; and took two pieces for herself.

'Father gets the cut above for his labours.'

'When will we ever get a cut above?' Gilbert asked.

Mama frowned, 'If and when your father has eaten sufficient of the loaf, we will all share in the cut above.'

'I don't mind the burnt bits anyway, they're sweeter and chewier than the top,' Gilbert observed, now blissfully nibbling his portion and biting each raisin in half to inspect the moist core.

'That was the most delicious thing I have ever tasted,' Agnes declared, licking a crumb from her lip. Margery, wasn't so sure; she liked the raisins, but was so used to plain pottage that the thick brown crust from the ginger loaf was a very new texture with a spicy flavour, though Gilbert was speechless in an ecstasy of savour as the caramelised crust, the heat of the ginger and the sweet raisins imparted a pleasure that was almost spiritual.

'You enjoyed that didn't you Gilbert?' Mama observed, now smiling benignly, 'But don't get princely ideas. He who is used to turnips must not eat meat pies.'

'I don't understand, Mama,' Gilbert responded, picking up a crumb from his breeches.

'It's an old saying of my grandmother. It means it's perilous to expect luxuries if you're not a rich man.'

'Why so?'

'For tis better to be content than always hunger for dainties beyond your reach. Many men have come to ruin who look beyond honest labour for gain, by meddling with dice or sultry queans. And I warned you hitherto that the Egypts carry many such of the devil's snares. Stay away from them.

'But I've said enough; we must ready to walk. Your father meets us at eleventh bell by the lych-gate so tie your bonnets girls and put your cap on, Gilbert.'

'Can we stay long at the fair, Mama?' Agnes asked eagerly.

'We will stay until the toll of two and then you will go Thomasing while your father tarries longer. Grab your basket Agnes, and Gilbert, the jug. You must meet father again at the lych-gate at the toll of four and pass him your gifts to sack home. I am staying to watch the players with you and for posset, but I must return early to add faggots and bake.'

'Hurrah for posset!' Agnes grabbed her little sister's hands and danced across the floor, all of them giggling.

'But can we not stay a while longer than four, Mama,' Gilbert whined.

'No young sirrah! That is time a-plenty for disports and I want you home before darkness. You must also return Master Eustace's food sack to the stores or Sir Anthony and Master Eustace will think us ungrateful sorners. Who can I trust to carry it?'

'I will Mama,' Agnes responded, still glowing from the approval she received for saying Grace.

'You mustn't lose it, Agnes. Here, put it in your basket, or better, let me tie it to you. Mama rolled the sack neatly and tied it to Agnes's girdle.

'I've tied it tight. Just tug the bow and it will free. When you leave the fair before Thomasing, run up the track and leave it with Mother Maisie in the kitchen and tell her you are returning Master's sack. Do not forget.'

'I will not forget Mama,' Agnes replied proudly as her mother pulled the cottage door to, securing the sliding latch.

Gilbert and Margery hurried on cheerfully through the beech wood, following the hoof prints from Master Eustace's stallion at a quickening pace, enticed by the sounds of the fair's distant hubbub.

'Slow down children and wait for your mother and sister,' Joan shouted.

Gilbert and Margery dallied briefly to show willing, but swiftly marched on ahead, running and skipping; Gilbert playing wolf behind tree trunks, leaping and growling while Margery shrieked, until they reached the village boundary a quarter mile from home, where the narrow woodland bridleway opened into a wider Roman road wide enough for two carts.

Ahead to the right was the Saxon church with its high boundary holly hedge obscuring the lane to the Common where the top of a large green double pavilion tent stood tantalising with its white scalloped trim just visible over the hedge top. Margery and Gilbert climbed over the stile into the churchyard and ran breathless to the lych-gate arch looking impatiently back for their mother and older sister approaching the stile with deliberate slowness.

'I wish they would hurry,' Gilbert said to Margery, 'It is Agnes showing off. She is playing the lady because Mama praised her.'

He picked up a thick stick and stabbed it in a puddle, digging a muddy slab of grassy clay and flicked it in the centre of a gravestone.

'In the Frenchman's eye!' Gilbert raised two fingers victoriously and balanced on top of the grave.

'I can see the fair!' he exclaimed standing tall above his little sister as his mother and Agnes came within yelling distance.

'So can I,' Margery squealed.

'Get down from there!' Mama protested angrily.

Mama lifted her kirtle over the hand post of the stile and stumbled forward, conscious of immodesty and irritable with her unruly son.

'What are you doing standing on the grave, you will bring an ill wind. Lord have mercy!'

Gilbert jumped down protesting, 'It's a papist's stone, so no shame.'

'Keep your mouth sealed thou dolt. You must not mark yourself with such opinion,' Mama blustered.

'And what did I say to you about running ahead? You should have helped me over the stile.'

Gilbert flushed, 'We didn't know how far ahead we were until we got here. I kept stopping to look back, but Margery ran on and I thought I saw Father on the road ahead and would meet him forthwith,' Gilbert responded sheepishly.

'Don't be pulling up fables from your dirty trough or you'll get more than the wooden spoon.'

'Mercy, Mama,' Gilbert bolted evasively into the churchyard with Margery.

'I'll go and find some berries for us,' he shouted back contritely.

'A berry won't stop me scolding your foolishness and for speaking lies, young sirrah!

'That brother of yours has the very imp inside him today.'

'What?' Agnes brought her hand to her mouth in alarm. 'Do you think a faerie abode in his boot in the night?' Agnes probed.

'By no means. I always upturn them after shutting-in. It is alas rife for boys to be impish on fair days.'

Agnes watched her siblings joyfully chase each other shouting wildly around the gravestones and hiding among the yew trees.

Joan detected Agnes was restless, balancing her mother's high praise with a desire to join them.

'Go and play, Agnes. It is good that you may keep them orderly. I'll watch for Father.'

'Thank you Mama.'

'I've found some!' Gilbert shouted excitedly as he hit a high branch with a stick. A flurry of red berries fell at the children's feet. They scavenged for a share.

'Ack, ack!' Mama shouted from the gate. 'Do not eat yet, come here. What is the rhyme I taught thee?'

The three ran back breathlessly holding the sticky berries.

'I can't remember, Mama,' Gilbert responded, 'but I know what not to do!'

'I know, Mama,' Agnes chipped in smugly,

'Pluck Yew berry red but spit the pip;
Nor roote nor branche imbibe;
A knave who gnaws the yew leaf greene
A headstone will inscribe

'Well done Agnes. You two listen to your sister and make sure Margery spits out the pips.'

'I swallowed a pip Mama,' Gilbert confessed fretfully.

'You dalcop boy!' She grabbed his chin roughly and opened his mouth. 'Was it just one? Did you gnash it?'

'No I just slurped it with the berry.'

'Then you will have no gripe. Stay here and stand with me for mercy's sake and wait for your father.'

Opposite the lych-gate the new corner house owned by Thomas Payne, Justice of the Peace stood majestic with first floor jetty overhanging a raised timber deck a foot above the rutted street. The cornerstone property had ebony black beams freshly tarred, contrasting with immaculately whitewashed plasterwork. The glass leaded windows reflected the pale December sunshine in diamond beauty. The house was only one of four black and white residences on the main street which included a workshop and smithy, a bakery and an alehouse; the remainder were drab, single storey timber-framed dwellings stretching a quarter mile to a drystone boundary wall by a forest bank that consumed the low sun in dark coniferous silence.

The street was unusually quiet for a Monday morning, most of the inhabitants abandoning their noisy trades for the fair, coal and wood smoke the only sign of tenure as the slow columns rose from each chimney, pooling unhealthily in a gauzy veil high above the thatched rooftops.

127

Ten yards to the west of the Justice's gable end was another stile wall. Father's familiar beige hat and black bearded face appeared with ruddy cheer as he eased himself down wearily onto the footpath, smiling. His boots were muddy from ploughing. The children ran to him excitedly. Agnes hugged him over his stiff leather doublet, though Margery was too small to reach and instead put her arms around his muddy legs to lean against his warm thigh.

'Father, lo!' Margery panted breathlessly, tugging him, 'We can see flags and bonny tents.'

Father grinned his familiar toothless smile and took his youngest's hand in his callused grip as she eagerly dragged him toward the field, her bright blue eyes more joyful than he had ever seen them.

'Whoa! We'll be there soon Margery, or would you forget Mama by the arch?'

The girls giggled, pulling their father impatiently across the street by his big hoary hands.

'We've got two little oxen here fit for plough, Joan. I could barely hold them,' he joked, kissing his wife and relinquishing his grip on Agnes as Joan handed him a cloth bundle of bread and cheese.

William stuffed hunks into his mouth hungrily as he led the way, wincing uncomfortably as he consumed each under-chewed dry mouthful.

'There are quintains and archers,' he mumbled swallowing, 'and goose-hawking; and minstrels and dancing aplenty.'

Agnes responded excitedly, 'Father, remember the sugared nuts you won last year with the horseshoe toss? Will you win again this year?'

'Mayhap I will; and don't forget I won a pie, pippins and an orange - as much as you and your brother collected Thomasing.'

'That orange was delicious, Father. I remember the room smelling of it when Mama peeled the skin.'

'It shone with the holly berries on the mantel,' Margery chipped in, 'It was like sun and stars.'

'Yes Margery, it was almost a shame to eat it. Perhaps you will get an orange when you go mumping with your brother and sister while I sport with the men.'

'Can I not join your sports this year, Father?'

'Not this year; you need to help your sisters carry the Thomasing basket and jug.'

'Yes Father,' Gilbert replied downcast, his manly ambition thwarted.

'Quit long-facing boy,' father jibed genially. 'Did you know I tarried with Giles the postgater who told me of Lord Misrule's 'George and Dragon' play? It is trumpeted as a *most fiendish spectacle* with something like The Green Man, a cockatrice and river changelings.'

'Hmm,' Gilbert responded testily.

Joan laughed, her moodiness lightening in the presence of her husband. 'Oh those puppets Gilbert, they are dreadful when they snap their jaws,' she nipped him in the side and he recoiled, repressing a giggle. 'You won't be scared like Margery was last year will you?' she smirked, turning to Margery and nudging her playfully.

Gilbert shrugged, pouting. Margery responded with childish umbrage, 'No Mama, I am excited,' she stomped, 'I was just a baby last fair.'

'Hush my little pomander! We will see if it is fitting when we walk past the tents.'

A thrilling din escalated as they rounded the bend past the church hedgerow. Two hundred yards down the cart track the fence line stopped by a gate alongside a ramshackle collection of roofed stables, cattle sheds and locked grain stores. A pair of fiery braziers full of glowing ash logs warmed the hands and faces of the officials sitting at their table inside the first empty shed by the gate, the shrill piping of recorders and drums greeting the eager jam of visitors pressing to enter in.

The town clerk sat on his high chair by the oak board and trestle, guarding a studded box of farthings and halfpenny coins, assisted by the church warden and his wife.

'A halfpenny for each adult. Bairns enter freely.'

William fumbled in his purse reluctantly.

'We had none such tithe last fair, sir. What reason for the extort?'

'The *extort*, as you say goes to church coffers to fund St Thomas' loaves and other such; a little charity to whom few would deny,' the clerk scowled, 'Besides, entry gives you a free ale at spout head.'

'We had free ale last fair without tithe,' William shook his head and muttered, tossing four farthings into the box. Joan flushed and hung her head shamefully as she passed the clerk, ushering the children quickly through the gap.

'Charity be gone, Joan! One penny buys nigh a gallon of good ale. That bawd at his board constrains the hand of the poor to supply their own alms.'

'You are right, Sir, but tis but once a year and the bairns delight in the merriment.'

'Whose side are you on woman?'

'William, I am of course in agreement, but the day begs you be calm.'

'Fine. No more will be said, but I have little enough coin to pay for the merriment, so we shall be constrained in our choices.'

'I do not mind one straw, William; I come here not to be profligate with your wages, but only to watch the folk enjoy themselves; the Lord knows you have earned them, but the bairns heartily desire to watch the play.'

'I have halfpennies aside for that,' he grunted, tying his drawstring to his belt. Joan linked his arm.

'Let us enjoy the day, William.'

William shook his head stoically. 'We'll just hope the bairns do good a' mumping to recover the loss.'

130

Joan looked up at him and grinned, kissing his black-bearded cheek gratefully.

The couple relaxed, distracted by the bustle; greeting friends and strangers; dodging cattle and barking dogs, while the children ran and chatted excitedly to their peers. Gilbert diverted with some young friends to view a shin-kicking competition and William chatted to a group of drovers exhibiting prize black rams, while Joan nodded approvingly, waiting patiently to move on.

'Walk ahead with the girls, Joan. I will join Gilbert to watch the kickers,' Father affirmed as Margery became restless, tugging her mother's kirtle.

The Egypt camp was marked by a line of smouldering fires straggling untidily through the shrub land of the Common by the old cattle sheds. The travellers were barely tolerated and paid dearly for their presence by ditch-digging and farm labouring two days either side of the fair in return for permission to trade their wares; regale their mysterious talents; and lodge in the stables and dilapidated outbuildings on the fair perimeter. Their juggling, boxing, dicing and *legerdemain* tricks were seen as colourful, even necessary diversions for the locals during the St Thomas Day celebration where exotic music, dancing and divination were stomached for the hedonistic duration, but as soon as the fair was over, they knew to move quickly out of town before impoverished locals found an easy target to unburden their winter hardships.

Adjacent to the travellers' shelters, tree branches and shrubs were hung with scarfs and cloths for sale of unusual blue, crimson and yellow hues alongside embroidered cushions and drapes of such colour and depth of texture that it was refreshment for Joan's eyes as she strolled past.

As well as Egypt wares, various timber-poled English trader tents, most with open sides and stitched hide roofs arrayed local products from pottery and furniture to clothing; meat and provisions. Two ale tents, draped in russet-brown canvas aptly redolent of the strong beverage within, marked out the fair's topmost corners and were deliberately positioned to draw the crowds through the full extent of the stalls before refreshment could be attained. Similarly, the

131

popular posset tent with open front was striped yellow and white to advertise its deliciously sweet and warming eggy tonic within.

Rudimentary fencing of low poles and string marked sports areas including horseshoe toss and bandy ball and a rowdy kicking game using a knot of ropes. Archery and quintain were organised by locals, but the wrestling and fist fighting were managed by the travellers whose prize fighters challenged stout townsfolk to compete in bloodied bouts as the Egypt women rallied the crowds and took bets. Agnes winced at the sight of a bloodied local bandaging his bleeding shins and a local challenger from the boxing ring only just conscious as his wife bathed his two puffy eyes and gashed lip with a ball of rags.

Locals queued for palm reading and divination, while pretty Egypt girls enticed men into the most lucrative diversion—the dice game—set inside a warm canvased tent with a brazier –hired to them by Sir Anthony's men for a percentage of the takings.

In spite of the unusual merchandise Joan didn't like the rowdiness of the Egypt stretch, especially as a drunk, sore loser was ejected swearing and flailing violently from the dice tent nearly colliding with Margery, so Joan headed briskly away, guiding her girls toward the apex of the field where players and puppeteers for the afternoon's plays were readying their act, but Agnes had stopped to stare at the fabrics and an older Egypt woman in brassy headdress perceived her interest and hawkishly beckoned her to feel the wares, looking into Agnes's hazel eyes and holding various coloured fustian rough cotton squares to match across the spread of her dark, wrinkled fingers, settling on a blue square which she deftly folded into a triangle and swiftly tied around Agnes's chin before she could protest.

'Savvy?' Kushti. Chi Shugra. Trés jolie.' The Egypt woman put her hand on each of Agnes's shoulders and span her around to face Joan, smiling and nodding approvingly before tapping a gnarly finger insistently into the centre of her palm. 'Baksheesh. Un Penny. baksheesh.'

'Non! Non, non!' Joan reverted to the little French she knew, pulling off the scarf from Agnes's head and handing it back to the old woman who made an urgent hand-to-mouth sign and pointed to a young Egypt urchin sitting in the mouth of a wicker tent as she bellowed louder, 'L'argent, l'argent s'il vous plait? Aliments pour chauvis!'

'Non. Non,' Joan shook her head, shoving Agnes behind her and thrusting the scarf forward insistently as the Egypt held her palms up in affected outrage, shaking her head and refusing to take back her wares as though some blood oath had been reneged upon. Joan laughed nervously at the histrionics and turned on her heel, frostily throwing the scarf back onto the pile of cotton squares.

'Come at once girls. Leave her to her babblings.'

'Dinlow Gadjo!' the old woman snarled and gestured with her fingers like talons towards Joan; pointing at Agnes and repeating the gesture before retreating into the cattle shed where Egypt mules were huddled by a low cart of hay for feed and a young girl was mashing the dung with hay to make bricks for the overnight smoulder.

Joan was agitated but coolly eased back into the bustle of the strolling crowd, hastening to find William who stood alongside Gilbert cheering at an enclosure where two greasy topless men wrestled.

'By my troth an Egypt made a grab for Agnes to extort me and threw a curse at us,' Joan blurted angrily.

'Stay away from those lifters Agnes.'

'Yes Father, I had not wanted to...'

'Just stay close to your mother!' Father snapped crossly as Agnes hung her head, her chin quivering.

'Hold off crying, Agnes, the masters are passing.'

At that moment Master Eustace and Sir Anthony paraded by on their mounts, inspecting the sideshows and sports at slow pace, nodding to the bystanders. William doffed his hat and Joan bobbed a small curtsey, Agnes nuzzled into Mama's apron to hide her tears.

For Sir Anthony's part, today combined traditional handouts for farm labourers with a public social obligation to convey pleasantries, though his friendliness was solemn and as formal as his black Barbary stallion that stood a lofty seventeen hands with a high square pommel and curved cantle with ornate breastplate and crupper, reminding lowly tenants of their dependant status. The large green double pavilion tent belonged to Sir Anthony and stood tallest near the top right of the field. This was the hospitality and feasting tent for Master Eustace and his friends.

After undertaking the required rounds with his father, Eustace dismounted, relieved of the day's etiquette and tied his steed to one of the twenty posts erected especially for landlords and visiting wealthy from the neighbouring villages.

The wide timber-decked entrance of his father's tent had three glowing braziers filled with coals. Eustace's haughty stride declared his son-ship to onlookers as he flicked his soft hide gloves arrogantly against his palm, handing them to a curtseying maid servant. Cheers and laughter arose suddenly from a group of rowdy and prosperous-looking acquaintances, their raucous shouts, jesting, back slapping and ritualistic display of arm linking, cod-piece grabbing and spinning sending them into uproarious guffaws. Sir Anthony, though remaining on his horse stood at the entrance and laughed approvingly before saying a few words and flourishing his cap theatrically, trotting back through the field to the Manor House. This was a day for the young to affirm loyalties, discuss politics and feast and drink riotously. Sir Anthony had seen it all before; besides, he had better wine and provisions at home and a vast fireplace with good reading.

William and Joan surreptitiously glanced in at the affluent feasting and bawdy jesting as they strolled past, finding it difficult in their penury not to resent the profligacy of the wine barrels and roasting boar over the central fire spit.

'Mind not the rich Joan, they have their day; it is fleeting as smoke.'

'You are right sir, we have good conscience and our brood are fed and sheltered.'

Perceiving Agnes still had hurt feelings William gently rubbed the back of her hair through her bonnet with his big hand.

Today the fair was busier than previous years and by one o'clock visitor numbers had peaked. There were only a few townsfolk not visiting - the infirm and very old remained home to stoke fires and

134

protect dwellings from thievery, and to dole out gifts for the children during the afternoon's mumping.

In fair tradition, the town's tradesmen and farmers drank raucously at one of the ale tents or played bowls or kickball together while their wives and children were free to mingle, watch the displays and buy provisions and local crafts from the tents; minding the children and fending off a stream of Egypt hawkers. Village traders fared better - Joan bought a whipping top for Gilbert, a clay beaded leather thong necklace with glazed lozenge and engraved letter 'A' for Agnes; and a corn dolly in a painted flower dress for Margery. Agnes proudly wore her necklace, showing it to friends who pestered their parents to buy them one.

William and Gilbert were distracted by a bowls competition while Joan and the girls meandered towards the top of the field where the play was setting up inside a roped pentangle housing five inward facing open fronted trader tents with extended roof shades. The tents were positioned to obscure the performance area from none-paying onlookers, but through the gaps between them, Agnes and her mother could see inside the tents as they walked the perimeter. One contained two sulky carts with a variety of ropes and painted canvases while two more contained musicians, and a player dressing up in a dark green smock. The fourth tent contained a selection of wooden and fabric puppet heads. Agnes spotted one with a grotesque fish face being carried to the raised timber stage with its framed roof housing various rigging and pulleys. The men adjusting the rig looked flustered.

'Mama, look the puppets are fiendish!'

'This year seems to be a most elaborate romp,' Mama said, peering nosily with Agnes through the gap as a hand bell jangled startlingly behind them.

'Beware!' a man shouted suddenly as they turned in fright to see a handsome tout draped from head to toe in branches of evergreen and ivy, his white teeth stark against black painted lips and pea green painted face.

'Beware the river dragon and his cockatrice changelings,' he bellowed. 'Gather ye to see the noble London troupe performing a most exciting spectacle.' He winked at Joan, 'Can ye afford not to pay them homage today?' he added forebodingly, with a melodramatic bow. Joan flushed.

'Worry not my dearling dove,' he bent low to reassure a terrified looking Margery, passing her a small red apple from his pocket. 'Tis but a few of us silly men masqued up for laughs. You will do well to see the puppets with your sister before the play.'

He beckoned the two girls to the back of the puppet tent, and lifted the rope of the enclosure before putting his head in between the overlapped canvas flaps, 'Thomas, let these pretty fauntelets see the snapping crocodile before you carry it over.'

A man in the tent nodded reluctantly. 'Alright Jack. Inside the tent, but be quick lasses,' he grunted.

'Hurry through my doves. He is lugging them forthwith,' the green man directed.

'Say thank you girls,' Joan smiled coyly as they disappeared inside and she was left standing with the stranger, embarrassed at having been caught peeping. 'We expect to view the revelry directly,' she blurted.

'Excellent. There's room for fifty standing and fifty sitting. The first play is full and only standing room left for the others so buy your pebbles quickly at the gate. A farthing standing.'

Meanwhile, Agnes and Margery shuffled uncomfortably beside the grumpy stage hand and gave a fleeting review of the wires and pulleys of the snapping crocodile head designed to sit on a man's shoulders. Thanking him with a quick curtsey they darted back through the flap and under the rope to Mama.

'That was quick girls!' the green man quipped, 'Thomas would have let you tarry longer than three heartbeats,' he joked, turning back to Joan.

'Thank you sir for your kindness and advice,' Joan blushed, fluttering her eyes.

'Oh and be wary of lifters. There are plenty afoot, so cloak your purses,' the stranger warned.

William moved in suddenly from the crowd, stepping alongside Joan and draping his arm jealously over his pretty wife's shoulders. 'There are more vagabond sorts here today than I have ever seen, so we heed your counsel,' he snapped.

The green man bowed politely, unperturbed by William's possessiveness.

'Come Joan, we take our places twixt one and two,' William spoke curtly, annoyed at her perceived flirtation. I want two hours at sports and ale with the lads while the bairns are mumping.'

William queued briefly where a young lad stood behind a table draped with red and yellow striped cloth. In front were five small baskets filled with large and small coloured pebbles assigning entry to each of five performances. Red pebbles for the first play were sold out, but sandy, brown, white and finally grey pebbles for the last performance of the day remained.

'It's a penny for four standing if you carry Margery, or Agnes can take Margery to see the dancers, as she may be terrified or lack understanding.'

'No Father, for I will miss out,' Agnes protested.

'Then she must be brave. Will you do bravely at the play, Margery?'

'Yes Father, I am not afeard. The dragon's teeth are dolly pegs.'

'Good girl. Pass the lad my penny and take four sandy stones.'

William lifted Margery to pick out four sandy coloured pebbles from the basket.

'Return all pebbles for entry,' the lad at the table instructed.

They heard the first play starting as they walked to view the remaining trader tents along the field perimeter near the fair entrance. A dolorous drumbeat preceded the first strident narration and the audience periodically shouted or shrieked uproariously during climactic moments which, according to what they could hear over the hubbub seemed to be a rhyming tale about a lonely fisherman terrified by changelings and river monsters on his boat during a storm. Drumrolls and discordant flutes mimicked thunderclaps and howling banshee-wails.

'It sounds very frightening, William,' Joan observed, eyeing Gilbert and Margery giggling nervously with each tumultuous cheer. Margery, conversely was clearly apprehensive in spite of her assertion otherwise.

'Let us not tarry long at these stalls, Joan. We must be vigilant for the ending of the first play so we can hasten to our spots,' William advised.

Minutes later a loud cheer rang out from the audience signalling a climactic denouement. William led his family back towards the top of the field where a small crowd gathered for the second playing. On route they saw Master Eustace and three of his cohorts staggering from the cosy green hospitality tent, whooping and laughing as they diverted toward the Egypt dice game, allured by the smiles of the curvaceous Egypt girls at the tent entrance in their russet pleat dresses, head scarves, low cut blousons and black waistcoats.

'Let us take these vagabonds for every farthing,' Eustace boasted as he swaggered inside ostentatiously jangling his bulging purse in the face of one of the girls.

'You want what's in my sack?' he mocked as his friends guffawed. The beautiful Egypt tilted her head feigning a smile and opening the tent flap with fake subservience, her outstretched arm gracefully pointing the young men to the dice board.

'Master Eustace is a boorish one, not at all like his brother Eugene,' Joan whispered to William as they passed by, heeding the bell that announced the second performance.

'Children, take your pebbles,' William handed out the stones. 'Margery, we are sharing a pebble as I'm carrying you, but try not to fidget.'

Twelve benches were laid in three groups of four to the stage facing sides of the pentangle. The benches were filled by merchants and their wives while the farm labourers stood deferentially behind. Joan, Agnes and Gilbert stood in front of William who carried Margery now contentedly wrapping her arms around her father's bearded neck, fiddling with his earlobe.

The dolorous drumroll sounded again and the chattering audience immediately hushed as a large canvas curtain on the raised square stage opened to reveal a hunched man sitting on a low stool on a painted riverbank with a rod in his hand. Above him hung evergreen branches, wooden seagulls and painted clouds. Wooden waves painted grey and white obscured trapdoors where players and puppets would soon appear, while a backdrop canvas painted with trees and a gloomy high cliff set the riverbank scene for the first onslaught.

A narrator's voice boomed out suddenly across the silence and the audience jumped. He strutted theatrically to the left and right of the stage front, pointing and staring in the faces of the people in the front seats as he hailed:

Should you decide to sit alone
Upon a lakeside edge or riverbank in repose
Then ponder wisely on this tale
And on the secrets waters hold

Swerve your mind to strange wild things
That slink and skulk and shrink away
For there comes a time when darknesses
In carelessness themselves betray…

The narrator turned sombrely to stage, his hand extended to present the fisherman protagonist who picked up the narrative:

Twas just as this a time ago
The leaden light, the silent trees
When I was casting by this bank
In hope of decking nor'bound salmon
Headed for the seas.

With knuckles tingling purple
And numbing in the evening air,
I fumbled clumsy with the shot
And firmed it to the sturdy hair

The fisherman cast his line into the waters:

As shade grew dim increasingly
Along the aching vein of night
I sunk my chin down chestwardly

Wrapped in blankets, fire alight

My line was slack and water slopped
In groping rhythm along the duct
A living noise the channel made
As blow holes sneezed and runnels sucked.

A wistful recorder piped a sinister melody and plinking sounds from wooden clatter bars provided eerie resonance as the fisherman continued.

Some starry fire flecks wind-whipped sparkling
From the fire's soothing blaze
Like tiny faery spirits darting
Dreamlike to a tiring gaze.

I well expected fairly soon
To feel a lulling sense of sleep
From the languid river tongues
That whispered language old and deep

As smoke dispersed in rapid plummet
Up and sideways aimlessly
And louder pitched the breeze made buffet
Round and through the flustered trees

Another recorder piped up mournfully with low notes combining with the first and a tambourine shake simulated the rustle of leaves and approaching storm.

Soon the tilt to kip I felt
From slouching listless against the oak
Secure in blankets stitched from pelt
And staring trance-like at the smoke

So strangely did my thinking rove
That soon I slid in billows deep
Sinking swiftly into sleep

But of a sudden dreams grew black
And restless things moped morbidly;
All dismal did my dreamings tack
Through moaning reaches inwardly
That soon in jolts I scrambled swift

A shudder at my darkling drift...

A loud drum thud and crash of cymbals mimicked lightning and the audience screamed. Margery buried her bonneted head into her father's neck as she gripped him tight and began to cry as the fisherman carried on:

..Waking sudden; grey with quaking,
Round a scene as tho 'twas faking
The vision I had seen of yore
And sights that had perturbed my resting
In that deathly dream all festering
Scathing soul and reason raw

Then I saw it! Imp fish foul
Like crocodile and a banshee owl
It fast came marching up the bank
Its fiery nostrils with brimstone stank

A trapdoor under the stage introduced a black smocked figure wearing the snapping crocodile head. The figure heaved up onto the stage, turned its head slowly from right to left in predatory calculation of the audience and began swiping toward the seated onlookers with its black clawed gloves. A child ran in terror as front row adults reeled backward, some laughing, some in undisguised dread. Other smaller hobgoblin-faced fish puppets ascended from under the stage recess, held aloft by sticks which thrust forward towards the protesting crowd. The offensive continued against a commotion of discordant drum beats, cymbal clashes and trumpeting sackbut.

'This is exciting, but bedevilling for some faint hearts,' William remarked as Joan gripped Agnes' and Gilbert's shoulders protectively.

At the dice tent, amidst the intermittent hubbub of the play, Master Eustace cursed his Egypt hosts through gritted teeth. He could not accuse them of loaded dice for they had checked and approved the use of his own.

Three burly Egypt men appeared silently inside the entrance as though summoned by some egregore spirit sensing threat.

'You cheating knaves, you cast my dice craftily. Give me them back and take your devious gain.' Eustace snatched his dice and cast ten shillings in the face of the heavy set Egypt matriarch.

'Non, vos dés sont parfaits!' the big woman barked angrily, thick spittle in the corner of her mouth.

'My loss is a frippery,' Eustace sneered, 'You will lose double when I return,' he boasted, rising smugly from his stool. His two acquaintances had no gripe and were inclined to leave the tent peaceably; they had not placed the large bets of Eustace and had accordingly only suffered minor losses.

Eustace however was furious at his loss. It was easily a month's stipend and as he was filled with heady wine he childishly tipped up the dice board with a curt swipe of his arm as he left, spitting on the tent floor.

In a maelstrom of controlled fury, the Egypt men lifted Eustace from the tent in pillar fashion and carried him noiselessly onto the muddy thoroughfare. Unprotesting, Eustace's friends held up their hands and followed outside, the four men guarding the tent entrance with arms crossed.

'Vous êtes un perdant déshonorant!' the pretty Egypt girl proclaimed as a humiliated Eustace steadied himself on the slippery ground.

'Yaldson Egypt knaves! You dare to eject me from my father's tent?' he yelled as he sloped away crimson faced with his acquaintances.

'Let us return to hospitality for more wine and we'll watch the English players. I am sick of the sight dark Egypt skins,' he spouted, marching ahead, quickly regaining his bombastic composure.

'Lend me a shilling lads, I will gallop home for more coin anon.'

Meanwhile the play was reaching a denouement. The crocodile's final snapping onslaught caused the fisherman to drop wretchedly to his knees, where in a final despairing act he looked to heaven and cried for help. A shocking crash of cymbals heralded the sudden unfurling of a heavy curtain painted with a forest scene that

142

dropped from the rigging in a flourish of green fabric and hundreds of dry leaves. The crowd jumped as the crocodile, meeting its nemesis face to face, heaved backwards in terror. An angel in the form of The Green Man from English folklore parted the forest curtain with outstretched arms and stepped powerfully forth from his wooded domain, cloaked in a robe of evergreen branches with pea green painted face and headdress of ivy. It was the man who had startled Joan with the bell earlier.

Turning slowly to the left and to the right, his piercing eyes examined the faces of the silent audience with austere dignity, as the river dragon crouched motionless in terror.

Suddenly the green avenger whipped out a sickle from beneath his fir-tree layers, flashing it towards the reeling crowd, flailing the curved blade firstly towards the ruthless horde of demon cockatrices who fell back, spinning fearfully down into the waves before the evergreen angel turned finally to vanquish the crocodile. The beast opened its jaws and in one final snap of stubborn resistance lunged at The Green Man before succumbing to the downward swipe of his blade, disappearing under the stage in agonised snarling amidst a din of wailing recorders, discordant strings and banging drums.

The Green Man raised his angelic reaping hook victoriously before bowing toward the fisherman and the audience and vanishing behind the forest curtain in a camouflage flurry of wafted silks and falling leaves dropped from a pivoted basket above. The crowds cheered and the children rejoiced as the fisherman expounded his final swelling words:

When all seems dark and death is certain
Help comes quick from Heaven's curtain
Take the knee and shout out boldly
The Lord delivers who seek Him holy

'Mama, did The Green Man kill all the cockatrices too? They went under the waves, but did they die?' Margery asked, concerned.

'Yes my little mite, do not fear - they went down into the flames under the waters - which is a reminder I have to go home to keep the fire while you go Thomasing,' she turned to Agnes and Gilbert, 'At the toll of four by the lych-gate you must meet your father. Take the jug and my basket and don't forget to return the master's sack, Agnes.'

'Yes Mama, but Margery and Gilbert must take the basket and jug til I join them.'

'Yes. Agnes will help carry the jug and basket when she meets you, then Father will help you carry the alms when you meet at the gate.'

The four walked together back to the fair entrance, joining other young friends with their bags, jugs and baskets, excited to go mumping before sundown.

The children ran ahead as Joan walked home to rekindle the fire and bring in logs ready for shutting in.

'I will catch up,' Agnes shouted diverting down the quarter mile woodland bridle path to the stables and kitchen quarters of Sir Anthony's manor house; her brother and sister distracted in chatter and laughter among a huddle of their peers.

The low sun cast long shadows through the ancient woodland with its oak, beech and yew though the sky was still blue above the apricot horizon. It would be frosty tonight; her breath already steamed. She tried to remember how verdant the bridal path's grassy verges looked just four months ago; now they were a drab memorial of summer, but she knew from tomorrow the days would lengthen and the ground would soon yield hard green blades of bluebells.

A cantering horse approached from behind her. It slowed to a trot and she turned to see Master Eustace on his mount.

'You are William the ploughman's daughter are ye not?'

'Yes sir, I have come to return your sack.'

'Ah, yes, the sack. Did you enjoy the dole I brought this morning?'

'Yes Master Eustace, we are very grateful.'

'What is your name?'

'Agnes, sir.'

'A pretty name to go with a very pretty face. And what does a grateful girl do for her Master?'

'I return the sack to the kitchens. Thank you, Master Eustace,' she curtseyed.

'No, no, no Agnes,' Eustace laughed, shaking his head wryly. He dismounted his horse and tied it to a tree. 'Why not let me see what you've got hidden?'

Agnes began to untie the sack clumsily from her girdle.

'I am untying it Master Eustace, sir.'

'No, no, no, Agnes. What I meant was what can a pretty girl like you show their Master by way of thanks.'

'I don't know, sir. Loyalty?' Agnes responded, confused, struggling with the knot.

'Let me help you with that,' Eustace yanked the girdle lace and the sack was loosed. He stuffed it into his saddle bag.

'Do I not receive a kiss for my help? Here, come a little way into the wood and let me look at your duckies. That is surely a fair payback for my kindness.' Eustace pulled her in close to him.

'Oh, I am sorry, sir,' Agnes responded blushing, 'I would that you release me, sir.'

'Ah, but you are standing under a kissing bough, do you not see it?' He glanced up mischievously. 'I cannot leave without a kiss.'

'Master Eustace, sir, my Mama says that a gentleman cannot ask for a kiss without a berry.'

'Do you deny your master a kiss?' His tone was threatening as he pulled her into the wood.

'Your Mama and father will not be happy if I have to put you out of the cottage next year.' He put his fat face up to hers, his bulbous lips red with claret.

'No, please sir,' Agnes winced at the sour odour of stale wine on his breath as he pulled her in tightly.

'Just one kiss, Agnes and I will be on my way.'

She reluctantly gave Eustace's clammy cheek a brisk touch of her lips.

'That is no kiss; that is a wren peck,' he teased, 'I shall show you what a kiss is.'

Eustace pulled Agnes in towards him and Agnes pushed away, turning her head from left to right as he strained to plant his lips on hers.

'Hold still you mare,' Eustace grabbed her hair through her bonnet as Agnes pleaded with him.

'Please stop, sir, my father will…'

Eustace put his leg behind her and pushed, tumbling her into the damp leaves. Grabbing her kirtle and hitching it upwards, he fumbled with his codpiece, panting loudly. With a surge of energy Agnes arched herself upward from her shoulders, bringing her knees up and squirming from his grip. Her elbow struck him in the temple and he was purple with rage. He grabbed at her ankle and pulled her boot off as she hobbled painfully onto the clinker path, running terrified back towards the town track where she might scream for help, but Eustace gave chase. He lunged at her, grabbed at her kirtle and punched her angrily in the back of the head. She began to cry as he dragged her into the low shrubs by the conifer plantation wall, pushing her head down into the damp winter grass and tightening her leather neck thong until it snapped as he completed his grunting molestation.

Satisfied, he rose up and secured his breeches, brushing the leaves from his body. He threw the necklace into a muddy rill and lifted Agnes's limp, unconscious body over the drystone wall, dropping her into the wood before wheezily hoisting his own podgy bulk over.

'You should've let me kiss you,' he protested, 'What tenant would strike their master so. You deserved what you got,' he mumbled exhausted, dragging her to the ancient well-head hardly visible through the hatch of brambles. He pulled her to the ledge of dilapidated stones and heaved her in head first, hearing an unprotesting thud and low whimper. Wiping his hands and brushing leaves from his breeches, he slapped his gloves against his thigh and strolled satisfied back to his horse.

* * *

Wassail, wassail, through the town
If you've got red apples, throw them down;
Up with the stocking down with the shoe
If you've not got apples, a farthing will do

Margery and Gilbert joined an efficient Thomasing gang and quickly accrued a heavy and unwieldy burden of cooking apples; a barley loaf and three scoops of oats.

'Where is Agnes to help us, Gilbert?' A ruddy faced Margery asked, dropping her apple sack and slumping by the wool-carder's barn wall as the older friends ran down the street.

'Hurry, we have to go further, Margery. I want to go with my friends and I have no eggs or cheese in the jug, just tart apples.'

'But my arm is sore Gilbert. Agnes should be here and it is nigh cockshut time.'

'Just sit here and wait and I will see if Squint-eye will give us eggs, then we will go to the gate.'

Gilbert ran on with his friends and Margery clutched her sack of apples to keep warm. The few scattered clouds had turned bright pink in the setting sun and the air was suddenly chill. The main crowds were leaving the fair in droves leaving the men in the ale tents and Sir Anthony's guests feasting.

Gilbert ran back to Margery holding the jug up triumphantly.

'I got eggs and bacon from Squint-eye. Father will be happy.'

Margery, pale and exhausted rose up from the ground with her apples and shivered, 'Agnes is still not here. She must be at the gate.'

'She better be waiting,' Gilbert agreed, 'It's too cold and we have too heavy a load to lug without her and it is getting dark, so come now Margery.'

William was not at the gate, he ran up to them with two of his field lads accompanying. After some parting laughter he spoke.

'My children, your Father is very merry, but where is Agnes, is she with Mama?' He asked Gilbert, lifting Margery and her apples with one scoop of his powerful arm. 'Let me carry those my little mite, you have both done well by the look of it; oats, apples and eggs, God be praised!'

'And bacon from Squint-eye.'

'Don't let me hear you calling the almoner Squint-eye, lad.'

'But I heard it from you and Mama first,' Gilbert responded.

'I'm sure you did not, but that's not something you parley to others. Keep your manners, boy.'

'But I did, Father, at Mass; I heard you say to Mama…'

'Keep your rudder lashed, lad. That tongue of yours will take you to stormy waters.'

'Yes, Father, but Agnes is the one who needs chastisement as she did not help at all with the mumping.'

'I'll decide who gets chastised. I need no guidance from you, jack.'

'Agnes must have gone to Mama's after Mother Maisie's,' Margery said, sleepily.

'Why did she go to Maisie's?'

'The dole sack, Father. Mama made her promise to return master's sack,' Gilbert responded.

'She must have done messages for Maisie and will be home.'

Margery was asleep on William's shoulder when they reached the cottage door. William lowered her down as Mama opened up, the glow of the fire dimly lighting their faces in the twilight.

'Where is Agnes?' Joan asked, concerned.

'Not with you, then?' William responded.

'No. Not with me. And she was not at the gate?'

'No Mama. We waited past four bells and supposed she was with you,' Gilbert replied.

'I will hasten back through the woods. Take the bags,' William responded wearily. 'I will be back anon. There is a moon tonight.'

148

Joan lay Margery in her wooden cot and placed the fleeces over her. Before closing the door she watched pensively as William's burly outline was swallowed by darkness on the beech wood path.

The noises from the fair were boozy and rowdy as he passed the field to his right. He prioritised a knock on Mother Maisie's door to find out when she last saw Agnes.

'No William. She has not been here this afternoon. I have been stewing puddings and the mite always has time for a little chat. Oh that is a worry. I shall wake Henry. He's been at the ale tent and is sleeping it off. I will get him to help you search.'

'No Maisie, thank you, I don't need him slowing me up if he's sotted. If I need him I will knock.'

'Oh mercy, William. Do not tarry, go quickly to the fair and ask among the English traders, she may be lost or have hurt herself and is not able to walk.'

'Aye, lass, but all the townsfolk know my bairns and would've carried her home by now.'

'Yes, that's true. I am sure she will be safe with Joan when you return, William, but I will keep my ears pricked for news tonight. It is a mercy the crescent moon and stars shine some.'

'True, but frost is deadly if she lies injured somewhere,' William voiced his fears and turned swiftly back towards the fair, unheeding the squashed grass by the wall where Agnes was tipped just two hours earlier.

The December darkness fell quickly and the fair was difficult to traverse. Small lantern lights at the entrances of the Egypt sheds and the glow from within the ale tents emitted sufficient light for William to navigate without tripping over guy ropes. The top ale tent was still rowdy, but gradually emptying as most of the men had left, stumbling to their respective homes together, linked in the darkness, eyes growing quickly accustomed to the pale moonlight glow that marked walls and ditches. William thanked sheep shearer Boaz who controlled the slur of his speech sufficiently to inform him he had seen Agnes headed with youngsters to the main street, but William already knew of the Thomasing procession.

'Did you see her afterwards, Boaz. Alone? With somebody?'

'No Will, I passed them at smithy. She were walkin' with the wheelwright's girls, your boy and a ragtag of other mites, all going a' mumping.'

'I will knock all the doors to find her.'

Suddenly a ruckus exploded from the dice tent, Master Eustace was expelled in brandy-soaked fury, wildly twisting and kicking to unfetter himself from the grip of the three Egypt men; the same three who had ejected him earlier. Eustace had demanded to play another game with his own dice, but his second purse was also lost upon the Egypts' board.

'I will run you thieving Egypts out of town,' he gnashed as they lifted him onto the muddy thoroughfare with unruffled restraint.

Humiliated, Eustace made to return to the feasting tent as the three stood guard over their pitch like shadowy sentinels. In a feeble act of defiance, Eustace hurled a log from a pile by one of the fires, lurching drunkenly backwards to watch it glance off the cheek of the smallest and stockiest of the silent Egypts, making a gash. Though tempted to hit back the itinerant tribe knew that engaging locals was dangerous and wisely considered the best revenge was winning their money.

'Knaves and varlets all. Tell your pox-ridden punks their curses will come to naught!' Eustace blundered into the night, spitting vitriol; stumbling past a preoccupied William, too busy searching for Agnes among the hunched silhouettes of the Egypt women and children as they packed up for the night, pulling their unsold wares into dark stooped tents and dim stables.

William sought to discern Agnes's cries above the mumbling voices and warbling unfamiliar songs of the travellers as he floundered between the shadowy outlines of shelters, shouting in vain; imagining his daughter's muffled entreaties amid the alien strains of gypsy harps and fiddles now summoning the tribe to cavort like spectres around flickering bonfires.

As the final throes of activity in the fair diminished, so did William's hope. He knew the longest night lay ahead and he must now rouse the town to help him. Running along the street he banged on the doors of dwellings shouting, 'Friends, have you seen my daughter Agnes? Please ask your children when they did last set eyes on her.'

Groups of concerned neighbours opened up their shutters and leant out, talking gravely. One or two children were lifted from their straw bales to explain what they knew. The wheelwright's girls had little to offer except that Agnes had left them early – they knew not why.

Helped by the light of two tallow torches carried by Daniel the chandler and his boy, William hastened along the street all the way to the final cottage on the row. The old widow there had shuttered in early, ignoring the shouts of Thomasing children and did not understand William's predicament: 'I have little enough to spare myself than give to beggars at this late hour. Get thee hence,' she shouted through the door.

Walking back up the street towards the church, the almoner's door opened. He remembered Gilbert and Margery well, but did not see Agnes with them.

'I understand your grievous worry William, and you have done all you are able this night. Daniel's torches dwindle and you look exhausted. Return to your kin; eat and drink for strength, and we will rekindle at sunrise. As soon as dawn breaks I will ring the bells and gather the town together to find her; menfolk, women and children all.'

The men parted and William trudged home despondently, the cold biting hard into his fingers and toes as he vainly continued shouting for Agnes; praying she had warmth, even if it was from inside an Egypt tent.

'That Egypt crone did curse me for not buying Agnes the headscarf, I am sure of it,' Joan cried, clenching herself with worry. 'She did point her finger at Agnes.'

'No woman! They do fear a curse must settle back upon them if they jinx one of God's own.

'I know not what else to say, woman!' William roared fretfully, 'I can but search all night. Give me bread and ale.'

Throughout the night William stumbled through dark woods and repeated a forlorn search in the town until he stumbled home, cold and exhausted. At first light, after pottage, he rose again. Joan and the children followed an hour later, even as Venus still shone brightly in the early sky.

The couple waited anxiously at the church gate for the almoner. Joan shivered, huddling Margery in a blanket who was wan and tired from rising so early. A pale lemon horizon heralded the first rays of midwinter sun and Gilbert ran down the street, looking for Squint-eye who, upon his word, left his abode and walked briskly to the church, ignoring the needling pain from his gout-gnarled foot.

'He's coming, Father!' Gilbert alerted, eagerly running back to the gate.

'No sign then?' The almoner asked solemnly.

William shook his head, his tired eyes moist with barely repressed tears.

Squint-eye paced urgently to the steps of the church tower, crunching on the hoar-frosted grass, the iron key cold and heavy in his hand as the family trailed behind awaiting his counsel; watching his breath rise like incense as he unlocked the belfry door. Before entering, he turned to reassure them: 'We will find her; many prayers are offered up and the town will heed the chimes.'

Squint-eye heaved himself up the internal tower staircase three steps at a time. Catching his breath he pulled down hard on the bell rope as the deafening appeal rang out in jarring chimes, piercing the solemn stillness of the winter morning in hopeful clarity.

Presently the first of the neighbours appeared, leaving their warm hearths to support the family; gathering in courteous silence at the lych-gate as the sun rose. More of the town's craftsmen, farm men, labourers and their families followed, some carrying sticks, others scythes and hay forks to help in the search. They talked respectfully in subdued tones, nodding to William and Joan and offering words of support and comfort to the children.

As the townsfolk convened, William walked half way up the outside steps of the tower and addressed them, speaking gravely and politely:

'My good masters and mistresses, thank you for helping. I have searched throughout the night, but with your help we will go over the same ground again in sunlight. We should divide into four gangs and search the demesne, each charting a different point of the weathercock.'

The crowd promptly organised into four sets of around twenty people to walk north, south, east and west. William held up two small metal objects.

'I can lend two hawking whistles. Are there lads here who can shout a good call without one?' He looked around.

'You, Tim; you bellow a loud holler out at field; and the baker's boy – where is he? - Here lad, you be cockerel for the lasses there.'

The boy obliged, pleased to be helping the group with the pretty milking girls. William handed over the whistles to the other two groups.

'Any finding my lass must whistle six times. We will meet here straight after the toll of ten if no one finds her.'

William and Joan joined separate groups; Joan took Gilbert and William carried Margery. Joan headed west toward the manor road and conifer wood while two other groups went east and north. William went south on the fair path to inquire of the Egypts in daylight.

As Joan's group approached the entrance of Sir Anthony's manor two horses pounded onto the lane, steam puffing from the stallions' nostrils. Sir Anthony and Eustace rode up and halted, Sir Anthony's horse splatted steaming manure onto the lane.

'Maisie has told us of your difficulty. Which of you has lost the maiden? Have you found her?' Sir Anthony enquired.

'Joan, Sir,' she curtsied, 'Wife of ploughman William. It is our Agnes, she went missing yesterday afternoon,' she choked tearfully. 'We have split into groups to search for her, good sir.'

'A goodly strategy,' Sir Anthony responded, handing Joan a kerchief, 'But I have news which may give advantage in your quest. My son here will tell you what he saw.'

'Aye, sir. Indeed with my own eyes I saw the young maiden pursued and harried by one of the stouter Egypts from the fair, and had it not been for the threat of my whip, the rat would have taken her.'

Joan's group gasped and looked at each other, some nodding knowingly.

'Where did you see my Agnes last, Master? Which way did she go?' Joan entreated.

'Near to where you stand now, goodwife. Yes, I am quite certain of it.' Eustace twisted around to look back towards the manor woods, restraining his impatient horse with a sudden punch across the cheek. He turned to his father.

'I saw the Egypt knave nearing the manor bridleway in pursuit of the girl as I did leave our lane. I thought I had thwarted him as he did seem to turn and run, for I went once more to the fair and let it be, believing he was dissuaded.'

'Would you know the man who harried her?' Sir Anthony probed.

'Sir. I am quite certain I would remember him for he was warty upon his chin,' Eustace feigned disgust at the recollection.

'Those foreign knaves surely have her,' spouted Giles the postgater, gritting his teeth and wielding his scythe handle with grave intent.

'Yes. I am persuaded you speak truly, sir,' Eustace flattered. 'These devil Egypts bring their curses to our fair town each year and we pay the price. Why do we tolerate their presence? For a few scarves or trinkets?' Eustace looked to his father whose tacit nod inferred approval.

'We can very well do without their gaudy offerings,' Sir Anthony acknowledged.

'Or their thievery,' a woman shouted from behind. 'A basket of eggs was taken from under our eaves but yesterday and they were put by specially for Thomasing gifts.'

'Aye, we would surely starve if they stayed longer than the week,' another chipped in.

Eustace had roused the indignant townspeople into a frenzy of suspicion.

'Would you haste with us to the fair, young master?' Giles the postgate enquired. 'We need to find out who this devil is and where he has taken Agnes, before he carts off to his next encampment.'

'Towards the fair. Follow us. Make haste!' Sir Anthony commanded, 'Which jack among you will alert Sir Thomas Payne, the Justice?'

'I will, sir! He is back from London this last week,' spoke Giles the postgate, 'I opened his house for him.'

'Good man, then do it! Explain to him Sir Anthony requires he readies himself to judge a matter.'

'I will, Sir!' Giles ran back up the street excitedly.

William and his helpers entered the field where one or two local traders were quietly dismantling their structures having carted their unsold wares and trestles back into barns yesterday evening. All but one of the travellers' stables were silent. An old Egypt woman raked over the ashes of a fire and stooped to add kindle to boil up a steaming broth; its unfamiliar spices pungent to William's nostrils. As they approached the lodgings a sturdy mastiff heaved on its chain and barked aggressively. The old woman looked at the approaching crowd fearfully.

'Hear me woman. Where is your patriarch?' William's voice was hoarse with emotion as he wavered between courteous petition and accusatory threat. 'Rouse your families and make haste to leave your beds. I have lost a daughter and we must search your tents.'

The old woman began wailing and shaking her head as other Egypts stumbled nervously up from their fir-branch beds into the bright sunlight.

The clamour of hooves and the arrival of Sir Anthony and Master Eustace coincided with rising commotion and confusion among the travellers. An old greybeard Egypt shuffled out towards William and the bystanders to speak.

'Sastipe. Sar sijan? Quel est ton souci?' the old man spoke, bowing politely.

'I don't know what you say old man,' William exclaimed.

'Aye, they speak English clear enough when the dogs want to play us at dice or read the palm,' Eustace interjected.

'Lass? Girl? Where is she?' William interrogated, beckoning one of the wheelwright girls over, holding her by the shoulders and spinning her to face the old man.

'Lass? Girl? Gone,' he shook her, exasperated at the old man's apparent lack of cooperation. William apologised as the wheelwright girl winced at his strong grip.

The old man shook his head.

'You show us you are not hiding my girl. We have a watch on you knaves,' William blustered, looking to his left and right, frustration rising. He whispered into the wheelwright girl's ear.

'I need to show him what I mean and cover you. Please do not fret.' He grabbed a canvas from inside one of the stables and thrust it over the head of the girl, carrying her horizontally at the waist in mock abduction. She screamed at the unexpected lifting while William pointed accusingly at the line of stables.

'Ni razumiv tut, mais nous vous aidons,' the old man responded.

'Girl gone!' William exclaimed, 'Open up.'

'Na! Na! Na!' the old man threw his tattered sandal towards William in furious indignation. Bare-chested to prove their toughness, the same three stout men who guarded yesterday's dice game rushed from their shed to defend the patriarch. The battered Egypt pugilist joined them; his crossed arms showed he was poised for confrontation. Other Egypt men, women and children arose from their shelters and stood in support, holding the barking mastiff forward on his chain in defence of their tribal privacy.

'Jack. Do six whistles to garner the others.' William shouted, 'They need to see they are surpassed in number.'

The baker boy's shrill signal pierced the air as more Egypt women joined in the wailing, protesting at the approaching clamour of tool-wielding locals marching behind Sir Anthony's belligerent looking charger and Eustace's braying mount. The Justice, Sir Thomas Payne followed in the distance, walking with the almoner and leading the other townspeople, some on horseback, who had temporarily relinquished their searches to gather in the field.

Sir Anthony and Master Eustace dismounted and waited behind William's group to greet Sir Thomas who walked sombrely towards them through the now bustling crowd that parted respectfully before him. Sir Thomas bowed to Sir Anthony; though inferior in rank, he recognised Sir Anthony's superiority in ownership of parish land and property.

'I have been briefly informed, Sir about this very serious matter, so let me summarise the position as I see it,' Sir Thomas orated.

'Our parish, in spite of tolerating the passage of these itinerants over our common land has reason to suspect, though not conclusively, but with evidence mounting, that one of its young has been assailed by a member of their tribe. It is William the ploughshare who grieves the vanishing of his daughter, Agnes? Is that right?' The crowd nodded and mumbled affirmatively. 'And is this the good man standing before me?' William greeted Sir Thomas, Sir Anthony and Master Eustace with a bow.

'Yes, I recognise you from the village and saw you yesterday morning from my chamber window turning sods. It is my role to ensure your daughter is found and that any crime is punished in accordance with English Law. In certainty, the sooner we conclude the search for your girl, the sooner we may consider what crime, if any is done. Where have you searched?'

'Aside from these tents here and Sir Anthony's grounds, all the common land, dwellings, ditches and fields hereabout have been searched and my Agnes is not to be found.'

'Hmm,' Sir Thomas nodded, turning to the almoner. 'We are wasting time. How stands the hour?'

'It is nigh on nine,' Squint-eye responded.

'Then with your permission, Sir Anthony, it is pressing we search your grounds before we are constrained to search the sheds here,'

Sir Thomas turned toward the crowd, recognising the danger of a violent confrontation.

'Prithee, keep thy good patience and stay thy tools and swords until we can conclude this matter.'

Sir Anthony mounted his horse and stood up in the stirrups, pointing his whip. 'You Giles hasten with ten men and make a search in my grounds. Be fast and thorough. We have no desire to rend their tents, but if we mark the manor as searched, these Egypts must then be veiling honest enquiry.'

Eustace smirked vengefully, 'Yes Father, they have forgotten we turn a blind eye to their vagabonding and more, for charity's sake, and as many here we have heard speak in toad's tongue - Sir Thomas may yet confiscate their property and share it with our Queen and whomsoever else he warrants.'

For an hour the stand-off continued. The Egypt women hurriedly boiled pottage for their hungry tribe, some suckling babies as they did so or surreptitiously packed their pelts, pans and belongings, knowing that whatever transpired, they would be forced mercilessly back on the road.

Suddenly the whole crowd turned their eyes toward the field entrance. Three men sprinted towards them on the frozen rutted ground. William read the urgency on their faces and hastened to meet them.

'Hold off William they are nearly here,' the almoner put out his arm, 'We all need to hear their message.'

'Sir, sirs!' The out of breath young man turned to William, took off his cap and clutched it to his chest.

'The girl...Agnes, your daughter sir. She is..' his voice quavered, 'She is found. She lies dead.'

'Where? Take me man!' William beseeched, an agony of tears welling up.

'The tumbled well, up by the manor calsey; the one by the old kiln. It looks like she has been dragged there and assailed. Two lads roped her out. George the coal lugger carries her.

He says we would not have seen her if rain had filled the beck.'

William pushed urgently past and through the crowd.

'No sir, 'tis not a sight…' the lad vainly shouted, William's hopeless eyes fixed on the manor road as he bounded down the slight field gradient like a young ox, as others followed behind.

'Whoa! Stand your ground men,' Sir Thomas ordered. 'Let him be, he needs no eyes to behold his grief.'

William raced down the main street, but suddenly collapsed on his knees as men rounded the corner from the manor bridleway carrying the stiff, lifeless body of his daughter. Agnes's hair was wet and matted and her bonnet bloody while William gazed in horror at her sweet face now taut with rigor mortis along with her coiled limbs set in the position of her death.

There was silence in the crowd; the Egypts and the townspeople strained to see across the mid-distance at the convulsing grief of the big man just visible through the fence as he raised himself up and stood clutching his daughter to his chest, falling once again to his knees as the rescuers stood respectfully by.

'I told thee, the well is right near where I first saw the knave!' Eustace declared, breaking the reverential silence of the crowd.

'Show us the beast. Is he here?' Sir Anthony blurted through his grey beard, his face purple with indignation.

'Yes, I see that vagabond. He stands with those other brown curs,' Eustace pointed and the crowd turned towards the three Egypt protectors who immediately recognised their treacherous accuser.

'Lo! His cheek doth sport a wound where the poor maiden resisted her despoiling,' Eustace spouted while an Egypt mother wailed and pulled at her hair in mourning as the crowd moved vengefully toward the youngest of her sons.

'Na! Ce n'est pas lui, il n'a pas fait de mal,' she protested.

'You men, grab him and bring him forward,' Sir Anthony commanded. The strong men of the village hurled themselves into the Egypt vanguard like bulls, wrestling the three men to the ground, separating the young gypsy from the grip of his older brothers, a dagger held to his necks as their hapless siblings were overwhelmed and he was dragged in front of Sir Thomas. He dropped down and clenched his hands together, imploring mercy from the magistrate.

'You showed no mercy to one of our lasses and you expect it from us?' Eustace snarled.

'You are certain this is the man,' Sir Thomas lifted the chin of the Egypt up to Master Eustace?'

'Aye, this is the knave. I remember his ungodly countenance like a gargoyle on the parapet.'

'And you are sure there are none others alike him?'

'I am sure, his blunt stature and warts were notable.'

Sir Thomas shouted loudly above the heads of the crowd, 'Are there any other witnesses who can pledge?'

No hands were raised.

'English law doth state that 'From the mouths of two or three witnesses a thing is established', but of today, there is only one. Are there no others?' Sir Thomas looked around expectantly.

'Perchance when memories are searched other good men will present themselves and recall yesterday's events more clearly,' he turned towards Sir Anthony and Master Eustace.

'Today however,' he continued, 'I vouch that young Master Eustace's testimony is as good as two men since I discern he follows in the noble steps of his father.'

'My word is my bond,' Eustace bowed to Sir Thomas who nodded back courteously, before turning again to the crowd.

'If my honourable neighbour declares he saw the villain, then with certainty he speaks the truth and the offender must pay the price with flogging and if convicted, with his life. It is clear from the bloody welt on the knave's face that he did meet some resistance from the poor mite. Since he refuses to lodge a plea in English, we can do naught but whip this fiend today. Such wickedness must be swiftly judged as a warning to others in his vagabond tribe. I am obliged to bind him over until he can be carted to the quarter session in Leicester to try him for murder.

'To the whipping post.'

The Egypts protested the taking of their youngest, but with their strongest men subjugated, the remaining tribe could do no more than shout, their women wailing and tearing at their clothes begging for mercy. An old gypsy widow, the grandmother of the accused, fell down on her knees in hopeless entreaty in front of Sir Anthony's horse.

'Move yourself or be trampled.' Sir Anthony raised his whip and brought it down upon her scarfed head. She screamed and fell out of the way as the baying crowd dragged her already beaten grandson down the field. The Egypt patriarch hobbled with his stick, in between Sir Anthony and Master Eustace's horses, pawing at their boots in weak petition.

'Unhand my stirrup you wretch and warn your crones who do throw their curses at us that this parish will be minded to try them for witchcraft if they do not shut up their screeching,' Sir Anthony bellowed as he heeled his stallion forward nudging the old man into the thawing mud.

Master Eustace gloated as he rode proud as a knight alongside his father; scarcely disguising his duplicitous smirk. The vengeful crowd was preoccupied and no one saw through his vile trickery. None but one.

Standing some distance from the baying crowd stood an old Egypt hag in hooded robe, her wrinkled features indistinct save for the green intensity of her eyes that delivered a piercing glower into the pit of Eustace's soul like a gouging emerald shard. Motionless as a shadowy wraith on an old tapestry, her unblinking scowl prevailed so that his very essence seemed clasped by it, illuminating his dreadful secret. The clamour around him grew strangely muffled and a mournful whistling in his ears lifted him momentarily from reality as her vulpine eyes tracked him like a deer on the fringe of a herd.

Alarmed and pale, a deathly shudder finally shook him from the grip of her terrible gaze and he heeled his horse quickly into the protective throng of villagers.

He dared to look back but the hag had gone.

The crowd marched the Egypt boy to the town gibbet that doubled up as a whipping post and chained him there as the villagers waited for the birch rod to be collected from Sir Thomas's lock up. Giles the Postgate handed it sternly to Zebulun the blacksmith; the image of Agnes's stiff body still fresh in the mind of the locals as the young Egypt's shirt was yanked fiercely over his head while his tribe gathered around weeping and pleading in foreign dialects.

'Thirty birch lashes for the knave,' Sir Thomas decreed.

Collapsed and agonised, the young victim was unchained and dumped shivering into a low cart.

'Take him to the lock up and set a guard. I need six sturdy men to share daily and nightly rotations to guard the felon. They will receive a stipend to oversee his captivity until the session.'

Given the winter slowdown in the fields, there was no shortage of raised hands for the work. The six chosen men walked alongside the bloodied cart as it rattled down the street to Sir Thomas's yard and the dismal lock up.

'Low rations, one Egypt wench to visit for one hour to bind his wounds,' Sir Thomas instructed.

As the morning sun dipped below the rooftops, the villagers trudged homeward; as did the mournful procession of travellers who were warned to leave by tomorrow daybreak.

William and Joan lay Agnes's stiff cold body on straw, barely able to look at her ashen grazed cheeks as they tenderly removed the bonnet from her bloodied head and covered her with a rough wool sheet. Joan lit two tapers and placed one at her head and the other at her feet for the night watch. By daybreak her frail body would be relaxed and the women of the village could help wash her and bind her in a winding cloth, tying it around her feet and placing a small wooden cross on her chest before her burial.

Gilbert and Margery lay back to back sleepily on the hay bed in a confusion of silent grief, pained by their mother's wretched sobbing that intermittently convulsed her. Gilbert squinted through tearful eyes at his father mutely hunched upon his low stool in the fire nook, mindlessly raking the dying embers with a twig, his soul numbed by the death of his beloved daughter.

A year passed and St Thomas Eve fell drearily upon the cottage. The young Egypt had met his death in Leicester by hanging; the crime of vagabonding being used to justify the sentence as no witness other than Master Eustace could testify against him, for which William and Joan were somewhat dissatisfied.

Margery and Gilbert shivered by the shuttered window in the light of a single taper, occasionally peeping into the daylight through a small knot in the elm panel, awaiting again the arrival of the dole. After moderate snowfall earlier in the week the cold soil waited on a proper thaw before December ploughing could commence. Accordingly, William sat at home carving a spoon as he attempted to enthuse the family for Thomasing while Joan made cheerful chatter; last year's events still sharp as frost in her mind.

The whinny of Master Eustace's horse suddenly sounded above the loud crackling of sycamore logs on the fire.

'We hardly heard you approaching, Master,' Joan spoke as she bustled the children out. William joined them outside, removing his cap and nodding politely to Master Eustace, who appeared impatient and distracted.

'Come children, your rhyme,' Joan smiled.

'St. Thomas Day,
St. Thomas gray,
The longest night…'

'I have no time for rhymes today. I prepare for guests,' he turned his horse, reaching to the back of his saddle for the sack. 'Take your dole.'

He tossed the knotted sack towards Gilbert who caught it before it hit the hard earth.

'Thank you sir, we are grateful to you for your alms,' William responded, taking the sack from his son.

'In certainty,' he said, swinging the black mare around and trotting promptly away.

'I am surprised that given the day he offered no words of consolation,' Joan commented.

163

'No. Tis not strange. He hardly doth meet my eye this year, knowing I am grieved for Agnes. He would demean his position if he showed pity.'

'Yes, you are right. He did stumble to find words on the day of her burial,' Joan recalled.

As the sack was emptied upon the board, the provisions were gratefully though cheerlessly received as Joan and the children remembered Agnes eating her soup and sharing the raisins and ginger crust last year.

A large tear tracked down Joan's cheek and plopped onto the wooden platter as she carefully positioned the pie on a pewter dish. Gilbert and Margery fidgeted awkwardly, thankful when Father's deep voice relieved the difficult silence.

'We will share the pie together and rejoice that Agnes now eats manna at the Lord's Table,' William spoke as he watched Joan turn away to wipe a flood of tears.

'Now lass, you make the pie salty with your weeping,' William jested, stuffing a hulk of pie into his gob; grabbing his wife by the waist and looking up at her pretty face.

'Come and eat. Agnes would not have her mother crying while she rests in glory.'

'It is nice pie. Agnes would like it,' Margery enthused, 'And it is the same sack as last year.'

'The same sack? No it cannot be. It is not the same sack. Neither Mother Maisie nor any kitchen servants saw Agnes.'

'No Mama, it is the same sack. I remember the swan shape next to an owl face in the weave by the split. And lo, the seam is mended with new stitches.'

'How can this be so? Are you certain?' Joan probed Margery.

Joan inspected the seam.

'Yes, it is the self-same sack.' She turned to William who was silent, his mouth stuffed with pie crust, but he had stopped chewing.

William grabbed the sack and looked at it. He could see the owl and swan shape.

'You are certain this is the sack?'

'Yes Father, tis the same sack,' she started to cry at his unbelief. 'Tis truly the same; I hatched a tale of a sad owl in my mind,' she whimpered.

'Quiet lass, I believe thee. Eat thy pie.'

William arose suddenly and pulled on his heavy rough cloak, his face set like flint toward the town. Joan said nothing and the children were too engrossed in their pie to question his hurried departure.

*   *   *

'Maisie! Open,' William thudded his strong fist on the kitchen quarters' door.

'William! How dost thou?' Maisie heaved the heavy door open and William entered breathless from walking. She wiped her hands down the front of her apron before embracing him.

'How fare ye? All of us are mindful about you and Joan today, of all days,' Maisie's warm hands cupped his forearms affectionately under his cloak.

'You gave us quite a start,' she continued. Ruth thought it was the young master furious at something.' Maisie looked up kindly at his grave face. 'But you are very welcome even though you have brought the cold in on your coat. Take it off and warm by the hearth.

William shook his head, ladled himself a draught of ale and wiped his beard before holding out the limp hessian sack expectantly. Maisie looked at it, puzzled.

'What is it?' She took it from him. 'You need not have brought this to us so quickly, but thank you.'

'This sack. Did you stitch this?' William asked gruffly.

'No. Let me look, is it split? Ruth mended this one last spring, did you not Ruth?'

Maisie's young kitchen maid abruptly left her cabbage chopping, concerned at any criticism of her needlework.

'Yes, 'twas in the master's saddlebag with riding linen and so forth,' she said curtly, inspecting every inch of it.

165

'Master Eustace?' William relaxed, his instinct had not floundered.

'Yes sir. It is a good sack and I fixed it. And lo, the seam has not pulled away. My stitching is good and strong,' Ruth pulled the sack roughly in all directions.

'No, it is fine.' William was relieved his misgivings about his friends had gone undetected, 'I just came to return it and in passing say you both cooked a fine pie and loaf for our dole this year.'

'Oh, you deserve it William,' she said, a little puzzled. 'You and Joan have had a heavy burden to bear these past months,' Maisie touched his arm tenderly. 'You disport with such endurance in spite of your trials. Will you be going to fair today?'

He shook his head, 'No, but Joan and her sister may tarry awhile for the children's sake.'

'No Egypts this year, William. It is a blessing.'

He warmed his hands over the hearth and did not respond. Maisie cut him a thick crust from a white loaf and keeled it around a pan of warm bacon lard.

'For your walk home – finest flour and grease. Hide it under thy cloak until you are on the road.'

'I am grateful Maisie,' he turned and nodded to Ruth, 'thank you too, and may I borrow the sack again until tomorrow as I have remembered Joan's turnips to gather.' Ruth dipped a slight curtsy and handed the sack to William who turned and tramped homeward down the manor house track, 'Don't split my comely seam now!' Ruth joked as she heaved the kitchen door closed.

William did not respond, he was in no mind for bawdy jesting, neither were turnips, the fair nor Egypts on his mind - just a sack - a rough hessian sack; one of hundreds regularly used in village commerce and one of around fifty the manor house used for carrying grain, storing oats or vegetables and for distributing the yearly dole.

He pondered by what chance it was the sack had returned into the master's hand and into their home. It was after all just a common sack, with no mark or brand to determine ownership; nor was it pulled with Agnes's body from the well, for these things had been enquired of. In certainty Ruth believed Master Eustace had it in his possession. Perhaps it slipped from Agnes's girdle *en route* to the manor kitchens and someone simply placed it unthinking into the granary where it ended up much later in the master's saddlebag.

The more he thought about it, the greater his confusion.

In the cottage he remained hunched in his cloak, sitting in the fire nook; rubbing his bearded mouth pensively with a closed fist.

'Are you...' Joan began.

'Quiet! I am thinking woman.'

Joan saw the deep creases in her husband's care worn brow. He suddenly looked old. She ladled him a bowl of steaming pottage.

'Pour it back into pot, I have eaten.'

'But you must...'

William stood up. Joan perceived his dark brow set toward some dreadful end.

'Where William?' she implored. 'We cannot bring her back.'

'There are things that must be settled whate'er the penalty.'

He grabbed his axe and felt by his leggings for his dagger.

'Please sir, think of our precarious situation before you go.'

The colour drained from Joan's face. She knew a precipice once jumped could not be repented from. She hastened to bar his exit, grabbing his hem, her hip nudging the trestle and spilling the soup upon the board as Margery and Gilbert sat perplexed.

'I have weighed the matter. Unhand me!' he commanded as a chill draught and flurry of flakes gusted in as he slammed the door decisively.

'Does father leave early for the fair without us Mama?' Margery asked.

'I will go with him.' Gilbert reached for his coat.

'So will I Gilbert. Wait!'

'Sit back at board!' Joan thundered and the children jumped. They rarely heard their mother raise her voice. Margery's chin quivered. Joan pitied her.

'No one said you could get down from the board. Your father has gone to settle a matter, he will return anon.'

A fretful wind whistled through the closed shutter like a dirge.

Joan mopped the spilt soup and turned away, bending to rinse the rag in the corner pail, wringing it repeatedly; hardly concealing her stifled sobs as she watched ripples from her large tears unsettle the joyless water, distorting her features into a wretched image of her sweet Agnes freezing in the dim pool of the old well.

Margery padded over to pat her mother's bonnet sympathetically.

'It will be a fine day Mama. Father will return anon with wood and we will go to the fair.'

Joan buried her head in Margery's bonnet; the sympathy of her five year old prompting a juddering release of grief like a flooding beck, her wind-chapped cheeks sodden with tears. Gilbert rose up self-consciously from his stool and awkwardly rubbed his mother's shoulder as she slumped sobbing onto the cold flagstone floor.

*　　　　　　　　　　*　　　　　　　　　　*

The fair was strikingly different from last St Thomas Day. Apart from an inter-village wrestling bout and archery competition, it was just like any busy market day. The foreigners had departed along with their music, dancing girls, boxing and dice. In response to Queen Mary passing the Egyptians Act most of the travellers had fled to Scotland or dispersed onto farms and into towns, pledging integration into society to avoid arrest, though enforcement was haphazard and many towns still tolerated the itinerants, but from now on remaining a wilful gypsy or even being seen in their company could be punishable by hanging.

Given the exotic touch and amusing discord the travellers brought, many locals found today's event bland, not least Eustace. Lacklustre though it was, he and his acquaintances would still enjoy the riotous merriment of his father's feasting tent. Today he played *Pope Joan* and *Goose* with his friends, accruing a comely three pounds and four shillings, a little more than the dice loss of the previous year, so as he trotted home to the manor at sundown he was in good spirits and as his father was hosting a night of galliards and dancing he was looking forward to removing his wine soaked breeches, putting on a fresh silk shirt and doublet, and new striped hose to impress his visiting second cousins and their friends.

He was light-headed with good claret, but not so much that he couldn't dance and stay the course of the evening's celebrations. The quarter mile up the bridle path to the house was deserted, but through the tree trunks he could just discern the glowing braziers burning their welcome at the manor gates. The guests would arrive between 8 and 9, so he had abundant time to dress, but now he had to piss.

His urine thawed yellow lines in the hard rime as he swayed unsteadily. An eerie bird noise ululated somewhere near; he hadn't heard a bird like that before. A raven or wintering diver bird perhaps. He shivered and hastily mounted his horse. The bridle path wound to the right by the old well wall. The memory was still vivid. *It was her own fault for refusing her master and striking me*, he mused.

The mare faltered. A large man stood in the midst of the bridleway facing him. Eustace could not mask his shock.

'William the ploughman? It is you. How dost thou?' he said uneasily. 'You startled my horse.'

William said nothing, but slowly raised an outstretched arm holding the limp sack.

Eustace lifted his shoulder in a half shrug, averting William's probing glare. Eustace looked at the sack.

'What is this? You wish for me to have a bag? Oh, it is a sack. You keep it. I have no need for it.'

William remained silent and unmoved.

'Wherefore dost thou trouble me with such frippery? Are you drunk man?' Eustace stammered nervously.

'Why dost thou face grow pale? Tis but a sack,' William affirmed sarcastically.

169

'Aye, tis but a sack.'

'Yet this self-same sack was of some import to thee last St Thomas Eve, so much so that you didst demand we return it prompt and not to forget.'

'Aye, so if I did?'

'Hast thy father's goods become of no consequence of the sudden?'

Eustace laughed derisively. 'You set an accusation against me, your lord and master, and dare talk to me of consequence? Get thee hence or feel my whip. My father will hear of your perfidy.'

'You took the sack from Agnes did you not? Say her name.'

Eustace raised his right arm and urged his big stallion forward forcing William to jump to the side. Immediately he swung the horse into a forehand turn, bringing its hindquarters around to slam William fiercely against a tree trunk. William's face contorted in pain as he buckled to the ground gripping his ribs, unable to breathe. The big horse, misunderstanding the sudden manoeuvre panicked and reared, tipping Eustace from the saddle.

Eustace quickly pulled himself up, watching his horse canter into the woods. Wheeling around and puffing angrily he pulled out his bollock dagger, his fist tight around the shaft. He plunged his portly knees down heavily onto William's back whose arms were helplessly pinned underneath his own torso. William let out a desperate wheeze as Eustace sat triumphant, gripping William's fringe in his left hand and wielding the knife blade just above the big man's Adam's apple in his right; cold iron slicing the flesh through William's black beard as the youth's surprising bulk squeezed down mercilessly upon him.

Eustace drew his lower lip between his teeth, relishing his power over the hefty though constrained ploughman.

'What shall we do with an insubordinate?' he snarled, 'One who accuses me of killing his young trull?

'I remember your lass well. She was defiant. Are the rest of your brood like her?'

William squirmed and tried to kick his legs to roll over, the suffocation intolerable.

'I could kill you now or let my good friend, the Justice, do his worst. While you sit in gaol counting the hours to the noose, you can remember what a fine family you have as I turf them like vagabonds out of the parish, but perhaps for charity's sake I will separate the youngling out for manor service. She has comely features like her sister,' he snickered.

Eustace teased the knife in deeper and a strange bird trilled close by. William felt warm blood drip down his neck as his strength ebbed away and despair engulfed him like November fog. Momentarily, a strange detachment visited him like a presence and he saw a vision in his mind's eye; it was Agnes and she was speaking to him, softly, yet stridently echoing the rhyme of the fisherman from last year's play:

When all seems dark and death is certain
Help comes quick from heaven's curtain
Take the knee and shout out boldly
The Lord delivers who seek Him holy

Sensing death was imminent though strangely pacified by the mystical vision, William prayed for his family's protection as he focused on blissful eternity while Eustace's worldly taunts faded to an indistinct, tortuous rambling.

'I wonder if wandering in the cold will help your goodwife rethink her husband's rebel…'

At once, a loud crack of twigs precipitated a sudden guttural *whoop!* Eustace's mocking words ceased abruptly, his throat clacking in a desperate fight for breath as he was jerked backward against a rough oak by powerful and unknown executioners to his left and right.

William, in a blur of semi-consciousness craned his bloodied neck up from the leafy bridleway. The dense underbrush seemed suddenly alive as it disgorged two stout men concealed in mantles of evergreen vegetation with laurel crowns on their heads and ivy circlets on their arms, their tanned cheeks and bare hands the only indicators of their foreign lineage. Panting, he watched the muted struggle unfold in unflustered efficiency that barely ruffled the serenity of the winter wood.

171

Gargoyle-like, Eustace's fat lips spewed out a swollen tongue as pressure from the stiff branch across his gullet clamped his neck tighter against the rigid tree trunk. Wide-eyed, he could only gawp at the Egypt crone standing in cloaked judgement before him; passing sentence upon the false witness responsible for the execution of her precious son.

'Le salaire du péché est la mort,' she whispered as he vainly squirmed to free himself, his crimson face jutting grotesquely forward from the unyielding garrotte.

William watched in horrified satisfaction as his enemy flailed wildly for air and his dagger dropped to the ground. The old crone's two remaining sons hefted the stiff branch in one final surge against the tree trunk as Eustace fouled his breeches in a fittingly undignified end before his neck broke and his thrashing corpulence succumbed to the chill gloom of death; his final vision the eerie, dispassionate glare of emerald eyes veiled under a dark and ghastly hood.

Somewhere in the branches above, a raven gave a long, low caw as though signalling to Hades that an awful cadaverous supper was served at the down-casting of one more black soul into perdition.

The men wiped Eustace's dagger and returned it to its sheath then dragged his onerous corpse, following the stallion hoof prints into the depths of the wood, laying the young noble's bulk beneath a low branched sycamore where it would be deemed he had tragically broken his neck through the bolting of his wayward stallion – a steed who could no longer tolerate being struck in the head by a chubby, hateful fist.

William groaned and sat up while the hooded gypsy knelt down and pressed the folded dole sack tenderly against his throat to staunch the bleeding. They looked upon each other with words unspoken.

Though cultures and lands apart, the English ploughman and the old Egypt hawker recognised the sentiment that passed between them; a universal appreciation that justice, even if delayed would eventually be served and rottenness removed from the land.

///blows.onions.quarrel
"ANGRY"

The first 'incident' was locally noteworthy, though in the scheme of things, away from the quiet and prim community of Middle Bogwell, rather unremarkable.

While road rage was not unheard of in the area given the slow tractor traffic during the spring and harvest and the un-signposted humpback-bridge-bottleneck between Bogwell Farm Road and Hutherton, where it was contestable who had right of way, the 'incident' was unusually aggressive. The altercation involved a forty-something sales director-type in his BMW who had smashed up old Mr Jenkins' Ford Escort after a standoff on the brow of the said bridge.

Mr Jenkins, following local road etiquette had proceeded first, but the Beamer driver, clearly an outsider, believed he had right of way. Mr Jenkins tried to reverse, but accidentally put the car in first gear so his car almost shunted the Beamer. This apparent intransigence infuriated the other driver who pushed poor Mr Jenkins back down onto a verge and into a ditch. The man then got out of his car, reached into his boot and got to work on Mr Jenkins' car door panels and windscreen with a 9-iron.

Police were called, but poor Mr Jenkins was so traumatised he forgot to take the registration and although enquiries were made, without dashcam footage or eyewitnesses the incident was put to bed.

It was the next incident, coming only three days later, in late January that stunned the community; and not so much the episode in itself, but the perpetrators of it that was shocking.

Irene and Isadora, eighty year old twin spinsters from Barntock Edge viciously attacked members of the local community during a red squirrel conservation supper talk at Hutherton Village Hall. They had apparently bickered about the seating arrangement for the PowerPoint with Mrs Coxwain from the Village Hall Committee when the latter had muttered something under her breath. The laptop and the projector were hurled onto the parquet floor and the ceiling-mounted projection screen ripped from its fixture. Mrs

Coxwain's hair had also been pulled with such force that a part of her scalp had been torn off and Mr Coxwain had sustained a black eye and groin injury in defence of his wife.

The local rag, The Littleton Courier sent their junior hack out to interview the witnesses who were 'shocked and appalled' at the 'unpleasant episode' citing the actions of Irene and Isadora as 'utterly unbelievable' and 'out of character'.

In rapid succession more disturbances made the Courier's column centimetres; events quite alien to the laid back friendliness and affable charm Middle Bogwell and Hutherton villages had historically demonstrated.

There was a fist fight in the forecourt of the local Spar Garage instigated by a senior barrister; while in Sedgeley two miles north of Hutherton, a farmer had shot both his neighbour's Red Setters after finding dog poo on his lawn; meanwhile, back in Barntock Edge a greenhouse was deliberately rammed by a florist who could not get a signature for her bouquet delivery and a Hutherton Estate Agent threw scalding coffee in the face of a customer who was late returning keys.

The long twelve weeks from late winter to late spring overwhelmed the tiny two person police office in Hutherton. Deluged under paperwork, PC Garven and PC Lyle requested urgent assistance and resource reallocation from the twelve person team in Littleton town to help them process an additional eight unusually malicious disturbances occurring within a slack six mile radius of Hutherton village centre, the most serious of which occurred in mid-April.

A young tourist was shunted in front of a pod of cyclists by a middle aged lady who complained she was taking up too much of the pavement and had accidentally tripped into her. The young woman was hospitalised, but without conclusive evidence no further action could be taken.

'Surely this is an aberration, an unfortunate series of events,' Inspector Catherine Rusby reckoned. 'They do happen. The Force cannot afford to transfer resources; you will just have to knuckle down and get on with it like we do in the town centre every Friday and Saturday night,' she decreed unsympathetically to her hapless Hutherton colleagues.

And that was it. Inspector Rusby appeared to be right. PC Garven and Lyle's backlog was dealt with by early May and everything returned to normal for months; indeed the summer was unusually peaceable and apart from a hay bale falling on a car and a drink driving incident, the two constables had very little to report until late October during the first cool week of autumn.

Headmistress of Hutherton District High School, Ms Rula Spungeon had taken early lunch in the village and returned to school in the afternoon to supervise the Under 15s inter-school Choral Society performance. It was a scandal.

The Littleton Courier reported the fifty-five year old teacher had sullied an exemplary thirty year track record by clearing out the packed assembly hall with 'choice language' after the lighting rig failed to work during the final performance. She had refused to be placated by the audience who insisted it was a minor inconvenience irrelevant to the competition outcome; however, deeming the failure a reflection of her management Ms Spungeon furiously denounced the audience as 'unprofessional c's' telling them to 'go home' in so many f's. The finale of her foul-mouthed tirade saw the refreshments table tipped towards the stunned onlookers while she hurled a pile of saucers against the wall; an action that seemed to mitigate her fury, as witnesses noted she fell to the floor smiling with malevolent satisfaction.

Apologies were made and medical excuses ranged from stress, anxiety, tiredness; a one-time epileptic fit brought on by exhaustion; as well as the suggestion of a rare undiagnosed form of Tourette syndrome; however, The Education Authority had to be seen to exercise good judgement and Ms Spungeon was persuaded to take early retirement.

The paperwork backlog piled high again in Hutherton Police Station.

The fortnight leading to Christmas recorded a jarring spate of domestic incidents among the middle class residential neighbourhoods of Bogwell and Hutherton. It was hearsay at first,

175

then more and more villagers began reporting loud and implacable arguments between previously upstanding members of their local community. Strangely the social housing quarter recorded no such incidents aside from a quickly resolved drunk and disorderly logged on Boxing Day; indeed this year, the less well-off residents of the district appeared to be distinctly better behaved than their unruly and well-to-do senior peers.

Retired doctors Tony and Liz Graham had come to blows over a Christmas card list; Jackie and Ian Trevelyan, B&B owners physically ousted guests for complaining about hair in the shower and separated in late spring; while Birta and Gunnar Magnusson, Icelandic architects in their seventies, dissolved a fifty year marriage after a vicious fight about locating a bird box.

Littleton's 'Relate' relationship-support mediation team noted the influx of divorce applications from the Hutherton and Bogwell district as 'atypical' given the socio-economic factors and age range of the applicants. A scatter chart showed an unusually high concentration throughout the Bogwell and Hutherton area, possibly attributable to a kind of psychological contagion or copycat effect among peers, perhaps triggered by the pressures of the previous year's pandemic lockdown accentuating marital dissatisfaction.

The Littleton Law Courts too noticed a steep rise in separation filings during the winter and spring and although unusual the influx was disregarded, though family members found it odd that couples who had previously been devoted were experiencing such dramatically divisive arguments. Septuagenarians and even octogenarians were surprising their mature children with sudden announcements of separation citing incompatibility of temperament.

But by mid-May everything was calm again and PCs Lyle and Garven were back to enjoying their sandwiches in the layby overlooking the cornfields, ostensibly monitoring speeding motorists, but really bird-spotting yellowhammers and finches; the pressure of the previous six months abating as the barley gradually ripened and swallows darted low over the whitening ears. Late summer was unusually warm and pleasant and continued into late-

October when a sudden cold snap with gales and early frosts reminded the townsfolk winter was looming.

In early November the coach driver for Roman Heritage Tours' trip to Bath diverted into Hutherton Village to check the vehicle's oil light. The unscheduled stop gave the sixty or so passengers a ninety minute slot to enjoy early Christmas shopping in the village gift shops as well as tour the local church and enjoy the fayre at Valerie's Tea Shoppe.

The coach departed at 1pm; however, another unscheduled event occurred on the A46 by Dyrham Park when an argument over Brexit involving at least ten of the passengers fomented into a physical ruckus that exploded into the aisle. The driver pulled over as fighting spilled out onto the pavement and passengers phoned the police. Statements were taken and the ten shamefaced seventy-somethings made Littleton Courier's front-page under the banner: *OAP Bus Brawl*, while national coverage appeared in The Sun with the headline: *Roman Holiday Goes Gladiator*.

'Have you seen this?' Inspector Catherine Rusby tossed the paper to Sergeant Griffiths, smiling. 'It must be the first time Hutherton has made national news. It says, 'Val Downing café proprietor in Hutherton, Gloucestershire, said the visitors had been very polite and had enjoyed their lunch with no sign of an impending fracas'.'

'On the map at last,' Sergeant Griffiths chuckled. 'We should try it.'

'Try what, David?' Catherine quizzed.

'The café. Valerie's Tea Shoppe?'

'Oh right, the Hutherton café. It's a bit twee—very granny-ish—cheese scones, cakes and soups; little triangle sarnies of egg and cress or cucumber on a cake stand sort of thing; not your foot long meatball marinara mega-sub lunch. It's quite pricey too so keeps out the local riff-raff. You're looking at £12 for a sarnie and a cup of tea, or twenty quid if you have a cake.'

'Yeah, that is a bit pricey, but we'll treat ourselves next time we're passing. I'm sick of Ginsters pasties and Costa from the garage.'

'Agreed.'

'Though I'm not sick of McDonald's Happy Meals. The perfect size for adult snacking and you get a toy for the kids. Amazing value for money.'

'Quite, David, I don't think your stomach will thank you though, especially since you always order two.'

By February the over-60s divorce rate had stabilised in Middle Bogwell and Hutherton. It appeared the low-hanging fruit of relationships ripe for termination had fizzled out, though further road rage incidents and disturbances among neighbours continued to keep PCs Garven and Lyle immersed in paperwork until early summer when calm once again returned to the district.

Aptly, though unrelated to PC Lyle and Garven's continuing demands for more support, Littleton police installed a new technology hub in the station to provide an updated data analytics dashboard. Inspector Rusby called a meeting to enthuse her colleagues about the new system.

'Data are critical in helping the Littleton team respond to daily challenges,' Catherine explained, 'helping fairly redistribute work and enable Littleton, Bogwell and Hutherton become part of a multi-agency network sharing data for analysis with partner organisations, such as fire and social services, hospitals, and neighbouring police forces to deliver more positive outcomes for the community.'

The Littleton Courier scrutinised Inspector Rusby's press release that extolled the merits of the regional force's multi-thousand pound investment. Catherine was used to awkward questions from the local press about expenditure when officers on the beat were at their lowest level in years in spite of rising anti-social behaviour and knife crime. To stifle criticism, she invited a journalist or two for a working lunch and gave a practical demonstration of the software. After pork pies, crisps and M&S sandwiches, Kyle Askew from The Courier was shown how the team loaded data and analysed datatypes; how they looked for interactions; built models and created predictions based on the evaluation dataset. It was fascinating.

Kyle asked about postcode scatter plotting using historical data for burglaries. As anticipated the plotting showed a clear and rising correlation between the high crime rates near the employment centres where older properties were situated. Entering statistics for violent crime the big surprise was how common assault and road rage incidents showed an unusually high concentration around Middle Bogwell and Hutherton over a three year period.

'I may have input something incorrectly,' Catherine noted, squinting, puzzled at the measles rash of dots on the display. 'I'll leave it to my more techy colleagues to dispute the data on that,' she laughed apologetically as Kyle Askew made notes.

'I know my colleagues in Hutherton were complaining about a rise in paperwork and this does bear that out,' Catherine continued, capitalising on the apparent error, 'but that's why this investment is so useful, since with fewer Bobbies on the beat, it helps us allocate resources where they are needed most,' she crowed, content with her snappy retort.

Val from Hutherton tearooms was busy. She had been helping her daughter set up a similar tearoom to her own in Old Hambury village, a few miles to the north of Littleton, though still within Littleton Constabulary's remit.

Emma, Val's daughter had helped her mother in the Hutherton café for three years during holidays from university. Capitalising on a small inheritance from her deceased mother, Val encouraged Emma to take out a lease on an old schoolroom at the end of the high street near the very busy hikers' footpath. Emma called the new café 'Old Schoolroom Tea Shoppe and Deli' and after an extensive kitchen refit was confident about repeating the success of her mother's tearoom fifteen miles to the south. The tea shop soon became a lively hub for more affluent locals and coach tours passing through, but with only half the tables and seating compared to her mother's, Emma quickly reached capacity and so she adapted a section to provide lunchtime deli sandwich and soup takeaways during the busier months to capture trade from ramblers and cyclists exploring The Cotswold Way.

In October, the Littleton team noted a sudden rise in call outs to Old Hambury and its residential district. The data were clear. From late autumn, through winter and into mid-spring three Actual Bodily Harm assaults and an unprecedented number of domestic dispute callouts were logged, the latter notable for their proclivity among affluent retired residents.

On Guy Fawkes Night afternoon, a fist fight between a group of young German hikers and Chinese students took place in a campsite near Broadway. It was reported on the local television news that the campsite shop was ransacked and three of the Chinese students were hospitalised. The Old Hambury Tearoom and Deli served the German and Chinese tourists just two hours prior and Emma Downing was interviewed by Littleton police trying to understand the motive.

'They were all perfect guests and very well mannered,' Emma told the constable. 'There was no hostility I was aware of. Just nice friendly boys and girls.'

'Some football hooligans work solicitor's jobs during the week; it's well established,' the constable affirmed as he took notes and descriptions of the suspects. 'Were they drinking?'

'Not that I'm aware of and we don't have a liquor licence anyway. They just ordered the usual coffees, scones, cake and soup.'

Catherine Rusby, in spite of being in charge of supervising Diversity training could not resist the temptation to stereotype the German visitors at the Littleton debriefing.

'Towels on sunbeds, David,' she mooted to Sergeant Griffiths, peering over her laptop screen. 'Typical German M.O.—The Chinese had taken a spot pre-claimed by the placing of a German rucksack and everything kicked off.

'Annexing of the Sudetenland,' David smirked.

'Sudetenland?'

'1938, Czechoslovakia. A World War 2 trigger?'

'Oh, right, very funny,' Catherine forced a smile. 'Anyway, I can't believe they caused so much damage. The look of fury in their eyes on the camp shop's video camera. They were crazed and absolutely zero evidence of drink or drugs.'

'A drunk and disorderly charge would probably lessen the severity of any sentence they receive,' David surmised, 'I've only seen aggression like that on the terraces.'

Catherine pursed her lips. 'So unusual, yet broadly similar in scope and socio-economic profile to that episode with the Hutherton cyclists reported by Lyle and Garven.'

'Cyclists?' Sergeant Griffiths puzzled.

'That fight with the borstal lads on day release?'

'Ah yes, last March. Those dangerous old geezers who laid into those two lads who strayed into the road.'

'On a community service litter pick. Very similar levels of unwarranted aggression. I guess the country is just turning nasty. I blame Netflix in spite of having an account myself.'

'I think it's more 'county' than country David, which reminds me, the chief inspector wants to discuss our latest stats.'

Catherine Rusby emailed Sergeant Griffiths the next day as a reminder. *David: Can you ensure we put our heads together tomorrow for some explanations regarding the upsurge in the sixties plus and how we can identify areas where the organisation can improve?*

The 3040 violent crimes recorded countywide were 10% higher year on year compared to each previous year in a four year cycle; however, drilling down within postcodes, a rise in domestic disputes involving common assault and violence among many more affluent postcodes remained baffling. While prosperity was an uncertain indicator of likelihood to commit crime, in previous years, violent crime stats clustered towards the inner city and socially deprived areas whereas now both the location, seasonality and uncommon senior age grouping had shifted, causing Catherine's team to doubt clear statistical facts facing them.

Catherine clicked through a selection of colourful PowerPoint slides as the chief inspector gorged loudly on crisps and sandwiches, spluttering the odd query about pi-charts as flecks of his foody spit launched into the crisps.

'So you have determined the overall rise in violent crime has been largely driven by increases in the offence categories. Variables which are most subject to changes in reporting and recording practices. Is that a reasonable exposition of your assessment?' The chief inspector asked.

Even Catherine knew her vague explanation was unsatisfactory and there was something very amiss in her box-ticking overview. 'Yes sir, but we remain vigilant and will continue to look for other factors which may be influencing the results and how we can identify areas for improvement. The rise may of course be pure coincidence given the narrow time period of four years, which, in the scheme of things could skew the outcome.'

The explanation satisfied her distracted boss, now ramming the twelfth triangle of M&S sandwich into his mouth. But neither Catherine nor her colleagues could account for the seniority of the age groups, nor rationalise how previously exemplary citizens were suddenly manifesting violent outbursts towards others or their partners.

'I'm truly bewildered,' she confessed to Sergeant Griffiths afterwards. 'I'm just pleased the violence hasn't directed itself towards the police. In twenty years I've only taken my baton out twice.'

'Could it have something to do with an increase in EMF radiation?' Griffiths suggested.

'No, there are no more cell towers in the vicinity than elsewhere and if it was purely down to EMFs, then the lower socio-economics would be manifesting and they're not and because of their 24/7 operation no seasonal variations would present.'

'Something related to medications then? Are the older generation pill-popping something causing aggression. There's an opioid crisis in America; maybe it's spread here? It must be something like that.'

'Could be. They all queue up for their flu jabs in the autumn and the disturbances in Hutherton, Bogwell and now Old Hambury do cluster around the colder months, but the same clinics serve a much wider area and these areas are unaffected. The German boys were early twenties remember, so not the sort who queue up at a medi-centre with their sleeves up.'

'Seasonal Affective Disorder then—S.A.D.—could be that,' David suggested.

'True, but that afflicts all age groups,' Catherine clicked her pen top repetitively on her top lip, 'and doesn't S.A.D. make you withdraw, not aggressive?'

'Hmm. Might the decline in incidents be people simply being happier and more agreeable in summer?'

'You've been on the force as long as me, David; and summer antisocial behaviour and fisticuffs has up till now been similar to the rest of the year, often more so with the pubs serving snakebites; yet these Hutherton and Bogwell stats show weird seasonal upsurges over a five year period and it's clearly unrelated to boozing. Now we're seeing similar data for Littleton and Old Hambury, so what gives?'

'I still think the whole stats thing may be pure coincidence. The new software is showing us things we'd be blissfully unaware of if we didn't have it.'

'Try telling that to PCs Lyle and Garven. They're convinced it's something alien.

'You being serious?'

'I wouldn't put it past them, especially with that corn circle on local news.'

'They spend too much time in La La Land with their bloody binoculars while us Littleton bods have to deal with the daily indiscipline of the town centre's Great Unwashed,' Sergeant Griffiths scoffed.

'Give them a break, David, birdwatching is their coping mechanism. They have been under more pressure in recent months.

'Haven't we all, but let's see what unfolds in the next few weeks.'

The AI system that linked the multi-agency network contained an algorithm originally designed by the military to flag anomalous data that could indicate nascent hostilities in global hotspots;

indeed military digital ears pricked up when the Littleton Constabulary data went online.

The measles rash scatter patterns in Hutherton, Bogwell and now Old Hambury had been seen before, just prior to revolutions indicating seething civil unrest. It was a barometer for the government to detect the heat signatures of discontent and it was flagged by Sally in the ops team.

Here's something a couple of Intelligence Corps bods might be interested in investigating, Sally recommended in her email, but priorities and resources were internationally focused and the email was disregarded.

Catherine Rusby and David Griffiths however could not ignore their own rising tide of paperwork. Autumn in The Cotswold Way had become angry; very angry and Old Hambury was at the epicentre.

'Let's take a ride out. We'll check to see if that village has some new electronic infrastructure.'

'I thought you said it wasn't phone masts,' David responded.

'I know, but honestly David, I'm at a complete loss especially with yesterday's deliberate ramming of the Hambury school bus. It's a wonder no one was killed. I think we need to re-evaluate with boots-on-the-ground. We'll go plain clothes in an unmarked car.'

'Good idea. I might even buy lunch.'

Catherine and David were relieved to drive into the countryside away from the dirty and depressing Littleton social services' role they often had to perform before the real social services team could be mustered. The crisp October morning in Old Hambury smelled of wood smoke and damp leaves; delightful to nostrils used to the cloying whiff of dirty houses and ashtrays.

'Let's look at the old graves; it's good to remind yourself of your own mortality at times; helps you appreciate stuff,' David laughed. 'We could ask a few locals if they've noticed anything unfamiliar in the last year or so that might be cause or effect.' David nodded toward a man locking the vestibule door. 'That must be the vicar.'

'Good morning, vicar,' David greeted, 'We're admiring your lovely churchyard. How do you keep it so manicured?'

'I'm church warden actually, but hello,' the man smiled, scanning the neat lines of the graves, 'We keep it tidy with a team of volunteers; grass-cutters; flower arrangers; that sort of thing. We're always looking for help if you're offering.'

'No thanks, we're just admiring. Too far out for us,' Catherine laughed. 'I'm Inspector Catherine Rusby, Littleton Police and this is my colleague, Sergeant David Griffiths, we're out of uniform today, but here are our IDs.'

'Ah, is this about the stolen lectern?'

'No, I'm sorry, that's not why we're here, but if you have a crime number just phone the station and they'll give you any update.'

'Oh, so what *are* you here for? Is anything wrong?'

'No, we are just asking locals for their thoughts on crime levels in the village over recent months and whether or not they have noticed anything unusual.'

'It's certainly a talking point and we've had a couple of recent sermons relating to forgiveness and living peaceably with all men,' the warden replied, 'but I honestly don't know. In the old days they'd have called it witchcraft; blaming curses and the like and probably would have organised a purge of the old women,' he joked.

'We're thankfully a bit more civilised today, but I know what you mean,' Catherine responded, 'These incidents are quite out of character for the area. Has anything new happened recently? New people to the village? New infrastructure like phone masts or lamp posts?'

'Nothing new happens in Hambury, that's why it's called *Old* Hambury,' the warden quipped, 'and I have no clue about lampposts, but don't think so. That's your territory anyway surely,' he paused and scanned the tops of the trees looking for hidden phone masts.

'That's true, we haven't looked into Planning records yet, but it's on our list,' Catherine responded sheepishly.

'Nope, nothing stands out…' the warden turned to leave, briefly glancing back, 'Oh, the café is newish though, The Old Schoolroom; nice tearoom,' he pointed, 'on the corner, two hundred yards. You should go there for lunch and ask.'

'Great idea. Thanks.'

'My shout, David,' Catherine volunteered. 'You can get the next one,'

The bell above the tearoom door jangled pleasantly as a waft of warm savouries, fresh bread, cakes and ground coffee gratified their nostrils. Muted chatter merged with the sounds of Smooth Radio from speakers mounted on high rafters of the Victorian classroom.

'Nearly full at 11.40, must be good,' she nodded to David, 'and menus on tables, so guess it's table service. Top left corner if you like?'

'What is the soup of the day?' David asked the young proprietor, Emma Downing.

'Winter Warmer. It's tomato, vegetable and lentil with a ham stock base,' Emma explained, 'blended until silky smooth with a swirl of cream; my mum calls it her *Scarlet Taste Experience*, but there's a vegan option of butternut squash.'

'Oh, no thanks; give me the *Red Taste Experience* please,' Catherine said resolutely. 'And I'll have the ham and egg pie and an apple and cinnamon slice too with a cappuccino.'

'Yep, sounds good. Same for me, but a pot of tea rather than coffee, thanks,' David confirmed.

'Be right up.'

'That soup really is delicious—piquant— I don't think I've had a tastier soup. Fancy a second helping?' Catherine dabbed her tomato stained lips with the napkin.

'You're right, that was bloody gorgeous. Glad I didn't opt for butternut squash.'

'Can we get two more bowls please?' David asked Emma as she passed.

'Yup.'

'Where to next, Catherine? We could drive around to check if there's anything conspicuous; masts or the like?'

'Could do,' Catherine nodded as Emma arrived with two more bowls of steaming red soup. 'We commend your mum's recipe. Absolutely delicious.'

'Oh thank you. Ironically, my mum and I don't eat it as we're both vegetarian, but my dad's a butcher so we cook the best hams on the bone here and at my mum's café in Hutherton and use the ham and clove stock for the soup base along with organic onions and tomatoes.'

'Your dad's a butcher and you're vegetarian?'

'Yeah, the irony is not lost on him,' Emma smiled, turning to serve the next table.

'Thankfully his ham stock has a home here. I could eat third and fourth helpings if you let me,' David laughed cordially as a familiar tune came over the speakers.

'You hear that song, Catherine?' he tapped his saucer with his soup spoon to the beat. 'Very apt. Do you know what it is?' David quizzed Catherine.

'No David, but you're going to tell me,' she exclaimed with a roll of her eyes.

'It's *My Name is Jack* by Manfred Mann's Earth Band, from the 1968 Pop Art film *You Are What You Eat.*'

'Pray tell, how dost thou know such trivia, David?' she shook her head wryly.

'Did it in Film Studies at college. Weird old psychedelic thing.'

'David, stop tapping!' Catherine glared, embarrassed at David's continuing percussion.

'Goodness. You're a bit irritable all of a sudden.'

'Sorry, it's just that people are looking.'

'No they're not, Catherine. It was hardly noisy.'

'It was, David. Anyway, we'll finish up in five and get going.'

'Right. I'll settle up…' David got up from his seat.

'…No, let me, I said I was…'

'It's fine, I've got it covered; you can do the next one.'

David paid by card at the till.

'Flippin' heck. That was two quid shy of sixty, a right little gold-mine that lass has here.'

'We had double portions of soup remember, but here, take thirty,' Catherine fumbled in her bag.

'No, Catherine, I didn't mean that, I was just shocked at how much it was for a little lunch.'

'Yeah, it is quite pricey. Targeting rich locals and captive market tourists I guess. There's little else around apart from the newsagent or crisps and peanuts in The Armitage.'

'True. It's always been a boozer's pub.'

'My shout next time, right,' Catherine reminded. 'We'll drive up to the old kilns and loop back around, then head back to the station, okay?'

'You want me to drive?' David asked.

'No thanks, David. I've got the seat and mirrors just right so I'd rather…'

'No problem. You keep control of the car and I'll keep an eye out for corn-circles and strange happenings,' David replied sarcastically.

'Sorry? What? I don't understand why it's an issue David…'

'It's not, Catherine. Carry on. No issue at all; it's just that you seem to be a bit snappy this afternoon. Is it something I've said?'

'What? What are you going on about David? When was I snappy? Here, take the keys. I'm so not bothered; go on, take them.'

Catherine thrust the keys toward David's face, her mouth set in a hard line.

'You see, there you go again, acting up. I thought I was being helpful,' he brushed her hand away.

'Me *acting up?* You're the one with a face on, like you've spat your dummy out.'

'Oh eff off, Catherine. Time of the month is it?' he flushed angrily.

'What did you say?' Catherine fumed.

'Just joking,' he turned away, shaking his head. 'Look, Catherine, I'm sorry, I don't know what got into me.'

'You better be, David. I'll pretend I never heard that misogynistic outburst.'

'Right. Good. Let's just go shall we?' David opened the passenger door and slumped heavily into the squad car seat, his jaw muscle twitching.

They drove past the kilns, sullenly; each unwilling to be the first to communicate in the mutual silence.

'Nothing here,' Catherine stated brusquely, 'We should go back to the station. I'm thirsty.'

'If you say so,' David pouted.

'I do say so.'

Catherine exhaled loudly and drove down the bank to the Old Hambury village junction to join the road back to Littleton. Pulling out of the junction she was oblivious to the zebra crossing adjacent to the infant school. A lollipop man shouted, slamming his fists on the bonnet, guarding the children in his charge. Catherine's emergency stop sent her and David jolting forward.

'What the…? You're supposed to stop at the crossing. Those kids. Bloody hell, Catherine, do you want me to drive?'

Catherine wound the window down to apologise and the red faced lollipop man blurted something about *due care and attention*.

'Lucky we weren't in the squad car; imagine two coppers on report for nearly killing a bunch of five year olds.'

'I was distracted.'

'Well, you should've let me drive like I said.'

'Are you *sure* you're okay, David? I mean, *what is your bloody problem*?'

'I ain't got no problem, darlin''

'Darlin'? What the hell is wrong with you?'

'Just drive, might be good practice for you.'

'I'll remind you David, I'm your senior officer and while I don't like to pull rank, I think you'd better start thinking about being civil.'

'Why? What have I said? I'm just pulling your leg.'

'Okay, fine. Let's just head back now and forget this conversation shall we?'

David grunted, shuffling back in his seat, petulantly resting his head against the window and staring into the wing mirror.

The silence in the car was as taut as the muscles in Catherine's neck. She just wanted to get back to the station before her new contempt for her colleague burst into another slanging match, but it was too late, her magma anger needed release.

'How could you bloody well say that, David?' she snarled, heaving herself erect in her seat, clenching the steering wheel like a gymnast on pommel rings.

'I said I'm sorry already,' David spoke with deliberately irritating composure, 'What more do you want me to do? Beg for forgiveness? Or will you be like my ex-wife, who couldn't accept an apology until she'd played a few punishment games.'

'Punishment? Punishment?' Catherine's voice rose an octave higher as she turned to him icily, her brows contorting.

'At the very least I want an apology that sounds sincere. You've always resented me since I got the promotion you thought you so sorely deserved,' she raged as flecks of white spittle landed on David's sleeve. She was driving the vehicle like a rally cross.

'Slow down, Catherine, there's no need to…'

'I'm in full control,' she shouted, 'I'll slow down when I get an apology….'

'Watch out!' David screamed as they rounded the next bend. Two loose Friesian cattle lifted their slow heads and stared gormlessly at the speeding car approaching. Catherine jerked the wheel, slammed on the brakes and the vehicle pirouetted, skidding on loose chippings and hurtling into a hedgerow-covered fence. A series of thuds, cracks and bangs synchronised with the dizzying loss of control.

David waited almost serenely for the impact as the car turned onto its side and came to a clumsy stop without airbags deploying. David could see the sky up to his left and muddy crushed grass and hawthorn twigs down to his right, the driver's side windows mashed into the verge. Both he and Catherine were held uncomfortably by their seat belts.

'Bloody woman-driver,' David raged. The truth Catherine had spoken cut his dignity deep; he felt more emasculated than the gelded bullocks now munching the grass verge in the rear view mirror, oblivious to the hissing black saloon lying in the ditch, the smell of petrol pooling. Catherine wheezed, a wooden fence spar had pierced the car roof, pinning her shoulder onto her bloodied seat.

'David, David, I can't move, help me.'

'Why should I help you? Give me one reason. You stole that promotion from me and you knew it,' he scowled. 'I deserved inspectorship more than you, but you took it unfairly. I saw the look in your eye. You knew.'

'No David, you're wrong, so wrong.'

'Chief Super trying to tick equality boxes instead of promotion on merit. I was robbed.'

'Oh no, David, have you seen my shoulder, I've just noticed, I'm stuck, I can't move. Please help me, I'm bleeding.'

David leaned forward and saw Catherine's right side sodden with blood. To his shock the stake had punched through her shoulder and had gone through the seat back.

'I'm stuck myself; the seatbelt, my weight,' he strained.

'I think I know what it is,' Catherine puffed.

'It's the catch, I'm trying…' David responded, his panic moderated by sheer physical struggle.

'No, David, not that, I meant I know what the problem is – all the incidents in the last five years.' Catherine laughed manically at the clear revelation in spite of her pain.

'I don't understand...' David fought to depress the release button, his thumb white with the strain.

'*You Are What You Eat!*'

'I still don't get...'

'What do people eat in winter and not in summer?'

'Please just stay calm, Catherine, don't try and talk, I'll get us out.'

'No David! What do people eat in winter and not in summer?' she insisted.

'I don't know...' he writhed, '...Stews? ...Hotpot?'

'Ha, you're nearly there!' Catherine crowed delightedly, blood trickling from her mouth.

'I don't know...' David could see the colour draining from Catherine's face.

'Hot soup—it's the bloody soup—' she coughed, 'something in it, making us full of hell, I don't know what, but I never felt anger like that. You felt the same, I could tell.'

'Yes you're right! Anger like burning inside; minutes after we left the café, I was demented. It made me want to fight.'

'Angry soup. Posh tea-room. It explains the data... older, middle-class...'

'You're right. The soup. Yes,' David winced with cramp. 'Bloody red soup. I didn't mean the things I said, it was like... like an angry person inside me, venting. I've been so...'

'It's fine David, really,' Catherine gulped, 'I feel better now, it must be adrenaline...'

'Catherine. I can't undo my belt or reach the comms,' David caught his breath, 'It's hanging by your knees...Catherine? Do you hear me, Catherine?'

Catherine closed her eyes and her head slumped towards her chest.

A sudden *whoomph* heralded the merciless and agonising conflagration that rapidly overwhelmed the vehicle. Catherine had already expired, but David suffered, though somehow his torment was diminished by the cauldron of sheer pig-headed boiling wrath that revived within him at the first lick of flame.

The tragic deaths were met locally with great sadness. The Littleton Courier headline declared: *PC Comrades Die in Horror Crash.*

Meanwhile, the assault and domestic violence data for Old Hambury, Hutherton and Bogwell continued to show an atypical rise in late autumn through to mid spring with the mysterious and sudden tail off until late October when the cycle began again, but since PCs Garven and Lyle had received two extra support staff, there was nothing much to stress about; besides, there were many other pressing issues to worry about for the chief superintendent including his *Equality* and *Net Zero* targets.

The bell above the door jingled at Valerie's Tea Shoppe in Hutherton as the beautiful Russian couple meekly stepped into the soothing hurly burly of tinkling teaspoons and the siss and burble of a milk frother. Val was delighted to serve a swelling hodgepodge of international guests.

'Such delicious soup. We have recipe? Yes? Our friends in Ukraine will very be enjoyable with this.'

Val Downing flushed with pride, fumbling coyly with her notepad inside her chintzy apron pocket.

'Oh, most certainly, we do all we can to help our friends in the Ukraine. I'll go and jot it down for you.

'That is so very kind,' Stanislav winked at Anna who stroked his leg under the table with her foot.

'It is the kind of soup that gives, how you say? The fire fight? Will be good for soldier morals in Kiev.'

'I think you mean *fire in your belly*, and yes, I am sure it will. Didn't Napoleon say an army marches on its stomach?' Val giggled, unconsciously dipping a tiny curtsey. She bustled back through to the kitchen to apply fresh lipstick and to write the recipe in her best handwriting on a floral notelet.

'This is our unique recipe, but you must promise to keep it secret, Valerie teased – we don't want it falling into Mr Putin's hands,' she beamed before waddling back to froth more milk.

The handsome Russian placed the notelet delicately into his wallet.

'I promise,' he smiled, darkly.

WARNING: (The recipe for *Red Taste Experience Soup* is available on the following page. It really is rather tasty, but do not exceed two small bowls in one 12 hour period.)

RED TASTE EXPERIENCE SOUP

RECIPE:

Ham or gammon on the bone

2 litres of water

10 cloves (remove before blending)

Tin of Cream of Tomato Soup

1 pint of chicken stock

2 grated carrots

2 sticks of celery

2 medium onions

200g red lentils (pre-soaked and cooked)

Teaspoon of chilli powder

½ Teaspoon of Cayenne pepper

Tablespoon of fresh parsley, chopped

Dash Worcestershire sauce

Black pepper to taste

METHOD:

Stud gammon or ham with the cloves and place in pan of water. Bring to boil and simmer until the ham or gammon is thoroughly cooked. Remove meat for other use, but retain the stock.

Add the carrots, onion and celery and return to simmer for 30 minutes. Add the lentils, spices and herbs. Add tin of tomato soup and Worcestershire sauce and simmer for a further 20 minutes. Blend before serving.

///train.home.reap
"WALKMAN"

'Mum, how long have we had that picture?'

'Funny you should ask that, I was thinking about it too just yesterday. There must be something in the air. I commissioned it from a man in Wiltshire thirty years ago.'

The young girl, nine had never really scrutinised it before, it had always been reliably present above the impressive mantelpiece from as early as she could remember, but today she really noticed it.

'What does commissioned mean?' she asked her mum.

'It means if you want something specific painting; something really special you can ask the artist to do exactly what you want.'

'Like getting a party dress designed with your own colours and jewels?'

'Exactly like that, something unique, that only you would have; one of a kind.'

The picture was an extraordinarily beautiful hinged triptych; an intricate landscape of English countryside around four feet by five feet, ideally proportioned for the big stone mantelpiece above the cosy inglenook. It displayed hedgerows, patchwork fields, rivers, roads, villages and moors stretching from left to right across the four seasons. Narrower side panels represented spring and winter respectively. On the left, sunshine bathed trees and flowers in full spring freshness and songbirds flitted above hawthorn hedges, while on the right, a winter gale stripped sparse leaves from frost-bitten branches and a lonesome rook wheeled over craggy heathland.

The central panel was a delightful merger of summer and autumn showing children skipping, riding bikes and flying a toy aeroplane. The detail was mesmerising with archetypical village scenery complete with streams and pond, country pubs, fences, signposts, harvesters, cars and motorbikes on roads which snaked far into the distance towards a purple haze of distant suburbia. In the autumnal section, just off centre and the focal point of the triptych was a small

196

copse with a church and graveyard sad with mourners, while a distant train rumbled from the summer section over a viaduct towards autumn beeches.

'Where is it?' The girl asked wistfully.

'Oh, it could be many places, it's a kind of a visual metaphor for life.'

'A metalfork?' she asked, bemused.

'No darling - *metaphor*, like meta and number four.'

'Me-ta-four?'

'That's right. It's when you describe something meaningful using pictures or ideas; like: *her eyes were sparkling pools*; or *clumsy as a bull in a china shop*.'

'So what is it a metaphor of?'

'It's a metaphor to remember that life has seasons and no one knows how long each will last. I had it painted to remind me to value family and friends past and present and to remember to bless each day.'

Mother and daughter stood staring at the picture.

'Your dad's cousin made the picture possible.'

Mum stood entranced, pondering the summer zone, focusing on the Tudor style pub with a swan sign and a lone bicycle leaning against the wall.

The young girl was silent, thoughtful; about to ask something when her mother unclipped the top left and top right triptych corners and folded the two side panels inward to reveal a circular motif in gold and silver leaf, rather crass and gaudy, interspersed with line drawings of popping corks, champagne flutes, gold coins and ribbons and embellished with beautiful gilded script and ornate scrolling. Around the circumference read the latin words:

SILVAE PARVAE GENERANT CADAVERA

'I don't understand, mum.'

Mum stood with a benign smile, recalling three decades ago …

*   *   *

'You can sussur..stuff your scampi and bb..bollock your Ploughman's Platters!'

Ben waited for a few seconds to wait for a response which sounded like a whimper, then slammed the phone down clumsily, paused, and then lifted it again to hear the dial tone in case she was still on the line. He left the phone off the hook.

'Oh man, I stuttered and said 'bollock' instead of 'bollocks to'', he realised, cringing. 'Still, she got the message,' he thought, satisfied.

Ben had rarely felt more content. The closest he had been to feeling as good as this was early on Boxing Day 1972 with his Christmas toys and sweets arranged neatly on his candlewick bedspread. He remembered reading the *Shiver and Shake Christmas Annual*, propped up by pillows and chomping through a box of Rowntree's *Weekend* chocolates and candies as 'You're So Vain' played tinnily through the single earplug on his new pocket radio as his mum and dad slept. Today, he was similarly relaxed and elated as he munched through a bowl of cornflakes in the living room, watching a repeat of Arthur Askey's *The Ghost Train*.

It was rare for Ben to have Monday off work, especially on a busy Bank Holiday and he relished the leisurely sensation of watching the film and planning his day. He would cycle to the High Street for his long awaited reward, then go and pick up his pay packet.

The cornflakes were horrible. Ben had used icing sugar rather than normal granulated. The remnants of the sugar bowl contained only hard tea-stained lumps, but the icing sugar tasted repulsive on cereal, the second surprise of the past twelve hours, but this was the last time he would have to scrape through his dad's frugal cupboards and bare fridge shelves.

He had planned on saying something much more acerbic to Penny Putnam, assistant manageress of The Swan Hotel and Carvery, but bungled his lines ineptly when it came to the, 'I'm not coming in to work today or ever again' clincher.

It was weird, he thought he hated that blubbery podgeball Penny, but in that moment of stammered diatribe, he felt a strange connection to her and guilt about what he'd just said, in spite of her bossy, puce-nailed, short-skirted, corned-beef-legged persona.

198

Talking of irritating, Arthur Askey's character in *The Ghost Train*, an old-time comedian called Tommy Gander, was infuriating. It was really just Arthur Askey playing himself and although he'd seen that film twice before, he only realised at twenty years old that Askey wasn't very funny at all, just childish and annoying. He even looked a bit mentally handicapped. *A bit of a retard actually*, Ben thought, *especially for pulling an emergency cord on a train to retrieve his hat from the track*. Askey ruined the old black and white film, Ben thought; a film which otherwise had great spooky potential, especially the part where the old stationmaster warned the passengers about the phantom train bringing death to all who saw it.

Back to porky-pink technicolour Penny, though. She was certainly no film star and he would never have to follow her pug-faced orders anymore or listen to her blethering on the phone.

What is it with porky birds? Ben thought. *Why do they talk to you about people you don't know using their first names?:* 'So I says to Sharon about Chris, then Denise tells me that Rosalyn's going out with Dave from Rickmansworth who drives a red Triumph Stag, bore, bore, bore.'

Ben prattled his impersonation of Penny under his breath, wobbling his head and mouthing the words to himself as he evoked her screechy Buckinghamshire dialect.

He had fantasised about making some dramatic 'Farewell to The Swan' speech and had played it over in his mind, coolly and heroically strolling up to Penny on a busy Saturday night in the carvery and pouring Chef's bucket of batter over her dirty yellow blonde wedge in front of all the diners.

That was another thing, Ben thought; *how does she not understand her hairstyle looks like a mushroom before the gills show? Like that squeaky Buck Rogers robot, whatsitsname? Kiki or Twiki? Yeah, that's the one. She bustles around with that 'I'm so important' waddle, always flicking her head back like some Charlie's bloody Angel.*

He could picture her now on the way to the kitchens, bustling along the claret carpeted corridor in between the public and saloon bars;

her fat ugly-sister ankles stuffed painfully into overstretched white high heels and her brewery blouse pigeon-proud with those Jon Pertwee ruffles.

Oh man, Penny when she's on Reception sorting through the filing cabinet drawers; riffling through the folders like a bloody Hill Street Blues' detective; pouting and hmmm-ing and fussing to herself and licking her forefinger with that tubby wrist bent back.

So bloody irritating. She honestly thinks she's some sexy babe in that fat-arsed black pencil skirt, he thought as he pictured her sitting in her tidy little office, absent-mindedly sniffing her pink Papermate pen; pretending to file something important in that glossy pink clip-file of hers with the 'Love is...' cartoon couple sitting in a heart on the cover.

And that irritating phrase she uses when she bosses the waiters, 'Do you copy?' or that other one when she finished calling her mate, Caz in head office: 'Bye now, I gotta skitty!'

Man, she's Tommy Gander's bastard daughter, he sneered inwardly.

Arthur Askey's character had just made a big unfunny 1940s deal about dragging his heavy costume basket into the old waiting room, which meant he would soon make the Jewish joke about the caged parrot, and sing that cringy comic song about the seaside, irritating the posh bloke so much he would chuck Gander's gramophone on the track.

Talking of cringe, Ben recalled a very funny Swan Sunday lunchtime when Penny was doing her *Maître d'* act at the restaurant lectern when an old granny had said, 'I like your hat dear'. Penny had turned into Queen Crimson and snapped at the old bat, 'It's actually a modern hairstyle called a wedge!' she'd remonstrated before walking off all huffy. The old woman had felt so bad she apologised to Garry the bar manager, 'Will you tell the lady I'm so sorry, I didn't mean to offend.'—'Lady', she said, mind you—not 'girl'—Penny was twenty-bloody-four, but acted fifty-five.

Ben scoffed to himself: *Very unprofessional, Head Office wouldn't have been impressed. A disciplinary offence snapping at customers like that!*

200

He remembered the upset well. She busied off with her assistant manageress keys jingling, disappearing into the toilets and coming back half an hour later all bleary-eyed, Garry comforting her.

And that perfume she wears. What's it called? Oh yes, *Chic by Lèntheric.* Most women wear it and it smells sexy, so why does it smell manure-y on her? Hers should be called *'Shit by Manuric.'* Ben approved of his funnier-than-Askey wisecrack and jumped up enthusiastically from the greasy sofa to grab a can of his dad's stout from the garage and a cigarette from the nearly empty pack on the mantelpiece.

I'll never have to scrape chewed up gristle and pie crusts into the swill bin again, or touch those slimy pans, he thought, luxuriating in the crackle of the first draw of his cigarette. He slumped back onto the sofa with ashtray on his chest.

Although it was warm and sunny outside, he'd closed the short velvet curtains to stop the sun shining on the TV screen, except for a bright slit near the pelmet. He could see dust specks and his blue smoke curling in the sunbeam.

'Breakfast beer and a JPS Superking. Majestic perfection,' he said, raising his can to Askey and flicking ash. 'To a man who made a great film crap,' he jeered.

His dad's news last night was a shockwave. When Ben got home at 9pm, weary from his Sunday afternoon shift in the kitchens, he was mystified at seeing his dad staggering drunk.

'Sit down son, ah've got news. 'Ere, 'ave a beer!' he slurred. His dad pulled out a can of John Smiths from his swollen carrier bag full of them and handed one to Ben, trying to suppress a grin.

'Cheers son! Are you looking forward to workin' tomorrow then?' his dad asked playfully, flopping down into the saggy armchair by the TV.

'Of course, Dad, I can't wait,' Ben responded with sarcastic puzzlement.

'Go on, have a ciggie, son, and tonight you don't have to smoke it up the chimney.'

He hadn't seen his dad this jolly since mum was alive and never so liberal about his smoking in the house.

'Have you got a new job?' Ben queried. 'Did you get the job as depot inspector or something?'

His dad pried open the ring pull and the beer fizzed, pooling rapidly on top of the can. He slurped it loudly before it dribbled.

'Hmm, getting warmer, but still very cool,' he teased, smiling broadly.

'You got another job then, not at the depot?'

'You could say that son, you *could* say that,' he grinned and swigged another draught.

'And you want to know what the new job is then?' he beamed.

Ben just nodded, confused, watching his dad slop beer on his pants.

His dad leant forward.

'Well it involves houses with swimmin' pools, fancy cars and travelling places. Any clue? Go on, 'ave a guess.'

Ben paused, baffled; amused at his dad's cheerful inebriation.

'A chauffeur? It must be a chauffeur dad, because you're certainly not butler material.

'Close son, you're gettin' hot!'

Ben shrugged impatiently, shaking his head.

'I don't know, dad, just tell me!'

'I'm going to be – I mean – we're going to be, full time chauffeurs of ourselves.'

'Chauffeurs of ourselves? I still don't get what you mean…'

'Football Pools' winners, you daft bugger! We've won the bloody Pools son. In fact, you and I both are going to be full time Football Pools winners from now on.'

Ben looked at his dad suspiciously.

'Don't mess me around, Dad, I'm not in the mood,' though Ben was reading sincerity in his dad's eyes, now moist with emotion as a tear tracked down his cheek.

'Serious?' Ben interrogated. 'You're serious aren't you?'

'Yes, Ben, seriously. I've won £1.4million with 24 points. I checked the paper this morning and had Littlewoods on the blower to confirm. Your mum's watching over us, she truly is and she's given us both the day off tomorrow, and the next day, and the next day and the next, so that's why I've had a bit of a party tonight.'

Ben grabbed his dad and cuddled him and his dad stroked his head like he did when he was a young boy.

'It's no wind-up, is it Dad? You are telling me the truth?'

His dad bent his head down in a convulsion of joyful sobbing, clenching his can in his right hand and cradling the back of Ben's head with his left. Ben knew he wasn't kidding.

'You are bloody brilliant, Dad. Littlewoods have confirmed, haven't they, they really did get your coupon?'

His dad composed himself and wiped his streaming eyes and nose with his sleeve, 'Yes son, they got it. I get the money Tuesday. Littlewoods come around with a cheque and some kind of money adviser. I've said I want no publicity so no greedy buggers knockin' down our door for handouts.'

Ben just looked at his dad, bewildered and cuddled him.

'I've got a month's wages tomorrow too, so double joy! Ben said.

'Double joy, son; triple and quadruple joy!' he said, pulling out a fresh can for himself and passing another to Ben. 'Our troubles are over. And you make bloody well sure you go and pick up every penny you're owed. Rich or not, you earned it son and it'll look funny if you don't collect. I can't have my little cousin Garry finding out about our good fortune; I know he got you the job there, but you help them more than they help you and every bleedin' distant ingrate relative will come out of the woodwork like greedy termites if we give 'em even a sniff of the dough.'

'I didn't think we had any relatives, but don't worry Dad, getting that pay-packet will be the last time I'll ever have to step into that dump again, unless it's to be a nuisance customer,' Ben sniggered.

'Yeah, well this week I'm tying loose ends up; going to the bank first thing Wednesday to have a word with the manager, pay the loan off and tell him I'm moving to the TSB. I can't wait to see the idiot's face when I wave that check in front of him. Tomorrow though, I'm window shopping at the estate agent.'

In spite of being hungover, his dad was singing and banging around loudly in the shower early on Monday. Once dressed, he popped his damp head around Ben's door, grinning, 'Have a nice day off - I mean, rest of your life off, son.'

He cast his eyes critically around Ben's shabby room, at the orange woodchip paper and the single bed he'd slept in from five years old. Ben's size 11 feet were sticking out from under the thin, sun-bleached chocolate-brown quilt, too short for his six-foot frame.

'I'm off to find us something a little larger,' he chuckled. 'Any requests? Mansion? Mayfair townhouse? Castle? With caviar and servants or without? Might get a four-poster for you too instead of that old thing.'

His dad pulled something from his back trouser pocket.

'Oh, and just before I go, here's some pennies from heaven from your mum.'

His dad threw a wad of banknotes toward the ceiling over the bed. Ben watched open mouthed as the big green and blue confetti dropped on top of him like some Daily Mirror Bingo winner wallowing in £500 of smelly pounds and fivers.

'Wow, thanks Dad! That's bloody majestic, thanks so much.' Ben sat up, raking the money together.

'Thank your mum. She was keeping this back for your wedding day, but I guess you can spend a bob or two now. Even get that Walkman contraption you wanted,' he grinned.

His dad left the room, thumping down the stairs enthusiastically two steps at a time, singing *Pennies from Heaven* like a pub singer. Ben heard his dad's voice fade, the front door slam and the familiar squeal of his battered old Commer van reversing off the drive.

It was amazing how a cash windfall could override any urge to lie-in, though he knew he would still have to get up to answer the inevitable phone call from The Swan chasing him to do Monday's lunch prep; an unwelcome intrusion into his pleasure zone.

On cue at 9.15, the jarring *ring ring, ring ring* of the telephone dragged Ben downstairs to make his botched speech.

Oddly, Penny had sounded more sad and surprised than angry. Her unexpected reaction had taken the bile out of Ben's vitriol. He resolved to pick up his wages from Garry, the bar manager, his dad's thirty something cousin, while she was on her lunch.

Ben sparked up another cigarette.

This was the best part of the film, when the gas light went out in the waiting room and the door swung open by itself. A genuinely spooky moment. Arthur Askey was still playing bloody court jester though, even after the train rumbled past and the posh bloke pulled his gun out and drew blood in the tunnel.

And that was another thing that was really off in the film. When the train crashed killing all the Nazi sympathisers, Ben couldn't believe Arthur Askey was still wisecracking, even though his character was responsible for leaving the bridge open and causing the crash.

The death of an enemy still demands solemnity, Ben thought, pulling a Churchillian cigar-face as he raised himself up from the sofa. The draw of the High Street and a trip to the record shop overruled any desire to watch the closing credits.

Ben pulled on his baseball cap securely back to front, checked his blonde fringe in the shiny stainless steel toaster and entered the garage through the kitchen. He sat on his bicycle and swung the garage door upwards roughly from the inside, nearly breaking it, before slamming it shut noisily and freewheeling from the drive diagonally across the road.

The mile trip through side streets and alleyways was thrilling in the summer sunshine. Every flower and bird seemed to share in Ben's jubilation. Similarly, at Cavendish Sounds, the happy hippie owner reflected the brightness of Ben's joyful demeanour requiring no salesmanship to sell the most expensive *Walkman* in the shop. Ben simply pointed at the box in the locked glass cabinet, slammed £130 on the counter and asked for batteries which the happy hippie gleefully installed for free, feeling a little guilty his young customer could save 25% on his purchase by catching the bus to Curry's just four miles out of town.

Ben secured the headphones under his cap excitedly and dropped in one of his home-recorded C60 cassettes into the slot that opened and closed with a beautifully dampened sophistication. The tape contained a home-recorded Capital Radio and Top 40 medley; loud clicks marking the end of most of the tracks with *Are Friends Electric* by Gary Numan and *Golden Brown* by The Stranglers clumsily interspersed alongside DJ banter and clipped promotional jingles advertising *Vogue Interiors*, and *Kentish Garden Strawberries.* Ben was so accustomed to associating much-repeated tracks with individual jingles that whenever he heard them independently he expected the jingle or DJ voice to follow.

Ben hurtled on his racing bike to The Swan, *I Don't Like Mondays* by The Boomtown Rats thumping solidly in mono through the stereo headphones. He skirted over the level crossing at Flockwell Junction and along Switchback Lane to staff bike racks behind the pub toilets. He was sweating as he walked furtively up to the sun-bleached fly curtain by the open kitchen entrance.

Dropping his headphones around his neck, he peered inside and whistled for his friend, commis chef, Duncan.

'Dunc! Dunc! Over here, man!'

Duncan walked over briskly, wiping his hands down the front of his dark blue striped apron.

'Is she out?' Ben asked, nervously.

'Yeah man, she's on a late lunch thanks to you not turning up this morning. Where've you been, mate?' Duncan interrogated over the din of ventilator fans, utensil jangles and crockery clanks. He grabbed Ben playfully by the chin. 'You look well enough to me you skiving bastard. You hungover?'

'A little bit, but no more than any other day of the working week,' Ben scoffed.

'Anyway, Porky's not happy. She had to get one of the waitresses to help with the salads,' Duncan warned.

'I'm not skiving or ill, Dunc. I've quit; I've only come for my wages.'

'You've quit? What for man? Porky never said you were buggering off. What am I going to do without my best geezer around here?'

~~~~~~ was clearly disappointed at the loss of one of his allies.

~~~~~~ new job, self-employed with my dad; going
~~~~~~ keeping schtum at the moment.
~~~~~~ next week.'

~~~~~~ . And you'd better ask Garry
~~~~~~ r gets back. He's the only one

~~~~~~ replied, walking towards the waiter
13 Aurant just as Dunc grabbed Ben by
~~~~~~ and to inspect the neat silver box

~~~~~~ w Walkman you got there geezer. Nice looking piece of kit... you nick it?'

'Hey, I told you man, self-employment pays. It's just a small treat before I start my new career,' Ben grinned.

'Yeah, right man,' Duncan remarked sceptically.

'Well, if you need someone with scampi frying skills...' Duncan jabbed both thumbs into his own shoulders and pulled a face.

Ben responded by grabbing The Sun newspaper from the staff table, tapping the picture of the topless model on Page 3.

'I'll be hiring some sexy bird like this before I give you a job, mate,' Ben snickered, striding away to find Garry.

Garry seemed flustered but fine and gave Ben his pay packet from the office cabinet, locking it and the office back up.

'I could see you weren't enjoying it much here Ben, but you and your dad are a couple of dark horses. Got something good going on then, the both of you? He's packing his job in driving buses to do what? It all seems very sudden. You sure he hasn't been sacked? He was a joiner once wasn't he?'

'Yeah, I mean no, he hasn't been sacked, and yeah, he was a joiner; just sick of the whole *On The Buses* malarkey and early starts, so we discussed how we'll be working on kitchen and conservatory jobs and probably swimming pools for bigger houses.'

'I thought your dad packed in joinery because of arthritis?'

'Yeah, he did, but I'll be doing the hard sawing and drilling bits, while he does the easier stuff.'

'Hey well, best of luck mate. My mate Col says that every pound you earn self-employed is worth a fiver employed. It'll be a hundred times better than working as a grubber for the brewery at any rate.'

'Cheers Garry. I appreciate it and I'll catch up soon, but I'd best leg it before 'Assistant Manageress' gets back.' Ben stuffed the pay packet into his back pocket.

Reaching the staff bike racks, Ben kicked his front tyre, vexed, and turned on his heels back to the kitchen.

'Dunc, I've got a bloody puncture,' he shouted, 'I'm going to have to leave it here until tomorrow, if that's okay. My dad will pick it up in his van to save me wheeling it.'

'Sure man,' Duncan responded with an apathetic flourish of his arm, now concentrating on slicing bread on a bacon slicer for Melba toast.

'Here: You want to gob on The Swan's finest Melba toast as a final farewell?'

'Nah, not today mate, but you can though,' he joked.

*   *   *

Penny Putnam felt as deflated as Ben's tyre. She took the 5pm train home from Low Beacons to her parent's bungalow in Flockwell. There was an uncomfortable forty-minute delay for a journey that normally took five minutes due to some commotion by the industrial estate.

The carriage was muggy and airless, but the interval gave her time to think and read some verses from a small hotel Gideon's Bible opened covertly inside her pink shoulder bag.

Walking home the extra half mile from the station in the hot sunshine was draining. A police car flashed by the T-junction at the end of her street as she stuck her key in the door. She was used to the faint smell of excrement from her Brother Timmy's colostomy bag as she went inside; though today in the humidity, it was stronger and blended with the whiff of carroty mince from the kitchen hob, like a bad school lunch.

Profoundly disabled from birth with cerebral palsy, Timmy would never taste the nutritious meals his mother daily prepared for the rest of the family, as he had to be fed with special liquid feeds through a tube in his stomach. It was all he had ever known and he was uncomplaining.

Timmy loved his sister Penny dearly. Every night he would whirr into the hallway in his battery wheelchair at 5pm and wait for her to walk up the drive, anticipating her blonde shape through the knobbly glass of the front door.

She hung her bag over the radiator and tenderly kissed his head and whispered, 'What's your best sis got for you today, Tim?' She lifted his deformed flexed wrist and long bony fingers, pressing a fuzzy magenta ball with googly plastic eyes and a dark blue ribbon stapled to the underside into his palm. The ribbon displayed The Swan Carvery & Bar logo with telephone number and 'See you again soon' printed in white text alongside. She let him feel the fuzzy texture momentarily and then took it back, rubbing it on his cheeks giggling, before peeling off the backing and sticking it on the arm of his wheelchair. Timmy made delighted shrieks.

'Do you know what it is Tim? It's a promotional logo-bug from work to advertise the carvery. A big box of them came today. I gave one to my boyfriend Ben, so the two men in my life have the same one.' Timmy squealed, delighted at the connection with Ben and the outside world.

'How is Ben?' Penny's mum piped up from above the persistent hiss of the pressure cooker on the hob. 'You must bring him to meet us one of these days, Pen. I know the situation here isn't ideal, but he sounds like a lovely young man and Timmy can't wait to meet him. If you invite him for tea your dad can rig up the barbecue and we'll all sit in the garden.'

Penny nodded her head and started to cry a little. 'He is lovely mum. You would really like him. He's so handsome and he really looks after me in the pub. He's so reliable too but he's just been way too busy to come.'

Penny's mum realised she looked upset and walked over to her, flinging her oven glove over her shoulder, giving her a hug and cupping her cheeks lovingly.

'You know Mum, we had a bit of an upset this morning and he's not speaking at the moment,' Penny flushed as her eyes welled up and her mum made to hug her again, but Penny shook her head and dashed along the L-shaped hallway to her room at the back of the house. She closed her bedroom door and sat on the edge of her Barbie-pink bed, holding back tears, her clenched fist to her mouth.

'Oh dear, love, don't get upset,' her mum spoke, concerned, with her ear to her door, 'he'll be fine. Young men can be ever so fickle and insensitive. I'm sure you'll both be patching things up again in no time.'

'It's okay, mum, I'm okay, really,' she answered, repressing tears.

Mrs Putnam persisted, 'Are you sure, love?'

'Yes, Mum, I'm sure,' Penny lied.

'Good. Anyway, your tea's going to be ready in five minutes, but I'll keep it warm if you want me to.'

Penny dried her eyes and picked up a plastic name badge with the brewery logo on it. It said Ben Deane, Kitchen Staff. She unclipped her badge from her frilly white manageress brewery blouse and placed it on the bedside table next to his, as she did every evening.

*   *   *

Ben strode homewards enthusiastically, pushing through the broken fence by the train tracks to the swell and the ebb of Duran Duran's *'Save a Prayer'* now thrumming loudly through his headphones. As the song played, he felt confident and unstoppable, imagining himself in a music video, partying with Simon le Bon and a bevy of sexy women on a yacht. He spun his baseball cap around the right way to keep the hot sun from burning his cheeks.

In the short term, he know he would never be a popstar, but he was certainly going to nail his driving test, buy a cool car and dress to impress. It was the beginning of one long Ben Deane celebration.

Ben took the square manila envelope from his pocket and squeezed. It felt like the usual month's pay, but there was an unusual soft lump inside. Curious, he tore it open and along with the payslip in the bottom corner was a magenta fluffy ball with eyes.

'Urgh, a small cuddly toy bonus for all my months of service,' he jibed, '*I'll stick it on the toilet cistern*,' he sang in tune with the lyrics, '*Save it til the morning after.*'

He held the logo-bug ribbon in his mouth and checked the payslip tallied with his wages.

The train from Low Beacons to Flockwell was no phantom. It didn't whistle like a banshee and it didn't come *a steamin' and a rollin'* like a *Casey Jones* loco with a bison bar. It was a dirty British Rail diesel clattering mundanely around the slow branch-line bend by the industrial estate; a journey so routine the driver was oblivious to Ben walking adjacent to the track; neither did he hear the muted thump of impact. Another driver on the 3pm return leg had spotted Ben's body.

It took days for the autopsy to confirm cause of death and a further six months for the transport investigation to submit its findings. Ben had died from blunt force trauma, a broken neck and brain haemorrhage. Old Tommy, the driver hadn't seen him because of the bend on the track where branches of a weeping willow tree somewhat obscured the view ahead. Even if he had been concentrating and not birdwatching the heron in the reeds over to his right, he rationalised he still would not have had time to pull on the brake. Ben had simply sidestepped too close to the train.

Local news station, Look South interviewed an official from the rail company who flagged up the danger of walking on the railway line. A broken fence was repaired and a Do Not Trespass sign put up. Parents warned their children to remove headphones and 'Look and Listen' near any traffic.

When Penny heard the news on the Tuesday morning, she took the day off sick, convulsed with grief. Her parents and Timmy thoughtfully gave her space.

Penny picked up a heart-shaped picture frame and held it to her chest, slumping onto her pink pillows. She wept for hours. The frame contained a blurry Polaroid cut-out of Ben holding a bottle of beer from The Swan Hotel & Carvery New Year's bash with Penny standing behind him smiling.

Penny prayed.

'Dear Lord, I never got to say goodbye to Ben and I want so much to see him again in Heaven. I don't know where he stood with you, but I pray you would reach out to him before he died and save his soul.

'Father, even though Ben died before I prayed this, because you exist outside of time you knew I would be saying a prayer for him the morning after.

'And because all things are possible with you, please, if it is your will, can you apply this prayer retrospectively, and can you give him some sign that I cared about him and I was thinking about him. That would be a blessing to me. In Jesus' name, Amen.'

*   *   *

The impact was heavy, yet strangely painless, and coincided with the fade out of the song: *Save it till the morning afterrrr.* A willow branch had caught on Ben's hat, pulling it off and Ben had made to grab it clumsily, knocking it onto the track.

Unthinking, he dodged to his right to pick it up, seeing a large shadow loom behind him, but before he could make any sense of it, he smashed headlong into the grey ballast, seeing stars and birds tweeting with the concussion, just like in a cartoon.

He groaned, wheezing and wounded, facing the grass at the base of the wooded embankment that led up to the industrial estate fence. His Walkman lay shattered by the trackside and his manila pay packet and wad of notes drifted over the sleepers in the shimmering slipstream of the train.

Alongside the weed-strewn verge, his eyes focused on a familiar shape, an immature puffball mushroom ripening in the rough grass with the magenta logo-bug alongside.

'It's a little Twiki mushroom,' he whispered, barely breathing, as a strange warmth covered him. *She wasn't so bad, Twiki,* Ben pondered, smiling, a breeze touching his bloodied forehead like a soft kiss. He remembered that night at the New Year's do when he was so drunk he had snogged Penny in the back of the taxi. *Oh man, the embarrassment the next day.* Thankfully, no one else knew.

Simon le Bon's lyrics repeated in his head: *Some people call it a one night stand, but we can call it Paradise.*

I wasn't very nice to Twiki, Ben reflected, ashamed at calling her all the porky names. A pang of genuine remorse and sadness stabbed right through him.

I gave her the wrong idea because I was so smashed that night and Dad said never to give a fat, ugly or handicapped bird false romantic hope.

She's really never done or said anything bad to me and I really only slagged her because other people did and I kind of got sucked in, caught up in the name calling, like it was The Swan kitchen staff thing to do, slagging the assistant manageress. She's not even that fat, just a little bit podgy. She's even got a sweet face, just a bad hair style. She's pretty good at her job too and was always fair to me.

Yeah, Twiki's okay, Ben concluded.

Remembering the hat on the railway track scene from The Ghost Train earlier, Ben had another thought: *I bet Arthur Askey was probably okay too. It must be difficult trying to be funny and putting on an act all the time, but people expect cheeky chappies to be jolly even on their days off. Must be so bloody tiring...*

Presently, he felt very tired too, his hands and feet tingly alongside an ebbing-away sensation. He jerked awake again as adrenaline fired a jolt of clarity. Ben feared he was dying and an urgency to pray hit him like a coal shovel.

'Owwrr Farrtherrr,' he slurred, 'Forgive us our trespasses…'

213

Blood misted from his nose as he garbled exhausted through the only prayer he knew, until satisfied, he reached a final mumbled 'Ahrrmenn.'

The ribbon of the logo-bug flapped gently alongside the cute small fungus and the words 'See you again, soon' came sharply and momentarily into focus, fading, as a warm breeze blew right through him, lifting his soul.

The next day, Ben's dad sat on the edge of his son's silent bed weeping; staring at the carpet pattern and clutching Ben's empty can of stout that he had used as an ashtray.

Two smiling men from Littlewoods Pools ding-donged the doorbell

*   *   *

'So why did you commission the picture, Mum?'

Penny smiled a sad smile.

'A long time ago before you were born, your dad worked in a pub with me. It's how we got together. His cousin left him a lot of money unexpectedly when he died. It's how we managed to buy Granny and Gramps the specially designed house for your Uncle Tim with all the ramps in the big garden. You know how good it is for all of them.'

'Yes, it's so cool. But what happened? What did Dad's cousin die of?'

'We think he died of grief—a broken heart— he drank himself to death within a few weeks of his son getting killed on a railway track.'

'Oh, Mum that's so horrible. So he left Dad all his money?'

'No, well, yes, indirectly, because Dad was the nearest surviving relative. His cousin had won something called the Football Pools and no one knew about it, but your dad was a surviving relative and benefited.'

'The Football Pools? I don't understand.'

'It was a similar sort of thing to the lottery when I was your age. Your dad and I had started going out with each other and then the brewery closed the pub we worked at. We both lost our jobs on the

214

same day and didn't know how we were going to cope, then one evening your dad had a knock on the door from a solicitor who told him he was the only living relative.'

Penny nodded almost imperceptibly, her eyes glistening with tears.

'Are you alright, Mum?'

'Yes hon, of course I am.'

Penny's fat forearm squeezed her daughter's shoulders reassuringly as she kissed the crown of her head.

'The picture is a reminder that money has its seasons; times of scarcity and abundance - but you must never put your trust in it because no matter how much you have, it can be taken away in an instant.'

Penny's focus shifted to the triptych and the distant teal and yellow diesel train rolling ponderously over the viaduct like an indifferent assassin.

For a few seconds mother and daughter stood in silence before Latin words breezed from Penny's lips: *'Silvae parvae generant cadavera.'*

'What does that mean, Mum?'

'It's Latin. It means copses cause corpses.'

The nine year old wrinkled her face and shook her head.

'Copses?'

'Just little woods, hon…' She gazed at the detail of silent mourners in the leaf strewn October churchyard and sighed, 'Just Littlewoods.'

///moment.pans.burn
"SUSPILIO DAY"

Suzy was stuck behind the log laden articulated lorry, moving perilously closer to its rear bumper as she tried to gauge her timing and acceleration to nip out in between the speeding traffic in the fast lane.

She was mad with herself for getting trapped like some old nana, especially given that her Mercedes could out-spurt most cars, but the stream of over-takers in the rush hour was unrelenting and the bulky timber load ensured the HGV was living up to its lumbering credentials in spite of the driver flooring it, evidenced by the thundering rumble of its engine.

Now she was tailgating and it was much too slow to change lane safely; her view of the road ahead concealed by cross sections of heavy tree stumps. She felt compelled to take a risk.

'Slow down and chill out.' It was a clear instruction.

Suzy was amazed to hear the calm, though emphatic male voice from *inside* her head.

'Who the…' She'd never heard a voice from inside her head before and it was weirdly familiar. Suzy checked her mirror and saw there was no one immediately behind her so she obediently took her foot off the accelerator and slowed down, putting a hundred yards distance between herself and the slow lorry. Suddenly a raucous gold sports car skidded out in front of her from a layby just after the roundabout, cutting in front of her outrageously, with cylinders firing like two gunshots as a ruby profusion of brake lights ahead screamed danger.

She swerved suddenly to the left to avoid clipping the delinquent coupé and snaked onto the verge of the carriageway raising a cloud of dust and parched grass as gravel clattered under her wheel arches.

'Morons!' she screeched indignantly, her car now unmoving, though she continued to grip her steering wheel like a security blanket, now utterly riveted by the sight of a big redwood log sliding ponderously from the back of the lorry like a slow motion

216

caber toss, thudding onto the tarmac and careering to a slow diagonal halt across two lanes while horns blared and vehicles skidded in a chain reaction of brakes and hot rubber.

The Trans Am dodged the log and shot off into the outside lane, disappearing into the summer haze as the traffic behind came to a screeching and silent stop—except for one solitary white van veering and swerving in her rear-view mirror, weaving from lane to layby in a clumsy slalom like a vengeful dodgem. Finding nowhere to decelerate safer than the grass verge it shunted into the back of her beautiful Benz. The Mercedes airbag exploded into her face like a stupid, big bellied bouncer.

Suzy was pinned to her seat. Stinging and dazed she fumbled in the centre console to retrieve a crumpled KFC napkin to dab her bleeding nose and mouth. She could see that a box-file full of letters, DVD discs and keepsakes from her Dad's bedroom drawer had spilled into the passenger side foot well and she started to cry.

*   *   *

'It doesn't get much better than this, does it?' Jim commented to Suzy, his eleven year old daughter, as they relaxed in a double raft that meandered pleasantly along *Mellow Creek* in the South Carolina water park.

'No, Daddy, it doesn't.'

Suzy trailed her hand in the water and watched sun dapples move over her ivory-white fingers making quiet laps and burbles depending on the tilt as she moved it like a fin, ruddering the shocking-pink inflatable along the serene indigo channel.

The *Mellow Creek* attraction snaked the perimeter of the popular park which was wholly bounded by tall palms and twelve foot high dazzling white walls swathed in pink, purple and orange climbing bougainvillea. The full ensemble delivered a haven of tropical luxuriance which was a triumph in discrete urban concealment considering the park's proximity to busy interstate, retail outlets, industrial parks and scrubland adjacent.

Enhancing the oasis vibe were artificial rock outcrops, fountains and waterfalls draped with tropical vines and fragrant oleander;

exotic shrubbery that attracted ruby throated hummingbirds to sip early nectar from the overhanging orange trumpet creepers.

'Wow, Dad did you see that gorgeous hummingbird? It just flew into that lovely flower.'

'There's three of them, look,' Jim pointed.

They tried to stop the raft by grabbing onto the fake rocks of the shrubbery to stare longer at the iridescent birds flitting and darting, but the current was inexorable and spun them briskly around the next meandering bend toward a bright canopy of white frangipani flowers that dropped petals into the stream like big confetti, their heady scent almost too sickly so early in the day.

No other tourists were in the park when they had first arrived half an hour ago and had sauntered over from the nearly empty parking lot to the ticket booths at 8.15am.

Yesterday, jetlagged from the Manchester to Charleston flight, they had picked up a hire car at 10pm and reached their motel room by 11pm. By 5am they were wide awake, having eaten a McDonald's breakfast and were the first to arrive at *Tropic Al's Waterganza Flume and Wave Park* just off the State Highway.

The park opened at 8.30am and the girl in the ticket booth tried to mask her annoyance that someone was waiting for her to open up before she'd even had a chance to flick the coffee percolator on, but reaching deep into her American Travel and Tourism training managed to eke out, 'Have a great day y'all,' on the dot of 8.31 as she handed out tickets and a fold-out map of the park.

'It's like a beautiful *Suspilio Day* today, Daddy.'

'A *what* day?'

'Suspilio Day, pronounced *sir speel ee oh.*'

'So does that mean a nice day?'

'It can do, but it might not.'

'I don't understand. What do you mean?'

'A Suspilio Day is a day when everything feels completely different or weirder than any other day. It's a day with a mood you've never felt before,' Suzy elaborated.

Jim paused.

'So I think you mean a day with a unique and surreal feeling to it. Is that right?'

'Does surreal mean weird?' Suzy asked.

'Yes, it can do; a bit dreamy and odd.'

'Yes that's okay then. To be Suspilio it must have that weird unrealness to it, because you can still have a unique experience on a day with a familiar mood. For example, you could go up in a hot air balloon, but the day might feel like any other day, normal, but not surreal.'

'I'm still not really sure what you mean, Suzy. Going up in a balloon is pretty special.'

Suzy chatted as she slipped into her bathing costume in the Family Changing cubicle as Jim slid his swim shorts on under a towel.

'Do you remember the paint chart that Mum got for the bedroom with all the hundreds of colours?'

'Yes, I know the one.'

'Okay, imagine every single colour on that chart gives you a unique and dreamy mood. That's more like Suspilio.'

They stuffed their shoes and clothes excitedly into the low locker 111 and Jim put the key band around his wrist as they strolled from the air conditioned coolness into the humid South Carolina air, stepping in the disinfectant pool as they walked out.

'Always best to choose a memorable number in case you lose the key,' he advised.

'Yeah, that is a good idea and it's a kwinky-dink,' agreed Suzy.

'A Quinky-ink what?' Jim asked.

'A kwinky-dink; it's what Mrs Taylor, my teacher calls a coincidence.'

'Oh, I see, but why is it a kwinky-dink?' Jim puzzled.

'It's our hotel room number too,' Suzy reminded him.

'Ah of course it is, I must have subconsciously chosen it for that reason.'

'There's no such thing as kwinky-dinks, Daddy; everything happens for a reason, Mrs Taylor says.'

'She might be right, Suzy. Phew it's warm out here.'

The low morning sun was obscured behind the tall palm tops rising behind the massive marine-ply mural of the currently motionless wave pool. The mural showed a surfer riding on a giant wave under the park logo. Soon the wave turbines would be turned on and the glassy waters would churn with whitecaps until closing time at 6pm.

'So what is today's colour on your Suspilio chart?'

'Hmmm,' Suzy scanned the waterpark, taking in the giant fuchsia coloured tubular slides and white log flume ride flanked by the jungle greenery. It was indeed odd, and lovely, to be standing in a giant park, just her and her dad, the only two people here other than a distant pool attendant wearing a branded fuchsia tee shirt, bright blue shorts and carrying a mop and metal bucket. The rattle of the bucket disrupted the muffled stillness of the air where the only other sound was the odd slap and gurgle from inside the pool filter units and gentle gushing from a pink and white mushroom cascade in the distant kiddie pool.

'I suppose it is a peachy kind of brightness with pale blue and Barbie-pink mixed in. Most Suspilio days though are probably just one colour, like a dull grey or a milky green.'

'So it's a uniquely strange mood that you could match on a colour chart, kind of feeling.'

'Yes, that's a good way of thinking about it, but you must remember that there is *bad* Suspilio as well as *good* Suspilio.'

'*Bad* Suspilio?'

A huge pelican glided suddenly above, disturbing the misty stillness.

'Wow, did you see that? We don't get any of those in England.'

'It was like a pterodactyl wasn't it, Daddy?'

'Yes; a very big bird to what we're used to; adding to today's special Suspilio vibe,' Jim chuckled. 'Keep your eye out for a good lounger spot. That raised area up the steps looks good; on its own and away from the busiest part where the loos and snack station are.'

'There's a sunshade and table and some nice bushes if it gets too hot,' Suzy added.

They ran up the steps and scanned the scene from their new vantage point.

At the bottom of the steps, litter bins surmounted by a metal pole with clamped tannoys and a fake driftwood signpost directed *To Mellow Creek and Waterspout Café.* Jim tallied their position on the waterpark map.

'Yes, that's perfect, Daddy, this lounger area has *good* Suspilio.'

A tropical dew soaked the white, blue and fuchsia PVC ribs of the striped loungers in the shade of the palms. They tipped the water off and dragged them side by side under a dark blue and pink sunshade, marking their tenure with carefully laid towels, swim goggles, a paperback and beach bag.

'Time to explore,' Suzy grasped her dad's hand and led him back down the steps excitedly, mindful of the yellow signs positioned in the sandy grass verges repeating the warning: *No Running* and *No Corra,* for Spanish speakers. They passed *Lazy Lianas,* a Polynesian beach hut-style refreshments shack, with bar stools matching the loungers. It was shuttered up, too early yet for Coors beer and corn dogs.

'Let's grab a double ring and go to *Mellow Creek* for our first ride,' Suzy implored.

At the creek entrance large netted enclosures held stacks of big pink inflatables. Jim grabbed a two seater raft with handles and they splashed eagerly down the wide steps into the shallow launch pool. Jim held the chrome rail and steadied the raft while Suzy slumped bum first in an armchair position, grabbing the handles. Jim followed, his weight momentarily rocking the taut inflatable. They sat back to back.

'The water feels like you can't feel it,' Suzy commented as they floated pleasantly under high palms and cactus planted slopes, the hot sun prickling their English skins.

'That's because it must be around blood temperature, so it just feels wet.'

Another fake driftwood sign scrawled in pirate handwriting warned of *Cool Cascades ahead* which explained the swelling roar of a waterfall. They rounded the next bend and the river divided into two channels, one leading to a cave with gushing falls at the entrance and the other a continuation of the mellow stream.

'You can choose waterfall or cop out into the big-baby stream,' Jim said, mischievously urging the raft towards the waterfall.'

'No Daddy, my hair will get all wet,' Suzy giggled at the futility of her protest as her dad heaved the raft into the perilous channel.

They both gasped as water thundered down heavily, pummelling their backs and thighs and spinning them breathless into the coolness of a mock rock tunnel.

'It looks like one of the props from Star Trek,' Jim said just as a pirate voice from a speaker above warned, *Rapids ahead, hold tight or be shark bait!*

They were propelled under another cascade of water at the tunnel exit into a gushing current that quickly carried them to the end where the big-baby channel converged into a soothing quiet stretch of stream. Suzy gazed thrilled at the mini-whirlpools where the swollen current converged with the calmer water.

'Ah, luxury!' Suzy said, relieved to bask in the instant warmth of the hot Carolina sun as she looked up in awe at the white tubular spaghetti of a scary looking log flume ride towering above her against the dazzling blue sky.

'So you mentioned *bad Suspilio*, Suzy. What does that feel like?'

'Well, sometimes I get a horrible depressing mood that makes me feel so anxious, like watching black and white vintage cartoons on a grey Sunday afternoon in January and you'd much rather be in school, even doing double maths.'

'I know what you mean, those old cartoons are creepy, and that glum loneliness you get on a Sunday afternoon in winter, I don't even like talking about it. But you can still get a really downbeat mood on a bright, sunny day.'

'Yes, I know, and I call that *Cheesy Light*.'

'What? Cheesy as in embarrassing?'

'No, cheesy as in that light you get in supermarkets in the cheese section. It's really bright and cold. I always feel a bit headachy when I see it; a bit sickly and miserable like that time I was off school with flu for about two weeks.'

Jim laughed at her description of fluorescent chillers.

'Cheesy light is that sunlight you get in winter or early spring, but there's something much nicer about summer sunlight. You can still feel weird, but somehow you feel less anxious.'

'You're warm for a start,' Jim rationalised.

They floated by a cactus-planted atoll midstream with a giant resin pelican perched on an old fashioned round buoy with mast and lantern. The red and white buoy was painted with the words Pelican Point.

'The pelican we saw has been turned into plastic,' Suzy joked.

'Along with a volcano,' Jim pointed to a fifteen foot high mock rock volcano with fake magma spilling over the brim. 'The sign says *Vulcan's Vista* with *Ye Old Bubbler Geyser* right ahead.

The same pirate voice from earlier instructed: *Geyser ahead, keep left to stay dry, me hearties.*

'We have to keep left it says,' Suzy advised, excitedly.

'Let's get wet then,' Jim laughed, paddling urgently to join the right hand current.

Blasts of icy water rained down on them from a water fountain located behind the volcanic cone.

'That was freezing, Daddy,' Suzy objected while laughing hysterically.

Around the next bend, another atoll with a wrecked skiff hull draped with fishing nets was backdrop to a pirate skeleton wearing tri-corn hat, tattered shirt and ragged knee high breeches, sitting astride an open treasure chest with gleaming coins. A sign nailed to the broken mast read *Don't Feed the Sharks*. A hidden speaker played the menacing *Jaws* theme: *durrm, dum…durrm, dum…*

Suzy and Jim laughed to be confronted around the next loop with a giant fake shark with open mouth, but that was it.

'I thought at least it was going to squirt us,' Jim said, disappointed.

'Maybe it was meant to, but needs to be fixed by the park men, because there's a tube in its throat. Oh look we're nearly back to where we started.'

They could see the shallow *Mellow Creek* entrance approaching ahead.

'We've completed one circuit,' Suzy observed, 'it looks like someone else is going to get in. Hurry up so they're not right behind us, I don't want anyone too close.'

'No, and I can't be bothered to speak to anyone yet,' Jim added, sweeping his arms like paddles to move ahead hastily.

They passed a young mother with toddler and an older women, perhaps in her late forties. The mother adjusted the young boy's sun cap and applied white sunscreen like goose fat to the parts of his body not covered by his UV-protect swimsuit.

'It's a shame someone else is coming into our little river, we had it all to ourselves,' Suzy complained.

'I know, the park will start to fill up quite quickly now as it's the May holidays. By eleven o'clock there'll be loads more people here.'

In the distance they could see a family of four pulling two loungers together and setting their bags and towels on top.

'Still, it's very quiet on the stream, so we should stay here longer,' Suzy suggested. 'I hope that little boy doesn't wee in the water.'

'It's a common problem and that's why there's so much chlorine in it,' her dad replied. 'A little toddler's wee isn't going to harm, but

'I don't like the thought of him doing a poo. That would clear me out of the river for the rest of the day,' Jim laughed, but he was quite serious.

'It would certainly spoil our nice Suspilio morning,' Suzy added.

'So how would you improve this Suspilio Day, Suzy? How would you make it perfect?'

'Daddy – I've already told you; Suspilio is a feeling like a never-felt-before mood with each mood a different colour on the paint chart.' She paused pensively and wagged her finger aloft like a professor having a *Eureka* moment. 'Actually, a big bag of marbles is a much better way to describe Suspilio.'

'Loved marbles when I was nine or ten, I was obsessed with them,' Jim smiled, remembering his brushed-denim string-pull bag as pendulous as a bull's scrotum.

'Yes Daddy, so was I. I had a favourite glassy one with a bright yellow and pink flame shape swirl. It looked like a strawberry and lemon Starburst had melted inside.'

'Mm, good enough to eat, and probably why kids choke on marbles.'

'Do they?' Suzy asked, concerned.

'I would guess so, probably; well, toddlers or babies anyway - just one more thing for parents to worry about.

'Do you remember I ate a crayon when I was little, Daddy. It was a lovely pink one and I just thought it would taste like the colour.'

'Yes, I remember! Do you think marbles are good representations of the uniqueness of Suspilio then?'

'Uh huh.' Suzy shifted her lounging angle in the pink inflatable as her legs and back had started to stick to it uncomfortably. She splashed water on the pink PVC to cool it.

'Yes some marbles, I think the rusty brown shades with thin wispy flames make me feel Suspilio sadness; but sometimes cosiness,' she said thoughtfully, 'but bright ones with oranges and yellows and pinks and bright blues and light greens make me feel Suspilio happiness or a mixture of happy and sad feelings, like clothes

225

flapping on Mum's washing line and playing teddy picnics in the garden when I was little.' She paused in remembrance, gazing at the overarching oleander blooms. 'But I had another marble with a big dark blue wisp that made me feel sad, like a faraway land.'

Jim smiled benignly at his daughter's poetic musings.

'You have more Suspilio days when you are very young, Daddy.'

'How's that?' Jim asked.

'Because every day is more likely to have that dreamy feel to it when you are young and innocent.'

'And every experience is new?' Jim suggested.

'Yes.'

'The hummingbird zone is coming up again soon, Suzy, keep an eye out.'

'I suppose marbles are a bit like snowflakes or little Suspilio planets, then,' Jim said, 'because each one is unique from another.'

'Yes.'

There was just one hummingbird on the trumpet flower now. The other two had flitted.

'Isn't it amazing how metallic and shiny the feathers are, Daddy.'

'Yes, stunning; a miracle of aerodynamics and engineering.'

Jim spun the ring round so Suzy was facing backwards.

'Just changing my aspect, so I can face forwards a bit.'

'Okay.'

'I wonder how it could be improved—not the hummingbird—your Suspilio Day. How would you design a perfect Suspilio Day?' Jim probed. 'This mellow river is a pretty good start isn't it?'

'Yes, I suppose so, but the really happy Suspilio mood was at the beginning when the sun was just coming up after we left the changing rooms and we had the whole park to ourselves. Now people are in the park, it has changed the mood a bit, not terribly yet because the two ladies looked kind and the little boy was very cute.'

'Ah, yes, other people do affect your mood,' Jim reflected, remembering the ignoramus on the plane who reclined his seat to sleep when he was still eating his breakfast, slopping orange juice all over his tray.

'Some people make your mood better, like best friends and people in your family.'

'Your tribe you mean. All of us like our own tribe.'

'Yes, so, today for example, the good Suspilio would be more likely to stay if it was just us, or only people from our tribe.'

'Careful now, Suzy, some people would call you racist for not wanting to welcome other people,' Jim quipped.

'No way! I don't mind other people as long as they're nice and skin colour is so irrelevant.'

'You mean people who share your views.'

'Yes, mostly, as long as your views are nice ones. I mean you don't want people arguing about stuff.'

'So you want people with the same culture then.'

'What is culture, Daddy?'

'Well, it's common beliefs and attitudes towards things; like, erm the clothes we wear; the food we eat; the music we play; and how we treat each other and animals.'

'I don't mind people wearing different clothes to me or liking different food or music to me as long as they don't force me to wear the same things as them or eat the same things that they like, that I don't.'

'As long as they're kind and thoughtful, you mean.'

'Yes, and they must be gentle and love animals and nature.'

'That makes perfect sense.'

'They mustn't be greedy either. Some people are greedy and hate to share.'

'Some greedy people are greedy because they're insecure, they try to grab as much as they can in case someone else takes it from them.' Jim contemplated, 'Rulers and politicians and other people who make money from war.'

'Well yes, that's right. In a perfect Suspilio world greed wouldn't be a thing because you would always have enough of everything, whenever you wanted it.'

'There's still people who have so much and still crave more, but anyway, how would you make sure of that, Suzy?'

'Make sure? People would just make and share stuff because they loved each other.'

'Okay, so say I wanted a bag of flour to make bread. Who would make the flour? You would still have to have someone doing lots of hard slog to plant the wheat, harvest it, grind it, take it to shops and sell it.'

'Yes, but work would be happy. You know when you really like someone at school and you look forward to French or physics because you're in class with them? It would be the same in perfect Suspilio, because greedy people wouldn't be there, people would just work because it needed to be done and they enjoyed it too and you wouldn't need money because you would just share in each other's harvests.'

'You young idealist, you,' Jim smiled.

They passed under the icy waterfall and through the tunnel, laughing.

'That seemed much colder this time. Probably because it's warmer in the sunshine than before.' Jim shivered.

'What clothes would you wear in these good Suspilio worlds?' Jim shouted over the gushing rapids. Suzy clung on and waited for the calmer water before responding.

'Completely organic stuff, I guess.'

'Like grass skirts and coconut husk Hawaiian bras. A bit uncomfy don't you think?'

'I didn't mean that, Daddy, but you know, things like swim suits and silk dresses and shorts, or if you were in snowy Suspilio world, cosy jumpsuits.'

'When I was young we all thought we'd be wearing *Star Trek* type clothes and have purple hair by now,' Jim paused, musing.

'So would you make your own clothes? Swimsuits are made from polyester and nylon, an industrial process, and for a decent weave you need complex high speed jacquard weaving machines so you would still need heavy industry and jacquard operators and maintenance workers at the very least on the Suspilio planets.'

'Stop being boring with techy stuff, Daddy. And no, you wouldn't because all the industry could all be done on another planet or underground by robots that were programmed to love their boring work.'

'Ah, like Morlocks! Do you remember that old film with the blue monsters—The Time Machine—I let you watch it when you were a little girl and you were terrified.'

'They weren't robots, Daddy, they were blue apes with white hair and glowing eyes.'

'Yes, you're right, they lived underground with all the industrial machinery. They were supposed to represent the future Working Class I think and no wonder they were mad, because they were doing all the graft and the people up top were just relaxing in the stream, a bit like we are today.' Jim laughed. 'So the girl in the kiosk is a Morlock while we're chillin' on the stream and there are Morlocks in the hot kitchens preparing our pizza and chips for lunch.'

'Yes, I just thought that exact thing too!' Suzy chuckled, 'and they're fries, not chips here, Daddy. You said chips.'

'Oops, you get a bag of crisps here if you ask for chips, or iced tea if you don't specifically say hot tea as I discovered in McDonalds.'

'Faucet instead of tap too,' Suzy added, 'and cookies, not biscuits.'

'Yes, and sidewalks instead of pavements and restrooms instead of toilets.'

'When I first saw the restroom sign in the airport I thought it was a place where people could go if they were tired. I imagined lots of old people sitting in armchairs with their cases and shopping bags, having a snooze,' Suzy commented, laughing.

'I know, it's confusing at times,' Jim was still thinking about industrial processing. 'Your idea of getting robots to do the really tough jobs isn't a new one,' Jim said. 'It takes jobs away from people who need the work though.'

'I know Daddy, because cars are made by robots. But remember, in a perfect Suspilio world people would be happy to share and really enjoy giving to each other. All the greedy people who loved money would never be allowed in remember.

'You wouldn't need money for a start because you'd be a part of the living ecology of each world and you would never be short of anything you needed. All the people would just fit in with nature. Like the hummingbirds get their nectar every morning and they are really happy. You wouldn't harm any of the places you visited and every place there would be food and clothes for you. And anyway, most of the planets would have lovely warm weather, unless you specially chose a cold one for sledging or skating, so you really wouldn't need many clothes.

'Animals would be your friends too and they'd be just like living teddy bears, not just cats and dogs and hamsters, but all the animals, fish and birds as well. We wouldn't kill them because we wouldn't need to eat meat and animals wouldn't kill each other.'

'Ah, yes, the lion lies down with the lamb,' Jim remarked, 'Like a Garden of Eden. Trouble is, I really like meat, Suzy. Where would I get my juicy steaks?'

'I like meat too, especially cheeseburgers, but in a good Suspilio world you would have so much variety with vegetables and fruits you wouldn't worry about not having meat. Anyway, in the Garden of Eden, you probably wouldn't have craved meat. Anyway God would still be able to design plants that copied the flavour and texture of meat and fish if you really wanted it, but you'd be so happy anyway and satisfied with other stuff, you seriously wouldn't be bothered.'

Suzy paused, gazing up at the bougainvillea flowers wistfully. 'You know when children are at parties or playing and their mums shout for them to come in for dinner, they don't want to because they're having so much fun. It's only greedy adults who think about their stomachs all the time.'

'You're possibly right about that,' Jim said, slapping his round belly.

A commotion and splashing up ahead distracted them.

'Daddy, where did those men come from? How did they push in ahead of us?'

Two Hispanic looking men in their early-twenties floating in single rings were raucously holding a third red-headed and heavily freckled man stationary in his ring under the cold waterfall, laughing riotously; keeping him fixed under the deafening deluge as he flailed wildly and gasped for breath.

'They must have got in when we were around the other side. Their language is terrible, Suzy, I know they're just young lads, but they should watch their language especially with children around.'

Suzy and Jim reached the split stream and pushed away into the left hand channel to avoid the ruckus. The three were oblivious to their presence, and continued to swear and wrestle each other. The deluged man upended in his ring and came up panting for air out of the tunnel, chasing his ring through the rapids and cussing the other two good-humouredly. He stood at the end of the intersection and waited for his friends to join him before clearing both nostrils into the water vulgarly and taking a bow like he was on stage.

'That's disgusting doing that,' Jim observed. 'All that snot now floating on the water for children to swim into later on, bloody disgraceful. No wonder people get ill and catch ear infections in pools. It could spoil someone's holiday that.'

'They wouldn't be allowed in my perfect Suspilio.'

'Nor mine,' Jim fumed, reddening. 'Let that bunch get well ahead of us, with their snot too.'

Jim and Suzy hung back in the slacker water, slowing themselves by grabbing onto the channel sides.

'They might be allowed in if they promised to be thoughtful and stop fighting.'

231

'What?'

'My perfect Suspilio. They might be allowed in if they stopped fighting and being disgusting.'

'Hmmm. Really? That's very generous of you. Do you think they'd change?' Jim mumbled, sceptically.

'I don't know, one of them might, but maybe not all of them.'

Jim had a flashback about something he'd done in his mid-twenties.

'Well, you may be right. I suppose we all deserve a second chance,' he mused.

'Anyway, continue with your Suspilio ramblings, I was enjoying them.'

'Okay, so I'm thinking that perfect Suspilio means the sensation you are enjoying has to keep on going. I mean this holiday, for example, it kind of spoils a holiday when you start counting down the days for it to end.

'You know my diary Daddy?'

'You mean your, *what I had for dinner today and watched on TV* diary?' he winked.

'Ha ha, very funny, yes, my TV dinner diary, which you MUST NOT read!' She wagged a finger. 'But anyway, it's memorable to me and I do this thing when I'm looking forward to something; I count how many days left, say thirty days, then I count back thirty days and remember what I was doing then and think to myself, wow, thirty days just feels like a few days ago and I get excited because it just flew by. But it works the other way round too—when you're having a nice time— like now, because I know we have twelve full days left here and I've started to think that twelve days ago it was the school trip to the Natural History Museum and that feels like just yesterday.'

'I know exactly what you mean. The finiteness of pleasure means you can spoil it as soon as you start thinking about the end of it. Did you know that a famous poet, John Keats talked about that feeling? It's called *transience*. I had to study that for A-Level English Lit. It was a very memorable lesson. And my genius

232

daughter has come to the same conclusions as one of the world's greatest poets!' Jim nodded approvingly.

'Well, it is quite a normal thought, I would say,' Suzy glowed, trying to show humility.

'Anyway, a perfect Suspilio would be that happy feeling going on forever.'

'Sounds like Heaven to me.' Jim said.

'Yes.'

'Actually, the marbles make me think of Heaven, Daddy.'

'How's that?'

'Well, I heard on TV that the universe is made up of trillions of galaxies and each galaxy has billions of stars and trillions of these stars might have planets like earth.'

'We really don't know that for sure, but continue.'

'Some people think that Heaven is a single place, but it might be a collection of worlds with loads of variety, or just one giant world with loads of variety, I don't know, but imagine if you had a massive bag of trillions of good Suspilio marbles; the Starbursty ones and every marble was like a heavenly planet.'

'So Heaven might be a huge bunch of exciting themed planets which you can explore.'

'Yes, that's exactly what I mean.

'So, the Heaven part would be exploring beautiful worlds with that permanent lovely feeling we had this morning when we arrived here.'

'Yes, that would be amazing.'

'And the lovely peaceful feeling would be different across the spectrum of colours that each marble, or planet gave?' Jim suggested.

'Yes, so one planet might be lit by two or three suns - a pale pink one, a peachy one and a white one so you got a different lovely vibe every place you visited.'

'So an infinite variety of lovely moods with billions of differently themed happy zones.'

'Yes, so one place might have that nice South Carolina early morning vibe, but another one might have a cosy autumn feel and another one might have a Christmas Eve feel. And you get to flit from place to place using wormholes or something, so you could hyperspace into a different happy mood planet or part of Heaven if you fancied something different; just playing all day, relaxing in lovely waterlily ponds with gorgeous creatures and birds everywhere, that weren't afraid of you and nuzzled up to you.'

'Sounds amazing, but wouldn't you get bored just relaxing and having fun all the time.'

'No way! Besides, if you had a lovely feeling inside and you were really interested in everything you did, you would never be bored. Anyway, Jesus would probably give you jobs to do that you really enjoyed, like designing flowers or birds of paradise and then giving the design to him so he could make it. Or making delicious tray bakes and multi-coloured meringues to share with everyone. Jobs would be more like playing with your birthday presents than work.'

'You have a great imagination, Suzy. You know, Heaven may be even more different, beautiful and amazing than anything you've described. I remember a tapestry picture in the school hall when I was a little boy that read, 'Eye has not seen, nor ear heard the things that God has prepared for those who love him.'

'So it's going to be even better than anything that I can imagine. That would be awesome, Daddy.'

'Awesome? You're turning American already using adjectives like that,' Jim smiled.

'After the worm-hole hyperspace bit, how would you travel on the planets?' Jim queried.

'Anti-gravity craft that whirred, with no fumes.'

'Ah, I see.'

They approached the entrance to the creek a second time. An overweight middle-aged fat man and an equally large woman waddled wheezily to the water's edge, their inflatable rings contrastingly diminutive. The woman's ring tipped back as she launched out midstream and all her hair and face got wet.

'Talking of American culture, now there's a couple of examples for you,' Jim spoke quietly.

The large lady gasped and spluttered as she wiped the water from her face.

'Yer gonna help me or just let me flounder?' she sniped in a South Carolina accent, flustered.

The big man flushed, embarrassed, 'You rushed in like a roly-poly bug, before I had a chance...'

He jumped backward into his ring, causing a wave and the woman sniped at the man restrainedly as Jim and Suzy passed by.

'Push us ahead Daddy, so we stay ahead,' Suzy whispered as Jim put ten metres between them.

'I was surprised their bottoms fitted into the rings, Daddy,' she snickered.

'Stop staring, Suzy,' Jim whispered through his teeth like a bad ventriloquist.

'Like the man on the plane we thought would never fit in the seat, but his fat just squidged over the arms,' Suzy reminded Jim, giggling loudly. Jim turned away to hide his wide grin from the red-faced couple.

'We're far enough away, they can't see.'

Jim swept his arms in broad paddles to get further ahead.

'There's always a skinny person underneath trying to escape,' Jim decreed, chuckling.

'I think they saw us laughing, Daddy.'

'It's your fault if they did.'

'No it's not, just keep paddling. They probably thought we were laughing at something else. I feel bad now, Daddy.'

'They'll get over it, don't worry,' Jim reassured.

Suzy sat up hunched in her ring, brooding.

'The nice Suspilio vibe has gone now,' she griped, 'everything feels normal again.'

'There's always something comes along to bite you in the bum,' Jim said, 'or someone,' he added.

'Not in perfect Suspilio there wouldn't be Daddy. You wouldn't be allowed in unless you were prepared to follow the rules. You wouldn't be able to spit or snot in the ponds or rivers or have fights and arguments. All the selfish people who like to do things like that, showing off, or hurting other people and hurting animals would be sent to their own bad Suspilio worlds where they could fight and argue with each other, but they'd never be allowed in to the good Suspilio worlds because they'd spoil them too.'

'They can all go to Hell you mean,' Jim challenged, cynically.

'I hadn't thought of it like that, but yes, Hell might be all the bad Suspilio marbles, like scary worlds of fire and deserts with dust storms and horrible winds, or just miserable places like industrial estates or lonely high rise cities where it always rains and you have no friends or family and you are constantly looking for a way out, but it's just a world of city.'

'Suzy, that sounds horrible, you're making me depressed; how does a girl of your age think of things like that?'

'I have dreams like that sometimes, Daddy and I wake up crying.'

'Dear me, Suzy, that's awful, I hope you don't have dreams like that very often.' Jim looked concerned, glancing ahead.

'We're catching up to the yobs. I'll slow us down a bit, but not so much that the fatties catch up too.'

Jim jumped out of the raft and held it back for a few seconds until the men had another ten metres on them.

'It sounds a bit unfair that some people would be sent to these places without any way of escape and not be given a second chance, because we all fight and argue, Suzy - and do things we're ashamed of from time to time.'

'Yes, I know, but once we know the two options we have, we either have to stop doing what we are doing or we're not allowed to enter.'

'I understand your reasoning, but it would be difficult to stay perfect even for a short time.'

'Yes, it would be difficult, but the people who really wanted good Suspilio they would make an effort and would admit their faults so they could be given new DNA without any of the selfish bad bits and then they'd be free to go wherever.'

'So the hope of good Suspilio at the end would be an incentive?'

'Definitely. Wouldn't everyone want that?'

'You'd hope so.'

'Uh oh, we're at Pelican Point again, stand by to be soaked…'

Ye Old Bubbler Geyser reliably doused them.

'I think I'm going to get out soon and read my book. Do you want to get out next stop?'

Suzy nodded, 'Yes, I'm a bit bored now so I might go and look at the log flume ride next.'

Dripping wet, they dumped the raft back into its net and padded briskly to their sun lounger platform to fetch twenty dollars hidden inside the paperback.

'The ground is so hot, Daddy, I need to stand in the shade,' Suzy whimpered as they scooted towards *Lazy Lianas* refreshments shack. She hopped up onto one of the bar stools to take her feet off the ground, though the dark blue parts of the PVC strapping were just as uncomfortably hot to sit on.

Jim ordered a Cappuccino and a Nehi Grape Soda for Suzy.

'Daddy, I don't like the Nehi Grape Soda, it tastes of medicine.'

'Jim sipped the purple drink from the plastic cup as his coffee was being frothed. 'That's an acquired taste for sure; I guess Americans are used to it. A bit like us giving them Marmite,' he whispered.

'I don't like Marmite either,' Suzy said.

'How about one of those Jungle Juice Slush Puppies instead?'

'Yes, please. I'm going back to get my crocs.'

'Okay, I'll order it and stay here.'

Jim sat at the beach bar and waited. The swash from the wave pool and the sounds of children having fun now echoed around the park along with a tinny soundtrack playing some indistinct rap music.

Jim wondered if *Tropic-Al's* had an ASCAP public broadcast licence to play the music and figured they almost certainly did as the fines for copyright infringement could be colossal. He recalled a friend of an American friend was fined for playing Jukebox music in a small Arizona café when some guy from the record label just happened to be passing and reported him. The Jukebox Licence Office of all things got in touch and fined him and he was fortunate they'd intervened because the record label wanted to go much further with a personal lawsuit, but the judge let him off with a warning. *An innocent mistake can cause a whole bunch o' trouble,* he mused, adopting American slang into his thinking.

Where was Suzy? Her Slush Puppie was turning to dark green slop. Jim drained the dregs of his cup and put down a dollar tip when three barefoot men came scampering urgently from around the corner, scanning around fretfully. One pointed at Jim. They were the two Hispanics and the freckled red-head, who'd cleared his nose in Mellow Creek.

'Sir, sir? Do you have a young blonde daughter, about eleven or twelve?' the freckled one said.

Jim jumped from his stool and the colour drained instantly from his face.

'Yes, where is she…Wh...? What's happened?' he stammered in rising panic.

'It's okay sir, she's had a trip, I think she's fine and there's an older couple with her and a First Aider's comin'. Follow us.'

Jim ran with them around the bend and could see a small group of concerned onlookers at the log flume entrance where a bloodied Suzy was being comforted by the big fat man from the creek. The fat lady crouched down alongside, holding a wad of wet tissues on Suzy's lips, pink with blood. The fat man cradled the back of her head tenderly.

'Ah, your pop's here now young lady; lookin' very worried about ya, but we'll show him it's not as bad as it looks, you've just had a nasty shock. I can see the First Aid man a-rushin' over now too.'

'I wanted to see the log ride before I came back, but I tripped on my crocs on the steps Daddy and the man caught me,' she blubbered with difficulty through the wad of tissues.

'I saw her trip and bang her mouth on the hand rail,' the fat man said, 'but I just caught her head before she fell face first onto the bottom step. In the right place at just the right time is my motto.'

The fat lady turned to Jim, smiling sardonically, 'He caught her head, but I think she's scuffed her arms and legs by the look of it.'

Jim mouthed a dry 'thank you' to the fat man who relinquished his position and stood while Jim bent down to cuddle Suzy who was crying convulsively. The fat lady cautiously removed the dripping wad when *Tropic-Al's* First Aider, Hank knelt down and took Suzy's hand.

'You gotta slight cut on your lip, but we'll get you into our nice cool sick bay and one of the girls will grab you a soda while we patch you up and make sure you ain't got no bad cuts or bruises,' Hank advised. 'You okay to carry your girl, Pop?' he asked.

Jim nodded and lifted Suzy up as she put her arms around his neck.

The fat couple shuffled behind, carrying towels.

'You need us for anything else, sir? You got a wife or other kids we need to holler for?' the fat man asked, concerned.

'No, it's just us, but thank you,' Jim responded.

'Recognised y'all from the lazy stream back there an' well, if you need us to do anythin', I'm Archie and this is my sister, Carla.'

'No. But thanks again. We'll be okay and appreciate your help so much. I'm Jim and this is Suzy.'

'English huh? Had a good friend over there in '44. Flew *Screamin' Weemies* outta Duxford. Loved your English pubs and girls, but didn't like the warm beer.'

'Archie, he don't wanna talk about the stupid war, he's concentratin' on his little girl.'

'Sure. Sure. Sorry,' Archie shook his head, raising his big stubby hands apologetically. They halted outside the First Aid door as Jim and Suzy entered.

'Now you get better quick for yer friend Carla,' she urged kindly.

Suzy nodded, tears still running down her cheeks.

'So I guess we'll leave you guys to it, but just ask if you need anything.' Archie snapped the lid of his waterproof money holder shut and held out a business card.

'Thank you,' Jim mumbled as he pocketed it in his damp swim shorts.

'You're lookin' okay young lady, just a few scrapes and a bit of a swollen lip.' Hank turned to Jim. 'Sir, I don't think it's serious, but we always recommend that you leave the park and get checked by a medic and we'll refund your tickets. There's three hospitals you could go to: The Trident, St Francis or VA depending where you're staying; real easy to reach by cab from here, but if you want to stay in the park, we have to insist that you sign the waiver sheet here to say you've been advised and waived the recommendation to leave. You okay with that, sir?'

'I think I'm okay now Daddy,' Suzy said, red eyed.

'Are you sure?' Jim looked at Suzy who nodded. He scanned the paper and signed it.

'Thank you for your help and for the soda.'

'Sure sir, you and Suzy have a great rest of your day now.'

Suzy sucked the Mountain Dew clumsily through the straw as she hobbled slowly back to the loungers. She had a thick lip, as well as a grazed shin and a sore elbow which were both in blue waterproof bandages.

'No broken bones or missing teeth today, sweetheart, just a bit sore and feeling sorry for ourselves, huh? You lose concentration for a second and that's when accidents happen. Like when I nearly burnt the house down with the chip pan.'

Suzy nodded again, sniffling.

They reached their loungers and pulled them into the shade. They sat spectating the crowds in the wave pool and the children screaming down the slides. Suzy seemed calmer now.

'I think I'm having a Suspilio moment, Suzy,' Jim surmised, smiling and tapping Suzy's thigh reassuringly.

'No, seriously, I've got a kind of *déjà vu* feel, like everything feels echoey and strange, but nice again.'

'I think I know what you mean, Daddy. It's been a weird morning. All the people we were saying mean things about ended up being nice.'

'I know, Suzy, I feel terrible about that. I was thinking the same. I hated even the look of them earlier, but now I feel a real affection for them.'

Minutes later, the young freckled red-head came up the steps holding hands with a girl about Suzy's age.

'How ya doin' guys? I told my kid sis' about the pretty English girl who hurt herself and she's come over to say hello and to see if you want to play.'

Jim got up to shake the young man's hand. 'Jim and Suzy. And you are?'

'Kurt and this is my baby sis, Grace.'

'I'm not a baby!' Grace objected, pouring out the contents of a large fluffy purple zipped pencil case onto Suzy's lounger towel containing various toys, sweets and stuff onto Suzy's towel like a lucky dip. The girls chatted excitedly and played for a few minutes, while Jim talked about sports cars with Kurt.

'Grace and I are going on to ride the log flume, Daddy,' Suzy interrupted.

'Okay, just be careful and no running, watch your step. Kurt and I are going to that big café around the corner for some lunch and you girls should meet us there in half an hour, okay? You know where it is, it's just past the refreshment shack near the Mellow Creek entrance.'

'Yes, Daddy.'

Suzy and Grace galloped across the park toward the high zig-zag steps of the *Log Jammer* flume slide, Suzy quite forgetting her cuts and bruises. Meanwhile, at *Waterspout Café* Jim ordered beers and nachos and Archie and Carla who were eating wings and fries, waved them over and the new acquaintances joined each other and chatted animatedly.

When Grace and Suzy arrived an hour later, they half-heartedly rushed down a pizza slice each, leaving the crusts and ran back into the park to spend a happy afternoon on slides, rings and rafts; sporting blue tongues from bubble gum lollies until the palm tree shadows lengthened and a stilled wave pool signalled the 6pm close.

The little tribe parted at the changing room doors with high fives and handshakes. Suzy gave Grace one final wave as her big brother and his friends wheelspun out of the hot car park in a metallic gold Pontiac Trans Am V8 that sparkled as golden as the rays of the evening sun. Suzy thought her dad's little hire car shamefully small as they drove back into Charleston, skins glowing, to a chilly air conditioned motel room, the base for the last throes of youthful innocence before she transitioned into a new school in England, difficult teenage years and the highs and lows of adulthood.

*   *   *

She could taste blood in her mouth as she fumbled crossly with the airbag, pushing it down as it slowly deflated, giving her opportunity to look in her rear view mirror at her split lip and then at the shocked gentleman in the vehicle behind; and beyond him, at the long queues of traffic building up for miles behind on the motorway, probably all the way to High Wycombe. It was the first time she had ever been at the front of a traffic jam.

Her face stung and a tear tumbled down her cheek as she looked at her swollen lips. The pain revived the vague memory of getting a fat lip a long time ago, yet the stinging was mingled with a trembling exultation of relief as she realised she had narrowly escaped death from a rolling log thanks to the Pontiac cutting her up.

A rap on her window interrupted her contemplation. The man in the van was checking on her. He was uninjured, though shaken and said that the police would be arriving soon. No one else seemed to have been hurt.

As she waited, she picked up the contents of her dad's bedside drawer and swept them back messily into the open box file.

She would eventually get home and her cut lip would heal and her car would get fixed and the file would be put in another drawer somewhere, and she would move on with her life, shifting the box and its contents from cupboard to cupboard; house to house; town to town.

In another thirty years, one lonely Sunday afternoon in January, she might—just might—pull it out from the under bed drawer and remember the day the care home staff handed it to her when he died. She would open its fusty lid and discover a dog-eared business card used as a bookmark inside an old paperback titled *Slow Down and Chill Out: Finding Your Peace in a Stressful World* and she would scrutinise the title and something might just click.

And on the old card she would read a name, *Archie from Angel Holdings Inc.,* with a Charleston address and she would remember going there. She might get around to asking her grandson, a vintage computer whizz, to download the files from that old disc. Possibly.

If she does, she will be transported back to the warmth of a forgotten South Carolina spring; the splashing of wave pools and hubbub of children having fun on flumes and remember her dad taking that photo of those half-remembered friends on the sun lounger deck, evoking the memory of a sore elbow and shins under the blue bandages and how hard it was to hold a smile with a thick lip. She might even connect the name on the card with the fat man on the photo and remember his soothing voice and how he caught her head in his big hand when she tripped. She would certainly never know this side of eternity how Archie Angel protected her from suffering a life-changing neck injury on the steps.

And the sweet little red headed girl whose hand she was holding on the photo? Would she ever recall her name? Maybe. She would certainly remember her waving goodbye in that gorgeous gold car of her brother's; what was it again? She would have to look up vintage American sports cars.

Curiosity might compel her to focus on the sun lounger just in shot and enlarge the scattered contents of the fluffy purple bag lying on a towel just in frame. She would smile at the jumble of Starburst sweets; animal figurines; crayons; rubber pterodactyl and marbles and she might—just might—have a small epiphany about *kwinky-dinks*.

And as bleak rain patters on her window in the glum January bedroom, her thoughts might wander to a warm and misty morning when she floated carefree under canopies of flowers and laughing waterfalls, as the memory of a Heavenly conversation with her Daddy whispers a faint but living hope, tender as a waft from a hummingbird wing, one good *Suspilio Day* a long time ago.

///strong.atomic.boom
"THE GAMBLERS"

On Monday morning, Jean and Jack Symonds sat down in the small tea room satisfied. This was how their days would be from now on, leisurely and pleasant.

They had driven the half mile to the town centre from Foxglove Cottage and Jack had secured the envied two hour disabled bay outside Iceland supermarket, perfectly large enough for the Audi Estate, courtesy of Jean's sporadic, though light, arthritic knee issue. They had walked the two hundred yards to their favourite tea room briskly as they saw the late May shower approaching.

Life was agreeable and as pulchritudinous as the large cheese scones and cream filled coffee meringues served in the oak beamed Dickens-themed tea room where they sat, overlooking the harbour.

This week's morning routine for Jack and Jean had consisted of a lie-in until 8am; BBC News in bed; a flick through the papers; a potter in the garden; sunbathing on the patio and a swipe through the last minute cruise cancellations on Jean's iPad. They had polished the gleaming stainless steel in the new kitchen obsessively and plumped up the sofa cushions countless times. Jean was however quite concerned about some sticker adhesive still remaining on the newly fitted hob and microwave door, so today's mission was finding solvent glass cleaner in a hardware store to ensure the kitchen was optimally gleaming.

If the weather continued cool and changeable, Jack suggested they might take an impromptu week away in the Southern Caribbean; there was a golf course in Antigua he was keen to visit, after all, they had nothing else pressing.

The couple's predictable and plush retirement future had been mapped out thanks to Jack's prestigious career in Local Authority Health Care in London, with its excellent Public Sector pension scheme. Jack had employed Jean as a secretary some twenty years previously and made sure, after they were married, that she was promoted to a very nice position in the Housing Department, such was his influence. It was an ideal role in that it didn't overstretch her and was 9 to 5 rigid, so that she could still find time to cook her wonderful cuisine in the evenings.

Jack had easily wangled work experience for their two children in the Local Authority too, aware of the unwritten, though well acknowledged foot-in-the-door rule, that they had a job for life if they wanted it, simply by turning up, attending the easy courses that pushed them inch by inch up the promotion ladder without the hazards and uncertainties of life in the Private Sector jungle where their mediocrity and languor would be quickly weeded out.

Jack's Finance expertise had enabled him to deliver healthcare-on-a-budget and he was reaping the rewards of early retirement at sixty with the chocolate-box-beautiful three bedroom dormer cottage in Broadstairs, Kent, with stunning sea views as well as his five bedroom London home skirting Barnes Common.

Jean and he loved a bargain. They couldn't understand how the coffee houses and tea rooms could turn a profit, given their great value for money cake and cream teas for a meagre £4.50. These venues afforded them the opportunity to feed more cheaply than they could cook for themselves as well as meet other like-minded folks. Importantly, it would enable them to glow with pride when someone would ask, 'Are you locals or are you on holiday?'

'Oh, we're a bit of both these days,' Jack said smugly, responding to the shadowy, well-spoken gentleman silhouetted against the small window by the corner table. As their eyes grew accustomed they saw he was dressed in a black, tailored, pinstripe suit with black waistcoat, burgundy shirt, dark claret tie and claret hanky in his breast pocket. The scar from his left eye to his chin and his azure eyes delivered a clichéd Nazi-villain appearance. Furthermore, his slight lisp carried a menacing tone that created both trepidation and subliminal respect. He placed a folded Times newspaper to his right and proceeded to make calculations in a Moleskine notebook, occasionally running his fingers through his thick sweepback grey hair.

'Jean and I are recently retired and hale from Wimbledon.' Jack surmised that Barnes was sufficiently close to Wimbledon to justify its location to a Broadstairs local who probably didn't know South London.

'Wimbledon. The town or village? I would occasionally visit clients for lunch in The Fox and Grapes. It overlooked the pond by The Common? Next to Cannizaro Park?'

'Actually, I *said* Wimbledon, but it's *really* Barnes. We often say that in case people don't know Barnes, but everyone knows Wimbledon.'

'Ah, I see, said the stranger,' closing his notebook and securing it with the red elastic bookmark.

'Jean and I have just purchased a holiday home here; used to come here a lot as a boy you know, always loved the Kent coast. Are you local?' Jack blurted, embarrassed at the Barnes' *faux pas*.

'Yes, I've lived here a good number of years now.' The grey haired stranger leant back in his seat and smiled, eyeing Jean and Jack unsettlingly over the rim of his vintage oval spectacles.

'Jean and I like to pop in for a morning coffee before heading up the cliff promenade for a breather, hopefully missing the showers,' Jack laughed, as though the comment was funny.

'Yes. It is a very pleasant walk to North Foreland Lighthouse.'

'Yes very nice. Lovely, lovely,' Jack replied, clumsily.

The smart gentleman was still the only other customer in the tea room. Mondays were often quiet until the lunchtime trade and Jack felt compelled to keep the conversation going rather than manage the difficult silence or attempt to converse banalities with Jean, given the proximity of the stranger.

'Jack and Jean Symonds,' Jack announced awkwardly.

'Arthur King,' the stranger responded, easing himself up leisurely from his seat and walking the three paces to their table. He loomed over them, his arm extended.

'Oh, er, how do you do,' Jack and Jean offered elbows, conscious of contamination, 'We hope you don't mind not shaking hands, it's just …'

'I understand,' the stranger nodded, refusing the elbow nudge and withdrawing his arm. He ambled back to the window seat. Jean flushed and fidgeted awkwardly with her napkin, wiping her teaspoon.

'We've both been a little poorly recently and wouldn't want to give you anything,' Jack said, defensively.

'It's not a problem, one has to be careful when meeting strangers,' Arthur King picked up his folded newspaper, flipping it open with a jerk.

'And you are dressed very smartly for business, Sir,' Jack flattered, keen to override any offence he had caused; drawing the conversation down a monetary route.

'I run a small premises in the town,' Arthur said vaguely, lifting his espresso cup slowly to his mouth while scanning the Times crossword in front of him. He set the cup back down unhurriedly in the saucer.

'An office or retail establishment?' Jack enquired, feigning interest.

'King's Penny Arcade,' Arthur replied, precisely articulating each syllable.

'Oh,' Jean and Jack responded simultaneously.

'It is a small and traditional establishment.'

'Ah yes, the amusements arcade just off the High Street?' Jack nodded.

Arthur King folded his paper and laid it down again.

'I prefer to call it a Family Fun Venue,' Arthur corrected.

'Oh right, sorry. I think we know which one you mean,' Jean chipped in, 'I would imagine there's some good trade in Broadstairs with all the visitors.'

Arthur King turned his head to the window, and brooded for long seconds at the ocean horizon before responding. 'It is seasonal, but adequate,' he replied, returning focus to his coffee, stirring it slowly and silently,

'I clear enough to keep the place going. I have a few *Space Invader* type video games and pinball tables, while a small bread-and-butter profit is made from coin-pushers and crane-grabbers that help with

248

the overheads. I have a range of customers, mostly tourists but three or four regular locals who play the slots.'

'The slots? Like the Vegas machines?' Jean asked.

'Yes, fruit machines, typically £25 and £50 jackpots,' Arthur King opened his notebook and scribbled something.

There was a long pause and Jack leaned forward about to speak, but Arthur continued unexpectedly.

'I have a £400 jackpot licence, so nothing like the large Vegas pay-outs. I'm limited by my premises description of Family Entertainment Centre.

'You'll have to come and pay me a visit, and perhaps …' Arthur paused, adjusting his notebook position neatly and levelling his gaze on Jack and Jean, '...you can pick up some essential winning tips.'

'Winning tips?' Jack was surprised at the invitation and folded his arms protectively thinking of how to politely decline the offer.

'I remember spending my pocket money in arcades when I was a lad and always came away impoverished. I learned my lesson early,' Jack looked at Jean, 'we're not gamblers are we Jean?'

Jean shook her head with a brief wobble, mouthing a silent 'no' as she brought her cappuccino to her mouth, mopping the froth self-consciously from her top lip with her napkin.

'Aren't you?' Arthur quizzed, 'Are you sure about that?' he smiled probingly, targeting his piercing blue focus at Jack who squirmed uncomfortably in his pink Pringle sweater.

'Well, yes, of course, the odd lottery ticket withstanding,' Jack responded brusquely, 'To be honest, I've always considered arcades and casinos, well … a little … unscrupulous.'

Jean nudged Jack, embarrassed, 'Oh, Jack you can be very opinionated at times, I do apologise for my husband's directness.'

Arthur King removed his spectacles, smiling, tugged his claret handkerchief from his breast pocket and wiped the lenses.

A breezy waitress bustled a tiny cup and saucer to King's table, breaking the silence.

'There you go Mr King, your top up.'

Arthur acknowledged his second espresso of the morning with a polite nod, replacing his glasses and handkerchief.

'Yes, indeed,' King responded drily, 'they can be most unscrupulous.'

Jack and Jean flushed, unsure how to respond.

'But my little 'amusements arcade' is now more than ever, necessary,' King continued, staring into his cup for long seconds as though divining something in the dark brew. He plopped a sugar cube in and stirred it silently.

Jack shuffled in his seat uncomfortably, pushing the table forwards and his seat backwards, increasing the distance between himself and the stranger. Jean shuffled her seat closer to Jack.

'Necessary?' Jack asked, bemused.

'Yes. It provides an essential service for some of my most loyal customers.'

'What? Gambling? I wouldn't call that essential,' Jack snorted.

'Do you have any idea what it's like to run a Family Entertainment Centre, Jack?' Arthur continued.

'Well, n...no, of course not,' Jack stammered slightly, 'I would imagine it has its challenges like any trade,' Jack replied regaining confidence.

'Would you like to learn?' King directed his keen blue eyes once more at the couple.

'Well, I'm not sure, you see Jean and I er …'

'There's no hurry, please enjoy your scone and meringue. I will give you a short tour. It will take just half an hour of your time. You may find it invaluable.'

'Well, if you really insist. Are you okay with that Jean?'

Jean nodded demurely.

'Just half an hour you say? You see we have car parking to attend to and a few errands as well as our walk …' Jack knew he had an hour and a half before risking a ticket.

'Half an hour, I promise, but we'll wait out the shower,' King nodded at the waitress, pointing to Jack and Jean's table. 'My tab.'

'Oh, er, thank you, that is very kind of you,' Jean's voice faltered, nervously.

Jack and Jean felt obliged to rush their coffee and cake to get the chore over with. The shower was short lived and the sun shone brightly over the harbour as they crumpled their napkins and pushed their plates forward neatly to indicate they were ready.

Arthur King drained his cup, stood up and politely motioned them toward the exit with outstretched arm and a slight click of his heels.

'It's only a very short walk,' Arthur reassured as he pulled opened the coffee shop door and stood aside with a slight bow, guiding Jean and Jack into the warm May sunshine.

The High Street was much busier now at 11.30am, loud with cars and chattering families walking excitedly down to the harbour and beach.

King looked like a City man, incongruous against a backdrop of gift shops and their postcard racks; swollen nets of neon beach balls, buckets and spades; and bins of kites and plastic windmills butting onto the wet pavements now steaming in the sun. The bistros and café owners were dragging seats onto the street after the early showers ready for the lunchtime trade.

Arthur King nimbly stepped around the puddles in his polished black brogues as he shepherded Jack and Jean into a side street where they could faintly discern the familiar sounds of an amusement arcade. They turned another corner to hear more clearly the muffled thump of techno music, laser sound effects and explosions along with thudding pinball flippers and sirens and a muffled baritone video-game voice droning: *You have sustained a lethal injury. Sorry, but you are finished here.*

Jack and Jean gawped at the brash arcade over the road to the right, lit up like a fairground with flashing lights tracing around the perimeter of the Amusements sign in a maddening, repetitive sequence.

'Here we are,' Arthur clicked his heels again and extended his arm, directing the couple to the left where three steps led upwards towards an open shop frontage, two feet higher than street level.

'Please you go first,' Arthur instructed.

'Oh, I thought …' Jack hesitated.

'You thought the large amusements arcade opposite was mine?'

'Yes,' Jack turned surprised scanning the discreet red neon sign above the shop which read: *King's Penny Arcade*.

'Nothing quite so large or ostentatious,' Arthur said, smiling. 'I prefer small and understated.'

Jack and Jean walked hesitantly into a plush, plum-carpeted room about twenty feet wide and sixty feet long. Cosy with pinballs, fruit machines, video games and a central *Penny Falls* with two crane grabber machines containing soft toys, bagged plastic toys and various stacked boxes banded with ten and twenty pound notes. It was dark and strangely comforting to be out of the glare of the late morning sun. The three sauntered quietly towards a change kiosk located at the top left where a young woman with long chestnut brown hair sat counting coins. The sounds of the arcade opposite became gradually muted and distant in the softly carpeted tranquillity of the room.

'Denise, I am showing a couple of friends, Mr and Mrs Symonds around the arcade and then you can pop out for your lunch at noon.'

The young girl smiled and motioned a thumbs up through the booth screen. Arthur turned back to his guests, 'Very loyal and reliable girl, Denise. You need people like that.'

Arthur led Jean and Jack to the centre of the arcade.

'You can see the arcade has a good selection of traditional machines. *The Penny Falls* is the oldest; 1950s; adapted the first time in 1971 from old pennies to new decimal penny and two pence pieces; again in 1985 to take five and ten pence slots; now it takes fifty pences and one pound coins. That's inflation for you.

'The crane grabbers and video games pull in the family trade and the fruit machines cater for the gamblers. Our operation is unique in Broadstairs. We never pay out tokens, only cash.'

'Why is that?' Jack asked.

'I feel duty bound to reward the gamblers with real cash, not fake money. Many of my competitors require you buy tokens to play the machines, and even though you can change them back to money it is a psychological ploy, because most people will simply put all their token winnings back because they do not value them in the same way as they would traditional pounds and pence. I view that as a dishonest sleight of hand.

'My personal favourites here are the pinballs. Genuinely good family fun. We have five machines, two modern virtual pinballs which are cheaper to maintain as well as three classic mechanical pinballs, all vintage machines. Here is a 1979 *Stern* and next to it are the two vintage *Bally*.'

Arthur caressed the machines proudly, polishing a smudge off the glass with his claret handkerchief.

'The 1980 *Stern Meteor* is themed on destroying an incoming asteroid, while the 1975 *Bally Air Aces* here is based around World War 1 dogfights. My personal favourite however is this old 1970 Bally piece, *Camelot* - aptly named you might say for an Arthur King,' he chuckled, his scar more pronounced and his eyes glinting ominously in the faint glare of the machine.

'The main trade starts from lunchtime onwards,' Arthur slowly turned to face his guests as he deftly dropped a two pound coin into the medieval-themed pinball, 'So while it's quiet …' he summoned Jack and Jean closer, 'I think you should don your armour and mount your steeds. Happy jousting, Jack.'

'Er, no it's okay, thanks, I haven't played pinball since …'

'I insist,' Arthur guided Jack central and placed his hands on the buttons with his palm in the small of Jack's back. 'Stand up straight with a slight lean in towards the game. Now relax. Breathe and listen to the sounds of the game.'

Arthur pulled back the plunger and fired the first ball, his sinister edge diminishing somewhat with his enthusiasm for the game.

'Connect the sounds with the things they do and you'll stay ahead,' Arthur instructed.

'The pop-bumper bells and kicker-bar clicks and knocks will tell you the machine is keeping the ball moving. The siren sounds when the machine is about to launch the ball at you hard, so listen and enjoy the experience. The more bells and noise, the more points you're racking up. The important thing is to return the ball to the top of the playfield and not let it drop between the flippers.

Jean stood awkwardly by as her sixty year old husband appeared ridiculous in his golfing best sweater and pants playing a teenager's arcade game.

'Don't flip both flippers, Jack. Use only one flipper at a time when you need to or you'll drain the ball. After you flip the ball let the flipper drop immediately or you'll leave a big gap for it to fall between. Ah, too late! Let's fire up the next one.'

Arthur pulled back the plunger and fired another ball.

'You'll find by holding the flipper up at the right time, you can stop the ball dead.'

The word *dead* echoed disquietingly in Jean's head. Presently, by some fluke Jack caught the ball in the trough of the flipper.

'Well done, Jack! You're *Camelot's* new Merlin. Time to take a breath and think of what you want to aim for in the playfield. You've got four mushroom bumpers straight up, but you need to look where the big points are. See the red light by the jousting lane on the left, that will give you 300 points and an extra ball. That's your target.'

A grin crossed Jack's face. He took aim and flipped the ball smoothly up the lane. The machine lit up with pleasant chimes and thunks like a vintage typewriter. His Player 1 score was 760 on the backboard with one ball down and one in play.

Jack was confident as the ball bounced back and forth in the top bumpers, succumbing to gravity and ratcheting up more points as it fell down through the top columns, sliding into the central mushroom cluster with delightfully percussive repetition. Suddenly the ball just dropped toward the outlane around the back of the flippers into the gate. Jack lunged his bodyweight forward trying to prevent it and the flippers froze.

'Oh, shoot!' Jack exclaimed, frustrated, 'The flippers have stopped working.'

'Ah, the over aggressive nudge, Jack. You're Sir-Lancelot-like-enthusiasm has caused the tilt sensor to paralyse your game and your end-of-ball bonus points are cancelled. Don't get me wrong mind you, a little judicious nudging is considered perfectly fair play in Camelot, and done right, can save a ball that might otherwise be lost. Unfortunately, machine abuse in Arthur King's Camelot automatically ends the game, but let me say Jack, I could detect the thrill in your eyes when you achieved that first free ball.'

'Yes, but my gamble didn't pay off,' Jack smiled, his palms moist with the thrill of the game.

'And you said you weren't the gambling type, Jack,' Arthur added, sardonically.

'Well, perhaps I did get a bit over excited with that last nudge,' Jack stepped back from the machine rubbing his hands together.

'Would you like another go Jack? How about you Jean? I think Meteor would be fun. Let's get you prepped to face the incoming threat from space …'

Jean shook her head and Jack responded, 'No thank you, that was fun, but our time is pressing, so please carry on with the rest of the tour.'

'Are you sure? It's never too late to learn new skills Jean and see if you can beat your husband and clock up some points without nudging.'

'No, really, no. I mean no thank you. It's definitely not my thing,' Jean asserted, blushing.

'That's quite alright Jean, no pressure,' Arthur said soothingly. 'Though talking of nudges and machine abuse, let me lead you over to The Penny Falls. Do you know how many lolly sticks we pull out of our coin pusher during the summer season? We daily have to deal with about twenty machine alarms a day.'

'Lolly sticks? Why?' Jean questioned.

'Children are very resentful of losing their hard-earned pocket money and the bent lolly stick is the classic method for recouping losses, especially when you see a tantalising ledge of teetering coins. Those sticky lolly-wielding fingers are the ideal way to nudge fifty-pences back into the trough. We feign outrage of course; but aside from cleaning tacky finger marks it really makes no difference to us, because the kids simply put the salvaged coins back into another slot.'

'You see Arthur, that's why I said I thought arcades were unethical, you take money from children.' Jack spoke exultantly, justifying his earlier criticism.

'Sweet shops do too, but we don't give kids cavities or diabetes,' Arthur rebounded.

'Yes, but …' Jean was about to say something, when someone in the far corner won a jackpot on the machine. The tinkling of coins into the win tray put her off her train of thought.

Arthur turned to face Jean, 'Another King's winner,' he winked.

'Let me explain something about *The Penny Falls* Jean. Your husband views this contraption as bit of a children's bully, stealing their pocket money. Conversely, I view it more as a strict schoolteacher with a cane in his hand …' Arthur clapped his hands together suddenly with a loud crack and Jack and Jean flinched as Arthur continued, '… teaching children an important life lesson.

'When children lose their money, it delivers a short, sharp shock, certainly not life threatening, Jean, and as Jack confided earlier, losing money in arcades gave your husband an early warning; a setback that he learned from. You could say it was like catching childhood measles; a little unpleasant at the time, but being struck by it when you're young prevents a greater malady later in life.'

'Are you saying a kid's bad run on the Penny Falls can stop them gambling as an adult?' Jack sneered, looking to Jean for support.

'For some, yes, Jack. But not all.'

'I'm not convinced, that's just an excuse for profiteering,' Jack harrumphed.

'You call it profiteering, though if you realised the low payback on this machine over running costs, you would understand why I call it entertaining. What is the difference between my Penny Falls taking pocket money from a child to a fashion brand extorting hundreds of pounds for a pair of status trainers or for a media organisation charging children for downloading the latest movie or music video?'

'Yes, but a movie or a music video is harmless fun and with a pair of trainers you still have something to show for your money,' Jean interrupted timidly.

'Training shoe and fashion brands are renowned for exploiting children in Third World sweat shops, and movies and music videos are far from being harmless fun, Jean. My Penny Falls or pinball games don't sexualise your grandchildren like *Rihanna* or *Lady Gaga*. They don't glamorise drug taking and knife crime like rap artists. Can you remember how *The Beatles* and *The Rolling Stones* made you rebel against your parents?'

Jack's face contorted disagreeably.

Arthur continued, 'The fruits of Sixties' free-love delivered a world of social problems, not least STDs and drug addiction as well as two generations of bastard children, millions of abortions, impoverished single mothers and emasculated or absent fathers. The spirit of rebellion and its influencers, the high priests and priestesses of popular culture continue to teach our children that revolution is cool.'

Jack pursed his lips. Arthur could detect he was trying to formulate a counter argument.

'And what is your trade Jack? You haven't told me that yet. What purity are you involved in peddling?' Arthur eyed him provocatively.

'Well, I'm retired now as I told you earlier, but I was a highly dedicated Medical Officer for the NHS,' Jack affirmed proudly as Jean shot him an admiring glance.

'A very responsible role Jack, for which you were doubtless highly regarded—and rewarded—by your peers,' Arthur responded wryly, Jean and Jack barely detecting his ironic lilt.

'The NHS does indeed provide excellent emergency treatment, but on another layer the organisation is profligate. Indeed, some might

257

say your role involved channelling taxpayers' money to buy expensive and addictive drugs from government approved cartels while deriding powerful and cheap natural remedies. The NHS is also a gateway for pharmaceutical corporations to literally get under the skin of every person, cradle-to-grave, over-diagnosing and over-treating patients with services and equipment that people neither need nor want.'

'That's bloody ridiculous man,' Jack reddened, finding the eloquent assessment difficult to refute.

'Well yes, of course it's ridiculous, the NHS is marvellous,' Jean added indignantly, 'Look how healthy people are these days,' Jean said.

Arthur was silent, understanding debate was futile.

'Look Arthur, Jean and I have to get going. We thank you for the pinball game, but really we have a lot to be getting on with.' Jack was curt, unhappy at the direction of the conversation. He began leading Jean towards the sunlight at the arcade entrance.

'Jack and Jean, I understand you want to leave, but you haven't finished your tour. Please, you really must indulge me a few minutes more. You are here to learn, remember. I want to acquaint you with King's Customer Service.'

'Really Arthur, we must be going, the thing is, we've got to get back to the car and …' Jack protested, but Arthur interrupted with a plea:

'Mr and Mrs Symonds, please, indulge me,' he tilted his head and smiled disarmingly, 'Just a few more minutes from your schedule, I insist. And if you get a ticket, I will reimburse you double the fine.'

His firmness was resolute and irresistible and the idea of a small profit in a worst-case-scenario did not go unheeded by Jack.

The arcade was seeing a trickle of late morning visitors as tourists finished their breakfasts and headed to the beach. Absorbed by the pinball session and the debate, Jack and Jean had not noticed the influx or the woman sitting on a stool by the fruit machine on the left wall near the entrance. Diagonally adjacent to The Penny Falls,

258

her bulky form was silhouetted against the sunny street. Gradually her features came into focus as Arthur led them closer.

'Good morning, Meg. How are you today? It sounds like you had a little good fortune earlier.'

Meg was engrossed by the spinning reels, and didn't immediately respond to Arthur or notice the two strangers alongside, though Jack and Jean were scrutinising her overweight form with veiled derision; her liver-spotted hands sporting an array of big, cheap rings and neon-orange false nails in a lurid clash with her nicotine stained fingers.

With her right hand raised she fed the coin slot as though nourishing an insatiable mechanical beast, while her left hand hovered over the square flashing buttons, poised pianist-like over the reel-hold options.

'Hello Arfur, darlin'. I'm doin' fine thanks, other than me usual dodgy hip, but hitting the jackpot doesn't half help take the aches and pains away temporary, like.' Meg's phlegmy voice rasped moistly as though her throat was filled with sea shingle and oysters.

'Meg, delighted you've won this morning, and I would like you to meet my friends, Jack and Jean who are new to my establishment.'

Jean nodded quickly at the two strangers, returning her attention to the spinning reels. Arthur continued, 'Perhaps you can share your passion for your favourite fruit machine with them and teach them a thing or two.'

'I'm with you in one minute my lovers; I just need to hold on to Arfur's cherries here,' she laughed coarsely, as two cherries plonked gratifyingly into the win line. The overweight fruit machine aficionado pressed the hold and start buttons spontaneously in quick succession and watched the blur of outer reels excitedly. To her dismay they stopped on a lemon and BAR symbol.

'Oh blast, you've put me off my streak you lot!'

Arthur reached into his waistcoat pocket and dropped three pounds into Meg's grateful hand as recompense.

'You're a darlin', Arfur,' she said, turning bulkily on her stool and putting her ring-heavy hand forward. The couple's germ-phobic reluctance to shake was evident, but Meg's reach prevailed as her pudgy digits gripped Jean and Jack's hands in succession.

Jean vented a frail-sounding 'Oh,' relieved she had alcohol wipes in the car.

'Meg, tell my friends why you come here,' Arthur asked.

'To see my friends, Arfur and Denise of course,' she flashed her stained teeth in a broad grin and her eyes sparkled.

'Aside from that it's the best arcade in Broadstairs, with my favourite bandit here that pays in real money. You and Den look after your friend Meg, don't you Arfur?'

'We certainly hope so, Meg,' Arthur winked. 'Denise will be off to get lunch shortly so if you have any sandwich requests, let me know.

'Oh thanks Arfur, a chicken tikka baguette with cucumber would be perfect.'

'That's fine Meg. Can you tell Jack and Jean how long you've been a regular here?'

Meg was around sixty, her salt and pepper hair in a tight greasy ponytail ironed out some of the care worn wrinkles on her tanned face.

'About fifteen years at a guess. Every Wednesday morning when I get my social I come for a flutter, and every Friday afternoon after Mass. It's my special club, innit Arfur? We're a close little family here.'

'I'm very flattered you think of us that way, Meg,' Arthur patted Meg's forearm gently. Meg continued to feed the machine while Jack and Jean shuffled impatiently.

'Thank you for your time, Meg. I was hoping to introduce Jean and Jack to Billy, but it's a little early for him yet, he normally comes in after twelve. His favourite game is the *Adders and Ladders* isn't it? I know you're not a fan, but Billy reads that Snakes and Ladders fruit machine like a book. He has a knack of knowing exactly when it's going to pay out and he really gets quite resentful when he sees anyone else cutting in on his investment.'

'Too right he does,' Meg responded, momentarily distracted by another successful spin as two pound coins thudded into the tray, 'He'll stand next to you breathing over your shoulder in the background pretending to help, but really he's just waiting to pounce,' Meg's voice rattled as she pumped her winnings back into the coin slot.

Arthur turned to Jack and Jean, 'You may have seen Billy already if you've been in Broadstairs long enough. Old-fashioned-nautical chap with pipe and a beret. He's been a regular here like Meg for years. White hair, white beard, looks like Captain Bird's Eye, but he fancies himself more as The Ancient Mariner. Visitors to the lighthouse think they've seen a ghost when he goes crabbing with his old bucket.'

'A bloody pirate more like,' Meg countered, laughing coarsely. 'Always in that navy pea coat and beret. He needs to get those smelly rags in the washing machine.'

'I'm sure Billy wouldn't be so flattered by that assessment, Meg.'

'You're right, Arfur, I'm jesting, he's a good friend of ours is Billy.'

'Meg is right about Billy's coat. It could do with a dry clean, but Billy himself is very well kempt, unlike many visitors to the arcade. We had our fourth lice infestation here last year, had to get the carpets sprayed.

'Case in point, please follow me.' Arthur glided towards the centre of the arcade. The Penny Falls had three grubby looking young boys engrossed in play, wearing damp swim shorts and tee shirts, keenly shuffling around one of the slots, their bare legs and feet covered in sand. A clatter of fifty pences fell into the trough followed by whoops of pleasure. Arthur stood alongside and glared at them.

'You boys, have you seen the sand on your feet and legs? Would you go indoors at home like that? Get out of my arcade and clean yourselves up. You wouldn't dare walk on your living room carpets with sandy legs and feet, so why do you think you can do use my

261

carpet here as a beach towel? Are you going to do the vacuuming? Arthur lunged his hand into the coin trough, crossly. 'Here, take your coins and get out and don't think about coming in here again.'

The three boys scurried out of the arcade, one of them saying a sheepish sorry.

'A seaside arcade owner's daily irritant, in spite of the sign at the window, *No Shoes, No Entry.*' Arthur faced Jean and Jack and was about to speak further when he perceived they were looking over his shoulder. A pretty young woman stood silently behind him. Denise, the girl from the Change Booth held the key fob for the booth door and was standing politely for Arthur to finish his conversation. Arthur turned apologetically.

'I'm so sorry Denise, I've been a little longer than expected and you need your lunch. Would you kindly add a chicken sandwich for Meg to the order and I'll take over in the booth. Do you have enough petty cash?' Denise pulled out ten pounds from her phone case and nodded.

'Jean, Jack are you sure you wouldn't like Denise to fetch you a sandwich from the deli too? The chicken tikka with salad is a very good option, or they do cheese or ham salad, tuna and sweetcorn or egg mayo. Denise, here's another ten and would you get a selection just in case Billy wants something too; usual for me please.'

Jack responded, 'No thank you, Jean and I really won't have time for lunch here.' The couple looked yearningly at the warm spring sunshine beckoning as Denise hurried out of the arcade into the bright street.

'Please follow me to the centre of arcade operations,' Arthur politely guided Jean back towards the Change Booth. Red faced, a reluctant Jack followed behind.

Arthur unlocked the door of the Perspex booth, it was only a little larger than a gas chamber. 'It's tight in here so I will be very brief.'

Inside, a single step led down to another door into what Jean and Jack presumed was an office area.

'Do you feed many customers?' Jack asked, impatiently in the cramped booth.

'No, only the regulars. It keeps them from going over the road to my competitors, who don't feed them, but who happily fleece them, but they're still not the worst.'

'Fleece them? Isn't that what you're doing too, Arthur?'

Arthur's blue eyes levelled with Jack's who folded his arms defensively.

Jack continued obstinately, 'Well you call it what you will, but I call it fleecing. Take Maggie or Meg there, you can tell she's down her luck, but you're letting her just get pumped by your machines. You were so enthusiastic about it too. You're just like a dairy farmer leading a cow to the stall to be milked.' Jack was pleased with his analogy.

Arthur responded earnestly, 'Tell me, Jack, should a farmer treat his herd cruelly or should he nurture them? Most cows like to be milked because it relieves the pressure. Some line up outside the milking parlour in anticipation. Would you have me uncaring toward my cows? Or would I neglect them so they wander over to a stranger to be milked?'

'Well, perhaps not, but this business of yours, it preys on the weaker members of society.'

'You are correct Jack. The gaming industry makes merchandise of people. It disproportionately affects the poor. It also pretends to have protections in place with trite sayings like, *When the Fun Stops, Stop*, and *Play Safe* but it's completely disingenuous, because the industry wants people to keep on spending even when they're on their knees. It will see a gambler and their families begging on the streets, even starving and will show no mercy. The people behind the industry are evil and covetous. That's an old fashioned word, Jack, *covetous*, but the dominant powers behind the gambling industry are some of the most evil and nasty people you could come across and you would be amazed how many of them hide behind respectability. Arcades these days are a tiny tip of a highly exploitative iceberg.'

'So you agree with me then?' Jack responded, 'Your business is unethical, but you appear to be separating yourself from this harsh assessment of evil covetousness you bestow on others.'

There was a sudden sharp rap on the change booth window. Jean flinched. The three swung around to face a white haired, bearded man with wizened features grinning back.

Arthur smiled at the surreal figure leering at them through the counter shield.

'Good afternoon Billy, enjoying some early summer sunshine I hope,' his greeting eased Jean's shock.

'Aye, Arthur,' the old man responded, 'I sees you've gotten some business callers, so I won't keep you; I just be needing a tenner's worth please.'

Billy slid the ten pound note to Arthur through the small counter shield opening. Arthur responded by pressing two levers rapidly ten times from a range of antique metal tubes with slits, and a cascade of coins clattered from a hopper into an external coin deposit cup. Jack was irritated the debate had been interrupted and surreptitiously nudged Jean as Arthur continued to chat with the man.

'I presume that's the seafarer he wants us to meet,' he whispered, 'He speaks like a bloody pirate and he's dressed like Granddad off *Only Fools and Horses*,' he mocked.

'Have a good day Billy, and I hope you climb more ladders than slide down snakes today,' Arthur finished.

Billy looked to check no one had usurped his position at his favourite machine, 'Thank you, Arthur, methinks them vipers are going to be a little hyper today when I cleans 'em out,' he cackled, shuffling away, muttering into his beard. 'And going to be another downpour soon, I reckons,' he shouted back to Arthur.

'Indeed you may be right about that,' Arthur affirmed, squinting toward the darkening street.

The booth contained a cash draw with lockable boxes and Arthur explained how the tubular coin dispensers had been reliably operating for over ninety years with some adjustments when decimalisation took place. He also briefly explained the CCTV monitor with split screen and how you could zoom in and check on suspicious customers.

264

'Some years ago we had a fraudster on a bandit using a coin with fishing line around it. He would have the other end tied to his forefinger and could deftly notch up hundreds of credits by yo-yoing the coin in the slot. It was down to an aberration from a sloppily manufactured sensor, but before the chap was caught he made thousands of pounds driving up and down the country seeking out the particular machine and emptying them. Broadstairs was not his last stand, but we got him on camera which enabled the police to match him to other demeanours in motorway service stations and pubs and clubs throughout the land.'

'Well done to him I say,' said Jack, 'Just taking back some of the ill-gotten gains from you lot.'

Arthur responded: 'Robin Hood, while reaping worldly admiration was no less a thief than Nottingham's corrupt masters.' Arthur looked at Jack to let the statement sink in, 'Though you will be pleased to know, Jack, the judge gave the villain nothing more than a slap on the wrist.'

Jack smiled triumphantly.

Denise suddenly hurried into the arcade with a carrier bag of sandwiches, shaking her damp hair. The dark shower cloud had prompted a street light to turn on and people sheltered under shop canopies as big plops of rain and hail pattered down. She pulled out a brown bag and passed it to a grateful Meg who put it on her lap, then, scanning the writing on another passed a corned beef and pickle sub to Billy who pocketed it, saluting her. Meg and Billy knew the rules that the sandwiches had to be eaten outside, but they would wait until the rain stopped.

Denise walked to the Change Booth and said, 'Mr King, I came back early to dodge the rain, so you can have these now.'

'Thank you Denise, it's impossibly cramped in here for another person, so I'll take our guests through until the shower's over and if you wouldn't mind manning the booth on your lunch, I'll see to it you can leave an hour early today.'

Denise nodded gratefully and Arthur led Jack and Jean down the step and through the back door into an airy and spacious L-shaped office with modern skylight windows and plum carpeted floor.

To the immediate right, a small section of the room had polished white floor tiles and housed a kitchenette with fridge, sink and cooker. A smoked glass table with six chairs was central with a Smart TV on the left wall above it playing news silently. In the far left hand corner by the fire exit stood a large, old fashioned safe with intricate brass relief scrolling, anachronistic to the modern units and computer work station adjacent.

Jack escorted Jean to the corner and ran his finger over the brass safe plaque which read: *British Made - The Guard Safe, Fire and Thief Resisting.* They turned to look into the adjoining room to the right, it was double the length of the room they stood in and contained a three-tiered wall of floor-to-ceiling racking stacked like a mini-supermarket warehouse full of boxes with catering sized tins of fruit and vegetables, soups, canned fish and meat, shrink-wrapped cartons of powdered milk, tea bags, sugar and coffee. One of the racks was heavy with shrink-wrapped catering sized bags of rice, pasta and flour and underneath shrink wrapped pallets contained pet foods, cigarettes, tobacco pouches and various types of spirits.

'I didn't know you were in the food and drink business as well Arthur,' Jack commented.

'I'm not really…' he paused, '…Yet.'

Jack's mouth opened to ask a question, but Arthur interrupted.

'This is the inner sanctum. Not many people get to enter the king's chamber, but you'll have to put up with an oblong not a round table,' Arthur joked, 'Please sit. Are you sure you don't want to share a sandwich?'

'No thank you, we're fine,' Jack insisted.

'Don't worry about the time, I'll run you to your car in ten minutes and we can check if you've got a ticket,' Arthur reassured, noticing the impatience on their faces.

'So let me tell you why I've brought you here. Meg and Billy are just two of hundreds of thousands of people in this country who are compulsive gamblers. I find them very easy to recognise because my father was one; he killed himself, so I feel duty bound to protect them and others like them.

266

Jean and Jack looked at each other, bewildered.

'I don't understand... I'm sorry to hear about your father, but let me get this right - you're telling me your idea of protecting a problem gambler is encouraging them to gamble? Surely having an arcade is acting like a drug dealer; giving people their fix so they can get their temporary high and you can make a daily profit.' Jack barely veiled his sneer.

'Profit we do make. Yes. The success of this business of course depends on other people playing the games and parting with cash, but if Meg and Billy were not patronising King's Arcade, they would spend their money gambling at another arcade that paid in tokens, that didn't feed them and they would be in a considerably worse state than they are today. They are the fortunate ones, believe me. I ensure they get fed here and they enjoy some camaraderie.' He looked up at the hail clattering on the skylights, 'And although I don't pry into their living situation, they can come in and shelter from the elements. It is a little social club for them.'

'You think buying a sandwich is protecting them? Even the casinos in Vegas provide free food,' Jean commented.

'This is Broadstairs, Jean. The arcades and the bookies do not feed their clientele.

'I assure you, for a committed gambler, this small arcade is a safe place to be. Meg and Billy and others like them are looked after here.'

'Safe place? This is Temptation Central for a gambler with all the flashing lights of the fruit machines. If you care so much about Meg and Billy, why don't you stop feeding their habit and let them hit rock bottom so that they seek help at The Salvation Army or Gambler's Anonymous?' Jean suggested.

'The Salvation Army and Gambler's Anonymous are excellent organisations, yes, and they do deal with many social ills that fall through the net of Social Services. Do you contribute?'

'No, we don't,' Jean replied. 'I don't know anything about Gambler's Anonymous and The Salvation Army is a religious organisation and we have our own preferred charities, don't we Jack? We do Cancer Research and British Heart Foundation.'

267

'Is that for personal reasons, or because you are banking you may garner some benefit in the future? Many people put money in the medical charities because deep down they're terrified of death, either their own or a family member's.'

'You are a very cynical man Mr King,' Jack interrupted, increasingly uncomfortable at Arthur's ability to read them.

'Anyway, some gamblers can't be helped, just managed. Some will have temporary breaks from gambling, but it always pulls them back in, like it did my father. I see my little arcade here as a less evil option than letting them get on with their addiction somewhere else. It's like a mother or father buying their junkie kid heroin to protect them from prostitution or loan sharks.'

Arthur picked up the TV remote control and aimed it at the wall.

'After my father killed himself, I decided I could either fight a losing battle against the system in entirety like Prohibition tried to do in the US against alcohol, or I could take a pragmatic approach; feed the addicts, let them play here and try to keep them from being exploited by uncaring venues elsewhere. Look what I'm up against.'

Arthur got up from his chair and moved to stand like a weather forecaster alongside the screen as he flicked through the channels, pointing out gambling sponsor logos and underscoring them with his finger. Jean and Jack suddenly understood. They had never really paid much attention before to the profusion of online betting sponsors on every channel, especially sports.

'Sport and entertainment is undergirded by this evil. The TV companies rake in millions from online gambling which loves to shove their brands in our faces with commercials or direct sponsorship. Sports were once a healthy pursuit, but these covetous organisations use them as a platform to immorally encourage the reckless use of resources, destroying lives; old and young alike. Once it was tobacco and booze, now it's almost exclusively gambling that is promoted. Most insidious of all is the psychology they use to lure children. Like paedophiles with the lure of puppies or lollipops, they now appeal to smartphone-savvy children with their fantasy games and gaudy colours; Pied Pipers using the siren-song of escapism as a lure. They know their psychology these devils.'

'I'd never looked at it that way before, or even noticed it,' Jean commented.

'It was bad enough in my father's day, but at least he was constrained by time. He would wander home dishevelled from the bookies most Saturday afternoons with his ten shillings doled out by my mother from his pay packet—my mother struck a deal with his employer that his wages be picked up by her every Friday— today's gambling addicts have no such protections. You can place your bets online 24/7. Addicts can cloak themselves in suburban anonymity; in a hidden digital world of despair behind bedroom doors and louvre blinds and many are women who would never have dreamed of entering a betting shop, but now they can gamble themselves and their children into dire poverty overnight. The demographic of the gambler has transformed.

'I am grateful that Meg and Billy are limited by their lack of access to and understanding of technology. They do not use smartphones. If they did, they'd inevitably be drawn into higher stakes games— and their lies the rub—it's a question of stakes. There is a limit to how much money you can lose in a day in a Family Entertainment Centre as opposed to high stakes bookies, casinos and online. My slot machines take very small coinage, unlike high stakes Fixed Odds Betting Terminals that take £30 maximum bets. The thing is, to a slot machine addict the pull isn't all about the money, it's the game that matters and the excitement of watching the reels fall into sequence. It's why many traditional and all online fruit machines pay in tokens; it removes the connection between real money, honest labour and reward, changing it into fantasy tokens that a gambler does not value in the same way as solid coinage. Similarly, the online gambler converts real cash into worthless digital coupons to gain digital rewards. Even if they win, there is a great deal of effort required to reconvert the winnings into money and back into their bank account, so the temptation is to keep on playing until you lose all your winnings.

'You call me unethical, Jack, but I'm honest about what this set up is. In an ideal world these places would not exist. I have not yet met

269

an ethical arcade owner. They are highly unscrupulous; they prey on their customers and many have links to organised crime and other dark vocations. Like those kids on the Penny Falls, I'm letting my customers get a taste of losing early on, so that they don't fall prey to the sickness of gambling when they're older. Let me ask you both. Is it better to be sick on Babycham or Cherry-B when you're eleven and be put off drinking for life than to die of alcohol poisoning at seventeen, downing a bottle of vodka at a party, your liver unprepared for the shock?'

'Yes, but you could also say you're getting them into the habit early,' Jean countered.

'That is a valid statement, Jean and yes, I agree; if this was the only game in town. There are some people who have that inclination, but with a blanket ban, like banning alcohol, the underworld will find a way to reach the addicts and feed their habit through illicit means.

'Meg and Billy are problem gamblers, but their precarious situation is restrained by me. They have reached a point where they aren't even interested in the money. It really is something else controlling their obsession; not just physical, but spiritual. They hit rock bottom at times, but always pull themselves up sufficiently to play the bandits again and again and again. Every now and then they have a good day, claw a little back and that feeds their dopamine pleasure sensors sufficiently to keep them believing they'll do it again next visit. Some gamblers think they will eventually recoup their losses and stop for good. That doesn't happen; they throw everything back during a losing streak.

'In Meg and Billy's case, I encourage them to limit the amount of time they play and we have an agreement that I also restrict the amount of money I change for them in one trip. It's the best I can do for them.

'Well, I'm not convinced it's the best approach,' Jack responded.

'I'd love to hear a better remedy Jack. Do you and Jean eat out? Do you expect a restaurateur to limit your intake of smoked salmon; steak and chips; dessert? Do you give pub landlords a hard time for serving beer? A bar manager always recognises the alcoholic sitting in his bar. Does he serve them? If he is a good landlord and sees the person staggering he will advise them they've had too much to drink, but if their behaviour is exemplary, he can't stop serving them. Even if he does they'll just go and drink some more at another pub, or at home, or in the gutter; he can only treat them with civility.

'There's nothing I'd like more than to see people like Meg and Billy released from their bondage, but hitting rock bottom often means either death for people like them or just a temporary hiatus. Social Services and homeless charities pick up the pieces and for the sake of the rest of society so they should. There but for the grace of God go you and I.'

Jack shook his head in disgruntled denial. 'We are not gamblers, Arthur. We haven't got it in us, so that accusation is unacceptable. Those people need to fill their lives with an alternative to gambling, like some hard work and they might find society gives them something in return, like self-respect.

'Personally I think you are jumping through hoops to justify your operation. I'm just pleased Jean and I were never tempted by your industry. We would never gamble our livelihood away, nor would we invest in gambling or promote it,' Jack looked at Jean with a smugness that verged on loathsome.

'Oh, I agree with you Jack, gambling addiction can often be traced to laziness and greed; a desire to get rich quick without working hard. How many of us don't have one of those vices at some point in our life? You've already confessed *you* dabble in the Lotto from time to time, but that aside, you and Jean are dangerous gamblers with much more to lose than Meg and Billy and don't even know it.'

'How so?' Jack snarled, banging his fist on the table, 'You keep suggesting we have some bloody gambling vice, but we don't.'

'Jack!' Jean reprimanded, embarrassed at his loss of control.

'Not overtly, Jack. Not overtly,' Arthur rested his elbows on the glass top calmly, deliberately setting Jack an example; clasping his fingers together in an arch, forefingers touching his pursed lips. He paused, then laid his hands and brought his eyes up to look at them. 'Have you heard of the long game?'

271

'What, well of course we have. You mean golf?' Jack tried to inject some humour, a little ashamed at his outburst seconds earlier. 'That's a very long game in my book, especially when I play it with Ted, eh Jean?' Jack and Jean chuckled at the mention of Jack's friend. Jean patted Jack's arm affectionately. Arthur's silence prompted another response, 'Ah, I get it, I think you probably mean a long game of poker that goes on for days, is that the long game you're referring to?'

Arthur smiled, shaking his head slowly, 'No Jack. While those are indeed long games, it's not what I am alluding to. The long game is an old confidence trick well known by villains; con being the key syllable. Let me explain.

'The *modus operandi* of the traditional long game was to set up a small business dealing in high value items such as jewellery or high value electrical. The crook would begin by winning trust; buying jewellery or electricals from a few suppliers, a little and often; cash up front. The suppliers deliver, pleased that the crook's credit is excellent and that he continues to buy in ever increasing quantities, always paying up front and increasing the order size gradually. This approach continues for six months or a year, perhaps longer; and because his credit is excellent the suppliers treat him as a high value customer, even wining and dining him occasionally. Over dinner he confides in them he is thinking about expanding and they get very excited at the idea of supplying even more product. He suggests volume discounts and they agree because they trust him implicitly and extend their credit terms. That's when the long game's big sting happens. The crook puts in a massive order on credit and collects, then he clears out his stock on a big lorry and disappears from the face of the earth with all the stolen goods.'

'Ah well, that may have worked before video cameras and facial recognition, Arthur, but not anymore,' Jack commented.

'That's very true Jack, long-cons are not as straightforward today. Successful outcomes depend on a more sophisticated strategy. You have to make sure the victim never understands they've been conned. Perhaps you're familiar with that well-known movie, The Sting?'

A nervous Jean edged closer to Jack.

272

'The Sting was a successful con because the victim didn't know he'd been had. In spite of losing money, he believed the cons had helped him escape from the law and he was grateful.'

'So how on earth does that apply to Jean and me?' Jack quizzed cynically.

Arthur stretched back in his chair placing his hands with fingers interlocked, behind his head, 'Where do you put your money Jack? Property? Pension? Shares? Probably a mixture. That's just gambling with public approval. Do you know how corrupt things get at the Stock Market level where your pension funds are invested?

'Anything you invest in that you can't get your hands on instantly is probably a long con. Do you have a private pension scheme? Stock market investments? ISAs? Bonds? These are all generic long cons designed to keep you under tight fiscal control, ultimately benefiting a financial elite who are not at all desperate and who have plenty of time on their hands, along with a controlled media to promote their schemes. In fact, the longer a long con goes on, the more trust it garners and the more money the perpetrators rake in from their victims.'

Jack shook his head and smiled disparagingly. 'I'd hardly call Jean and I victims of our investments,' he scoffed.

'You don't think so, Jack? But certainly other people are victims. Do you have a clue how many sweatshops are killing kids tied to corporate profits that help you indulge in your trips abroad and cruises when you retire, thinking yourself a mighty-fine upstanding individual? Well, I don't know the specifics of your pension scheme, but the typical private pension is linked to the military industrial complex and the continuous conflagration of war and suffering around the globe.'

'I get it, the world is corrupt and there's nothing we can do about that, but how are we victims of our investments?' Jack seethed.

'Okay, let's take your pension scheme. It required you paid a certain percentage of your wages into it every month. You are coaxed into doing so because the fund managers tell you that there are tax benefits for high earners like yourself. You are charged a management fee for set up and regular management fees throughout the course of your investment: That is the first claw-back, but you barely noticed it because you were so busy. Then you find out half way through the scheme that your initial investment wasn't as much as you thought because of deliberate stock market manipulation or some war or crisis somewhere destabilising the fund, so you are 'advised' to top up your pot just in case. That is claw-back number two, a manipulated financial shortfall that meant you lost some of your investment to 'the vagaries of the market'.'

'Oh, come on, the stock market is bound to go up and down,' Jack countered.

'You're right. It's designed like a casino; an arcade with glitzy names for various funds and schemes to draw you in, backed by apparently trustworthy megaliths. Like fruit machines with their *payback percentage,* which is substantially less than what goes in. Casino management has that information in something called a par sheet, but players never have access to that info. Some punters will win a jackpot once in every thousand spins and walk away flush. The Stock Market with its shares and stocks operates along similar principles. Every stock, fund or pension scheme has a payback percentage, but the outsiders, the general public, who don't control the Stock Market version of casino par sheets; the long term investors in stocks, shares and pensions; usually lose much more than they put in, though some lucky ones will walk away from the table at the right time and stand proud, acting as ambassadors to pull in the next generation of punters.

'The casino managers or the City bankers know exactly when and how long a player will reap success and they also know how much to rake off or when part of the investments will dry up or go bust, because they control the system. One of their hidden stings is inflation, a deliberate devaluation of money so that even if it looks on paper like you've made a pretty penny you still don't have a fair return on your original asset, and when you come to cash in you are further depleted by taxes on the withdrawal.'

'I disagree Arthur, my excellent pension scheme has had a few riskier stock investments certainly, but we also have property which is the best investment of all we think, don't we Jean?

Regarding inflation, our rising property portfolio thrives on it and it's what has enabled us to enjoy such a good standard of living today. So we have plenty of fall back options and so we don't have all our eggs in one basket.'

'For the moment you and Jean are sailing pretty because you believe you retired at the right time and you feel you got a pretty good deal, just like Meg and Billy on their good days you feel you've hit the jackpot. Property prices are high and you think you can eat, drink and be merry for the rest of your days; indeed, depending on how long you live, you might just eke out that dream. God knows.'

'You're a very negative man Mr King and let me say, you're making quite a few judgements about us that are frankly damned presumptuous.'

'No, I'm being truthful because you need to be warned.'

'Warned? About what man?'

'You want to know your biggest gamble, Jack?'

'Go on, enlighten me, oh wise counsellor!' Jack moved his seat back, readying to leave.

Arthur shook his head, dismayed, 'Your biggest gamble is trusting the system. You will have no resilience when it fails, and it will. Meg and Billy out there will be more resilient than you because they're used to hard knocks.'

'You really are completely mad, man,' Jack turned to Jean and signalled to her to leave.

'See this scar?' Arthur traced his finger slowly down from his eye to his chin. 'My father's loan shark couldn't get to him, so he got to me, but it pushed my father over the brink and my mother ended up putting us into care. It was the day I stopped trusting in the system.'

'That's something that happened to you because of your father borrowing from crooks.'

'No. I didn't get this scar from the crooks, they just threatened me to intimidate my father. I got this scar from fighting off a paedophile in the care home I was sent to. I cut it trying to jump

275

through a window, but he came off worse than me in the end. The glass shard that cut my face provided a nice little weapon that severed his ardour permanently. Unfortunately, I went to borstal for assaulting a peer of the realm. I learned then that the system protects its own, that it is deeply corrupt, but it also exists on a knife edge. My father's situation and my unjust incarceration was just a *micro* version of a *macro* global condition.'

'The fact that you and Jean and so many others in the world are experiencing a period of prosperity and peace for so long means that the controllers of the system are deliberately lulling you into a sense of false security and are about to pull a sting. Prosperity, Jack, is not the default position unless you are a controller. It is used to take our eyes off the ball so we are distracted while draconian legislation is passed in Parliament or good laws are undermined. You may not feel the iron grip of tyranny today, but if you are distracted by your glittering trinkets, your grandchildren will.'

Jack rose from his seat suddenly, trembling with anger.

'That is quite preposterous, I am in full control of my finances and our children's and grandchildren's future. You are talking like a bloody conspiracy theorist. The system is too big to fail.'

'Jack, hear me out. You think you've got the rest of your life mapped out, one leisurely day after another, but I'm here to warn you that the system is going to fail and unless you are physically and spiritually prepared, you will be in great danger. What have you got other than a pension, bank savings and property alternatives? Have you invested any of your time and money in acquiring survival skills? Do you know what you would do when the grid goes down or if you couldn't buy food at Tesco or Sainsbury's?'

'Come on Jean, we are leaving, I have had quite enough of this gentleman's rantings for one day. Good day to you, sir; parking ticket be damned, we're out of here.'

Jack moved Jean's seat back and helped her up. Arthur rose calmly from his chair, buttoned his jacket and walked gracefully to the fire exit door where Jack was fumbling agitated for the latch. Arthur calmly pushed the bar down and opened the door wide. Jack and Jean bustled into a back lane. The rain had stopped.

'The High Street is left and left again. Are you sure I can't give you a lift to your vehicle?' Arthur asked.

'No thank you, Sir! I need fresh air and even if we get wet it'll be better than sitting in here listening to your drivel,' Jack responded rudely. Jean shook her head, mouthing an embarrassed 'no' without looking Arthur in the eye.

'Your car, what is it? Petrol? Diesel? Electric?' Arthur asked.

Jack turned around pompously, chest raised like a pigeon, 'Petrol. Audi Estate V8 if you must know. Goodbye,' he said pompously.

Arthur smiled, 'Enjoy it.'

Arthur secured the fire exit door and did a visual inventory of the shelves stacked with provisions. He stood doubting, momentarily unsure of himself; wondering if his experience and circumstances had jaded his thinking. Perhaps Jack and Jean were right, perhaps there was no conspiracy, perhaps Broadstairs and England would always remain peaceful and safe.

He glanced over at the TV news playing the same repetitive loop, smiled and shook his head, 'Tut, tut, tut. I really must stop doubting the evidence,' he whispered to himself.

*   *   *

Jack and Jean were on a beach in Fuerteventura when it happened. Jack was hungover and Jean was feeling a little sick after a large breakfast. They were grabbing another hour or so in the warm waters of the bay before sauntering back inside the hotel to shower and take their cases to the hotel reception. They wanted to be refreshed and ready for the airport coach to pick them up for the Heathrow flight.

Jean had put down the boring Pulitzer Prize Winner, noticing people were rushing about talking fretfully to each other and gathering their bags quickly from the sun loungers. The deathly pallor on the thirty-something woman's face adjacent as she scooped up her three year old and ran towards the hotel building

277

signalled to Jean something alarming was happening. She woke Jack from his snooze.

Jack and Jean gathered their belongings hurriedly and didn't bother to dust the sand from their feet as they entered Reception. Staff had abandoned their posts and were skidding dangerously out of the hotel car park, in packed electric cars and bikes. The owner of the hotel was trying to explain in various languages that there was nothing he could do and people would just have to wait for news, but that all flights had been cancelled because air traffic control was 'down'.

There had been some kind of explosion. Huge. Tidal waves and earthquakes followed. The whole system had been taken out, destroyed.

Some rumoured nuclear terrorism because of the sheer strength of the atomic boom, but it was actually a huge meteorite as big as a mountain, hurtling from space like a fiery pinball and slamming into the ocean. There were no Hollywood heroes to flip it back; no United Nations' cooperation or ballistic missile space-shields to counter its unexpected lethality. Not this time.

No one knew exactly which part of space it had come from or where exactly it had hit; The Pleiades Probe and the giant new space telescopes had apparently missed it, but the result for the system was unfixable brokenness.

The TVs were blank; the pick-and-go stations in the shops were frozen. The power grid and infrastructure was a heap. Localised generators kicked in for a while, but the financial network was irreparable as its central hub and all its back-up systems were gone.

Only a few understood what was happening. Previously, economic crises had been man-made, deliberately manufactured. This time it was the controllers who were surprised.

People waited frightened for three days, but then grew terrified as they gradually realised the government, army and police were not going to help them. It was everyone for themselves and it got ugly, fast. Police, soldiers, politicians, rich and poor, young and old in every country joined in the looting.

The rich were a mess. They thought they'd always be able to fall back on something, but the poor fell on them, violently.

People had chosen to be physically wired up to the new 'fairer' digital system that promised to remove poverty and improve global health. It was so trusted that people didn't carry wallets anymore, relying instead on tokens in their bi-ome chips; everything, including their healthcare records, in one safe and convenient under-skin basket.

A remnant of people in every nation had opted out - typically the 'Biome Rebels' were already homeless; viewed with mistrust and derision for their refusal to bend to progress; especially as the popularity of the world leader and his cadre of celebrities grew, demanding that people comply so that the full benefits of the system could be enjoyed by everyone. But now the unsinkable blockchain infrastructure was sunk.

Initially, those with guns had the upper hand, but even they were overwhelmed by the frenzied mobs, then suddenly all the food stores with their digital right-of-entry gates were looted; the roads were gridlocked and people trudged home, trembling and hungry; frightened their neighbours would steal the last of their provisions.

People lost hope as the destruction got worse and looting spread from city to city; town to town; house to house. The supermarkets and warehouses were marauded first, then everyone's home was a target. Cars were traded for a can of beans. Pets were pushed out into the woods, but most came wandering home, emaciated to die alongside their owners.

*   *   *

Jean and Jack hunkered down in their hilltop hotel room. Big waves had flooded the buildings on the lower shore, but nothing like the tsunamis elsewhere. Jack had pompously voiced his indignation to the hotel owner explaining 'how disgraceful it was' that the Spanish Authorities had not intervened and that the hotel owner 'had a duty to his guests' etc. They were allowed to stay in the hotel room a week longer, but had to trade their valuables for food and water which ran out quickly. They had to drink from the swimming pool when the taps suddenly ran dry.

Eight days after the calamity, the hotel owner said that planes were being readied in the airport and all remaining guests should make their way there. It was a lie, but he got the guestroom keys back and secured the premises.

Jack and Jean strode optimistically the twenty miles to the airport overnight, Jean's arthritis apparently cured, but they never made it back to England. They collapsed exhausted in despair when they saw the plane carcases burning on the runway. People sat on kerbs with their heads in hands waiting for rescuers that never came. Children slept on top of folded clothes in open cases like cots while parents scavenged scraps and boiled sweets from the airport cafes and shops and smashed vending machines. The signs on all the shop doors and windows *No Biome, No Entry* in four languages were irrelevant now as some five hundred or so families of different nationalities competed with Jack and Jean for the last remnants of food, and to get back home. Some wandered with gaunt, frightened children into the Fuerteventura countryside hoping to be taken in by farmers as labourers or to scavenge the land.

Jean and Jack gave up. Their last meal was a rock hard sub Jack found kicked under a counter in the abandoned airport cafe. They softened it in moist coffee ground residue from the smashed commercial coffee machine. Jean licked sugar residue from a saucer and wept.

No one ever came looking, but if they had, they would have found their bodies locked in a parched embrace in a dark corner of the video games zone.

*   *   *

In Broadstairs, Arthur King had refused to exchange his wealth for digital tokens and instead had put every real coin and asset he owned into a smallholding and secure food storage lockers before the full digital transition took place; but even for him it was only a matter of time before the perishable supplies were gone or plundered by the dwindling hungry mobs who grew weaker every day, contending as they were now against a festering form of flesh-rotting leprosy caused by the bi-ome chips. You could smell death on the digitised population long before they succumbed.

Arthur still had a few secret stashes of long term cans and dried pulses and had established a network of small community growing hubs with other renegades. They had learned how to grow and hunt and harvest and although survival was narrow they were now the only ones who could adequately feed themselves or their children. The days of subsistence farming and seasonal foraging were back.

Jack and Jean's idyllic sea view dormer cottage was perfectly appointed for two old Broadstairs' toughies; an old sea farer and his pal, Meg. The microwave in Foxglove Cottage's kitchen was a convenient store cupboard for Meg's copious tobacco stash.

Billy looked more like Merlin than Captain Bird's Eye as he stooped with his long beard straggling over the limpet, crab and sea radish stir-fry sizzling in one of Jean's prized *Le Creuset* pans, charred as black as a cauldron by wood smoke on the BBQ pit by the French doors.

The stylish patio was now an outdoor cooking area for Meg and Billy; a rabbit casserole with hogweed and ground elder stewed alongside the stir fry—a delicious medieval feast fit for a king, or to be specific, their very special friend, Arthur King—the unofficial Regent of Broadstairs who would soon ride over the fields on horseback to visit along with his handsome, shotgun-wielding son and his gun-toting daughter-in-law Denise.

The three riders dismounted and the horses whinnied as they were hitched to Jack's sturdy car port posts.

Meg and Billy greeted the three friends who brought elderberry wine and barley bread.

After dining *al fresco* in the warm September dusk, they went indoors and slumped onto the plush leather sofas and Billy lit two oil lanterns and candles. Once the bowls of stew had been cleared from Jack's gorgeous round table, Meg thought she might break out a deck of cards for a hand of poker or two. She had learned that playing with shells by candlelight was nearly as much fun as playing for money.

A grateful Arthur strolled onto the patio with his glass of elderberry wine and lifted up his head to the heavens, hopefully.

///organs.showed.alive
"THE FORGOTTEN SENTENCE"

Anais was sullen. Her three year old little sister was playing in the large terraced garden with a bucket and spade while she up-swiped her screen from the sun lounger listlessly looking at *tiktoks* and occasionally glancing down to check her sister wasn't going near the koi pool.

It was already warm and Anais was chasing shade, dragging her sun lounger closer to the large hydraulic sliding doors of the indoor swimming pool as the morning sun climbed over the meadow beyond the walled garden to the south east. As the final tract of shade was swallowed up she squinted at her iPhone screen to find the house controls app to open the pool doors and pull her lounger inside the shaded enclosure.

She juddered the heavy recliner irritably over the threshold of the door as soon as the hydraulics had opened it sufficiently in its tramway and slumped down crossly on its luxurious cushioned fabric, half in, half out of the room. At least her legs could tan while she read her phone screen in the shade. A striped green sunbed drifted on the still pool surface behind her as the outside breeze unsettled the stale chlorinated air in the most underused room in the whole of the big house.

Her dad occasionally took a dip on a Saturday morning before golf in one of his half-hearted keep-supple efforts to which she would always mock, 'Desperately trying to prolong your Middle Class lifestyle, Dad?'

'How long is he effing going to take?' she looked at her screen. 11.41 am. The delivery driver had promised he was only half an hour away nearly an hour ago. Her delivery of Ralph Lauren 400 matchstick jeans which she'd ordered yesterday was essential for the party tonight. She texted her frustration to her friend on WhatsApp.

'It's not as if we're difficult to find FFS! Meadow Mansion, biggest house in village, durhh.'

Villagers called the three houses at the base of the bank, *Millionaire's Row* and she liked that. Of course, when she had to go to the village store she would don fake humility even as her mother or father flashed up in white Range Rover or black Maserati-opulence to buy farm eggs or artisan bread as lynchpins of local community patronage.

Locals were not taken in. Her mum was an entitled bitch and the village knew it. She flounced around in sarong-thonged minimalism in a manicured shimmy of blondeness and Botox, gliding from room to room on white marble under-heated floors to dust expensive kinetic sculptures from Harrods that silently rocked and whirred-out the final throes of her modelling career now consisting almost wholly of hand modelling.

This week had been, well…exhausting. She'd tapped a jar of face cream approvingly with her forefinger for a TV ad; broke warm scones for an M&S summer commercial and was stand-in hands for a famous female chef who bit her nails and who needed close ups of fluffy peak meringue whisking. Exhausting indeed. Today she was treating herself; lunching with one of her vacuous friends from the Lipo Clinic.

Accordingly Anais was doing the babysitting. Again.

Her little sister Annabelle clambered up the terraced steps clutching a toy bucket of soil and stones, panting excitedly.

'Look, look Anais! Tweasure.' Annabelle delved into her bucket enthusiastically and like little Jack Horner pulling out a plum, she proudly held a dull triangle of Willow Pattern china and a muddy fragment of clay pipe stem aloft in chlorophyll-stained fingers.

'Lovely,' Anais muttered scornfully.

Annabelle didn't quite grasp sarcasm, she just looked bemused before quickly regathering her enthusiasm as she squatted down by the foot of the lounger, rummaging in the gritty bucket while humming *Twinkle Twinkle Little Star*. The sheen of her blonde bob wisped angelically in the sunny breeze as she thrust her hand up again triumphantly.

'A pweshus pwezent for you,' she gushed.

'It has a letter on it.'

Annabelle held a muddy lozenge of clay pottery with the initial *A* graven into it just an inch away from her big sister's recoiling face.

'Not right in my eye; I've told you before, I can't see when you put things so close.' Anais snatched it grumpily and focused on it at arm's length. It was crude, thick and dark brown with some ancient glaze on it and a hole at the top.

'Oh yeah, great, don't suppose you can dig me up some Ralph Lauren jeans while you're at it.'

'What are Wafflorrin jeans?' Annabelle asked, confused.

'Nothing, forget it.'

'Anais, it is a very pweshus tweasure. It pwobbly belonged to a wickle girl who lived here.' She looked at it wistfully, 'You must keep it safe.

And I have somefing else to tell you...'

'Shush!' Anais commanded impudently thrusting her finger in Annabelle's face as the rumble of a delivery van gunning along the gravel driveway from the gatehouse distracted from her sister's sweet ramblings.

'You hurt my feelings about what I was saying,' Anais said, eyes glistening and chin quivering, 'and it is very important.'

Her sister continued to ignore her, heeding the pleasing squeak of a cheap van door opening and banging shut. Anais dashed from the lounger and raced around the pool perimeter to the room exit, impatiently pushing the automatic swing doors as they slowly opened, cursing their sluggishness before pelting along the cool side corridor to the mansion's trade delivery door.

A fish-eye video monitor showed the delivery driver fumbling for a doorbell under the pillared baroque portico, oblivious to the butler bell with cast-iron pull hanging out of sight.

No doorbell durhh. It's a mansion FFS, Anais whined under her breath, unbolting the door and grumpily snatching the parcel.

'You said half an hour a bloody hour ago. I've been stuck in waiting for this.'

284

'Sorry love, nothing I can do about tractors and combines. You get stuck behind one and…'

Anais slammed the heavy door shut before the driver finished his excuses or had a chance to photograph the parcel. He shrugged, stepped back and took a picture of the oak studded portico door, joining his colleague who skidded out of the driveway and slewed up a wave of gravel onto the neat paving by the ornate orangery.

Anais ran to the white steps of the curved glass balustrade staircase and along the right hand marbled landing to her room, ripping open the package while glancing at the long sweep of garden. From the middle arched window she could see Annabelle crouching with her yellow plastic bucket over a low box hedge that traced the perimeter of two ornamental scrolled flower displays on the second garden terrace above the fountain and koi pond.

Good. She's not near the pond.

'Alexa, play *Sia, Chandelier*' she commanded, strutting inside her walk-in closet to get undressed by the full length mirror.

Pulling on the skin tight jeans, she admired the perfectly comfortable fit as she sang along to the thumping track: *'One two three, one two three, three… I'm gonna swi-ing… from the Shander-lee-ah... the Shander-lee-ah. You only get… what you choose to pay for…what you choose to pay forrrr'*.

She flicked through a hundred or more coat hangers containing tops, vests and blouses, many still new with tags; pulling and pushing valet poles; trying on top after top; opening drawers and rifling through organisers in the built in cabinetry.

After twenty minutes she eventually settled for a Dolce & Gabbana brocade and lamé floral design jacket with an Alexander McQueen tee shirt, rotating her automatic watch winding case to find suitable wrist wear.

She was satisfied with her choices, but there was something nagging her; some small thing she had forgotten.

The butler's bell rang again. *Who the hell is that?* She sighed histrionically.

'I'm sorry love, but the gaffer told me to run back to photograph the parcel while he finishes his round.'

Anais looked on impatiently.

'Words.pool.fetch,' the man said emphatically.

'What? What did you just say?' Anais looked troubled.

'It's the what3words app we use: words.pool.fetch. Takes me to the exact spot of your back door here so I can take a pic for the courier insurance,' the delivery driver fumbled in his green overalls for his iPhone, which he had inadvertently left in the van, but Anais only heard the three words: words.pool.fetch that blasted through her like a lorry's klaxon.

'Wait!' she exclaimed, as the colour drained from her face.

'You alright?' the man asked.

'Annabelle! The pool!' she screamed as the image of a muddy square of crockery with embossed 'A' and her sister's yellow bucket flashed through her mind. She hurtled down the corridor and saw the automatic pool doors closed again. To enter from this side she needed to punch in the key code - 'R2D2' - on the panel. Unable to see anything through the frosted glass she cursed the door's slow opening and shouldered her way through as soon as it was ajar, when to her dismay she saw ripples unsettling the usual mirrored surface.

Annabelle was face down in the water, her bucket floating alongside her and stones lying in the bottom of the pool. It was the shallow end but not shallow enough for her precious three year old little sister.

She jumped in and lunged her sister up onto the poolside then followed, heaving herself out breathless; her saturated jeans heavy, taut and restrictive.

Trembling in panic, she tried to remember the First Aid lessons with a plastic dummy at Venture Scouts. Something about clearing the airway and tilting the head, but didn't she have to press on her back to squeeze water out of the lungs first? She couldn't remember.

'Help, help, help!' Anais screamed, paralysed in panic. Seconds later the delivery man ran into the pool room and quickly assessed the situation.

'Is she breathing?'

Annabelle screamed, 'No she's not! Do something.'

'Move,' he said assertively, 'Get an ambulance.'

The delivery man performed CPR until the ambulance arrived and the emergency team took over.

Annabelle was admitted to paediatric intensive care, but some of her organs were failing.

Apart from a blurted summary of what had happened and having been distracted, her mother could not speak to Anais or even look her in the eyes. There were no excuses worth giving and her mother didn't push it. She knew she had to take some responsibility and would suffer a backlash if she dared mention *selfishness* or *thoughtless behaviour*. Anais had an arsenal of vitriol she could unleash about being a surrogate mother to Annabelle because the three year old's real mother was too engrossed in lunching; modelling; car valets; or her precious manicures to prioritise her children's wellbeing.

Anais lay unresponsive, her body rigid. She stayed on a ventilator for twelve long days and the hospital prepared them that she might not make it and if she did she would probably have brain damage. When she came off the sedation medicine their worries were confirmed, she was paralysed in a vegetative state with severe brain injury. Discussions about wheelchairs and feeding tubes horrified them.

In the days that followed, eating and drinking was a laborious chore for the family. The joy of life had gone. Music was an irritant and silence a comfort. Every waking moment felt like pushing through dark molasses, but for Anais the despair was intensified by a terrible pining.

Not only was she desperate for her little sister to know how sorry she was, but the last words Annabelle spoke to her on the patio kept replaying over and over in her head. Maddeningly she wasn't certain of the exact phrase, but she remembered it was something *really important* she wanted to tell her. If only she had listened. If only she hadn't been so preoccupied with her bloody jeans; a stupid pair of overpriced denims. The yearning to know ate away at her. She tried guessing what it could have been, but surmising made it worse. She thought she was going demented.

Friends had slowly stopped texting. They had all done their duty with sympathetic messages: *'If you need anything, please just call'* and the *'You okay, hon?'* and *'Don't forget we're just a phone call away if you want to talk',* but Anais knew they were going through the motions and life was progressing just the same for them after they pressed *Send*.

How could they know? How does anyone understand tragedy unless they experience it? Even the death of Annabelle may have been less traumatic than seeing Annabelle connected to monitors like a vacant blob. At least death provides closure and opens a door to time's healing touch.

Anais resolved she would give everything she owned both now and in the future just to say sorry to her sister, and to know the forgotten sentence. The regret of casting such pearls aside and the yearning to know hung like a ball and chain.

After a month of bedside vigils the doctor advised, 'Annabel has suffered anoxic brain injury due to lack of oxygen, but I want you to consider an option; it's an experimental treatment called hyperbaric oxygen therapy; a new approach for paediatrics, though it's already a routine treatment for decompression sickness or *the bends* in scuba diving and to treat serious wounds and infections. In Annabelle's case because of the brain damage, I believe she has nothing to lose in pursuing it. It involves taking in pure oxygen in a pressurised chamber or through a tube.'

The doctor recognised in their collective body language his words were like a ship on the castaway's horizon, energising hope.

'I must manage your expectations, because it is experimental…'

Anais's mother cut him short. 'We will try it. Please tell us next steps.'

The three were buoyant. In the lift to the car park Anais's mother clasped her hand. Exhausted and relieved to feel her mother's forgiveness they hugged all the way home in the back of the un-valeted Maserati. Anais noticed two of her mother's nails were broken.

Five weeks after the accident, Annabelle received oxygen through a nose-tube for 45 minutes, twice daily. Rapidly Annabelle seemed more aware and her movements resembled a child sleeping rather than vegetative insentience. In a week she opened her eyes and stared for short periods.

The doctor was confident she was ready for hyperbaric oxygen therapy. She was ambulanced to the clinic for treatment in the pressurised chamber for an hour five days a week and after a couple of sessions she could speak in small sentences and her vocabulary grew. Soon she held her head up and then could sit up on her own. By the last few sessions, she was taking her first shaky steps.

'My colleague calls it a mix of God and science, but since I believe God is the origin of all knowledge the delineation is questionable,' The Filipino doctor asserted, 'because I think we have seen a miracle here. I am truly inspired by this.' His words were accompanied by tears of gratitude.

The family also sought to thank the delivery man for his intervention; strangely they couldn't find a record of a delivery to that location, though the what3words geolisting was in the garden of Anais's first childhood home in Taplow where she buried her pet dog.

As the mid-august sun shone through the hospital roller blinds, Annabelle, propped by pillows, licked her ice lolly and drew pictures with the crayons the nurse had given her.

'That's a lovely picture, Annabelle,' Anais remarked.

'A wickle girl wiv a doggy,' she responded happily.

'Can you remember speaking to me on the patio and you got upset? You said you had something really important you wanted to tell me?'

'Yes, I wemember you hurt my feelings.' She pulled a sad face.

Anais grabbed Annabelle's hand and put it to her mouth to kiss it, tears running down her cheeks.

'I'm so sorry,' she choked, 'so very, very sorry for not listening, please will you forgive me.'

'Yes, Anais, but your cwying is wetting my picture,' she scolded.

'So what else was it you were going to tell me?' Anais couldn't hold back her desperation. She knew the answer to that riddle was the one thing she had inwardly pledged she would trade everything to hear.

'I wanted to tell you how to make a bag for a bee with petals. It's very easy you know, you just…'

Annabelle chatted into the evening, her family rapt by every word of her innocent imagination that shone more exquisitely than sultan's jewels; her sweet voice and enthusiasm uplifting; her presence more valuable than anything they had ever owned—fancy cars; homes; gardens; fountains; holidays or expensive kinetic sculptures—they counted them all dross compared to the nuggets of glory that dropped from the mouth of the precious three year old.

///courier.void.reply
"EPILOGUE"

The last time I saw him was in the wing mirror standing by a verge on the A3024. He raised his arm in a slow, final wave as I flashed my hazards in acknowledgment, pulling off towards Bourne End via Holyport to pick up my repaired van.

I was weepy; actual tears, can you believe it? The very man whose gaze I dreaded to make contact with earlier that morning, now left me watery-eyed with that rueful lump-in-the-throat sadness you get saying goodbye to someone you know you may never meet again— the holidaying couple you spent a nightly table with on a cruise ship, or the kindly old schoolteacher you assure you'll visit again, though you know you never will.

I clicked the radio on. Oddly, all the stations were now crisp and clear. Radio2 *Drivetime* swiftly put me in a more upbeat frame, then just as I rounded the bend by The Jolly Gardener I spotted it; the folded mass in the door pocket.

I drove a mile to swerve safely into the nearest side road and spin the van around, hurtling back east towards Fifield, but he'd gone.

The lift he was waiting for must have come just after I dropped him off. I told him I'd wait until his boss—was it Arnie or Archie?— came by, but he insisted I should leave in case the garage closed.

Nearly five years have passed since the ride and I'm a little older and greyer. I guess he's still somewhere doing his thing.

Regrets? Certainly. He was pleasant company and a good help. I wish I'd taken his business card or number. Having said that, I never did see him with a phone – probably stuck somewhere in the long pockets of those grubby green agricultural overalls, the ones he pulled that equally grubby old sack out of to protect the van seats; my daily reminder of him, residing there.

He continually fiddled with that sack like a security blanket as he regaled me with his tales. Why he carried it who knows? I've seen smarter potato sacks covering the compost heap, but I haven't the heart to chuck it out. It contains seven coloured stones which sometimes clack and rattle when I drop below 1000 revs; it was obviously something he valued otherwise he wouldn't have folded it so neatly.

Funny, my eye is often drawn to the crumpled seam where the fibres overlap making a little owl face. Wise old owl, Jack, eh? I vaguely recall an owl in one of his stories, or was it a raven?